Kim Cummins

National bestse
Lynn Ku...

W9-BST-167

"Ms. Kurland is an author to watch for . . . She compounds amazing mixtures of passion, history, and humor to create tales that leave the reader with a thirst for more of her unique brand of the unusual and the fanciful."

—*Rendezvous*

"I dare you to read a 'Kurland' story and not enjoy it!"
—*Heartland Critiques*

"A bright new talent . . . Ms. Kurland seems destined for a most promising career." —*Romantic Times*

Phenomenal praise for Lynn Kurland's debut novel
Stardust of Yesterday

"Lynn Kurland has created a true knight in shining armor who will capture your heart the moment you meet him. This is a brilliant first novel you won't want to miss."

—*New York Times* bestselling author
Constance O'Day Flannery

"This lighthearted contemporary fantasy is a fine effort by first-time author Lynn Kurland." —*Atlanta Journal*

"WOW! . . . If you want absolute incredible joy, then make a special trip for this one . . . An awesome book sure to have readers raving for a long time to come." *Rendezvous*

"Incredible! . . . This one sets the standard."
—*Heartland Critiques*

Turn the page for more remarkable
reviews of Lynn Kurland's novels...

A Dance Through Time

This Is All I Ask

Lynn Kurland

JOVE BOOKS, NEW YORK

THIS IS ALL I ASK

A Jove Book / published by arrangement with
the author

PRINTING HISTORY
Jove edition / August 1997

The Putnam Berkley World Wide Web site address is
http://www.berkley.com

ISBN: 0-515-12139-8

A JOVE BOOK®
Jove Books are published by The Berkley Publishing Group,
200 Madison Avenue, New York, New York 10016, a member of
Penguin Putnam Inc.
JOVE and the "J" design are trademarks
belonging to Jove Publications, Inc.

PRINTED IN THE UNITED STATES OF AMERICA
10 9 8 7 6 5 4 3 2 1

To my mother

who always thought reading was more important than chores

and who still laughs in all the right places.

This Is All I Ask

prologue

THE TWIGS SNAPPED AND POPPED IN THE HEARTH, SENDing a spray of sparks across the stone. The cauldron bubbled ominously, the thick brown contents slipping up to the edge and almost over, much like a youth looking into the abyss of sin and toying with the idea of leaping in headfirst.

"Magda, mind the kettle!"

A wizened old woman jumped as if she'd been stuck with a pin, pushed her white hair out of her face with a plump hand and hastened to the fire.

"Sweet Mary, I think I've burned it again!" Magda cried.

"By the Fires of Hell, I do hate it when you use those saintly epitaphs," the second said, coming over and taking away the spoon. She tasted, then cursed. "Lucifer's tocs, must I do everything myself?"

"Oh, Nemain, what shall we do?" Magda exclaimed, wringing her hands. "I cannot bear watching them lose this chance when the Fates have worked so well in our favor thus far!"

Nemain grumbled as she pulled the pot off the fire.

"Berengaria, come taste this. I say 'tis the worst love potion Magda has burned yet."

Berengaria didn't answer. She was far too busy staring out the window and watching the past unfold into the future. It was a gift she had, this Seeing. It had amused her in the past to see what the future held, to know how kings would die and lands be lost. It had also come in handy to know beforehand when whatever castle she lived near was to be besieged, leaving her time enough to pack her belongings and seek out new lodgings before the marauders arrived. But this task that lay before her now was her most important yet: to bring two unwilling and, frankly, rather impossible souls together. Aye, this was worthy of her modest arts.

She felt Magda tiptoe over to her, heard Nemain curse as she stomped over with her worn witch's boots, but she didn't pay them any heed. Failure had been but a breath away. Had the lord of Blackmour possessed a bit less honor, he would have ignored his vow to protect and defend a woman he hardly knew. Perhaps honor wasn't a wasted virtue after all.

Berengaria let the present pass before her eyes, watching the dark, dangerous knight the Dragon of Blackmour had sent as his messenger. She scrutinized the battle-hardened warrior and was pleased to see that he wouldn't falter in his errand. He couldn't, or all would be lost. There would not be another chance such as this.

"Magda, by my horns, that is a foul smell," Nemain snapped as she retreated to the far side of the hut. "Pour it out and start over again. And go carefully this time! It's taken me a score of years to find the thumb-bone of a wizard and you've almost used it up. I've no mind to venture up to Scotland again to search for another!"

"Stop shouting at me," Magda sniffed. "I've only been at this a few years."

"I daresay even the lowliest priest could tell that. He would sooner think you a nun than a witch."

Berengaria ignored the renewed bickering. Instead, she watched a homely woman-child of a score-and-one years who practiced with her forbidden sword in the garden at Warewick. The girl's father wouldn't be pleased with her disobedience, but with any luck the Dragon's messenger would be there before Warewick could learn of her actions. Berengaria nudged the knight a bit more, like a pawn on a chessboard, forcing him to urge his horse to greater speed. Satisfied he would arrive in time, she turned her attentions back to the young woman.

"Just a few more moments, my child," Berengaria said softly, "and then your new life will begin."

one

THE TWIGS SNAPPED AND POPPED IN THE HEARTH, SEND-ing a spray of sparks across the stone. One of the three girls huddled there stamped out the live embers, then leaned into the circle again, her eyes wide with unease.

"Is it true he's the Devil's own?"

" 'Tis the rumor," the second whispered with a furtive nod.

"He was spawned in the deepest of nights," the third announced. She was the eldest of the three and the best informed on such matters. She looked over her shoulder, then looked back at her companions. "And I know what happened to his bride."

Gillian of Warewick paused at the entrance to the kitch-ens. She didn't like serving girls as a rule, what with their gossiping and cruel taunts, but something about the way the maid uttered the last of her boast made Gillian linger. She hesitated, waiting for the girl to go on.

" 'Tis said," the third began, lowering her voice and forcing the others, including Gillian, to edge even closer, "that his lady wife found him one night with his eyes as red as Hellfire and horns coming out from atop his head. He caught her before she could flee and she's never been heard from since. 'Tis common knowledge that he sacrificed her to his Master.''

Gillian felt a shiver go down her spine. Her knowledge of the world outside the castle walls was scant indeed, but she could well believe that England was full of witches and ogres who wove their black magic in the dead of the night. Her brother had told her as much and she'd had no reason to doubt his tales.

"He never leaves his keep, or so *I'm* told," the second girl said suddenly, obviously trying to sound as important as the third. "He has his familiars see to his affairs."

"Perhaps he fears someone will learn what he truly is," the youngest of the three offered.

"A monster he is," the second stated, bobbing her head vigorously. "There isn't a soul in England brave enough to face him. A mere look from his eyes sends them fleeing in terror."

"And no children in his village," came the third voice, as low as before. She paused. "Blackmour drinks their blood."

Gillian gasped in horror and her wooden sword clattered to the floor. Blackmour?

The girls whirled to look at her. The eldest girl hastily made the sign of the cross, then fled, pulling the other two after her.

Gillian stared after them, speechless. The wenches had been talking about the very Devil's spawn himself, yet they crossed themselves against her?

"Lady Gillian, your father is waiting."

Gillian spun around to find her father's man standing behind her. She thought of asking for time to change her garments, then thought better of it. The longer her sire waited, the angrier he would be. When he saw how she was dressed and realized what she had been doing, he would be angry enough.

She picked up her wooden sword and forced herself to stand tall as she walked behind the steward, even though the mere thought of facing her father's temper was enough to make her cower. She whetted her lips with a dry tongue as she followed the seneschal up the stairs and down the passageway to the solar.

Gillian left her sword against the wall before she trailed her father's man into the small chamber where her sire conducted his private affairs. Her heart pounded so forcefully against her ribs, she was sure both men could hear it. Oh, how she wished William were alive to protect her! She took a deep breath and clutched her hands together behind her back.

"You sent for me, my lord?"

Bernard of Warewick was a tall, heavyset man, a warrior who had survived countless battles and would likely survive countless more. Gillian forced herself not to cringe as he turned his substantial self around and looked at her, starting at her feet and working his way up—his eyes missing no detail. She felt as if her boots were caked with twenty layers of mud, not just one. She was painfully conscious of her worn tunic and patched hose. Her hair, which was never obedient, chose now as the proper time to escape its plait. She felt it fall around her face and shoulders in an unruly mess.

Her father's eyes narrowed.

"Can you not do something with those locks? They look like straw."

Gillian's shoulders sagged.

"And I expressly forbid you to set foot in the lists. Perhaps you need to have your memory refreshed." His eyes slid pointedly to a birch switch leaning against the wall.

"I wasn't in the lists," Gillian whispered. "I vow it."

"You were in the bloody garden!" he roared. "Damn you, girl, I'll not bear such cheek!"

Before she could move, he had snatched up the rod and brought it across her face.

The sting told her the skin had broken, but it could have

been much worse. She took a step back, ready to drop to her knees and curl up to protect her face from more painful blows.

"My lord," the seneschal put in quickly, quietly, "perhaps you should wait. Until after," he added.

The sound of the cane cracking against the far wall made Gillian jump. At least the switch was far from her. She looked up to see the tic under her father's eye twitching furiously. Sweat began to drip down his face and his breathing was a harsh rasp in the stillness of the chamber. He fixed his man with a furious glance.

"Bring the whoreson in. I'll beat respect into this wench after he leaves."

The moment her father's notice was off her and on the door, Gillian scurried over to a corner. She put her hand to her cheek and found the cut to be only a minor one. Oh, how was it all the other daughters in England bore such treatment? She had lain awake nights in the past, wishing she had the courage she knew other maids had to possess. She imagined them bearing up bravely and stoically under the lash while she herself was reduced to tears and begging after only a stroke or two. Lately, just the thought of the pain and humiliation was enough to make her weep.

Her brother had sheltered her as much as he could, but he had been away much of the time, squiring and warring. But when William had been home, he had shooed the maids from the solar and taught her the rudiments of swordplay—with wooden swords, of course, so no one would hear. He had even fashioned her a true sword, a blade so marvelously light that she could wield it easily, and so dreadfully sharp that she had once cleaved a stool in twain without much effort at all.

But her sword was currently hidden in the deepest recesses of her trunk and it was of no use to her. Her brother was buried alongside her mother in the deepest recesses of the chapel and he could not save her. Gillian again put her fingers to her cheek, the feel of the broken skin reminding her all too well what she would suffer at her father's hands once his man had departed for safer ground. She never should have gone out to the garden. If she hadn't thought her father would be away for the whole of the day, she wouldn't have.

The door burst open and a tall, grim man strode inside. He was dressed in full battle gear, as if he expected to sally forth and slay scores at any moment. Perhaps he had expected a battle in Warewick's solar. Gillian would have sold her soul to have relieved him of his mail and donned it herself.

The man made her father a curt bow.

"Lord Warewick, I bring you greetings from Lord Blackmour. He trusts all is in readiness."

Gillian paled. The Dragon of Blackmour? What could he possibly want with her father?

"Aye, all is in readiness," Bernard barked. "But he was to come himself. I'll not bargain with one of his underlings."

The man smiled. It wasn't a pleasant smile. "My lord Warewick, I am Colin of Berkhamshire and I am not an underling."

Gillian caught her breath. Merciful saints above, Colin of Berkhamshire had a reputation for violence and cruelty that spread from the Scottish border to the Holy Land. William had traveled with him on the continent and told her tale after bloody tale of the man's lack of patience and his love of slaying those who offended him. It was said he'd once cut down five knights his size because they dared comment on the style of his tunic. Seeing Sir Colin in the flesh left Gillian with no doubts the tale was true.

She looked quickly at her father, wondering if he had realized his error. His expression gave nothing away, but the tic under his eye twitched with renewed vigor.

"Hrumph," Warewick grunted. "Even so, I'll not have Blackmour insult me by not coming himself."

Colin's smile grew chillier and Gillian pressed herself harder against the wall, ready to duck should a fight ensue.

"I'm of the understanding that you can find no other mate for the child," Colin said. "As she is far past the age when she should have been wed, I should think you would be anxious to rid yourself of her. My lord has accepted your rather ordinary and unimaginative dowry and done it willingly. Perhaps you would be better served by keeping your pride on a tighter leash. There are other maidens with more attractive holdings than hers."

Colin's words sank into Gillian's mind like sharp daggers, painful upon entry and excruciating as they remained. She wanted to draw air into her lungs, but her shock was too great. She stood still, listening to her father and Colin of Berkhamshire discuss her marriage.

To Christopher of Blackmour.

"Nay," she whispered, pushing herself away from the wall. "Father, nay!" She crossed the chamber and flung herself down at his feet. Her terror of Blackmour overcame all the fear she felt for her father. Anyone but Blackmour, anyone at all. He had horns, he drank children's blood, he danced under the moon as he worshipped the darkness. "Father, I beg you—"

"Silence, wench," he thundered, backhanding her.

Gillian went sprawling. She rolled herself into a tight ball, preparing for the inevitable blow to follow. She cried out when she felt hands haul her to her feet.

But the chest she was gathered against and the arm that pinned her against that chest were not her father's.

"Hush," a deep voice commanded. "I've neither the time nor the patience for tears."

Gillian had never been so close to a man other than her brother or father and she found she didn't care much for the sensation. Not only was Colin of Berkhamshire only slightly less evil than the Devil himself, he smelled.

"The child comes with us. Now. The ceremony will be a se'nnight hence. The banns have already been read."

Gillian closed her eyes and began to pray. *Oh, God, not to Blackmour!*

"The bold whoreson! I might have changed my mind."

"Indeed?" Colin drawled. "You rid yourself of your daughter and gain a powerful son-in-law with the same deed. I suspect that changing your mind was the last thing you intended to do."

"Begone," Bernard snapped, but there was no fury behind his word. "And take that sniveling wench with you. The sight of her sickens me."

Gillian was too terrified to argue. She squeezed her eyes shut as Colin swung her up into his arms and carried her from the solar.

"Your chamber, my lady?" he barked.

Gillian couldn't answer. She couldn't even find her tongue to ask Colin to pick up her training sword—not that wood would have served her where she was going. Steel was the only thing of use against warlocks, or so she'd heard.

She listened to her father's steward give Colin directions, respectfully spoken of course, then felt herself being carried up the steep, narrow steps to the tower chamber, a pitifully small place where she had passed all of her days.

"Pack only what can be carried easily," Colin said curtly as he set her down on her feet. "Your husband will provide you with whatever else you may need."

Husband? The Devil's own spawn? Despoiler of maidens, scourge of England, ravager of Blackmour? Aye, she knew much of Christopher of Blackmour and the tales were grim ones indeed.

He had driven his wife mad, killed her and then buried her unshriven. He was known to take the shape of a wolf, loping over his land with long, lanky strides, ripping the throats from sheep and unwary travelers alike. It was rumored he practiced his dark arts by candlelight in his tower chamber, for ever the shadows could be seen dancing wickedly therein in the deepest of nights.

She had no doubt that all of what she'd heard was true. She believed in witches, and magic, and in men changing their shapes when the moon hid his face. And she could readily believe the rumors of Blackmour's harshness, of the beatings he dealt his servants, of the cruelty he showed to every soul who crossed him. And now she was to be his. Exchanging one prison for another, with like jailors.

For a brief moment, she toyed with the idea of taking her own life. She could pull the sword from her trunk and fall upon it before Colin could stop her.

A firm hand grasped her by the chin and forced her face up. She looked into Colin's grim expression and quailed. It was no wonder he was so feared. There was no mercy to be found in his gaze.

"The cut on your cheek is not deep," he said. "I should kill Warewick for having marked you, but my lord will be displeased if I rob him of future sport. Gather your belongings and let us be off. We've a long ride before us and I'll start it before more of the sun is spent on this ill-fated day."

She was surprised enough at his words to hesitate. Had he come near to offering to defend her? He wasn't going to simply ignore Warewick's treatment, as did all the rest in the keep?

"I've no time to coddle you, girl," he said, releasing her face abruptly. "Don't stand there gawking. Your father has sold you to the only bidder and you've no say in the matter. Pack your things and let us be away, while my mood is still sweet."

The saints preserve her if she ever saw him when his mood was sour. As for the other, she readily recognized the truth of it. Her father could have sold her to a lecherous dotard or a five-year-old child and she wouldn't have had a say in either. That he had sold her to Christopher of Blackmour only proved how little he cared for her. Aye, her fate was sealed indeed.

Unless she somehow managed to escape Colin between Warewick and Blackmour.

She turned the thought over in her mind. Escape was something she had never considered before, knowing it would have been impossible to get past her father's guards. Now things were different. She might manage it.

She turned to her trunk, her mind working furiously. Aye, she would escape, and she would need clothing that wouldn't hamper her as she did so.

She reached for her two gowns, ones she had worn to please her father, to make him look on her with favor— gowns that had tears in the back, reminders of just how futile her efforts to please him had been. Nay, those garments wouldn't serve her while she fled. And, should she by some malevolent bit of misfortune arrive at Blackmour, she had no intention of anyone knowing how her clothing had been ripped so she might be beaten more easily.

She pulled tunics and hose out instead, things of William's she had cut down to fit her frame. No matter that they were patched and mended a score of times. Indeed, such mending would perhaps make others think she was merely a poor lad in search of supper. She would beg a few meals, sleep a night or two under the stars, then find herself in London where she would seek aid from the king.

Assuming, of course, that London could be reached in a day or two. How large was England, anyway? A pity her father had been too ashamed of her to let her outside the inner bailey. It would have helped to know where she was going. No matter. She would watch the position of the sun, as William had taught her, and go south. London was south. She would reach it eventually and find the king. He wouldn't refuse to aid her. After all, she was the only child left Warewick, flawed and unworthy though she was.

Clothing decided upon, she dug into the bottom of her trunk and came up with her sword, wrapped in a tunic.

It was torn from her hands and Colin barked out a laugh. "What is this?"

Panic overcame her. Nay, not her true sword. Not the sword William had gifted her . . .

" 'Tis naught of yours," she said, making a desperate lunge for it. Her sword was the one thing in the world she could trust to protect her and she would never relinquish it.

Colin held it above his head, far out of her reach. "You'll have no need of this, lady. My paltry skills will assure your safety."

"That is mine, you . . . you swine," she blurted out, using William's favorite slur.

Colin's expression changed and she knew her cheek would cost her. In an instant, her choices paraded before her, showing themselves in their fullest glory. She could defend herself, or she could die. She might have survived a beating at her father's hands, but she knew she wouldn't survive the like at Colin's. She grasped for the last shreds of her courage and brought her knee up sharply into Colin's groin.

He dropped her sword with a curse and doubled over, choking. Gillian dove for her sword, then lurched to her feet, fumbling with the wrappings. She jerked it free of its scabbard and brandished it.

"I know h-how to use this," she warned Colin's doubled-over form, "and I wouldn't think t-twice about g-gelding you if need be."

"Pox rot you, wench," Colin gasped. He lurched toward her, still hunched over.

Gillian leaped backward in terror. She caught her foot in her gown and went down heavily, dropping her sword along the way. It skittered out of her reach. Gillian cried out in fear, for she had lost her one advantage. She knew it would be impossible to retrieve the blade before Colin reached her. So she did the only thing she knew to do: she bent her head and cowered, waiting for the first blow to fall.

"Pick up your sword, girl," Colin said, panting. "I've

no stomach for beating women. And I remember telling you I wanted to be gone before the morn was wasted. Your father's house feels more unfriendly than a camp full of infidels. I'm certain you're as eager to leave as I am.''

Gillian froze, hardly able to believe her ears. When she felt no blow come, she lifted her head to see what Colin was doing. He was staring down at her, but his hands were clutching his thighs. They were not clenched and held high, which, to her way of thinking, boded well.

''I said, wrap up your blade, wench.'' Colin straightened, then limped over to her trunk and looked inside. ''What of these gowns? None to suit your finicky tastes?''

Gillian couldn't manage an answer. Colin hadn't struck her. Indeed, he seemed to have forgotten her insults. She watched him in shock and not just a bit of suspicion. She had wounded more than just his pride and he wasn't going to repay her for it? It took nothing more than the thought of such an act of defiance crossing her face for her father to punish her. What manner of man was this Colin of Berkhamshire?

Colin picked up a gown and looked at it closely. Gillian wasn't a skilled seamstress and the gown showed clearly how oft it had been torn. There was even blood on the garment he held, a mark she had scrubbed repeatedly, and unsuccessfully.

Colin flung the garment into the trunk and slammed the lid shut. ''Christopher will have other gowns made for you. You'll not wear those in his hall. Saints, but I'd pay for the pleasure of meeting Warewick in the lists,'' he muttered.

He turned, strode over to her and drew her to her feet. He retrieved her sword, scabbard and dropped clothing, then shoved it all into her hands. He took hold of her arm and kept hold of it as he pulled her from the chamber, down the circular stairs and across the great hall.

Her father stood at the door to the hall, his mouth open and likely full of more words that certainly wouldn't please

Colin. Colin shoved him out of the way, then herded Gillian and the rest of his men to the waiting horses.

"You can ride?"

"A bit," she managed the moment before he tossed her up into a saddle.

They were through the inner gates before Gillian had the chance to find her seat astride her horse. The outer gates had been reached and breached before she could catch her breath or find her wits to marvel at the dumbfounded look on her father's face. Whatever Colin of Berkhamshire's other flaws might be, he certainly had a way about him that annoyed her father. The memory of her sire's spluttering was almost enough to make her smile.

Colin set a brisk pace and by the time Gillian thought to look over her shoulder, her father's hall was small and becoming smaller by the hoofbeat. She clutched the hilt of her sword and stared back at her prison in fascination. Odd how a place that had held her captive for the past one-and-twenty years seemed so puny and insignificant when viewed from a safe distance.

"Watch your mount," Colin barked, snagging her reins. "I've no time for coddling your tears."

"Oh, but I've no tears to shed," she assured him quickly.

"I shouldn't think you would have," Colin said, tossing her reins back at her. "Look sharp, lady, and don't force me to halt for you. I haven't the patience."

Gillian nodded and took hold of her reins, contenting herself with that tiny bit of control. It was, like her freedom, not destined to last more than the time it took them to travel from Warewick to Blackmour.

Unless she could truly wrench destiny to her own pleasure.

She looked about her at the score of grim-faced warriors and her heart sank. How could she elude them? Or escape them once they took up her trail? There wasn't any hope. She was doomed to be carried off to another prison likely as terrifying and stifling as the one she had just left.

Courage, Gill. You'll not live forever at Warewick. Someday a handsome lord will take you away and make you his, and then think on how happy you'll be. I know it will be so.

William's dying words came back to her, making her want to weep with despair. What William couldn't have known, what even the most fiendish of village witches couldn't have imagined, was that she wasn't going to a man who loved her, who had offered for her out of affection, or even lust.

She was going to the Dragon of Blackmour.

two

THE DRAGON OF BLACKMOUR SAT IN A CHAIR IN HIS BED-
chamber with his feet up on a stool and cursed the fool
who had invented ale. Saints, it was poison! His head
throbbed. The fingers he put to his head throbbed. He
could have sworn the soles of his feet throbbed, but he
wasn't truly sure as he couldn't feel anything past his
knees.

He fingered the rolled parchment he held, then cast it
aside, not caring where it came to rest. It wasn't as if he
couldn't remember every bloody word written there. He
closed his eyes and leaned his head back against the chair,
allowing the words to swim before his mind's eye.

*I, William of Warewick, send greetings to Christopher
of Blackmour. Time is short, my friend, for I know I
am approaching my end. I adjure you to remember
your vow, the one I begged you to make in the event
of my death. You are the only one I trust with such a
deed, Christopher, and I implore you not to fail me.
Upon your honor, hold fast to your oath and see to
what I cannot. God will bless you for your goodness.*

I write this by my own hand, this fourth day of April, the Year of Our Lord, 1248.

William had penned those words a year ago. At the time, Christopher had thought William had slipped too far into his cups and was imagining his coming demise. With his own head currently paining him nigh unto death, Christopher could well understand the feeling.

But now he knew William had been in earnest.

And it was all because of the vow. By the saints, he had been daft to ever make such a promise. The very last thing he needed was a bloody wife!

He rose with a hearty curse and left his bedchamber, making his way with care down to the great hall. Too much ale had made him clumsy and he had no intentions of misjudging his step and tumbling down the stairs.

Chris, I'm trusting you to see to Gillian if anything ever happens to me. Do whatever you have to do to take her from my sire. You know as well as I what her fate will be otherwise. I know she's not beautiful, but there are qualities more desirable than beauty.

Christopher smiled bitterly at the thought. Aye, qualities such as loyalty, something he knew firsthand.

"My lord, I brought you something to eat."

Bile rose in Christopher's throat at the mere smell. "Take it away, Jason!"

He listened to his squire scurry away, then sighed as he made his way to his chair at the high table. Jason of Artane should have had a better master, one who could have given him the training he needed. Christopher had tried to send him away three years ago, after the wounding, but neither Jason nor his father would accept it. Christopher had been left with no choice but to allow the boy of ten-and-six to remain, to become indispensable to him. A pity, really. Jason deserved better.

"My lord, here is herbed wine. If you'll hold your nose and drink it, your stomach will be settled."

A cold cup was pressed into Christopher's hand. He held his breath and downed the contents, then waited for the nausea to come. He leaned back against the chair and closed his eyes, remaining still until he was certain his stomach wouldn't reject Jason's brew, then he nodded and handed the cup back to his squire. A calm belly was no blessing, though, for it gave him nothing to think on but his own black thoughts. Saints above, what had ever possessed him to promise William anything at all?

He hadn't given much thought to the vow he'd made his friend, though he remembered well enough the giving of it. It had been during the time he and William had been squiring together at Artane. Christopher had been watching Lord Robin, a man he worshipped to the depths of his soul, pick up his young daughter and carry her back to the house, giving her gentle words all along the way. He had followed, then run bodily into William, who had been staring at their lord with a grief-stricken expression.

Christopher had never forgotten the look on William's face. He had never known his friend to be anything but merry, but that day William had turned to him in obvious torment.

"Promise me," he had said, his face ashen. "Promise me that if anything happens to me, you'll take my sister away from my sire. Vow it by the Holy Rood, Chris. Vow it now."

Christopher had been too unsettled to do anything else. Once he had given his word that he would see to William's sister, his friend had slowly returned to his normal, cheery self. But from then on Christopher had marked the way William studied their lord with his daughter.

Christopher sighed and raked his hand through his hair. It had been years since he had given any thought to his rash words. He had been far too busy seeing to the tangle that was his own life. He'd had holdings to see to, a short, disastrous marriage to endure, then months to spend living in his own private hell as he recovered from the sabotage which had cost him so dearly.

Then had come the fateful visit from one of William's guardsmen. Edward had arrived half a year ago and given Christopher the tale of William's death—and the sounds of beatings that echoed in the stillness of the night at Warewick.

And of Gillian's attempts at pretending she wasn't the recipient of those beatings.

Christopher forced himself to release the arms of his chair, then flexed his fingers. It wasn't wise to let the tidings affect him so deeply. What went on at Warewick wasn't anything that didn't happen frequently in the whole of England. Christopher himself had endured several choice beatings at his father's hands.

But he had given William his word and William had called him on the bargain. His damnable honor had risen up like fat to the top of soup and he had choked on it. He had fought for air for almost half a year after William's death before giving in and sending his messenger to Warewick with his offer.

He had known he wouldn't be refused. As far as he knew there wasn't another man in the realm who would take Gillian's dowry, something he had no use for. Her gold could be spent in one trip to market. Braedhalle, her dower estate, was the most pitiful, overworked, barren bit of soil he had ever seen. Add that to her lack of beauty and it was a wonder Warewick hadn't packed her off to a convent years ago. Nay, not even the Church would have taken her. In their eyes, she had no value at all.

Christopher rose with a curse. As if he cared what anyone thought of the girl! The Church likely had reason for not wanting her. What would they want with a child who possessed neither beauty nor wealth?

He strode across the hall, wanting nothing more than to escape his thoughts. He had done the honorable thing and sent for her. He would wed her and give her the protection of his name. His word was fulfilled and now he could turn his mind to other things.

Without warning, he smacked his shin smartly against the end of a bench and gasped out a curse.

"Who put this here?" he bellowed.

"I beg your pardon, milord," a timid female voice answered. "I moved it to clean the hearth and forgot to move it back."

"Don't forget again," Christopher snarled and marched across the rushes. He marched carefully, though. His shin smarted worse than his pride, and that was smarting mightily at the moment.

He stepped outside the hall and a chill breeze caught him full in the face. It cleared his head far better than Jason's brew had. He moved over to the bench that sat near the door to the great hall, probing for it unobtrusively with his uninjured leg. Upon successfully finding it, he lowered himself with a sigh. The wall at his back was cold and the early spring sun a poor warmth, but he didn't care. He fixed a grim look to his face, one that was guaranteed to insure privacy. And with his precious privacy, he made a list of what he would not do.

He wouldn't let Gillian disrupt his life. He would bed her a time or two, get her with child, then never speak to her again. That was the only way to assure she didn't steal his heart, then rend it in twain.

He would also hide his flaw from her. She, like most of his household, would never know just how badly he had been injured.

"My lord?"

Christopher sighed at the interruption. "Aye, Jason."

"I've the missive you dictated to my sire, informing him of your coming nuptials. It requires your signature."

"Bloody Hell, I'm occupied now." Saints above, would this farce of a marriage never cease to disturb his peace?

"It will take but a moment, my lord. I've everything

needful on this board: ink, a quill, and wax. And you wear the proper ring.''

Christopher felt the indentations on the ring he wore. ''I knew that, Jason.''

''Of course, my lord. 'Twas merely a tactic to convince you of the ease of the task.''

''I don't want things that are easy, damn you!''

There was silence.

''A poor choice of words,'' Jason said softly. ''I only meant that it would be quick and painless, not that it was simple.''

''Aye, I know,'' Christopher said, with a deep sigh. ''My growls are just growls, lad, and not meant as censure. Here, give me what I need.''

Jason set the small board on Christopher's lap and put the parchment atop it.

''At the bottom, my lord. On your right hand.''

''In the usual place,'' Christopher observed dryly.

''You like things to be orderly. I try to humor you as I may.''

Christopher felt a smile tug at his mouth. If there was anyone who could charm him out of his foul mood, it was his squire.

''Such cheek from such a wee lad,'' he said. ''Perhaps we'll wrestle after I finish this great, imposing task, and I will repay you for using me as sport.''

''I would relish the challenge, my lord.''

Christopher felt for the edges of the missive, then lifted the quill.

''A bit more to the left,'' Jason murmured, so softly that Christopher barely heard him, ''and up. Aye, that's it.''

Christopher signed his name carefully, then lifted the quill. It was taken out of his hand and he heard Jason brush sand across the parchment. It was rolled, then Jason swore.

''Bloody Hell,'' he muttered, with the same inflection Christopher always used. ''The wax never goes where I want it to.'' He was silent for a moment or two more as he worked with the missive. "Here, now, my lord. 'Tis ready." He took Christopher's hand and guided it to the parchment. "Hold but for a moment. Aye, well done. With your leave, I'll deliver this to the messenger, then return for your sport."

Christopher nodded and waved the lad away, unable to speak. Life was a bitter taste in his mouth. He couldn't swallow past it, couldn't spit it out, couldn't drink to cover it up. As with his affliction, life was something he couldn't escape.

Saints, what would Gillian think when she learned?

three

GILLIAN HAD BEEN CURIOUS AT FIRST, WHEN SHE COULD see only a speck in the distance that Colin assured her was indeed Blackmour. She had envisioned a humble place, likely smaller than her own home, and rather more primitive. After all, it was rumored to be only a few days' ride from the Scottish border.

But now, as she sat but a few hundred paces from the outer walls, she realized just how wrong she had been.

Blackmour was enormous. It was a grim fortress that sat so far on the edge of the land that she fancied it ran the tremendous risk of slipping over the cliff and plunging into the sea—though how anything so large could have ever been moved she didn't know.

The first line of defense was a tall, smooth wall topped with unfriendly arrow slits. She watched the weak sunlight glint off the helmets of the guards who walked the walls, guards whose eyes searched out the landscape for any who might attempt entrance without permission. The drawbridge yawned open as she approached and a heavy portcullis was raised, its steel-tipped spikes hanging threateningly over the pathway through the tunnel.

She reined in her mount and simply stared at what was

going to become her home. How would she ever survive a lifetime in this gloomy place? From what she could see of it, the inner wall was no less tall than the outer and it boasted not only arrow slits but fixtures for the dropping of boiling oil onto whatever army dared topple the outer walls. Gillian suspected no foe ever saw the inner walls, much less stood underneath them to be boiled alive.

"Lady Gillian?"

She blinked, startled from her contemplation of her new prison, and looked at Colin. "Aye?"

"We'll stop again in the inner bailey and you'll look to your heart's content. I'll not linger outside the walls."

Gillian nodded and followed his horse up the final distance to the outer bailey wall. Her eyes adjusted readily to the darkness of the long tunnel under the wall and she suddenly found a strange comfort in knowing that the outer defenses were so thick. If nothing else, Christopher of Blackmour would keep her safe.

But that also meant that if no one could get in, she wouldn't be able to get out. Merciful saints above!

She only realized she had jerked on her reins when her horse reared.

"Whoa!" Colin exclaimed.

Without warning, he scooped Gillian off her saddle with one arm and set her down sideways behind him.

"Peter, see to her mount. Do not look down, lady. I'll not have you send us both into the abyss with your screaming."

Abyss? She looked down to her left and stifled a cry. They were nigh onto crossing the bridge that spanned the short distance from the whole of England and what she could see was the lamentably small island that served as Blackmour's foundations. She clutched the back of Colin's cloak as his surefooted mount trotted over the heavy stone bridge. In truth, the span was large and sturdy, but that knowledge didn't convince her to loosen her grip. The slightest misstep would have plunged them over into the sea.

"You never said it was perched out here on nothing," she ventured, clinging to fistfuls of Colin's cloak and praying she could keep her tenuous seat atop the horse's rump.

"A fine aerie for the Dragon of Blackmour, is it not?"

She could have sworn he was laughing, for his voice quavered just the slightest bit. She, however, saw nothing humorous about the Dragon's choice of nests.

"If one doesn't care for great tracts of land surrounding one's home," she muttered under her breath.

"Nay, lady," Colin said, "Blackmour suits those of us who live here perfectly. Christopher employs his own guard year-round and his men have grown accustomed to the lack of land about the walls. This isle is far larger than it looks at first glance, so you needn't fear for places to roam. You'll see that for yourself soon enough and no doubt find it to your liking.

"Of course,"—he cleared his throat suddenly and made a few gruff noises—"I couldn't care less if you like it or not. And I'll surely not have any time to show it to you. You'll see it or not by yourself."

Gillian pretended not to notice the slip in Colin's ruthlessness. It wasn't the first time it had happened. Though he'd complained loudly about every stop he had called for her sake, he had called them often and ignored her protests that she was managing well enough with his brisk pace. It was difficult to believe that a man of Colin of Berkhamshire's reputation could possess any sort of kindness, but she couldn't deny what she had seen. A pity her future husband was a sorcerer and would possess no kindness whatsoever. No warlock did. All the gentler emotions were burned out of them in the course of their mastery of the darker arts.

She forced thoughts of Lord Christopher's evil habits out of her mind as they rode out into the inner bailey. It did no good to think on what he was, for it would only increase her fear. She already had enough of that, and to spare.

She stared at the lists on her left. Mailed men currently trained with their weapons of war. The men trained very hard—likely in fear of incurring Blackmour's wrath. She would have trained just as hard in their place.

The lists gave way to a smaller wall that surrounded the inner courtyard. *Smaller* was, of course, an understatement. Indeed, all of Blackmour seemed to make a mockery of her home, a place she had considered quite large and fine.

Tucked into one corner of this smaller courtyard was the great hall. A chapel huddled a ways away from it, along with a garrison hall and, further still, the stables. A modest garden sat between the great hall and the chapel. A pity she would never know the peace of sitting amidst the herbs and dreaming.

Colin dismounted at the steps to the great hall, then held up his hands for her. She was deposited on her feet and commanded to enter the hall.

Gillian paused at the threshold, wondering if it were too late to turn and bolt.

She turned away, and her nose made immediate contact with Colin's broad chest. He put his hands on her shoulders and turned her back around to face the gaping hole of the hall doorway.

"Courage, my lady."

If she'd had courage, she would have drawn Colin's sword and run him through, then escaped on his horse.

But she was a coward.

So she crossed the threshold.

CHRISTOPHER CONCENTRATED ON COUNTING THE FINAL steps down to the great hall. He seldom miscounted and usually descended them with a confident air. Now he crept along like a bastard son of the lowliest tanner, afraid of even his own shadow. Ten-and-six, ten-and-seven, ten-and-eight. He inched the toe of his boot forward and encountered nothing but solid ground. He cursed under his breath. What had ever possessed him to offer for her? He was a fool!

He hadn't been waiting in the hall when she had arrived, though he'd been kept abreast of the happenings. Jason had been run ragged trying to see to Gillian's comfort and appease Christopher's demands for tidings at the same time. But the lad was young; he would bear up well enough under the strain.

The one person Christopher hadn't talked to was Colin and he was furious about it. He had sent Jason down with explicit instructions that Colin present himself with all due haste. Colin had sent word back that he couldn't possibly leave Gillian alone and if Christopher wanted to talk to him, he could bloody well haul his stubborn arse below to do it. There were times Christopher wondered why in hell's name he had ever saved Colin's sorry neck in the battle of Coyners. He was even sorrier that Colin was his brother-in-law and not his vassal. It made ordering him about nigh onto impossible.

Now, hours later, Christopher stood unwillingly at the bottom of his stairs, wondering why he found himself in this pitiful state.

He listened to the sounds in the great hall, trying to divine where everyone was. There was the usual racket from the kitchen: pots being washed, servants gossiping, kitchen lads being slapped and scolded for stealing treats. He heard the scrape of wood against stone as the trestles were dragged across the floor to the wall. A man laughed and others joined him. He heard Colin's booming curses, but he did not hear a woman's voice.

Yet he knew she was there. The hall smelled different. The faintest scent of roses drifted toward him.

"Gillian," he barked.

The splat of wine and the ping of a silver goblet hitting the stone floor told him he hadn't been mistaken. He could have sworn he heard her teeth begin to chatter.

"Come here," he commanded.

He heard Jason murmur soothingly and heard a chair graze the stone. He held out his hand, waiting for her to come put hers in it. Her shuffling step stopped; then cold fingers came to rest on his palm.

She was terrified. He could feel it in the chill of her skin and the way her hand trembled against his.

"Jason, she should be sitting closer to the fire," Christopher rumbled. "Her lips are blue."

That was a flash of inspiration. Her hands were freezing; her lips would surely be blue.

"Forgive me, my lord."

Her voice was whispery soft and tinged with terror. Christopher dropped her hand immediately and felt for the wall behind him. The saints help him, he was going to do something absurd, like haul her into his arms to comfort her. He backed up until his heels hit the bottom step.

"We'll wed at noon, five days hence. Do not make me wait when the time comes. I am not a patient man."

With that, he turned and walked back up the steps, concentrating on nothing but their number. He sighed as he reached the top, then went stumbling forward before he realized he had miscounted. He caught himself heavily with one leg, the impact shooting pains up through his foot to his hip.

"Bloody Hell," he muttered under his breath. He straightened, hoping no one had seen him, and continued on his way to his chamber.

Once there, he closed the door and made his way to the hearth. The lit candle was exactly where it always was and he started a fire quickly with the peat and kindling. He wrapped up in a fur and sat down with a deep sigh. The chill dampness of the ocean rarely bothered him, but tonight was different. The chill was in his heart. A few days ago, he'd complained loudly about what little Gillian had to offer him. Now he began to realize just how little he had to offer her.

A wet nose nudged his hand and Christopher sighed again as he scratched his favorite hound behind the ears.

"Women," Christopher muttered. "Wolf, my friend, keep yourself away from them. They'll cause you naught but grief."

Wolf growled softly and licked Christopher's hand. Christopher ruffled the hound's fur as he turned his face back to the warmth of the fire. There was much to be done in preparation for the ceremony. He knew he wouldn't be so fortunate as to have Warewick decide not to appear at his daughter's wedding. Nay, the man would come to gloat, if nothing else. After all, he was gaining a tie to Blackmour and all that went with it. A tenuous tie, to be sure. If Warewick thought to form any kind of friendly alliance, he was deluding himself.

Wolf lifted his head suddenly. Christopher stiffened along with him at the sound of a soft footfall behind him. He hadn't heard the door open. Thinking deeply behind an unbolted chamber door was never wise.

Wolf growled low in his throat, which narrowed down drastically who the caller could be. Wolf accepted few people: Jason, Colin and Christopher's captain, Ranulf. Anyone else was considered a threat and treated accordingly.

"Who is it?" Christopher asked, not turning his head.

"Janet, my lord. Master Jason thought you might be wanting something to eat."

"Put it on the table." He waited until he heard the sound of a wooden trencher being set down and the girl's footsteps retreating before he rose and bolted his bedchamber door.

Christopher forced himself to eat, though he had no appetite. Aye, 'twas the thought of marriage that soured him so on the idea of food. A pity just keeping Gillian at Blackmour wouldn't be sufficient to keep her safe. Marriage it had to be.

Christopher put the trencher down on the floor and let

the enormous black hound finish the meal. He couldn't bear the smell.

Rising abruptly, he walked over to the alcove and threw open the shutters, letting the chill sea breeze wash over him. Saints, he didn't want a wife! Gillian would expect civility, perhaps even kindness, and he had none of either to give. His heart was cut off from those foolish feelings just as surely as his keep was severed from the rest of England. He had no desire to change things.

Why should he? Life had dealt him the cruelest of blows. How could anyone expect him to bestir himself to care for another soul? He had his hands full with Jason and the running of his household. He had no need of any more complications.

And if it weren't for his damnable honor, he wouldn't be contemplating the thought of facing a priest with a woman by his side for the second time in his miserable life.

He closed the shutters with a bang, then turned and strode across the chamber. He snatched up his sword and stalked out into the passageway, feeling the intense need to cut something to ribbons. Perhaps a few hours in the tower chamber would take his mind off what his vow would demand he do five days hence.

Honor.

What a perfect waste of a man's energy.

four

GILLIAN SAT IN HER CHAMBER, CHILLED TO THE BONE. She had risen at dawn, dressed, then remained where she was. There was no sense in giving up the safety of a barred door, though the necessity of that was still in question. Lord Christopher had taken one look at her and fled back up the stairs, surely to retch over her ugliness in private. It was unlikely he would seek her out and she couldn't have been happier about it. She hadn't seen his horns the night before, but then again, she hadn't had much of a look at him.

A soft knock sounded on the door and she jumped. She wiped her suddenly damp palms on her skirts and crossed to the door.

"Aye?" she asked hesitantly.

"Lady Gillian, 'tis Jason. I've come to fetch you down to break your fast."

Gillian hesitated. What fate awaited her below? Would Lord Christopher be there? Would he beat her in front of the servants to show them her place from the start?

"My lady," Jason said, "should you fear Sir Colin's poor manners at the table, there is no need. He and my lord are shouting at each other in the lists and will likely remain there for the rest of the day. You may come eat in peace.''

Gillian opened the door slowly and looked out. Jason made her a low bow and smiled. Gillian returned his smile, albeit shakily. Jason of Artane seemed to be a sweet, gentle boy and she wondered what had possessed his father to send him to squire with a monster like Christopher of Blackmour.

''Come now, lady,'' Jason said, offering his arm. ''My lord gave me leave to eat with you and I never forgo the pleasure of serving a comely maid. Then, if it pleases you, I will show you about the castle.''

She nodded and took his proffered arm. If Jason noticed her hesitancy in doing so, he hid it well. He kept up a steady stream of chatter as he descended before her down to the great hall. Gillian paid little heed to Jason's words; she was far too busy gaping at her surroundings. In her fear the day before, she hadn't had the stomach to do more than stare at the floor and pray for deliverance. Now she wondered how she could possibly have been so distracted that she didn't mark anything about her new home.

Blackmour's great hall was the finest thing she had ever seen. It made her father's small hall, with its fire in the midst of the floor and the thick smoke clogging the air, seem barbaric. Lord Christopher's hall boasted four hearths set into the walls, with flues to carry the smoke outside. Gillian could actually look up and see the ceiling.

Not only was there a great lack of smoke inside, there was light from windows set up high in the walls. The weak spring sunlight filtered in and was absorbed by the fine tapestries lining the walls. It must have taken a score of seamstresses years to complete those hangings. Oh, how much she had missed in never having seen aught but her father's house! Either all of England was much richer than her sire, or Christopher of Blackmour had more gold at his disposal than the king.

The meal was certainly the finest she had ever been

served. There was white bread and tasty porridge in abundance, though she ate little of it. She had intended to use it to shore up her strength, but after the first time a knight had come bursting into the hall, she remembered again just what her situation was: She was a prisoner in the Bane of Blackmour's keep. The saints only knew what torments he had planned for her. Terror lodged in her throat, making it impossible to swallow her meal.

Jason, though, seemed to have no fear of his surroundings, if the relish with which he attacked his food was any indication. Then again, a lad of some ten-and-six years likely never let anything get in the way of filling his belly.

She jumped when she found he was looking at her. His brow was furrowed.

"The fare doesn't please you? Shall I call for something else?"

She shook her head quickly. " 'Tis wondrous, truly."

"Then why don't you eat, my lady? You're powerfully thin."

Gillian picked up a bit of bread and ate obediently. There was no sense in offending her future husband by having him learn she hadn't partaken of his food. She wouldn't give him reason to beat her—more reason than he would find on his own.

"Perhaps you would care for a bit of air?" Jason asked.

Leave the great hall? Venture out into the same place where Blackmour might be roaming? She felt her chest tighten and her breath begin to come in gasps.

"I couldn't disturb His Lordship," she managed.

"I spoke of the battlements," Jason said. " 'Twill give you a commanding view of the surroundings. I daresay Sir Colin didn't allow you much time to look about."

Gillian felt some of her fear diminish. Perhaps she could manage the battlements. If Christopher and Colin were in the lists, she would be safe above.

She nodded and then allowed Jason to help her up from her chair.

"I always go up to the battlements when I'm allowed time for myself," he said, as he walked before her up the steps.

"The view is so fine?"

Jason grinned. "Nay, I know that 'tis the one place I am safe from Sir Colin and his foul temper."

"And why is that?"

"He is terrified of being much further off the ground than where being atop his steed places him."

Gillian blinked, surprised. Then she smiled. The thought of the fierce and intimidating Colin of Berkhamshire being afraid of such modest heights was the most ridiculous thing she had ever heard. Why, even she had felt no fear when gazing down at the courtyard from her tower window at Warewick. Well, that was certainly something to remember the next time the man frowned at her to frighten her.

"I tease Sir Colin when I can," Jason continued, "by inviting him to come up and scout with me, telling him that my lord finds it too menial a task for himself. 'Tis usually at that moment that something pressing requires his immediate attention. I try not to laugh, but I usually can't help myself." He grinned again. "If I'm quick enough, I can flee to the battlements and escape his wrath, though he usually lies in wait for me below. A lad can only haunt the walls for so long before hunger drives him to descend."

Gillian froze in midstep. "He beats you then?"

"Of course not, my lady," Jason said, a puzzled frown crossing his brow. "He wouldn't dare. I belong to my lord Christopher and Sir Colin would surely answer to him if he took sport of me. That isn't to say," he added, with the twinkle back in his eye, "that he doesn't propose a wrestle now and then. He does his bloody best to crush the life from me, but I relish that challenge. There are few who face Colin of Berkhamshire and live to tell the tale."

"And your lord?"

"Even fewer, my lady, even fewer. Know you nothing of him?"

"Just rumors," Gillian said as she resumed the climb. "I know little of the world outside my home. This journey was the first I'd ever made out of the inner bailey."

"I see. Then perhaps 'tis best that I leave you to form your own opinions. Here we are at the door. You aren't afraid to go out, are you?"

She shook her head in answer.

"We'll make the circle then," Jason said, taking her arm and leading her over to one wall. "This wall faces west, over the baileys and inland."

Gillian looked down over the courtyard and saw the chapel and other outbuildings housing the smiths and such. Outside the courtyard wall the bailey was full of merchants milling about, dogs barking, men cursing, horses stomping and pawing the earth. The sound of hammer against anvil rang out in the morning air, mingling with the other sounds of castle life. It was a bit like Warewick; only here it seemed wilder, more untamed. The peasants at her father's hall lived in terror of attracting the lord's gaze. These souls either didn't care or were of much bolder stock, for they didn't cower.

In the lists mailed knights jousted, men fought with swords; still others wrestled with their mates or trained their mounts. Gillian looked for Christopher but couldn't mark him. From what Jason had said, she should have been able to hear him shouting at Colin from where she stood.

Jason took her hand and led her to the north wall.

"Scotland is to your left, though many leagues away. My home is also north, on the edge of the sea as is Blackmour, though Artane is not perched up on a bit of rock as we are now."

"Do you miss your family?" she asked, looking into his pale gray eyes.

He smiled. "Aye, I do. But I see them now and then. My father comes two or three times a year to assure himself that I haven't driven Lord Christopher daft. I am sent home each summer to present myself to my mother and prove that I am behaving as I should. But I return to Blackmour willingly. I am the youngest son and have no title, though my father has vowed to be most generous with his lands. In truth, I don't know if I want them. My lord has need of me yet and he will see that I lack for nothing." He smiled again and shrugged. "I am content."

With a beast like Blackmour? Gillian couldn't believe it. Perhaps the lad was more innocent than she thought.

"And now for the east. This is what I come to look at when I make the climb. You've never seen the sea truly, have you?"

She shook her head.

"Then close your eyes and let me lead you. Never fear, I am quite adept at this."

Gillian clutched his arm and followed him, stealing looks down at her feet as they went. Her trust only went so far.

Jason stopped and placed her hands on the wall.

"Now look."

She lifted her head and gasped in surprise, then backed away from the wall. Jason grabbed her arm and jerked her back from the edge of the parapet.

"Careful," he exclaimed. "Hold onto the wall, my lady. My lord would have me flogged if aught happened to you."

Gillian peeked over the wall and flinched as a wave crashed against the cliff below her. The sea surged and billowed, throwing itself against Blackmour's foundations. The white spray erupted below her with a fierceness that frightened her. How puny and weak a mere mortal woman was when compared to the savage forces of nature. She clutched the cold stone wall in an effort to reassure herself that she wouldn't tumble forward and become swept away by the violence of the waves.

And slowly, in spite of her unease, she fell under the

sea's spell. The ebb and return of the waves was hypnotic, teasing her into a strange, fragile sense of peace. At that moment she knew, beyond all reason, that her entire life had been naught but waiting for this, for the sea and for this place, this gloomy keep perched atop its steep cliff, pounded by the elements until it was weathered and beaten. Blackmour took that pounding and survived it. Gillian doubted that anything could ever tear down the keep beneath her. And in that strength was power. She felt it as surely as if it reached up through the rocks and grasped her in its embrace. Aye, nothing would ever shatter this keep. If anything, a man would break himself against it in the attempt.

And now this bleak, weathered place was to be her home for the rest of her life. She tightened her grip on the stone wall. The fierce beauty of the sea below her was almost enough to convince her to stay. To be allowed to look on that sight each day would be a great pleasure and she had had so few pleasures in her life. Perhaps the sea would be recompense for being wed to Christopher of Blackmour.

Devil's spawn.

Fear slithered down her spine. How could the sea possibly soothe her if it were viewed from Blackmour's tower chamber, the hellish place where he worked his dark arts? Would she see the waves one last time before he raised his knife and—

"South is next," Jason said softly, interrupting her thoughts. "The view is less fine, just the sea and a bit of land. I prefer the ruggedness of the north myself so I don't often look south."

Gillian took a deep breath to calm her pounding heart.

"London is south," she said, looking at Jason. "Isn't it?"

"Aye, London is south."

Gillian nodded, swallowing with difficulty. At least she knew in which direction she should flee.

"I think I've seen enough," she managed. "Would you take me back now?"

"Wouldn't you care to see the rest of the keep?" Jason asked.

She shook her head, praying she could keep her tremors at bay until she was safely locked behind her chamber door. There was no sense in letting Blackmour hear how terrified she was. It would only give him pleasure.

"As you wish, then, my lady," Jason said, with a bow.

He led her back to her chamber, built up the blaze in her hearth and left only after she assured him she truly wished to rest after her journey. Once she had bolted the door, she changed her clothes and dug in her trunk for her sword. Practicing her skills against imaginary opponents was a twofold blessing. It would take her mind off her fear and also sap her strength enough that she would sleep soundly. She knew she would be wise to sleep while she had the chance. It would be only during the dead of night that she would be able to escape Blackmour and she wanted no weariness to hinder her when the opportunity to flee arose.

The feel of cold steel in her hand caught and held her attention. She sized up her unseen opponent and began to work, watching for the inevitable false move that would give his weakness away.

GILLIAN TURNED OVER ONTO HER SIDE, SEEKING A COM-fortable position. After a few moments, she gave up and rose from the bed, shivering. She looked in trunks, under the bed, behind tapestries. Fruitless. What fool had decided that leaving her without a chamber pot would be fine sport? She drew her cloak around her and contemplated the heavy wooden door. It was either leave her chamber and seek out a garderobe or remain bolted inside and suffer.

Another cramp in her belly told her that suffering wasn't an alternative. She took her courage in hand and unbolted her door as softly as she could, which was very softly indeed. The door made no sound as she opened it and slipped out into the passageway.

Finding a garderobe at her father's house had never been difficult. Even if she hadn't known where they were, she could have found them by following her nose. Her father never emptied the cesspit unless it was nigh to backing back up the shaft and spilling out into his passageways.

Blackmour was, as in all other things, completely different from her home. Gillian walked until she was weak, seeking nothing but relief. It was only by sheer luck that she opened a door and saw the moonlight coming in the window slit.

She saw to her needs, then stepped out into the passageway. She'd become so turned about that she had to stop and give serious thought as to where she had come from. She looked to her left, then looked to her right.

That was when she saw the shadows dancing along the wall.

It was as if her eyes were possessed by a contrary spirit. The very saints in heaven knew she didn't want to look up, but she was powerless to stop herself. There, to her right, was a stairwell. There was obviously someone in the chamber at the top, for the light was coming from above.

But it was a tower chamber.

Christopher of Blackmour's tower chamber.

She wanted to flee back to her chamber, but her feet seemed to have something else in mind. Before she could stop them, they were carrying her toward the steps. Then she found herself climbing those steep steps. Her breath came in harsh gasps, her body trembled. She had no desire to see what the tower contained, no matter what her feet seemed to think about the matter. She already knew what awaited her above. It was Lord Christopher, practicing his dark arts.

She clapped her hand over her mouth as she climbed up to the landing. The tower door was ajar. Faint light spilled out, sending shadows flickering along the stone.

Her heart beat in her throat. She trembled at the sound of heavy breathing and grunting coming from within the chamber. She could have sworn she heard the ring of steel. Merciful saints above, was he hacking a sacrifice to bits, preparing to drink its blood?

A movement startled her and she froze as the biggest, blackest dog she had ever seen raised itself up and looked her square in the eye. Nay, it wasn't a dog, it was a wolf. His eyes gleamed in the faint light, his bared teeth flashed white. Gillian was too terrified to scream. Lord Christopher's familiar, his devilish protector was before her, ready to rip out her throat!

The wolf moved closer but Gillian didn't dare move back. She closed her eyes and prayed that death would come quickly and painlessly. She felt a cold nose against her palm and sucked in her breath so hard that she almost choked. The Hound from Hell snuffled her hand, likely trying to decide if biting her there first would be worth his time.

Then Gillian felt a tug at her sleeve. She opened her eyes and looked at the great black beast. He had the hem of her sleeve in his mouth and was pulling her toward the bottom of the stairs. Gillian was surprised enough to let him do it. Once the hound had led her down the steps, he loped back up them and disappeared into the darkness.

Gillian didn't wait to see if Christopher would come out and converse with his familiar about who their next victim should be. She fled down the passageway as fast as her shaking legs would carry her, tried several doors before she found hers, then bolted herself inside her chamber. She dove under the bedclothes, cloak and all, and jerked the blankets up over her head.

It was worse than she had thought. She might have discounted the rumors, if she'd had but a shred of proof they were untrue. But she had seen the flickering candlelight and the shadows that twisted and spun madly along the wall. She had heard the mutterings of a warlock spinning his dark magic. She had heard the ring of steel signaling the sacrificial knife doing its foul work. Aye, she knew the truth for herself.

Christopher of Blackmour was evil incarnate.

And in four days she would be his.

five

CHRISTOPHER WALKED INTO HIS BEDCHAMBER FROM YET another long evening spent trying to distract himself from his troublesome thoughts. His mood was worse than it had been four days ago and he knew exactly at whose delicate feet to lay that blame.

"Shall I see to your gear, my lord?" Jason asked.

Christopher shoved his sword at his squire, then stripped off his sweat-soaked tunic and mopped his face with it. He sat down on the stool before the hearth and heaved a sigh of pure relief. At least now he would be too weary to think of aught besides a cold cup of ale and a soft bed beneath his back.

"I wasn't able to lure the lady Gillian from her chamber again today, my lord."

Christopher scowled. Jason had been dropping little daggers such as that off and on for days, as if he were bent on bludgeoning Christopher with tidings.

"She'd never seen the sea before, you know."

Christopher let loose a snort of irritation Jason couldn't have helped but notice. So Gillian had never seen the sea. Why would she, when Warewick was nowhere near the shore? Christopher grasped the cup of wine Jason gave him and ignored his squire with renewed vigor.

"I thought she had enjoyed seeing the keep that first day, but perhaps it overwhelmed her. Warewick is rather small. And from what I understand, her father never let her past the inner bailey. I wonder why not."

Christopher took another long draught of wine, determined to let the pounding in his ears drown out Jason's babbling.

"She smiled, though, that first day. 'Twas a most pleasing sight indeed—"

"Jason!" Christopher exclaimed.

"Aye, my lord?"

Christopher could almost see the innocent look on Jason's face, as it had been one the lad had mastered by the age of eight.

"Your father was too lenient in your youth. He should have taught you how to hold your tongue."

"Forgive me, my lord."

Ah, blessed silence. Christopher enjoyed it thoroughly for perhaps a quarter of an hour before he stopped enjoying it and started to find it annoying. No doubt Jason had a great deal more to tell, and, despite his own desire to know as little as possible about his future wife's habits, Christopher knew he would be wise to listen to it. Forewarned was forearmed, as Jason's father always said.

"Jason," he barked.

"Aye, my lord?"

"Come sit you here and cease with your incessant straightening. Pour me another cup of wine and have one yourself. Your days spent tending the wench have likely driven you daft."

Christopher waited until Jason was seated on the floor, waited until both cups were filled, then waited some more as Jason had a drink and a hearty belch. Then he suppressed the urge to strangle his squire.

"Well?" he demanded. "Did she make you daft, or not?

By St. George's throat, lad, you're closemouthed tonight!''

"But, my lord, you said you wished to know nothing more about her."

Christopher mentally reminded himself of all the reasons that throttling his squire would be unwise. The only decent one he could come up with was if he did so, Jason wouldn't be able to provide him with the tidings he wanted.

"I've changed my mind," Christopher muttered. "Speak freely while you may."

"As you wish, my lord." Jason gulped more wine. "I found her to be a charming maid, though a most timid one. She seemed quite undone by the fineness of the hall and especially the view from the battlements. After I showed her the sea, she wished to retreat to her chamber and she's been there ever since. When I told her today that her sire had arrived, she refused to unbolt her door. She pled illness."

"Why didn't you fetch the leech?"

"Because she was perfectly sound. I daresay she was afeared to meet her father. She bears a mark on her cheek, the mark of a cane or perhaps a small whip—"

"St. George's bones!"

"Newly made it looked to me when she first arrived," Jason continued quickly. "Sir Colin told me that her father had given the mark to her."

"Why didn't you tell me?" Christopher bellowed. He hurled his empty cup at the wall to his left; it slammed against the stone with a hearty ring.

"My lord, you seemed to want as little to do with the girl as possible—"

"Not when she's been beaten," Christopher growled. "Put a guard in front of her door and see that no one enters her chamber without my express permission."

"I'll see to it immediately."

Christopher gritted his teeth and wished desperately for someone to strike, preferably Gillian's sire. The man was beneath contempt. There had been times over the years that Christopher had been provoked mightily by a piece of Jason's mischief, but he had never laid a hand on the boy. He'd shouted at him as loudly and fiercely as the deed merited, but to strike him? Not even when he'd been tempted had he done it. The memory of beatings at his own father's hand had kept him from it.

And to beat a woman? A child who couldn't possibly defend herself against a man superior to her in size and strength? Christopher remembered very well just how large Bernard of Warewick was and how formidable his temper. He could well imagine the hell Gillian had suffered, for he remembered vividly having seen her after just such a beating.

He had been a serious youth of a score-and-four with spurs on his heels and hard-won gold in his purse. He and William had just returned from the continent where Christopher had gone to try to regain the fortune his father had heedlessly squandered. Only pure weariness had convinced him to spend a night or two at William's home, as he certainly hadn't had the time or the heart for play.

Gillian had been waiting on the front steps, obviously overjoyed to see her brother. Christopher had watched as William dismounted and scooped Gillian up in his arms. She had cried out and he had set her down instantly. It hadn't taken any effort to note that her back was tender. When she'd turned to lead them into the hall, Christopher had seen the remains of blood on the back of her gown.

He had blanched. William had turned to him and given him a look that had needed no words, though Christopher heard them as clearly as if William had said them aloud.

If I cannot aid her, you must. Now you see why.

It had taken William almost a se'nnight to coax Gillian out from behind her defenses completely. Even so, Christopher honestly could not remember having met Gillian's eyes even a single time. She had been a skittish, terrified child who trusted no one but her brother.

And now he could blame himself for adding to her terror by having left her at Warewick's mercy for half a year longer than he should have. He ground his teeth at the guilt that washed over him. Saints, how he hated having any part of this affair!

Jason's lithe step sounded and Christopher whirled toward the sound.

"Well?" he demanded.

"Sir Colin himself will stand guard, my lord, along with Captain Ranulf. I assured the lady Gillian that she was perfectly safe, but I don't think she believed me."

Christopher forced his breath out through clenched teeth. "Take your rest, Jason," he said. "I'll wish to rise before dawn and see that Warewick stirs up no mischief before the ceremony."

"You mean to wed her, my lord? In truth?"

Marriage. The very idea made the noose tighten about Christopher's neck. He'd felt the first touch of the rope when he'd finally sent off his offer to Warewick. As the weeks passed, the constriction had increased until he wondered if he would ever again succeed in taking a normal breath.

Now it was all he could do to keep his hands down by his side, not clawing at his throat in an effort to loosen the pressure, however imaginary it might have been.

If he could have, he would have bolted. Anywhere. Away from his responsibility, away from a marriage that could only bring him grief, away from having to care for anyone but himself. Saints, he wanted none of it!

He found his fingers at the neck of his tunic, tugging. This time, he didn't bother to fight the impulse.

"My lord?"

"Aye," Christopher rasped, "I'll wed her. I gave my word."

And what a heavy word it was.

• • •

GILLIAN SHIVERED AT THE TOUCH OF COLD HANDS against the back of her neck.

"Forgive me, milady," the serving maid whispered. "Shall I stir up the fire?"

Gillian nodded, relieved to have the girl's icy hands out of her hair. She stepped closer to the fire and held her hands to the blaze. The day was doomed, if the state of her locks was any indication. Why couldn't she have had smooth hair, hair that was tucked easily under a veil?

"You look beautiful, milady," the servant said, touching the sleeve of Gillian's dress.

Gillian looked down at herself. Though she had no such illusions about her person, the gown of heavy emerald silk was indeed lovely. It was only one of the many gowns that had been provided for her soon after her arrival, and it had been the one to appeal to her the most.

When she had asked her maid about who had seen the gowns fashioned, the girl had confessed to knowing nothing about them. Indeed, the girl knew nothing at all, if her responses told aught. When Gillian ventured questions about Lord Blackmour, the girl would only shiver and refuse to answer. She had looked near tears more than once.

As if she had heard Gillian's thoughts, the maid clutched Gillian's cold hands in her own and started to weep.

"I'm so sorry, milady. So desperately sorry."

"But . . ."

"Oh, for you," the girl wept. "I'm so sorry for you."

With that, she dropped Gillian's hands and fled from the chamber. Gillian stared at the heavy wooden door and felt her trembles begin again in earnest. She had managed to reduce them to small shivers over the past three days, but that had likely been because she had been training. Concentrating on her swordplay had left her with little room for thoughts of her black-hearted betrothed.

But now she had no choice but to think of him. What, by the names of all the holy saints above, was she doing binding herself to the Devil's spawn? She had heard him in his tower chamber. She had seen his wolf-hound. The only things she hadn't seen were his horns and his red eyes, but she would no doubt have a fine view of those too, just as soon as he had bolted her into his tower chamber, where he could torture her in peace.

Was there any hope of escape? She looked around frantically but saw no exit but the door. She started toward it, hesitated, then gathered her courage and strode forward. She would flee while the others were busy with preparations for the ceremony.

Her fingers were but a hand's breadth away from the door when the wood came flying toward her face. She jerked back, the brush of air against her cheek telling her how close she'd come to being the portal's unwitting victim.

Her father stood in the doorway, his eyes glinting, his lips drawn into a disdainful frown.

"Even on your wedding day, you're no beauty. Saints, child, couldn't you do something with those locks?"

Gillian shrank back. Her apprehension about wedding the Dragon of Blackmour was quickly forgotten in her fear over being alone with her sire. She could but imagine what Christopher might do to her; with her father, she already knew.

Warewick folded his arms over his chest and smiled coldly. "Well, aren't you going to beg me not to leave you with him? Plead with me to take you away from this accursed place?"

"How much worse can it be here than it was there?" she blurted out, panicked at the thought of returning to Warewick.

"Hold your tongue!" he bellowed, his fist raised. He stepped toward her. "I'll do Blackmour a favor by beating you one last time to silence you. It will save him the effort."

Gillian backed up. Not in her new gown. Oh, not in her wedding gown!

"My lord Warewick, I would respectfully suggest that you lower your hand."

Jason stood behind her father. Gillian let out a half-sob of relief.

"You insolent pup! How dare you speak to me in such tones?"

Two burly knights stepped into the chamber behind Jason. They were men easily as large as her father and wore looks that equaled her father's fiercest frowns.

"Lady Gillian belongs to my lord," Jason continued, "and he doesn't take kindly to the beating of women, especially when that woman is his. Now, if you'll make your way to the chapel, I'll see your daughter escorted down with the utmost care."

"She isn't his yet," Warewick growled.

The hiss of swords coming from scabbards made Warewick's expression darken even more. Gillian had the insane desire to laugh. During the whole of her life, she had always dreamed of a rescuer who was enormously skilled, yet gentle and kind. Here she was being rescued by men even more fierce than her father!

Her father uttered a black oath and strode from the room, shoving Jason out of his way. Gillian looked at the boy as he straightened his clothes, rearranged his hair and came to her, making her a low bow.

"I have come to see you to the chapel, my lady. Now, if I might offer you my arm?"

Her relief at the rescue disappeared abruptly at the reminder of what her immediate future held in store for her. She tried to swallow past the fear that leaped to her throat, but failed. Merciful saints above, time was running out!

"Ah, I think I need a moment to see to my hair," she said, forcing a smile to her stiff lips.

"Why?" Jason asked. "It looks well enough to me." He smiled. "Come, lady, before my lord wears a trench in the chapel with his pacing."

"But . . ."

Jason took her gently by the elbow and tugged. "Trust me," he said, "all will be well. You'll see."

What she would see was Hellfire burning brightly in her husband's eyes; aye, she was sure enough of that.

"You're chilled," Jason announced. "I can well understand the feeling. You know, I first came to Blackmour when I was a wee lad of six summers and I vow my lips were blue until I was eight. You will accustom yourself to it in time, my lady, but until then you'll have to take care that you are always wearing a cloak. Already 'tis almost spring. We'll likely have warmer weather in a month or two. There is nothing quite like an afternoon of sunshine after the fog has melted away. I daresay you'll enjoy passing those afternoon hours in the garden. My lord doesn't care for it exactly, but I think it would do him good to be outside more often, spending his time in pleasure."

By the time Gillian had digested most of that, she found she was wearing a heavy fur cloak and she had descended to the great hall. Before she could dig in her heels, Jason had whisked her out the door.

It was dark outside, dark as twilight, though Gillian knew it was but midday. It looked as though even the elements were celebrating their dark prince's nuptials.

A drizzle began the moment her foot touched the dirt of the courtyard and she took that as a sign. Either those black, thunderous clouds were preparing to welcome her pitiful soul later that night, or the weather disapproved of Christopher's choice. Either way, Gillian knew she was doomed.

She looked around desperately for an avenue of escape but saw nothing but two rows of seasoned warriors flanking the path to the chapel. She looked back quickly over her shoulder to see the ranks closing in behind her. Her only choice was to move forward.

Jason pulled her up the steps to the chapel, then steered her off into the priest's private chamber. The priest himself was there, as were her father, Colin and another man or two she didn't recognize. But she did recognize the tall man standing before the priest with his broad back to her.

Gillian felt Jason urge her forward and she went, only because he was pushing her. She stopped alongside Christopher and looked up at the man who would become her husband in a matter of moments.

He was dark. Not only was his hair dark, his very soul seemed dark and brooding. She had to admit that he was handsome, as handsome as only the Devil incarnate could be. His jaw was stern and his nose finely chiseled enough, but that was where devilish handsomeness ended and harshness began.

His lips were compressed in a tight line, as if he were mightily displeased or on the verge of letting fly a fit of rage. His jaw was clenched, his brows drawn together, the muscles in his neck and shoulders tensed. Even his long hair was tousled, as if he had sought to rip it out by the roots. No doubt he'd done it in his anguish at setting foot inside a holy place, a place obviously at odds with his black soul.

He turned his head toward her and she lost her breath with a gasp of terror. Stern and rugged he was, and completely wrong for her husband. Despite all his other devilish flaws, he was cruel and unyielding. She could see that easily in the depths of his dark blue eyes. Saints above, she would never have a kind word from this man. What she needed was patience, compassion, mercy.

Christopher of Blackmour surely possessed none of those qualities.

As if to confirm that, he thrust out his hand, half a foot in front of her.

"You're late, wench."

She would have turned and fled if Jason hadn't had the flat of his hand in her back. She had no choice but to remain where she was. She put her hand in the Scourge of England's massive paw and prayed he wouldn't break her fingers.

Her father stepped up on her other side and she cringed.

"Don't stand so close to her, Warewick," her future husband growled, not sparing her father a glance. Gillian jumped when Christopher put his arm around her shoulders and pulled her closer to him.

She looked up at him, but his eyes were focused on the priest. She dropped her gaze and tried to accustom herself to the feel of Blackmour's heavy arm draped around her in a semblance of protectiveness. Then she almost laughed. As if such a thing would ever happen again! Nay, he would wed her and be done with her, or, worse yet, drag her up to his tower chamber and sacrifice her to his master.

Before she could even decide if she had enough courage to blurt out that she wanted to seek asylum with the king rather than wed with the Devil's spawn, the priest was asking for a recounting of her dowry.

She listened to her father name her portion and forced her shoulders to remain back, not slump as they so desperately wanted to do. Naught but Braedhalle, her father's poorest bit of land, and a paltry sum in knight's fees. He would have been kinder not to dower her at all.

Then Colin began a listing of what Blackmour would bring to the marriage and Gillian knew the full meaning of shame. His holdings were nothing short of princely! 'Twas no wonder his hall was so fine. Gillian felt her knees give way in humiliation. Her betrothed's arm immediately tightened around her shoulders.

"Steady," he whispered under his breath, his voice a rough sound against her ear.

She jerked herself upright and struggled to ignore the smug look on her father's face and the overwhelming fear she felt at being so close to Christopher and knowing what he was capable of.

The contract was laid on a flat stand before them and a clerk proffered a quill. Jason took it before she could reach for it.

"Allow me," he said, making her a small bow. He put

the quill in her hand and gestured toward the document. "You see the place for your signature, my lady, at the bottom on the left, not far from the edge of the parchment." His voice was soft, so soft she barely heard it. "You'll have to sign without any flourishes, I fear. There isn't much room for it."

Gillian looked at him, wondering if the chill had suddenly seeped into his brain. "I can see that perfectly well, thank you."

Jason only gave her a grave smile. "Of course, my lady. I was only trying to be of service."

Gillian signed her name, then looked down at it in surprise. She had just put herself into the Dragon's talons, without hesitation, without pause. Merciful saints above, she was almost his!

Unless he chose not to sign the agreement.

She watched Jason dip the quill into the pot of ink and put it into Christopher's hand, in much the same way he had done with her.

"There isn't much space for you either, my lord," Jason murmured, "as you can well see. Go carefully."

Christopher didn't hesitate. Gillian watched with a sinking feeling in her belly as Christopher felt for the edges of the parchment, then settled the quill over it.

Over the last few words of the document, rather. She looked up at him quickly. Couldn't he see he was about to sign his name where it couldn't be read?

"My lord, surely not," Jason whispered quickly. "Do you intend to blot out some of your holdings? A bit lower, perhaps."

Christopher's expression couldn't have been any more strained as he signed his name with careful strokes. Perhaps he couldn't read or write. Aye, that would be likely enough. The man was a warrior, and few warriors could even sign their own names. But he could certainly see what he was doing and he was coming perilously close to traveling completely off the parchment. She opened her mouth to warn him, but before she could say aught, the quill was back in Jason's possession and Christopher's heavy hands were on her shoulders, turning her toward him.

She stared up into his eyes in terror, expecting him to use her as roughly as she'd seen her father's knights do to the kitchen maids.

Instead, he gently eased a ring onto her finger, then kissed her very quickly and very chastely on the forehead.

It was over. Colin slung his arm around Christopher's shoulders and led him off to the chapel. Gillian followed with Jason, dazed. She was so surprised at Christopher's lack of brutality, she could do no more than sit where Jason placed her, next to her husband on a long bench at the front of the chapel.

Mass was long, far longer than she had ever remembered it being. Perhaps it seemed long because everything was so different. A signature on a scrap of parchment, a chaste kiss from the Scourge of England and suddenly her life was completely and irrevocably changed. The heavy gold band on her finger felt more like a manacle, shackling her to the huge man who sat next to her, squirming.

She stole a glance at him. He was shifting uncomfortably, much like a lad being forced to attend Mass when he would have rather been out stirring up mischief. No doubt Christopher was being needled by remembrances of all the poor souls he'd sacrificed over the years. Gillian couldn't help but take a tiny bit of pleasure in his discomfort. After all, he did surely merit it.

They were called forward to take communion and she rose. She was very surprised when Christopher rose right along with her. Didn't he realize he would damn his soul with his unworthiness? Perhaps his soul was already so black he no longer cared.

He took her hand without hesitation and started toward the front of the chapel, completely ignoring the woman kneeling directly before him.

"My lord," she whispered urgently, "you will step on her if you do not attend better."

He froze and remained motionless, but his jaw tightened as he clenched his teeth. Ah, so he was suffering pangs of guilt. Gillian looked up at him and, to her surprise, felt her terror recede at the small stirring of pity inside her. How could Christopher admit to his folk what he truly was by refusing the priest's ministrations? His soul was damned, but that was no reason to upset his household. Devil though he might have been, he at least had that much care for his people.

The ones he wasn't leading up to his tower chamber, that is.

Gillian tugged the slightest bit on his hand, urging him to the left. He obeyed instantly, probing the floor in front of him gingerly with his foot, like a blind man in a strange place. He knelt down with her before the priest and she could have sworn she heard him sigh lightly in relief.

Relief over what, she couldn't tell. Didn't the thought of even receiving the holy communion trouble his black soul? Or was he completely past feeling?

He accepted the priest's ministrations just as she did, without a hint of reticence. Gillian found herself past being surprised at his actions. Demon spawn were obviously much more complex beings than she had originally thought.

She made to rise, but he kept her kneeling with him with gentle pressure on her hand.

"I would pray yet a while," he said tightly.

Pray? She sank back down next to him, her hand still captured in his. By the saints, the man was a confusing tangle of contradictions. Surely he couldn't mean to truly pray, yet he knelt with his eyes closed and a very earnest look on his brutally handsome face. Either he prayed in truth, or he was a very convincing liar.

But what need had he to lie? Colin certainly hadn't remained at the front of the chapel for more time than

necessary. Her father hadn't even come forward. Yet
Christopher gave every indication of a man who was begging his Lord for some great boon.

He had even ceased to squirm, which she didn't know
how to take at all. The most surprising thing, though, was
that his hand around hers was warm. It wasn't the hand of
a warlock.

Wizards and warlocks being cold-handed, of course.

At that realization, other troubling thoughts came to her.
William had loved Christopher well. They had squired together, then spent a number of years on the continent, tourneying together. She even remembered when Christopher
had come home with William several years ago. Though
she had been terrified of the large, silent knight, William
had shown no fear. Surely William would have known if
something were amiss. Her brother was no fool.

A terrible suspicion began to bloom in her mind. Had
she been the fool?

The longer she knelt in the chapel, the more she began
to suspect that was the case. Had she ever known a serving
wench to tell the truth? Nay, she had not. And where had
she heard all the tales she knew about Christopher of
Blackmour?

From the kitchen wenches.

It was true that her new husband was a most imposing
man, but did that make him a devil in the flesh? Colin of
Berkhamshire had a most ferocious reputation, but hadn't
she found him to have rather a soft underbelly? Even dragons were rumored to have chinks in their scaly armor.
Perhaps Christopher was tenderhearted and only frowned
to hide that.

Christopher pulling her to her feet alerted her to the
finish of Mass. She looked up at her husband and stiffened
at the sight of his face. Nay, tenderhearted wasn't a possibility with a frown like that. It was entirely possible that
Christopher of Blackmour was a mere man and not a demon, but he was anything but gentle and kind. His ex-

pression was thunderous. She shrank back in fear, bumping into Jason.

Fortunately her husband seemed to have forgotten her. He was staring out over the chapel, no doubt looking at her sire who had started complaining already about the chill and the lack of creature comforts. Gillian winced at the volume of her father's charges.

Jason pushed her up to Christopher's side. "The feast is prepared, my lord, and none too soon. Lady Gillian looks nigh onto fainting from hunger, don't you think?"

Christopher agreed readily with his squire. Gillian knew she looked nothing of the kind, but didn't argue. The less notice she garnered, the safer she would be.

"My lord," Jason said, propelling Gillian forward with a hand under her elbow, "I daresay the last of these benches needs to be repaired. See you how badly 'tis worn? Aye, and the doors need to be cleaned. You can see the filth from five paces, can you not?"

Gillian was sure Christopher could, and she wanted desperately to tell Jason to be silent. Pointing out to the Dragon of Blackmour that his chapel was a sty was certainly not the way to endear oneself to him.

"And these steps," Jason continued, heedless of his precarious situation. "Aye, the priest needs to better watch over his lads. The chapel could be much cleaner, even here outside. Here, let me kick this straw out of your way. I'll have it seen to immediately. At least the courtyard is smooth, is it not? Lady Gillian, the path from the chapel to the hall used to be quite treacherous. I have a fine scar on my arm from where I tripped in this precise place, only a few paces from safety in the great hall. You, there, move out of our way. Why do these peasants insist on sitting upon the steps here? There are only four steps up to the hall, surely they could choose a more likely place to rest."

Gillian could see perfectly well what was before her without Jason's constant description of it. If he were seeking to put her at ease, he was failing miserably. She was certain it was doing nothing but angering her new lord.

Despite her attempts at warning the boy with her eyes alone, he kept up a steady stream of drivel right until the moment she was seated next to Christopher on the dais and the food began to come from the kitchen.

Supper was a long, unpleasant affair. Her father downed wine as if he were dying of thirst. His temper didn't improve because of it.

Christopher was silent and mannerless. He came close to knocking over his goblet half a dozen times. Jason rescued it the first time, then Gillian took over the task. Christopher knocked meat off the board, fingered the length of a loaf of bread before breaking off a piece, then dipped his hand in a cup of sauce before he realized what he was doing. The more clumsy he became, the more angry he became, which made him just that much more bumbling.

Gillian felt her patience begin to thin. The longer she sat next to her husband, the more she was sure the rumors about him couldn't possibly be true. Even the Devil couldn't have spawned something this inept.

At least Jason had stopped hovering. He had been sent to the kitchens on some errand and Gillian was left to see to her husband. He seemed not to notice her at all, which couldn't have pleased her more. The last thing she wanted was for him to remember she was there, for the saints only knew what he would decide to do with her now that she was his.

One of her father's men came to stand before the high table. Christopher didn't bother to acknowledge him either. The man remained silent, waiting. Moments continued to pass and still Christopher made no sign of even having seen the man standing before him.

"My lord, surely you should speak to him," Gillian whispered.

"Who?"

"My father's man who stands before you."

Had Christopher stiffened any more, he would have been less likely to bend than a sword.

"What is it, man?" Christopher demanded.

"My lord Warewick has complaints about the fare, Your Lordship, and I was sent to—"

"If he doesn't care for the meal, let him seek a place at someone else's table."

"And his bedchamber—"

"Let him bed down in the stables!" Christopher shouted, rising. He slapped his hands on the table and glared at her father's man. "Nay, he's likely to make off with my horseflesh. Let him sleep outside the walls. Indeed, take yourself and your men and begone!"

Gillian gaped up at her husband in shock. How brave he was to insult her father so thoroughly! Perhaps he had no idea what Warewick was capable of.

Her eyes fell to his shoulders, to the muscular arms his clothing didn't manage to hide. Then again, perhaps Christopher was aware of her father's prowess in battle and he just didn't find it intimidating. She looked at his face again. Nay, he wouldn't find Warewick intimidating, because he was so much so himself. Indeed, should it come to blows, she had the feeling her father wouldn't come out the victor.

"I'll not be insulted this way," Christopher bellowed. "Warewick!"

Gillian looked at her father, who had left his place further down the table and come to stand next to his man. Christopher continued to bellow for her father, as if he couldn't see who was standing right in front of him.

"Too much wine," Warewick slurred, "has clouded your vision, Blackmour."

Christopher started, as if he had just realized his father-in-law was before him. "Out of my hall," he snarled.

Warewick shook his head drunkenly. "I'll take the wench with me."

"When I'm dead," Christopher said, his voice cold. Gillian found herself snagged by Christopher's heavy hand and pulled up behind him.

She was shocked enough at making contact with his broad back to not protest his action. He held her pinned there, his long fingers a vise around her wrist.

Somehow, though, the sensation was not unpleasant. He certainly smelled better than Colin. His fingers curled around her wrist were tight, but not painful. His muscles were rigid with anger, but his words certainly indicated that his anger was directed at her sire, not at her.

And, best of all, his back made a handy shield between her and her father. She found she could tuck herself completely behind him, likely without even a hint of her gown showing. She pressed her forehead timidly against his back and closed her eyes, pretending that not a soul could see her to harm her.

"Begone," Christopher warned, his deep voice rumbling in his chest, "while my temper is still cool."

"You're drunk," Bernard snarled. "Too drunk to see aught but the bottom of your cup. Beware, Blackmour. That kind of blindness will be your undoing."

The hall erupted into a small war. Gillian felt Christopher shift, heard the hiss of his sword as it came from the scabbard, felt his hand tighten around her wrist. But she didn't move. She clutched the back of his tunic and kept her eyes closed.

The battle was, mercifully, very short-lived. Only a handful of moments had passed before her father and his escort were aided in finding the gates. Once the hall door was closed, Jason put his hand on Christopher's shoulder.

"The hall is cleared, my lord," Jason said softly, so softly Gillian almost missed his words, and she was standing close enough to feel his breath on her hair.

Christopher didn't relax as he guided Gillian toward her chair. He was looking at it, but obviously too angry to see it for he almost sent her sprawling to the floor with his gentle push. Only Jason's quick hands saved her from a tumble. Christopher groped for his own chair and lowered himself into it carefully, feeling for the arms as if he weren't sure where they were.

Gillian sat back and watched her husband. He fumbled for a piece of bread, tipped over a goblet of wine and poked himself sharply on the tip of the knife he'd left lying on the table, all as if he couldn't see what he were doing. She looked quickly at his face and noted that his eyes were not following the motion of his hands. She began to wonder if he truly *were* drunk.

Except she knew he hadn't touched his wine.

She froze. Christopher was merely clumsy, wasn't he?

"My lord, Warewick's men are through the gates," Jason said quietly.

"Are there any left in the hall?"

"Nay, my lord."

"How long had he been standing there while I bellowed for him, lad?"

"Long enough, my lord."

Christopher cursed fluently, but softly.

Gillian met Jason's eyes and felt herself blanch. Jason only smiled grimly, then clapped his hand on his lord's shoulder before he turned and walked away.

The merrymaking began again, despite the conspicuous absence of Christopher's guardsmen. Minstrels sang, pipers piped, food and wine continued to appear far into the evening. Gillian watched it all without seeing any of it.

Just as her husband did.

She clutched the arms of her chair, finding it to be the only thing stable in a world that had just become full of things she had never expected.

She had expected to have Christopher beat her. She had expected to have him ignore her. She had even expected to see horns pop out from atop his head and watch his eyes burn as red as Hellfire as he suggested a visit to his tower chamber.

But she hadn't, not in the deepest recesses of her soul, expected him to not be able to see her.

Merciful saints above, her husband was blind.

six

CHRISTOPHER SUCKED ON THE WOUND HIS KNIFE HAD left in his finger. Normally such things never happened. Perhaps he could be forgiven for forgetting where he had laid his eating dagger, given the circumstances.

A heavy hand clapped him on the shoulder, almost pushing him out of his chair. A body sat down on his right, belching loudly.

"Bloody hell, Colin," Christopher growled. "Leave me in peace."

"Time for the beddin'," Colin said. "Give me some aid, lads—"

At least Christopher's sense of direction hadn't been disturbed, for he managed to grab hold of Colin's throat easily enough.

"Silence," Christopher whispered sharply.

Colin gurgled his response, then knocked Christopher's hand away, laughing.

"Saints, Chris, don't seem so eager! Jason, go up and warm the blankets for your master's delicate toes—"

"Enough of this," Christopher hissed.

"And wine for the man. He'll need a goodly amount to strengthen him for his labors—"

Christopher almost missed the sound, it was so soft. But his ears at least hadn't failed him and he realized the muffled squeak of terror he had heard had come from his bride. And to be sure, he couldn't blame her a bit for it. Well, the sooner he got her away from the drunken idiots about him, the less miserable she would be. He could give her that much.

"Enough," he exclaimed, leaping to his feet. He reached down for Gillian and managed to grasp some cloth-covered appendage. He pulled her to her feet and put her behind him. "There will be no standing up tonight, so—"

"We'll see it done," Colin said, "won't we, lads?"

Christopher turned Gillian toward what he hoped were the stairs.

"If you've a grain of sense in your head, run!" he said. "I'll be right behind you."

She was rigid with terror, but Christopher could do nothing for that. He gave her a push.

"Go, child, unless you'd have me do worse than bed you."

Her sharp intake of breath was audible even over Colin's drunken babbling. Christopher released her wrist and heard her light footsteps stumble away. He followed her immediately, drawing his sword. Gillian cried out softly and he heard what sounded distinctly like wife and chair crashing to the floor. He groped for her but found nothing until he heard her shriek. Her terror ate at him, but he could do nothing but use it to his advantage. He followed the harsh sound of her breathing until he'd caught her and pulled her up to her feet. He kept hold of her with one hand while he grasped his sword with the other.

Blind though he might have been, his sword was none theless brutally sharp and not even Colin was fool enough to step in the path of its arc. Christopher pushed Gillian up the steps as he backed up them himself, waving his sword meaningfully at his former brother-in-law and personal guardsmen.

Guardsmen he would, of course, have flogged at his first opportunity in repayment of their sport.

Once they reached the landing, Christopher swiftly dragged Gillian toward his chamber. She was silent, frighteningly so. He would have thought she had fainted if she hadn't been moving with him.

Aye, that and her trembles. Christopher gritted his teeth at the remorse that washed over him, but he had no time to ease her fear. She would have to be terrified until he'd finished what he intended to do, which was provide his bloody mates proof that he'd bedded her well and truly.

He'd barely bolted the door before heavy fists began pounding and voices called encouragement.

"Silence!" Christopher bellowed.

Colin's hearty laughter came through the door. "Best heed him, lads. Wouldn't want to divert his attention to things of lesser importance."

Christopher dragged Gillian to the bed. Actually, Gillian dragged rather easily, for she was stiff as a post. He left her shuddering next to the bed while he felt for the blankets and quilts and flung them back. Gillian's breath caught in her throat, but Christopher paid her no heed.

He jerked his knife free from his belt and Gillian cried out.

"Good," he said, through gritted teeth. "Scream again."

"My lord, please," she whispered.

"Scream, damn you!"

Not waiting for her to obey him, he dragged his blade across his arm with a quick, violent motion.

Gillian shrieked so loud he flinched. He wiped his arm across the sheets, praying it would look convincing enough.

"Scream again," he said, yanking the sheet off the feather tic.

Unfortunately, his bride made no more noise. Christopher managed to find her without groping overmuch, and his fingers told him what his eyes never could. She was trembling from head to toe. More shrieks would have been convincing to the louts beyond the door, but Christopher knew Gillian wasn't capable of them. And he wasn't capable of forcing them from her. He was already sick from the terror he'd heard in her voice.

He resheathed his knife in his belt and jerked the sheets from the bed. He strode over to the door, unbolted it and shoved the sheets out into the passageway.

"Proof," he said coldly. "Now, leave me in peace."

"Saints above, Chris," Colin said, his voice unusually hushed, "you didn't have to hurt the girl."

Christopher slammed the door and shoved the bolt home with a vicious oath. It wasn't enough that he was wedded again against his will. It wasn't enough that he felt unwelcome pity for a woman he fully intended to ignore long into his old age. And it wasn't enough that he had cut himself too bloody deep on the arm and it stung like a dozen belts across his back. *Now* he had to listen to Colin accuse him of cruelty and feel the guilt of it, even though he hadn't touched a hair on Gillian's head!

He cursed again as he walked to his hearth and started a small fire. Midway through the task, he decided instead on a large fire. He could hear Gillian's teeth chattering from where he knelt.

"Don't just stand there gawking, girl," he said curtly. "Either come warm yourself, or get into bed."

There was no sound of movement, but the chattering of teeth ceased abruptly. The child was likely now too fearful to even shiver.

"I won't touch you, if that's what you're fretting over," he added. "Neither of us has the stomach for the deed, I'll warrant."

There was still no movement. Christopher conceded the battle. She could stand there all bloody night for all he cared. All he wanted to do was become warm, then to go to sleep—hopefully to wake and find the entire day had been naught but a foul dream. Merciful saints above, this had been a mistake!

It served him right for having given into his foolish feelings of responsibility. He could have just as easily ignored William's missive. In time the guilt would have faded and he would have been at peace. He also surely wouldn't be suffering from a slash across his forearm that smarted far worse than his pride. He ripped off his sleeve and held one end of it between his teeth as he tried to wrap the rest of it around the wound.

Cold fingers on his wrist made him yelp in surprise. There was a squeak and a sudden crash, as if a stool had been tipped over.

"Saints, girl, you startled me," he exclaimed.

Wood scraped against wood as the stool was carefully righted. Then he heard the faint rustle of skirts.

"I c-could bind that," she offered. Her voice was so soft, he had to strain to hear her words.

Christopher contemplated his choices. The offer was made kindly enough, but he wanted none of her kindness. On the other hand, he couldn't see his arm to bind it very well, and he didn't have two free hands at his disposal to do the task properly. There was no weakness in allowing Gillian to do the deed for him.

He thrust out his arm and held out the torn sleeve.

"Be quick about it."

He gritted his teeth as her chilled fingers skimmed hesitantly over the flesh near the cut. She was freezing and she was likely terrified. A wave of pity threatened to engulf him, but he pushed it back ruthlessly. Aye, he needed none of that to cloud his judgement. He had wed her because she was William's sister. He had made it seem that he had bedded her for not only his peace, but hers too. But to feel aught for her?

Not if it was the last thing he ever did.

"My l-lord?"

"Aye," he said, gruffly.

"Perhaps you should have stitches—"

"Just bind it!" he commanded sharply. "And if you cannot do it without babbling, leave it be. I've endured worse and survived."

The silence in the chamber was broken only by the crackle of twigs snapping and popping in the hearth. Gillian's movements were so slow and timid; not even the cloth made a noise as she pulled it together gently.

"Harder than that, girl."

"But, it will pain you—"

"By St. George's bones, child! 'Tis a paltry cut, not a life-threatening wound! Pull it taut, for pity's sake."

Either she was powerfully weak, or she feared to hurt him. As he suspected it was the latter, he bit off a curse and fumbled for one end of the wrapping.

"Hold, lady, while I pull."

He jerked the dressing tight about his arm and held it thus as she knotted the ends together. Then he sat back with a sigh and waited for her to get up and leave.

She didn't move.

"Well?" he demanded. "Are you going to sit there all night? Be off with you!"

She moved, but it seemed to be only a shifting of positions. Christopher suppressed the urge to toss her bodily from him. The very *last* thing he wanted, far and beyond all the other things he didn't want from her, was to sit and make idle conversation. Already he knew too much about her. Any more and he would surely regret it.

"Why?"

He blinked. "What?"

"Why did you? Cut yourself," she added slowly.

"So they'd leave us be, of course."

She was silent for some time, but he had the distinct feeling he wasn't going to be let off so lightly. Now would come questions about why he hadn't bedded her in truth

and what he intended to make of their marriage, farce
though it was. What was he to tell her? That he had wed
her only because of his vow to William? That he couldn't
bear the thought of speaking to her, much less allowing
himself to touch her? That even the thought of allowing
her into the crudely fashioned defense he'd built around
himself terrified him worse than any battle ever had? Nay,
he could say none of those things. She would have to think
of him what she would. He wouldn't explain himself.

"My lord?"

"Eh?" he asked, wondering if he'd missed something.

"I asked why, my lord. If you please," she added timidly.

"Why I cut myself?" he repeated. "I already told you
why."

"Oh."

There was a very long pause.

"Then, you had to cut yourself," she said, sounding
exceedingly puzzled, "so they would leave us alone?"

"Aye," he said, exasperated. "So they would think I'd
bedded you."

"Ah, I see."

The saints be praised for that. Now if she could just see
her way clear to go to bed and leave him with his own
thoughts . . .

"But you didn't bed me. Did you?"

The throbbing in his arm intensified in direct proportion
to the throbbing that had begun behind his eyes.

"Gillian."

"My lord?"

"Pour me wine."

Only moments later, a cold cup was pressed into his
hand.

"Gillian."

"My lord?"

"Go get into bed."

She gasped. "But—"

"Alone," he exclaimed. "Go get into bed alone and leave me be! Saints, child, you're worse than Jason with your questions and foolishness. Now, obey me, while my humor is still tolerably fine. I guarantee you it won't last much longer."

She obeyed him without hesitation, if her abrupt flight to the bed told the tale true. Christopher stretched out before his hearth and willed away the pounding in his head. If the girl couldn't tell whether or not he'd bedded her, she was far more innocent than she should have been, and far too innocent for him to face that night.

The pain in his head had finally subsided to a dull, irritating ache when his blissful silence was broken.

"My lord?"

He grunted in response, the only noise he could bear to make.

"You . . . you'll not g-go . . ." She cleared her throat a time or two. ". . . tower chamber?"

"What?" he barked. "Speak up, girl."

"Your tower chamber," she blurted out. "You're not going there tonight?"

"I'm not going anywhere," he groaned as he rolled toward the fire, pulling a fur up over his shoulder for warmth. "Go to sleep, Gillian. I beg you."

He heard her settle back into bed, then listened to the ropes creak as she shifted. Finally, all movement stopped. Christopher relaxed, waiting for sleep to claim him.

"Thank you, my lord."

He didn't answer, though he could have. He didn't want her gratitude. He didn't want her in his bed. He didn't even want her in his house, but there was no helping that. He had given his word she would come to no harm. His word was one of the few things remaining him.

But allowing her to stay didn't mean anything else would change. He would put her back in her own chamber come morning. Bedding terrified virgins was not something he enjoyed. Perhaps in a year or two he would give it some thought, for he would need an heir eventually. But he wouldn't think of it now. It was all he could do to keep himself from splintering into scores of pieces from his grief. Perhaps in another year or two his sight would return and he could think on other things. Now, he could do no more than survive each day as it came, thinking of no one but himself.

Thank you, my lord.

Her words rang in his mind. He smiled without humor. Aye, he'd certainly freed her from hell, hadn't he? He had rescued her from one loveless prison only to bring her straight to another.

He was such a fine example of knightly virtues.

seven

GILLIAN WOKE WITH A START, HER HEART POUNDING. SHE remained perfectly still, praying she hadn't already moved and alerted her husband to her awakened state.

There was, however, no sound of soft snoring within the chamber. She opened one eye a slit and found that the bedcurtains were open and the sun was struggling to slip through the few cracks in the shutters. She lifted her head up slowly, peeking over the top of the blanket.

The bedchamber was empty. Gillian sat up, hugging the blankets to her chest, and sighed in relief. She was safe.

For the moment, at least.

She tensed instinctively at the thought, then forced herself to relax. Christopher hadn't harmed her. Indeed, he had been as good as his word as far as the bed was concerned for he hadn't come to it. She would certainly be the one to know since she hadn't slept a wink during the whole of the night.

And he hadn't carried her off to his tower chamber to offer her up as a sacrifice. She was most grateful for that. She hoped he'd heard her say as much the night before.

Why he had cut his arm, though, was still a mystery to her—as much a mystery as why he'd thrown out bloodied sheets to Colin and his mates. Had they expected him to carve her up in some variety of ritual? Kind of him, to use his own arm instead of hers.

She leaned back against the headboard and stared out over Christopher's chamber, letting her questions and speculations settle about her like so much dust. Christopher had obviously been in no mood to give her any answers the night before, not that she would have demanded them from him. A timid robin did not stand forth and demand answers from the dragon looming over her. Gillian knew her place well enough and had no intention of stepping out of it. The moment she did, Christopher would notice her and then she would surely run afoul of his ire.

So, what to do? She fingered the rich quilt that covered her and gave thought to her choices.

She could flee. That would have certainly been her choice the morn before. Now, though, escape wasn't quite as appealing. Beyond Blackmour's thick walls lay London, true enough, but her father was also lurking about the countryside somewhere, likely abusing his peasants to appease his anger over Blackmour's treatment of him. Gillian had no desire to be in the same shire with her father.

She could stay, but remain out of sight. She turned that alternative over in her mind and found it rather to her liking. Surely she could snatch a few hot meals now and then and find a safe place to sleep. Jason seemed to be fond of her, at least enough so that he might help her escape Christopher's notice.

She sat up with a start. As if she would actually have to hide from her husband. The shocking truth she had learned the night before came back to her with just as much force as it had the first time. Christopher was blind. Even if by some terrible misfortune she did attract his attention, she could escape him. At the very least he wouldn't be able to see her to hit her. Closing her eyes, she sent a prayer of thanks flying heavenward. His blindness was a blessing indeed, one she would be ever grateful for.

She left the bed with a smile, feeling for the first time in years a bit of hope for her future. Perhaps Christopher might even begin to look on her as a younger sister of sorts and treat her as William had. Of course, he would never be as kind as William had been, but she could accustom herself to that. Perhaps in time Christopher would even forget thoughts of taking her to his tower chamber. Though she felt quite sure he wasn't a warlock, she wasn't at all sure that what he did at night was anything she wanted any part of.

A knock sounded on the door and she stiffened immediately. She looked around frantically for covering of some kind, then realized she was still wearing her gown from the day before. She dragged her hand self-consciously through her unruly curls, then approached the portal cautiously.

"Aye?" she ventured.

"Lady Gillian, 'tis Jason. My lord said you likely wouldn't want to come downstairs, so I brought you something to eat. Will you have it?"

Gillian opened the door and admitted her husband's squire, who set a wooden trencher laden with food on a table near the hearth. Jason looked her over carefully, then met her eyes.

"You are well?" he asked gravely.

She nodded, silent.

Jason hesitated, then shut his mouth and simply stood there, as silent as Gillian was. As time passed, Gillian began to grow anxious. She felt decidedly uncomfortable with the lad and could find no reason for it, save his own reticence.

"Jason, is there something amiss?" She paled as her thoughts continued down along that well-trod path. "Oh, merciful saints, have I angered him—"

"Nay," Jason interrupted quickly. He held up his hand,

as if to stop her from saying anything else. "By no means, my lady. He was mightily irritated this morn—"

She gasped.

"—at Sir Colin for his actions yestereve."

"Oh," she said, only slightly relieved. "You are certain?"

"Aye, lady." He paused, then looked down at his feet. "But you, my lady. You are well?" He looked up at her from under his eyelashes. "Unhurt?"

" 'Tis not me who was hurt," she said quickly. " 'Twas Christopher. His arm, you know."

"His arm?"

"Aye," she nodded, feeling another wave of gratitude wash over her. "He cut it, you see, to bleed on the sheets. I suppose it was done to spare me a trip to his tower chamber. I'm most grateful."

"Tower chamber?"

Gillian looked at the lad and wondered if too many years at Blackmour had driven him slightly daft.

"Where he works his dark arts."

Jason stared at her blankly.

"I'm fairly certain he isn't a warlock, Jason, but even you will admit he does devilish deeds in that tower. I've seen his Hound from Hell. I've heard the ring of his sacrificial knife about its foul work. I've no idea what else he does up there, but I have the feeling it isn't pleasant. I'm simply grateful he spared me yestereve."

Jason was staring at her so intently that she began to feel as if she'd said a great deal more than she should have. Perhaps Christopher didn't want anyone knowing of his kindness. Knowing his reputation, she had the feeling that might be the case.

"Jason," she said quickly, "please don't repeat anything I've said. I shouldn't have said aught and I'm not sure why I did." She paused, then tilted her head and looked at him thoughtfully. "It must be that I trust you. Aye, that's it, then."

She closed her mouth tight and simply smiled. She wouldn't add any more burden to Jason's keeping of her words.

He took her hand and bowed low over it.

"I am honored," he said. He straightened, his face slightly red. "If I may serve you in any way, lady, all you must do is ask."

"That is very kind of you, Jason. But I need nothing now."

He bowed again, then left the chamber.

Gillian ate slowly, savoring what was surely the best meal she had eaten in all her score-and-one years. It was either that Christopher's cook was far better than her father's or that she had, for the first time ever, peace in which to enjoy her food.

It was a most delightful pleasure.

SHE SPENT THE AFTERNOON STUDYING THE THINGS IN Christopher's chamber, hoping for a clue as to the character of the man she was now wed to. His things were generally very much like William's, save his clothes were better cared for than William's had been. Then again, perhaps it was that Christopher didn't have her doing his mending. William had never complained about her lack of skill, though Gillian knew he likely should have.

There was a small trunk near the window that she couldn't open. It was either full of implements of torture or merely personal things Christopher didn't want his servants plundering. Gillian ran her fingers lightly over the lock. She had the feeling it would contain things from the continent, not thumbscrews. William had brought her back many gifts from the times he had gone tourneying with Christopher. Her father had destroyed those gifts one by one after William's death.

Gillian rose quickly and walked away from the trunk. She would not let memories of her sire ruin her pleasure in the day. He couldn't harm her again. Christopher had

vowed to see her safe and she believed he would hold fast
to his vow. He was a knight. That meant nothing to her
sire, whose gold spurs had clicked against the stone floor
as he'd paced before his selection of whips, but she was
certain it meant much to Christopher.

There was nothing else that gave any clue to Christopher
himself. There were no baubles lying about, but she could
understand that. He wouldn't have use for much clutter.
The tapestries lining the walls were obviously there just to
keep out the chill, for they were worn and faded, as if they
were either old or had been chosen without care. She fingered one such tapestry and decided that something should
surely be done about Christopher's chamber. Though he
might not be able to see it, she certainly could and she
didn't like seeing her lord in shabby surroundings. The rest
of his hall was marvelously fine; his bedchamber should
also be so.

Aye, and such deserving treatment would begin that
night. Gillian walked to the door, the beginnings of an idea
already forming.

She opened the door to find one of Christopher's guardsmen leaning against the far wall of the passageway. He
was so obviously watching her door that she couldn't decide if she should be flattered Christopher was protecting
her so well or nervous that he was guarding her so she
didn't escape.

The man made her a low bow, though, and his expression was kind enough.

"My lady?"

"I need a thing or two," she began, chewing her lip
and sizing the man up. He looked too skilled to be fetching
her things, but she wasn't about to venture out and fetch
them for herself.

"Name them, my lady."

If he was going to offer, she wouldn't refuse him.

"I need a small tapestry, no bigger than the width of
your outstretched arms, a bottle of Lord Blackmour's finest

claret and perhaps some sweet-smelling flowers. Are there any in bloom yet?''

"Flowers?" the man echoed.

"None to be had, I see," she said, with a sigh. "Very well, then, the other items, if it wouldn't be too much trouble." She looked up at the tall knight. "Would it be too much trouble, Sir . . ."

"Robert, my lady. I'll fetch them posthaste."

"Thank you, Sir Robert. You're very kind."

The man nodded quickly, then turned and fled for the stairs. Gillian suffered a moment of panic when she wondered if he rushed off to tell Christopher that his wife was making free with his goods.

She shoved away her worry before it became full-blown terror. The man had asked what he could fetch for her, hadn't he? If he hadn't meant it, he shouldn't have said it.

Gillian wandered about Christopher's chamber as she waited. To her surprise, she felt almost at peace, if such a thing were possible. Perhaps it had been passing the day in her husband's chamber to calm her so. After all, he was only a man, as William had been. Her brother had a healthy temper, but he'd never turned it on her. Christopher might act the same way, if she didn't provoke him.

TWO HOURS LATER, SHE KNELT ON THE TAPESTRY SHE had thrown before the fire and surveyed her handiwork.

The fire burned cheerily, as well it should have for all the trouble it had given her starting it. Christopher's furniture was heavy, but she'd managed to move it back away from the hearth. The tapestry was an old one, yet it looked well wrought when viewed from the light of the fire. A goblet of wine sat on the stone of the hearth, waiting to be mulled once Christopher had arrived.

All in all, it was a very clever arrangement and Gillian congratulated herself on having thought it up. Now, all she had to do was remove herself to the alcove and stay out of sight while Christopher enjoyed his comforts after a long day training and doing his lordly duty.

The door opened and she hastily jumped to her feet, then backed up when she saw it was her husband. She escaped to the alcove, then watched hopefully as he strode into the chamber.

And then she realized the enormity of her mistake.

Christopher tripped over the stool, then bellowed out his surprise only a moment before he fell and smacked his head loudly on the corner of his chair. Gillian took a step forward, then froze as Christopher lifted his head and looked straight at her, the blood dripping down his forehead into his eye. The absolute fury on his face told of his rage more eloquently than any words ever could have.

She didn't have to be told to flee. She ran for the door, skidded around it and fled down the passageway to the bedchamber she'd slept in for almost a se'nnight. A heavy tread followed her, a tread she was positive belonged to her husband.

She gained her chamber, then slammed the door and slid the bolt home the moment before the wood shook from a single, powerful blow.

"Open the door."

The words were spoken with complete calmness and serenity, which terrified her all the more. How many times had her father seemed calm when he beguiled her into opening her door to him, then proceeded to beat her until she couldn't breathe?

"Gillian," the deep voice came again, even more calmly, "open the door, girl."

Gillian fled across the chamber to her trunk. Her hands shook so badly, she could hardly get the lid open. It fell down upon her fingers twice, adding to her pain and frustration. She pulled out her sword with a cry of relief.

Christopher knocked.

Gillian began to weep with fear. He would do more than beat her; he would kill her. She had no doubts of it. She had seen it in his expression when he'd lifted his head.

Aye, he would repay her for her stupidity and that repayment would be death. Hadn't he killed his first wife, then buried her unshriven? Gillian no longer completely believed he had horns, but she could well imagine him burying his bride in secret, denying her the benefits of a last priestly administration, all because of his fury over something she had done. She had no doubts he would do the same to her.

She dragged her sleeve across her furiously tearing eyes and struggled to gain control of herself. She drew her sword and held it up, putting it between her and the door.

"Gillian, I want you to come over and open the door."

"Never!" she croaked, shaking so badly she could barely hold her blade.

The wood quivered from the force of Christopher's slap, yet when he spoke again, his tone was no less pleasant than before.

"Now, Gillian, we must talk and I'll not do it through this door. Don't make me break it down."

"I'm n-not coming out," she said, gaining some courage from the feel of cold steel in her hands. "And you'll not be coming in. I have a sword, you know."

"Damn you, woman, I'll not be disobeyed!"

"I know how to use this!" she shouted back, then bit her lip. As if shouting at him would actually make things better.

"Break it down," Christopher growled to someone outside the door.

"But, my lord—" a man protested.

"Break it down!" Christopher thundered. "And the next one who makes my head pain me any further will have a hundred lashes by my hand. Now, *break down the bloody door!*"

The wood quivered once, twice, three times, then the bolt gave, the wood of the frame splintered and the door swung open and slammed back against the wall. Christopher stepped into the chamber, his face red from both anger and his blood.

The sword suddenly became too heavy. Gillian struggled manfully to keep the steel pointed at the man who would now take her life but found her strength deserting her. The blade clattered against the hard wood under her feet and she sank to her knees with a sob of pure despair. She folded her hands over her neck and cried out over and over again in terror. Never in her life had she felt such uncontrollable fear, not even with her father. At least she'd tasted the fullness of his wrath. Christopher's likely would go on endlessly.

She screamed as hands grasped her arms and hauled her to her feet.

"Gillian," Christopher shouted, "cease! I'm not going to touch you! By the bloody saints, I vow it!"

Empty words, as she well knew. She wanted to stop weeping, for she knew it would only anger him the more, but she was powerless to cease.

The next thing she knew, she no longer had her body under her control. It was only when she felt the softness of a bed beneath her that she knew Christopher had picked her up.

"Sheath her sword, Jason, and bring it to me," Christopher commanded.

Gillian went rigid with terror. Was he going to beat her with that first?

The hilt was held above her and Christopher fumbled for first her right, then her left hand and wrapped them about the haft.

"Your blade, lady," he said, his voice still tight with anger. "Don't ever, *ever* bolt a door against me again. I've no way of impressing upon you how much that displeases me short of beating you, which I will not do, or shouting at you until your ears ring, which I've no stomach for either. So, let this be the warning. I'll not have such patience in the future."

He straightened and walked to the battered door, then turned and came back. He glared down at her.

"And do not ever move anything in my chamber. If I want my furnishings moved, I will move them myself. They please my eye the way they are. Understood?"

"Aye," she croaked.

Christopher straightened and turned. "Come, Jason. You'll return my chamber to rights."

"But the Lady Gillian—"

"Now!" Christopher bellowed. "I have no qualms about beating you, insolent pup. Make haste, boy, before my hand moves any closer to my belt."

The pair of them then quit the chamber. Gillian turned her face to her pillow and let it muffle her great, wrenching sobs of terror. They lasted so long and were so violent that she finally had to seek the chamber pot.

Retching only made her weep the more. She remained on the floor where she was, pressing her flushed skin against the chill of the hard wood.

Oh, but Blackmour was worse than Warewick. She'd had hope that morning, hope that at last she had finally found a safe haven. She had fully intended never to attract Christopher's notice, for then he would never be irritated by her or her actions. What a fool she had been to remain!

But what to do now? At least Christopher hadn't struck her. He might have terrified her with his calmness, but at least he hadn't followed through with his belt this time.

This time. She had no way of telling what he would do the next time. She was certain, though, that it would be much worse than anything her father could do. Christopher was bigger and younger, and likely that much stronger.

Perhaps taking the chance of meeting her father in some unfamiliar shire was a safer choice than remaining where she was.

Tomorrow she would go, after she had rested and shored up her strength. She would elude Christopher's notice for the whole of the day, then flee just before the drawbridge

went up for the night. She would have to remember to ask
Jason in which direction south lay before she left, on the
off chance the eve was too cloudy for stars.

That was a detail she was certain she would need in her
travels.

eight

CHRISTOPHER RAN HIS FINGERS LIGHTLY OVER THE SPLIN-
tered wood of Gillian's door. It would have to be repaired,
but he couldn't think about that yet. His head pained him
too much for thought, and the pain only grew worse with
each passing hour.

He had no idea what time it was, but Jason had fallen
asleep hours ago and even Gillian had ceased to sob. He
couldn't help hearing her in the next chamber, damn her
to hell. It would have been wiser to lock her in his tower
where she could have wept in peace, and left *him* in peace.

Never in his life had he heard such terror in a body's
voice. Not even in battle had he heard men scream as she
had when he'd entered the chamber. Merciful saints above,
he didn't want to know the details of her life at Warewick.

He leaned his head against the rough doorframe and
sighed deeply. Jason had spared him no details while putting the chamber to rights. He'd heard all about the tapestry put there for his pleasure, the cup of wine ready for
mulling, the pillow plumped and placed close to the fire
for his comfort. How would he have known that on his
own? It wasn't as if he'd been able to see it. He'd almost
bloody killed himself falling over that stool!

He'd been angry at the bump on his head, and furious over the disruption, but in truth, he knew it was more stung pride than anything. It was hard enough to choke back his fear and walk forward confidently when he was certain there wasn't anything in his way. Surprises did not sit well with him.

How could Gillian have known though? She thought he could see. That in itself eased his embarrassment quite a bit. At least he had succeeded in keeping his flaw from her. She would likely credit his anger to his enviable reputation for violence. In time, she would learn that he would never truly raise a hand against her, but she would have to learn that on her own. He could afford to spend no time trying to convince her.

Which made him wonder why in Hell's name he was standing at her doorway, straining to hear even the sound of her breathing. He eased into the chamber and padded slowly to the bed. He reached down carefully and patted the quilts, wanting to make sure she was covered. All those tears had likely soaked her gown and she would catch her death if she weren't covered well.

To his surprise, he found the bed was empty. He remained perfectly still, certain he'd heard the soft sound of his wife breathing. He ventured out to the middle of the room, wishing he'd brought a cane or something to probe with. He grimaced at the thought. The sight of such a thing likely would have sent her into fits she never would have recovered from.

His foot touched something soft and giving, something that gasped.

"Nay," Christopher said quickly. "Do not start scream-ing again. My head cannot bear the sound."

She obeyed, but her breath came in harsh gasps just the same.

"Stand up, girl, and give me your hand." Chivalry might have demanded he lift her up himself, but he wasn't sure where she was and had no intentions of fumbling for her and frightening her more with his clumsy groping.

"My lord, I beg you," Gillian choked out, her voice hoarse. "If you've any mercy at all . . ."

Christopher squatted down with a curse and searched until he found her hands, clenched together. He took hold of the both of them and rose, pulling his wife up with him. Gillian shrank back, but he ignored it. He couldn't blame her. She was no doubt looking frantically at his head, expecting horns to pop forth at any moment.

He pulled her toward the bed, ignoring the soft, desperate sounds of distress she was making. They ate at him, making his belly hurt right along with his head.

Once the side of the bed hit his shins, he lifted Gillian into his arms and laid her out. He reached over her, pulled over the blankets and covered her as best he could.

He sat down on the edge of the bed and fumbled until he'd found her face. Then, without giving his foolish actions more thought, he stroked her hair, as gently as he knew how. It was something he'd done for Jason now and then, during the first few months of the lad's stay at Blackmour. He'd soothed his squire partly because Jason was Lord Robin's son and partly because Christopher had always thought of the boy as something of a younger brother. It was only right to comfort those more helpless than yourself.

Unfortunately, with Gillian the touch didn't seem to be working. Christopher pulled his hand away, dismayed at her violent shivers. Such gentleness should have soothed her; instead it had worsened her fear. Christopher searched back through his memories for what William had done that fortnight they had been together at Warewick.

Ah. Christopher nodded to himself as he dug out one of Gillian's hands from under the blankets. He laid her fingers flat in his left palm, then smoothed over her slight hand with his right. Her fingers jerked a time or two, then were still. At least they had ceased to tremble.

How long he repeated his gentle motions, he couldn't

have said. All he knew was her hand became warm and her breathing deepened and quieted. She even made the little twitches of a body falling asleep. Christopher slipped her hand back under the blankets and carefully tucked them up to her chin.

"Sleep on, Gillian," he said softly. "You're safe now."

He wanted to remain, just to assure himself she would sleep peacefully, but heard the sounds of his household rousing. It wouldn't do for him to be seen lingering at his wife's bedside, as if he had nothing better to do with his time.

He stepped into the passageway quietly. He closed the door as far as it would go, then paused and sniffed.

"What do you want, Colin?" he demanded.

"Saints, Chris, how is it you always know 'tis me?"

"The Sight, you fool. How else?"

He turned toward his bedchamber and started down the hallway. Perhaps Colin would use the few wits he possessed and remain behind. Christopher had no desire for speech, especially with his brother-in-law—even though Colin had apologized the day before for his actions the night of the wedding. Christopher had forgiven him readily enough after a wrestle during which he just happened to use Colin's nose as a place to rest his elbow numerous times. A broken nose, several bruised ribs and a swift kick in the arse had been repayment enough, to Christopher's mind.

"How is our lady?" Colin asked politely. "You were in there long enough. No screaming, so I assume you didn't bed her again."

Christopher stopped and looked in Colin's direction.

"Did I or did I not tell you yesterday that I had no desire to discuss my wife? With you or anyone?"

"Aye."

"Then why in the bloody Hell do you keep bringing her up?"

"I like 'er, Chris. I don't know why you don't."

"Whether you like her or not is of little import to me,"

Christopher said, ignoring the last. "She has my name and a safe place to sleep. Whatever happens to her beyond that matters not to me."

Colin stopped and Christopher didn't stop with him. He continued on to his bedchamber where he shut himself inside and contemplated going back to bed.

He turned sharply to the fire. He'd remained abed for three months after his wounding. It had taken him a month to be able to lift his head without retching and another to do the same without weeping over what he'd lost.

The final month had been what had almost killed him. He'd done nothing but lie on his back and stare up at the ceiling, telling himself that, aye, he was beginning to make it out. Two fortnights of deceiving himself. Two fortnights of sheer hell.

Colin had dragged him out of bed—bodily. Christopher had cursed his dead wife's brother so thoroughly and so hatefully that he now wondered why Colin hadn't just walked away. But Colin hadn't. He'd bullied and badgered and pestered Christopher until he had risen each day just to try to beat the whoreson senseless. It had accomplished what it was meant to.

Christopher sighed and dropped into his chair by the hearth. He put his head into his hands, then winced as his fingers made contact with the tender bump. He gingerly lowered his face into his hands and let his shoulders slump.

Someone should have warned him that his second marriage would be far more difficult than his first. It would have been the kind thing to do. Or perhaps someone should have warned him before his first marriage. That had been the start to all his troubles.

He closed his eyes and pretended he could see the flames dancing against the walls of his chamber. He could remember how fire looked as the reflection of it played over the sides of his silver goblet, how it had looked in Lina's pale hair, how it had caressed her flawless features. Angelic she had appeared, angelic and so beautiful that she had ever stolen his breath. Saints, he had been taken with her! It had been so from the first time he'd laid eyes on her.

He had gone to Berkhamshire at Colin's invitation, taken one look at Colin's sister and fallen face first into lust. Magdalina of Berkhamshire had been the most beautiful woman he had ever seen. Pale and delicate, as unattainable as a dream. Yet she had become attainable and only because of him, or so she had led him to believe. She had teased and flattered him, yet held her distance, prolonging the game. Christopher had found himself, for the first time in his serious young life, playing the fool. He'd sung for her, he'd danced for her, he'd made up foolish lays to tease her into smiling for him. He had laughed more in the six months he had courted her than he had before in his entire life. He had wed her willingly. She had been his beautiful Lina and he couldn't spend enough to see her clothed or adorned or entertained. He had laid his heart and his wealth at her feet and thought it would be enough to hold her.

He shoved away his foolish thoughts. It did no good to think of her. He knew well how skillfully her beauty had hid the ugliness of her soul. He smiled grimly. Perhaps he hadn't been served by sight in those days. Had he been blind, he might have listened more closely to what she said and paid no heed at all to her face. Aye, he would have been much better off without his bloody eyes to guide him.

Never again. He rose, then swayed at the sudden pain in his head. Never again would a woman touch his heart. It would hurt too much when she discovered the truth.

As Gillian would, and no doubt soon enough. He had been careful not to let on to his secret, but he wasn't sure how long he could keep up the ruse. It might be easier if he never had to speak to her. He promised himself a good evening's worth of thought on that when his head wasn't paining him so greatly.

Aye, he would find a way to keep Gillian away from

him, for then she would cease to trouble him. His belly wouldn't wrench at the sound of her frightened cries, his poor head wouldn't take any more abuse thanks to her attempts to please him, and his heart would not soften at the feel of her hand resting so trustingly in his. He could go back to wallowing in his miserable life. At least there all he felt was pain. Other emotions were unpleasant at best.

And frightening at worst.

nine

GILLIAN TOUCHED HER HAIR SELF-CONSCIOUSLY AND wished she hadn't been so foolish as to have cut it off eight years ago to spite her father. She had paid for that not only by the lash, but by her hair's subsequent defiance. Much as she wrestled with it, it simply would not stay tucked under a veil. Unfortunately, poorly coiffed hair would make a poor impression on the servants. She would have difficulty enough convincing them to obey her without her locks adding to her troubles.

She wouldn't have been facing the servants at all, but Christopher had demanded she leave her chamber and make an appearance before the household. That message had come by way of Jason, along with the admonition for her to stay out from underfoot, although Jason had phrased it kindly enough. Gillian, however, had heard Christopher bellowing the like, and knew what the original message had been. It didn't trouble her. All she wanted was to do nothing to foul her husband's humor. Not that she had seen enough of his humor over the past se'nnight to know what state it was in.

After that first night when he had broken down her door, she had been certain she would leave the next evening.

But when the next night had fallen, leaving had seemed rather unappealing. It was cold out and very dark. Who knew what sorts of things lurked in the darkness outside Blackmour's walls? At least inside she knew what she faced. And so she'd gone to bed, terrified that at any moment Christopher would come in through the door, having changed his mind and decided beating her was wise.

He never came, though. That had been enough to keep her from leaving. Every night she went to bed terrified, and every morn she awoke, untouched. It was a fragile peace, but it seemed more appealing than braving the wilds of England.

And even though Christopher did not visit her, Jason did. He came often, to see if she needed aught and to deposit meals on her table and carry off the untouched ones. After hearing Christopher's exclamation of displeasure over her neglecting her food, she had decided eating was much easier than enduring a flogging, so she had eaten all that was given her. Christopher hadn't come to express his opinion about it.

Toward the end of the se'nnight, she actually found herself becoming restless. The view of the sea from her window was indeed fine, but she longed to see it from the battlements and have something around her save the four walls of which she was growing increasingly tired. It was then that Christopher had demanded she take up her duties as chatelaine.

She smoothed her hand over her gown and stepped out of her chamber. She walked down the stairs to the great hall. The tables were put up and the servants lounged about, as if they hadn't a care in the world. She knew she should have done something, but what? One of the serving wenches looked up and stared insolently. Gillian looked away quickly and decided that impressing the servants would have to come another day. For now, all she wanted to do was escape their notice.

She left the great hall quickly, grateful to shut its door

behind her. It was chilly outside, but not unbearable. The
courtyard was full of folk working and children playing.
They were, though, far less interesting than the group of
men who cheered and clapped at the spectacle in their
midst. Gillian edged closer, wondering what it was they
watched.

Through the crowd, she could see that two men wrestled
in the middle of the circle. Normally she wouldn't have
paid any heed to such a thing, but she could have sworn
one of the combatants was Jason. Christopher wouldn't
like it if his squire were being abused. She certainly didn't
have the courage to stand up to whomever was abusing
him, but she could mark him and pass his name along to
Colin, who could in turn tell Christopher.

She approached cautiously and stood behind a broad
man, trying to peek around his shoulder. It just happened
to be Colin's broad shoulder she was trying to see around.
He frowned down at her. She looked up at him and tried
to smile. She knew it had come out as more of a grimace,
but Colin seemed not to notice. He turned around again to
watch the wrestlers, putting his elbow up on one of his
fellows' shoulders as he did so. It, quite conveniently, allowed Gillian full view of the battle. Somehow, that small
gesture cheered her. Feeling a bit more courageous, she
leaned forward and looked into the circle.

And then she wished she hadn't.

It was Christopher who wrestled with his squire, and he
was half-dressed and sweating profusely. Jason could have
been wrestling naked and Gillian wouldn't have marked it.
She had eyes only for her husband.

She had seen William before with his shirt off, but he
looked nothing like Christopher. Merciful saints above, her
husband was finely fashioned! Not a spare bit of softness
on him at all. Finely honed muscles rippled under his skin
as he moved, as he avoided Jason's grasp, as he lunged
for his squire when he came too close.

It was in the midst of her gaping that Gillian realized

that Christopher was actually managing the feat without seeing anything. She looked more carefully and noted that though he seemed to be watching his squire, in truth he was listening intently. And touching. Though he looked as if he were merely toying with Jason, he kept his squire within reach merely to know where the lad was.

"Don't be such a woman, Artane," Colin boomed. "Take your lord down!"

Jason lunged and tried to do just that. And though he was rather tall for his age, he could do nothing more than force Christopher back a pace. The men laughed and Jason's face flamed. Even Christopher cracked a smile at the bawdy jesting. Christopher held his squire immobile until Jason cried peace. Christopher released the lad and started to walk toward the edge of the circle. Jason moved and Gillian almost called out a warning. It was unnecessary. One moment Jason was lunging at Christopher's back and the next Jason was flat on the ground with Christopher's bulk pinning him there.

Gillian stood, silent and marveling, as the crowd broke up and moved away. Colin grunted at her on his way by, possibly his way of bidding her a good day. Gillian acknowledged it, then gave her full attention to her husband.

He rolled off his squire, then helped the lad to his feet. Jason stood with his back to her and submitted to having his hair ruffled.

"A fine showing," Christopher said, "despite your dishonorable attack."

Christopher was actually smiling at the lad. Gillian was hard-pressed not to gasp in surprise. Devilishly handsome he might have been when he frowned, but he was nothing short of beautiful when he smiled. For the first time she had seen something approximating gentleness on his face and the sight left her completely undone.

"Surprise is my only ally, my lord," Jason said, ducking away from Christopher's hand.

"You've made me sweat. That says something for your

strength, does it not? Your sire will be well pleased with you, I think.''

Jason kicked at the dirt at his feet. ''My lord, unless my sire comes here, I should leave within the month.'' He looked up at Christopher suddenly. ''Come to Artane, I beg you. My mother ever complains that you never accompany me.''

Christopher's good humor evaporated. ''I haven't the time.''

''My lord, 'tis an easy ride—''

''Damn you, Jason, I said nay!''

''But you know Artane as well as you do Black—''

Christopher put his hands on Jason's shoulders. ''Jason,'' he interrupted, ''does it not occur to you that I might wish to see your family? Do you think I haven't wished to roam again in the places where I passed my youth? But what would it serve me? To be led about by the hand everywhere I went, to appear weak and maimed?''

''But, my lord, it would not be that way,'' Jason protested. ''I vow it wouldn't.''

Christopher ruffled Jason's hair affectionately. ''Enough said, imp. Let us search out something edible as reward for our hard work, then I'll leave you at liberty to spend the day however you choose.''

Jason's sigh was heavy, but he readily followed Christopher into the house. Gillian stood in the middle of the courtyard and watched them go inside. Her father had never once given any of his lads a kind word. The kind of cheek Jason had displayed would have earned them a flogging, at the very least. Yet Christopher's rebuke had been nothing more than a few words, and gentle ones at that. What manner of man was this Christopher of Blackmour?

She walked over to the bench pushed up next to the hall and sat down, bewildered. Indeed, her life had become nothing but a tangle of confusion. She was captive in the aerie of a dragon whose reputation for cruelty and wickedness was flung far and wide, yet it was the one place she'd slept where she'd never been beaten. Her husband had broken down her door in anger, yet had then soothed her to sleep by stroking her hand as William always had done when she'd been frightened. Christopher was a fierce lord who obviously brooked no disrespect from any soul, yet he had been gentle with a squire who should have known better than to let his tongue run free at his lord's expense.

But the most startling revelation of all was Christopher's smile. By the saints, how that transformed his visage! In that smile was kindness and affection. It was a smile that would have laid the whole of England at his feet, if he had but used it to his advantage.

She leaned back against the chilly wall, tucking her hands under her arms to warm them. Somehow, after having seen that smile, running away from its wearer seemed even less appealing than before. Surely there was gentleness in him. If he could show it to Jason, perhaps he could show it to her in time.

And, even if not, at the very least she had a safe place to sleep. Her door had no bolt, but Christopher hadn't entered her chamber and that likely wouldn't change in the future. A safe haven, warm food and sturdy clothing: what else could she possibly want?

A black shape bounded over and came to a stiff-legged halt before her. Gillian froze. It was the Hound from Hell. Gillian pressed herself back against the wall as the huge wolf came closer, sniffing tentatively at her shoes, then her dress. He transferred his attentions next to her hand, his cold nose sending chills through her. She could almost feel his teeth sinking into her flesh.

What she felt instead was a pink tongue tickling her fingers and a heavy head soon coming to rest on her leg. She hesitantly reached out her hand and patted the beast. The moment she stopped, he bumped her hand with his nose as if to tell her that he was pleased with her actions and wished for more of them.

Gillian hesitantly reached out and patted the hound, then scratched him behind the ears. He truly enjoyed that, for he pressed himself up against her legs that much harder, as if to make it easier for her to see to him. Feeling extraordinarily brave, she patted the wolf with both hands.

Then she shrieked as he leaped up and planted his front paws on the bench. Her heart beat wildly against her ribs as he thrust his face close.

Then a pink tongue came out and swiped her liberally across the face. Gillian couldn't decide if she should laugh or burst into tears from the fright. She chose giggles instead. She pushed the hound away, but he only woofed low in his throat and continued to torment her.

"Cease," she gasped, finally taking hold of fistfuls of his fur and forcing him back. "Leave me be, you murderous hound."

Said murderous hound only sat obediently, wagged his tail a time or two and smiled as best he could with his tongue hanging out the side of his mouth. Gillian patted his head affectionately.

"Is your master so easily tamed?" she asked.

"Nay, he is not," a deep voice growled. "Wolf, come."

Gillian looked up at Christopher who stood fully dressed at the door to the hall. Color flooded to her cheeks at the knowledge he had overheard her foolish words.

"Go back in the house, lady," Christopher said curtly. "You'll chill outside."

Gillian jumped up as he turned to leave. "My lord," she said quickly, "I . . . I—"

Christopher turned and looked at her. It was unnerving how clearly his sightless eyes seemed to focus on her.

"Aye?" he demanded.

"I . . . I think I would like to be of some use," she blurted out, mustering up all the courage she had on hand. "If you please, that is . . ."

"Then be of use. Clean the hall. Terrorize the servants. Just stay out from underfoot and leave me in peace."

"But—"

He was halfway down the steps before she got the word out. He didn't bother to stop. Gillian stared after him, wondering if their encounters would ever become anything pleasant.

Christopher didn't seem too concerned about it, if his haste was any indication. He walked swiftly, with a confident air, as if he saw every stone and twig in his way. Wolf trotted alongside him, a fierce black shadow that only a fool would have tangled with.

Gillian turned away from the sight and looked at the open hall door. So she had leave to be of some use. She wiped her hands on her dress, wishing she'd kept her mouth shut. To someone else, it might have looked as if the dragon of the keep had just departed. As far as she was concerned, the dragons waited within, ready to mock and scorn her for thinking to order them to do their work.

She took a step forward and was almost knocked over by the body that came flying out the doorway. Jason caught her by the arms and gasped out an apology.

"I didn't see you," he exclaimed, then he grinned. "You're looking well today, my lady. I'm very happy to see you outside."

"Thank you," she managed.

"A good morrow to you." And with that, he was down the steps and racing toward the gate where his master was headed.

That was not a boy who was being mistreated. Indeed, he seemed to love Christopher deeply. Gillian felt a curious gnawing in her belly, a feeling she had never experienced before; she hardly knew how to identify it. She watched Jason catch Christopher and saw her husband sling his arm around his squire and give him a quick, rough hug. The feeling intensified at the sight. She turned away as she realized what it was she suffered from.

Envy.

A sudden longing for William's company rose up in her. She missed her brother's teasing, his ferocious hugs, his constant attention when he was home. The thought of never enjoying any of those things again was grim indeed.

Unless Christopher could be persuaded to think of her as a sister. It would be far better than having him treat her as a nuisance, which was exactly how he seemed to feel about her at present.

The first step was to do something to please him. She was good at least at attempting to please people. William had always appreciated her gestures. Christopher might, if she tried hard enough. If he wanted her to be useful, then useful she would be. She took her courage in hand and walked into the great hall and over to the kitchens.

A small group of wenches huddled near the fire. Their words were easy to hear and Gillian was reminded sharply of the conversation she'd listened to the day she had learned she was to be Christopher's bride. It boded ill indeed for her peace of mind now. She hesitated, torn between curiosity and good sense.

"I say he'll put her away."

"Oh, aye, and what do you know of it?" a second voice scoffed.

Gillian frowned and remained where she was. Of whom did they speak?

"He didn't take her, much as he'd like the sheets to tell a different tale. And if he didn't take her, that means he doesn't want her."

"I say she's blessed he left her be," the third added in a low voice. "Likely would have killed her."

"And *I* say he'll send her back to her father. What reason does he have to keep her? She's of no use."

Gillian felt the floor become unsteady beneath her. She searched blindly for the doorframe to hold herself upright. They spoke of her! And their words—by the blessed saints above, could they be true?

"Aye, not even as a breeder," the first agreed. "If she'd conceived, he would have kept her."

"Perhaps his tastes have changed," the second voice said with a low laugh. "He's not having any at all, unless he's bedding his squire—"

The other two laughed heartily over that, offering their own suggestions as to how it might have been accomplished. Gillian put her hands over her ears in horror. She turned and fled. She ran all the way to her chamber, then shut herself inside.

She leaned against the door and let the shivers come. So he planned to send her away. There was no denying the truth of their words. Christopher hadn't bedded her. The wenches had said as much. She knew he hadn't even been close to her in a bed, so it must be true.

Then it followed that he hadn't bedded her because he didn't want her. Hadn't he told her to stay out from underfoot and leave him in peace? Nay, he didn't want her in his house, nor in his bedchamber.

And if she proved to be too great a nuisance, he could very easily pack her off to Warewick. Indeed, what was stopping him from doing that immediately? For all she knew, he could have been planning her journey at that moment.

Gillian walked across the chamber and sank down onto the bench in the alcove. The bedding was the key, obviously. Christopher certainly hadn't seen to the task in truth, despite the cut to his arm. She wasn't sure she wanted him to. She had seen servants and knights with their mouths locked together and she had winced at the moans the wenches had made. 'Twas a sketchy knowledge she possessed, but she wanted no more of it than she already had.

But there was an heir to think of. There was certainly no reason why he shouldn't want a son. Aye, it was the only thing she could give him, for she certainly had nothing else with which to appease him. Her dowry wasn't incentive to do aught but toss her out the gates. Her skills as chatelaine were nonexistent, just another reason for him to have Colin deposit her inside Warewick's puny walls.

She rose and wandered restlessly about her chamber. Desperation made her continue moving, as by doing so she could escape the feelings that plagued her. He would send her away! There was absolutely no reason for him to keep her.

Unless she could give him a child.

She latched onto the idea with the tenacity of a damned soul clutching at the faint hope of salvation. Perhaps she could help him drink too much wine, then place herself in his arms. That was all there was to the bedding, wasn't there? Surely he wouldn't resist a willing female. He would take her, do whatever he had to do to get her with child, and then she would have a place in his house.

But if he had slipped into his cups, how would he remember doing the deed? She stopped and frowned. Worse yet, would he be too bumbling to accomplish it?

Nay, there had to be an answer to her problem, something she could do to assure herself of a place in Christopher of Blackmour's life.

She walked back over to the window and threw open the shutters. Merciful saints above, there was nothing underneath her but the ocean beating ceaselessly against the rocks below. She flinched each time a wave came crashing against the rocks; then slowly she felt herself begin to relax. She closed her eyes against the cold sea winds. The sea was beautiful and terrible and more majestic than even William had ever been able to make it seem. The power frightened her, made her feel small and awed.

Nay, she knew she could never leave Blackmour, and it had nothing to do with her father. All it had taken was one glance to forever enamor her of the ocean and she wouldn't give that up. No matter what she had to do to stay, she wouldn't give up what she had found.

She needed a plan, a scheme to bind Christopher to her. If she gave him a child, he wouldn't put her away. And if he tried, she would beg him to let her stay in his hall—as a servant, as a page, however he would keep her. He wouldn't send away the mother of his child, would he?

She could learn to be sweet, and perhaps she could even learn to be whorish like her father's wenches. How much worse could it be than what she had endured in the past? Or what she was likely to give up in the future if Christopher cast her aside? Aye, the pain she knew she would suffer at Christopher's hands couldn't be worse than a beating. And if it was, so be it. At least she would be suffering it at the hands of someone besides her sire. Christopher of Blackmour would find his way into her arms, take her and perhaps wonder what had possessed him to do the like. But at least he would take her. The very thought made her ill with terror but she would bear it.

She left her chamber, her purpose fixed.

ten

CHRISTOPHER BANGED HIS CUP DOWN ON THE TABLE AND felt the wine slosh over his fingers. He hadn't slept a wink in almost a fortnight thanks to his worry over his bride, a worry that galled him to the very depths of his soul. As if he bloody cared that she wept each and every night until the wee hours!

Nay, he didn't care. He'd been pacing in his room each night because supper had been upsetting his stomach and sleep seemed to be eluding him. It had nothing to do with his wife.

But this. *This* was another matter entirely.

"She went *where?*" he thundered, reaching out and snagging Jason by the front of his tunic.

"To the midwife, my lord," Jason said with a squeak. "Perhaps she doesn't know that Alice earns most of her keep from whoring."

"Oh, she does," Colin interrupted. "Asked me herself who I thought might be the one to discuss such matters with." He chuckled softly. "Poor lamb was screwing up the courage to speak to me for hours. She stuttered and stammered enough for a dozen wenches, then blurted out the words 'heir' and 'gold.' I figured she could only mean she was looking for a few new ways to please you, Chris, and was willing to pay for the learning."

Christopher felt a chill steal over him. Pay for the learning? To what end?

"Glad to know you and the lass are getting on so well. I still say she's a mouse, but at least she's biddable. You can't be too unhappy with that."

"Be silent," Christopher snapped. He rose and pushed Jason away. "Jason, fetch her away from the whore and bring her to me upstairs."

He left the great hall and walked up the stairs by memory, for he was too shocked to count them. It was suddenly all too clear to him. She wanted a child. And it was for bloody sure she didn't want to give him one out of the goodness of her heart.

Nay, she had discovered him. She had noted his blindness and had decided she would have none of him, save his seed. By the bloody saints above, how was it he had been a fool not once but *twice* in the same lifetime? He never would have suspected it of Gillian. But hadn't Lina warned him well enough?

Blackmour, you're not fit but to sit in the muck and beg in your rags. No woman will ever want you. Strong and fine you might be, but without your eyes, you're worth less than nothing. Mark my words, beloved. The moment a woman finds out how useless you are, she'll take your gold and seek out a man who is whole.

Lina's parting words hit him like a fist in the gut. He stumbled up the remainder of the steps and walked unsteadily to his chamber. Lina had deserted him only to meet her end at the hands of ruffians. Gillian would likely meet the same end. The only difference between the two women would be that he fully intended to have a say in Gillian's departure.

He slammed his bedchamber door closed behind him and began to pace, his fury deepening with each step. Aye, Gillian was far more clever than he had given her credit for being. So she planned to get herself with child, then leave. It would certainly assure her of an income far into her old age. Perhaps she had already selected one of his fiefs in which to hide while her child was reared.

But that wouldn't happen. He would send her away before she could see her plan accomplished and he would count himself well rid of her. If only he had known before he'd put himself through months of agony, stewing over her life at Warewick! It had been agony wasted. A pity William couldn't have included a few more details in his description of her.

But, nay, William hadn't been home enough to know the black depths of his sister's soul. Christopher knew he couldn't lay the blame at his friend's feet. But when he met William in heaven, he would look the man full in the face and count himself justified. He had fulfilled his vow. He would be absolved of any guilt, for Gillian had indeed forced his hand with her actions.

"My lord, she is in her chamber."

Christopher whirled around at the sound of Jason's voice, then pushed past him and made his way to Gillian's bedchamber.

"Out," he said, once he had entered. He pointed back toward the door. "Get you out of this chamber and out of my house. I never want to smell you in my hall again."

"But, my lord," Gillian gasped.

"Out!" he thundered. "You conniving slut, get you gone! I'll be slain before I'll get you with child. Take nothing of mine but what you wear. Slink home to your father and take your bloody pitiful dowry with you. I don't want either of you."

"Oh, my lord," she pleaded, "I beseech you."

"I said go!"

"I'll do whatever you wish—"

"*Go!*" He took a step toward her, his fist raised.

She fled. The echoes of her light footfalls remained behind her in the chamber along with the sounds of weeping.

Saints above, the wench could still affect him with her tears! As she had likely affected her brother. 'Twas fortunate indeed William hadn't known what kind of creature his sibling was. It would have broken his heart, for he had loved Gillian deeply. It was a love that was certainly undeserved. Christopher didn't intend to be the same kind of fool her brother had been.

At least her treachery had been exposed while his heart was safe. Saints, he should have learned the lesson the first time. It hurt worse this time, far worse than he had expected. He hardly knew the girl and her betrayal wounded him. How would it have been had he been in love with her?

He strode out of her chamber before that feeling could engulf him. This would be the last of his marriages. The Blackmour line would just have to die out. Perhaps Jason could be adopted. It would certainly save the current lord a great deal of anguish.

"Christopher, what have you done?" Colin yelled from the top of the stairs. "Did you beat the girl?"

Christopher whirled around. "Not another word, Colin. See that she leaves and give her nothing to take with her."

"Bloody Hell, why do you want her to leave?"

Christopher walked down the passageway and into his bedchamber, slamming the door behind him. As if Colin couldn't guess the reason!

The door opened and shut.

"Saints, man, have you lost your mind? She has nowhere to go! You swore you would keep her safe!"

"That was before, when she didn't know I was blind," Christopher said. He walked to the alcove and forced himself to breathe deeply. "It seems she had just recently discovered it," he continued, trying to sound uninterested, "likely just before she came and asked you of Alice. I would guess she was secretly plotting to steal me blind." He laughed bitterly at his words. "She wanted naught but my gold, just like my first wife, the bitch. Excuse me. My first wife, *your sister*, the bitch.''

Colin's heavy tread came over to the alcove rapidly. "You fool, she knew after the ceremony.''

"She did not,'' Christopher snapped. "She couldn't have.''

"You imbecile! She couldn't tear her eyes from you all day long.''

"Nay, I was far too careful . . .''

"Saints, man, *Warewick* likely noticed!''

Christopher found he had no reply for that. He dragged his hand through his hair, then rubbed his fingers over his face. Then he turned, threw open his shutters and let the stiff breeze from the sea blow into his chamber. It chilled him immediately, bringing with it a small return of sense. Colin was right; he hadn't been careful, not as careful as he should have been. And even if Gillian hadn't noticed the day of their wedding, she surely would have suspected something was amiss when he walked right into a stool he should have seen clearly at a dozen paces, then fell and struck his head on a chair a sighted man could have easily avoided.

Aye, he conceded with a sigh, she had known. But that still didn't change the fact that she had gone to Alice to buy the knowledge to seduce him. What other reason could she have had other than to hold his babe as ransom, demanding gold in payment for its return? And if she had known of his blindness from the start, that meant that she had been plotting against him from the start.

"You should find her and apologize,'' Colin said.

"Leave me,'' Christopher said, not turning from his window. "I'll speak no more of this.''

"Chris—''

"I said leave me!''

"Bloody *stubborn* whoreson,'' Colin muttered.

The door slammed with a resounding bang and Christopher found himself alone with his thoughts, finally. He

sat on his heavy wooden bench and let the sea air brush
over his face, tug at his hair. Usually the smell and the
sharpness of the wind's touch pleased him. He wasn't surprised to find it had no effect on him at present.

So she had known from the first. All his posturing, his
valiant efforts to appear normal, all had been in vain. Why
had she bothered to remain by his side so long? He sighed
deeply. He would have the marriage annulled, then send
her back to her father. At least he'd had the good sense
not to bed her.

He leaned forward and dropped his face into his hands.
His wife was likely weeping in the chapel, so there was
no hurry to go fetch her. Knowing Gillian, she wouldn't
have the courage to venture further than that. He would
send Jason for her after a bit, then have Colin take her
home.

I'm trusting you, Chris, to see to her.

Christopher ignored the voice in his head, the voice of
a man who had no inkling of what his sister truly was.

It was a good thing William was dead and couldn't see
it for himself. It likely would have killed him.

GILLIAN WASN'T STOPPED AS SHE FLED FROM THE HALL,
through the inner bailey, through the outer bailey, over the
treacherous bridge, and across the drawbridge. That not a
one of Christopher's men tried to learn of her intentions
was only another sign of how little she mattered in the
grander scheme of life at Blackmour. It wasn't every day
that a woman ran from the keep as if the Devil himself
chased her. Nay, she would die in a bog and no one would
be the wiser, nor would they stir themselves to care.

And though the desire to fall into a ditch and weep until
she was ill was very strong, her fear was stronger. Christopher had every intention of sending her back to Warewick. Why he had even wed her was something she would
never understand.

One thing was certain; she would die before she returned

to her father. There was little threat in that, as she was certain her father would kill her if she dared show her face at his hall.

She would go to London. It couldn't be very far. Aye, London was the only safe haven left to her.

She ran until her legs were unsteady beneath her and her lungs were on fire. And when she could run no more, she dropped to her knees and gasped for air. Just a tiny rest, then up again. At her current pace, it wouldn't take her long at all. It had seemed to take several days to travel from Warewick to Blackmour, but that was likely because she had been so apprehensive.

She was apprehensive no longer; she was determined. Christopher wouldn't have the satisfaction of casting her away and her father wouldn't have the satisfaction of beating her. She would beg the king for mercy and thwart both her father and her in-name-only husband.

By the time she could breathe again, the fog had rolled in from the sea. It was an eerie mist, one full of ghostly shapes. She jumped up and ran, praying she was still going south. It was impossible to tell, as she couldn't see anything but her hand in front of her face, and that not very well at all. There was no light from the sun.

She ran, then she walked, then she ran some more. Soon she had no more energy for tears, just enough for drawing in great, gulping breaths.

Soon she had no more energy for even that. She stumbled a last few paces, then saw a tree loom up before her suddenly, and then more trees beyond that. The forest. She had seen the forest to the south, but it had seemed much further away.

She had obviously made good time. She dropped to the ground and panted until she had finally caught her breath. Then she lay back, pulled several handfuls of rotting leaves over her and closed her eyes. She would rest for a bit, then rise again and perhaps find something to eat. Aye, that was a sensible enough plan. Just a short rest to regain her strength.

Peace stole over her as her racing heart slowed and her breathing eased further. Soon even the chill bothered her no more. She relaxed completely, lulled into a deep sleep.

And she dreamed of a lone dragon circling his aerie perched on the edge of the sea.

eleven

CHRISTOPHER KNEW THE SUN HAD SET ONLY BECAUSE HE heard the distant sounds of preparations for the evening meal begin. He sat on a stool in the middle of Gillian's unwarmed chamber and let the cold sink into his bones. The bitter chill was keeping him sane. When a body was on the verge of freezing, he didn't have the energy or the heart for simpler emotions such as guilt or fear.

Both of which threatened to overwhelm him.

He fingered the flat of the blade laid across his knees. It was a light weapon, a weapon fashioned especially for a woman's strength of arm. Gillian's blade. It was, he knew, the last shred of hope she had clung to as he'd broken down her door on the night after their wedding.

And now that hope rested on his knees while his wife was outside his gates, unprotected.

He had waited too long to see what had become of her. He had expected her to have run to the chapel. She hadn't been there when Jason had gone to fetch her, nor had she been anywhere else in the keep. In truth, she had vanished.

Then he had found the sword. He had been searching through her trunks like a plundering servant, half expecting to find bags of his gold stashed away for her future use.

Instead, he had found a length of cold metal sheathed in a finely tooled scabbard. Especially cold were the two stones set in the hilt.

William had once said he planned to have a sword fashioned for his sister. Christopher had given William an emerald to use, merely in jest. He realized then that William never jested about his sister. Abashed, he had listened to William describe in detail how innocent she was and how he had struggled to teach her to defend herself. But Gillian would never need the knowledge in truth, for if something happened to William, Christopher would be there to see to her. Wouldn't he?

Christopher ran his finger over the hard gems in the hilt and wondered which of the two was his unwitting gift. For the first time in years, he felt the hot sting of tears form behind his eyes. Not even when he had learned he would never see again had he wept. The urge he felt now had everything to do with the innocent who was outside the impenetrable walls of Blackmour without the one thing she could have used to defend herself. Saints, he had been a fool!

The memory of her terror on the night of their marriage caught him full in the chest and left him gasping. Terror? She would know it in full measure out in the dark.

At least William was dead and couldn't come disembowel him. Christopher knew he would have deserved it for having let the child from his sight. She likely couldn't tell bloody east from west and now he was crediting her with conceiving a plan of ransoming his babe? He was the one with the darkness in his heart. He had no right to believe the same of her.

He lifted his head at the sound of a light footstep.

"Aye?"

"No word, my lord," Jason answered, crossing the chamber. "The men have searched the village and found nothing. I heard one of the guards say he thought he saw someone hurry across the bridge, but he cannot remember who it was, what he was wearing or what he looked like.''

"He cannot remember!" Christopher exclaimed. "Are my men such fools they cannot mark who comes and goes inside my gates? What of the other guards?''

"I don't know, my lord. I will return and see what else is to be learned. Can I not see to your comfort first? A fire, perhaps, or some wine—''

"I need nothing," Christopher said flatly. "Nothing but tidings.''

Once Jason had gone, Christopher wrapped Gillian's sword up and placed it in her trunk. He would find her alive and well, and she would be pleased to know her sword had not been disturbed. It would come in handy when he opened his arms and invited her to run him through.

"Christopher!" The faint voice grew in volume as it drew closer. "Chris, where in the bloody Hell are you?''

"In here.''

"By the saints, I can't see a thing. Where are you?''

"Stand still, Colin. What did you learn?''

"She ran through the gate just after noon today. None of the guards stopped her, as they assumed she intended to come back. She hasn't. The fog's thick, Chris, but we have to search. I'll organize a party and we'll leave post-haste. I'll send word as soon as may be.''

That message delivered, Colin's boots retreated swiftly from the room, carrying Colin with them.

Christopher stood in the center of Gillian's bedchamber and fought with himself. He hadn't been outside his gates since he had been carried in them three years earlier. Inside his keep he was safe. He knew every inch of his hall, of his baileys, of his battlements. But outside? Outside his gates was terrain that had changed since he had been blinded, terrain that terrified him worse than any battle ever had.

He turned away from the door. Colin would manage it.

Colin always did. He was a fine tracker with good instincts.

But Christopher knew he himself was better. He could move about in the fog as if it weren't there. His squiring days at Artane had only honed the skill he had first learned at his own home. He could track a rabbit in the rain for leagues and find it in time for supper. And, if the truth were to be known, he did know the area surrounding his home. He knew where the gullies and bogs were, where the forest began and ended and what lay in between.

He could use Jason as his eyes. More than that, he could use his own instincts. Gillian was running blind. Who better than a blind man to follow her?

He left her chamber and walked slowly to his. He dressed in hose and a handful of tunics, worn one on top of another. He would need the warmth; it would also give him something to put on Gillian when he found her, for she would be chilled.

His fingers were stiff and uncooperative as he tried to buckle his sword belt around his hips. All his foolish suspicions came back to haunt him vengefully. Gillian had known from the beginning that he was blind. She hadn't been plotting to hurt him. How could she plot betrayal, when all she had wanted was a safe place to sleep?

Wasn't that why he had wed her in the first place?

He was sure he couldn't bring himself to trust her entirely, but he wasn't going to be the cause of her death. He would bring her home, explain what he did and did not want from her and the tale would be finished. She would remain, but she would remain out of his way. She would be free of her father's beatings and he would be free of her foolish plans to seduce him.

He snatched up his cloak and strode downstairs. He heard Colin's gasp the moment his foot hit the floor of the hall.

"By the bloody saints, what do you think you're doing?"

Christopher smiled grimly. "You're beginning to sound like my mother, Colin, so I suggest you leave off. Jason, come with me and we'll discuss our strategy."

Jason's shoulder was suddenly and quite conveniently under his hand.

"Command me, my lord, and I'll do your bidding with gladness."

Christopher felt his chest tighten at the tone in Jason's voice. There was pride there that he hadn't heard in years. Three years, to be exact. It had to have been difficult to go from being squire to arguably the fiercest warrior in the realm, to being that self-same warrior's nursemaid.

Christopher put his arm around Jason's shoulders. "Think you she knows north from south?"

"Doubtful, my lord. I know she won't go to Warewick, but I wouldn't be surprised if she went to the king."

"Aye," Christopher agreed, "but she couldn't have gotten far today. We'll fan out and search south, then pull back and go west. And, Jason," he said, lowering his voice, "you'll have to be my eyes. My brilliant stallion won't let me run him into a tree, but I'll be useless beyond that."

"My lord, it would be an honor to serve you this way. I shall not fail you."

"Of course you won't, lad. Artane's son doesn't know the meaning of the word."

A quarter of an hour later they were riding across the drawbridge. Colin was behind, minding the men, and Christopher rode before the company with Jason at his side. Jason talked only loud enough to be heard over the clatter of horse's hooves, though at present he could only describe the suffocating darkness.

Christopher could imagine that perfectly well without any help.

GILLIAN WOKE TO THE FEEL OF A COOL HAND AGAINST her brow and a voice that murmured soothingly.

"Hush now, child."

"Berengaria, will she live?" a voice asked, from a distance.

"Aye," the voice that belonged to the hand said, "she'll live. She's strong."

Gillian wanted to speak, but she was too weary. She kept her eyes closed and slipped back into her dream. She had started out dreaming of Blackmour and a dragon; then she had begun to walk. Whether it had been only in her mind or she had risen to her feet in truth, she couldn't say. The mist had been relentless, blocking out all but the faintest of light. She could have walked for an hour, or she could have walked for days. All she knew was she had been, and still was, bone weary and cold.

And sometime during that interminable night, she had felt herself falling. Gentle hands had caught her and laid her on a soft bed. It was then that she had first heard the voices.

"Not that, Magda, you fool! 'Tis a pinch of *un*derstanding you want, not *mis*understanding!"

"But the pots all look the same to me."

"Aye they would, to a pitiful novice such as you. Only a full-fledged witch could tell the difference. Now, take you some of this understanding and add it to the potion. The lad is hopelessly pigheaded and Gillian will never win him without some aid from us."

"He is handsome though, isn't he, Nemain? And she so fair. What fine children they will have together."

"Lucifer's knees, Magda, cease with your mooning! Keep stirring, lest you burn this again."

"Hush, you two," a third voice had said, the weathered voice Gillian found so pleasing. "The child needs rest, not your potions."

"A love potion is never wasted," the second voice lectured.

Gillian finally forced her eyes open and saw an older

woman leaning over her, a woman with soft blue eyes and silver hair.

"Good morrow to you," Gillian whispered.

The woman smiled. "And to you, child. Rest now. Your lord will come for you soon and you don't wish him to see you with your eyes red and swollen."

"But he cannot see me," Gillian said, fighting to keep her eyes open.

"Your knight is learning to see things his eyes never could, girl. Be patient with him."

Gillian closed her eyes and tried not to weep. After all, the silver-haired woman was trying so hard to make her feel better; not weeping was the least she could do in return.

Unfortunately, she knew the woman was wrong. There would be no reason for her to have patience with Christopher for he didn't want her in his house.

She knew the thought should have troubled her deeply, but she had no energy for being troubled. She was hard pressed to stay awake.

"What is your name, my lady?" she managed with the last of her energies.

"Berengaria, my child."

"SHE ISN'T HERE."

Christopher dragged his hand through his hair and blew out his breath in frustration. He turned to Colin. "You looked everywhere?"

"Aye. Not a sign of her."

"Then we go north. Perhaps she lost her sense of direction in the night."

"Chris, the men are weary. We should let them rest for a few minutes—"

Christopher reached out and jerked Colin close. "My wife is out there, likely frozen to death or worse, and you speak of weariness?" he hissed. "Damn you, Colin, I will not have her suffer for my foolishness!" He shoved his brother-in-law away from him. "Go home, if you wish it. I'll go by myself."

He heard Colin walk away, then heard him give the command to mount up. Christopher swung up into his saddle and let Jason's voice lead him. Two days. Two fruitless, eternally long days of searching and finding nothing. Gillian wouldn't have gone north. Surely even she knew that Scotland lay to the north. The only answer was that she had become lost and wandered off in the wrong direction.

He forced himself to think of the things that could have befallen her in the past two days. Death by exposure. Death by becoming supper to any number of wild animals. Each and every second of her suffering would be more drops of blood on his hands.

He cursed himself as he urged his mount forward. He had treated her abominably and he deserved whatever anguish his actions would bring upon him. Gladly would he make his penance if by some miracle he could find her alive and unhurt. Perhaps a pilgrimage to the Holy Land. On his knees. William would certainly have suggested the like, had he been alive to do so.

Christopher felt the light touch of rain against his face. Perfect. It wasn't enough that Gillian had been wandering outside for two days. Now she would likely catch her death from the ague before he could reach her.

"Jason," he said quietly.

"My lord?"

"Does Wolf appear to be following anything?"

"Nothing but your steed, my lord."

Christopher cursed under his breath. "Damned useless hound," he muttered. "Why didn't I take that black runt your uncle Miles offered me two years past?"

"I believe you feared Wolf would have the pup for supper, my lord."

Christopher grunted. "Likely so—"

"Wait, my lord," Jason interrupted. "There's a clearing

ahead. Why, even Wolf seems to have taken an interest in it. I'll follow him.''

Christopher reined in immediately. "Nay, let Colin go first. I'll not risk you, Jason." Saints, that was all he needed, to lose Robin of Artane's beloved youngest son and have that blood on his hands too. "Colin, press on ahead," Christopher called. "Bring us tidings posthaste."

Christopher's horse shifted restively under him; Christopher fingered the reins just as impatiently. This was the very last time he intended to pass a pair of days thusly. Saints, he had been a fool!

"She's here!" Colin yelled.

Christopher swung down from his mount immediately. He felt the dips of the uneven forest floor beneath his feet and took a hesitant step forward. The toe of his boot caught the arch of a tree root and he froze. What he wanted to be doing was running toward Colin's voice, but what he did was force himself to remain where he was. There was no sense in doing his own self in before he could rescue his wife.

"My lord," Jason said, catching him by the sleeve. "Here, follow me."

"Aye," Christopher said. He put his hand on Jason's shoulder and pushed his squire ahead of him.

"Low branches," Jason warned.

Christopher ducked accordingly, then straightened when he felt Jason do the same. The going wasn't as quick as he would have liked, but at least Jason wasn't plowing him into anything solid and immovable.

"Fifty paces, my lord," Jason said quietly. "There is a hut ahead."

"Hurry then," Christopher said, urging his squire forward. "See you any signs of other souls?"

"Nay, my lord. But the rain and mist obscures the surrounding trees. 'Tis possible there are others about, though surely Wolf would have given a warning. And I see Captain Ranulf sending his men out to scout in the shadows.''

"Perhaps she has rested here undisturbed," Christopher said, praying it was the case.

"We'll know soon enough. Ten paces, my lord."

Christopher pushed Jason out of his way and ran for the direction of Colin's voice. How many times he stumbled he couldn't say, but finally his hands found the wall and then the doorway. He stepped inside, his hands up before his face, seeking.

"She's here, Chris. Alive, but feverish."

Christopher found Colin's broad shoulder, then dropped to his knees and reached out, patting lightly until he felt Gillian.

"Oh, Gillian," he said hoarsely, running his hands over her gently. "Colin, can you see if anything's broken? Merciful saints above, she's burning with fever." He stripped off his cloak and put it over her. He slipped his arms under her back and knees and started to lift her. "Colin?"

"Nothing's broken that I can tell. She looks hungry and cold. You're too distraught to carry her. Give her to me."

"Nay, just help me find my horse."

"You can't ride and carry her at the same time."

"Then I'll bloody well walk home!"

Colin sighed heavily, then took Christopher's arm and turned him toward the door. "The doorway's thin, so mark how you carry her that you don't bump her head."

Christopher soon found himself flanked by Colin and Jason. They led him quickly back to his mount. Christopher was grateful for the aid. It was all he could do to keep hold of Gillian's limp form and not sink to his knees and pray. Even so, he prayed as he walked. Gillian shouldn't have to suffer for his foolishness.

"Here," Colin said, "give her to me and mount up."

"I will carry—"

Colin growled in frustration. "I'll merely hold her while you mount. Now, let me have her!"

Christopher relinquished his wife unwillingly, then mounted and held down his arms. He lifted her up, frown ing over the lightness of the burden. He would have to see her better fed.

He gathered her close and tucked her head under his chin to shield her from the rain.

"Home, lads," he said hoarsely. "Quick as may be."

The company didn't move fast enough to suit him. There was little he could do to speed things along, for it wasn't as though they were racing over open ground. How Gillian had managed to wander off into the forest some two miles north, he couldn't have said. 'Twas obvious she had lost her sense of direction. At least she'd found herself shelter instead of finding herself in peril. Christopher shoved away thoughts of all the dangers she could have run afoul of. That she'd stumbled into a deserted hut was indeed something to be grateful for.

She wasn't moving, though, and that unsettled him greatly. She didn't stir even when he shifted her in his arms. He closed his eyes and rested his cheek against her hair.

"Hold on, Gillian," he whispered. "Almost home."

It seemed hours before his mount was trotting over the stone bridge to the keep. Christopher allowed Colin to take Gillian long enough for him to dismount, then he retrieved his bride and made for his bedchamber, Jason close on his heels.

"Build up the fire, lad, while I put her to bed."

"Of course, my lord. Shall I fetch the leech?"

"Nay," Christopher said, laying Gillian down on his bed. "I can heal her well enough myself. If I need aid, you'll give it to me."

"Shouldn't I at least seek a woman from the village?"

"Nay, I'll not trust Gillian to some village witch."

Christopher stripped off Gillian's soaked slippers and stockings. Her feet were like ice. He covered them with a blanket, then made short work of stripping off her remaining clothes. The rest of her limbs were just as chilly as her

feet. If he hadn't felt the pulse at her throat, albeit a weak one, he would have thought her dead.

"Hot wine, Jason, as quickly as you can see to it."

Christopher set to chafing his lady's feet. Though it brought a slight bit of warmth to her toes, it did nothing for the rest of her. She continued to shiver from the fever and the chill. Christopher almost bellowed for Jason to hasten when he heard his squire rush into the chamber.

"Your wine, my lord," Jason panted.

Christopher took it and knelt down by the side of the bed, slipping his hand under Gillian's neck. He lifted her head and placed the cup of wine against her lips.

"Drink," he said, tipping the cup up. Gillian's teeth chattered badly enough to make forcing the wine into her mouth impossible. Christopher swore and pulled the cup away. "Saints, I can't see what I'm doing."

"Perhaps you should warm her yourself," Jason suggested, taking the cup. "I never lack for a place to lay my head. I like to think it is because of my skill between the sheets, you know, but I daresay 'tis because of the heat of my body."

Christopher smiled dryly. "Perhaps that might be the thing to do after all. See to the fire, then fetch some broth for my lady and something hearty for you and me."

"Aye, my lord."

Christopher stripped off his clothes and slid under the blankets next to his wife. Had his body had any notions of reacting to her nearness, it was disabused of them the moment he drew Gillian's icy flesh against his. He shivered right along with her, gritting his teeth as he tucked her cold hands against his chest. He rubbed his palm over the backs of her legs, then started on her back.

It was then that unbidden and certainly unwelcome tears stung his eyes.

His fingers told him what his eyes would never be able to. Her back was covered with the scars from the lash. Saints! Her father could have bruised her with a switch and not left any marks. But this, this flogging! Christopher was torn between weeping and roaring. What had given the man the right to take a lash to an innocent child's back? At that moment, Christopher vowed to see Gillian's sire repaid for his treatment of her. The saints only knew how he'd manage it, but manage it he would, if it took him the rest of his life.

It did no good to think on it presently, though. Anger would only sap his strength and his strength was better used tending his wife. He held her close with one hand and rubbed her back lightly with the other. Soon he wasn't shivering and neither was she.

When Jason returned, Christopher ate with one hand and kept Gillian pressed against him with the other. His worry stole his appetite, but he knew that tending his wife would take all his strength so he forced himself. And when he was finished, he sent Jason away and wrapped his arms around Gillian again. Slowly her flesh warmed and Christopher's worry eased. He tucked her face against his neck and closed his eyes.

Immediately, his instinct for self-preservation reared up and bellowed for him to leap out of bed and run while he could. It reminded him that he didn't need a woman to complicate his life, especially a woman who would be as much trouble as Gillian surely would be.

He pushed the blanket away and started to rise.

"Nay."

He froze, fully expecting Gillian to start screaming once she discovered she was naked and so was he.

Instead, she merely snuggled closer to the shoulder he hadn't managed to remove from beneath her head. The little sigh of relief that escaped her was the killing blow to his bloody common sense.

With a sigh of pure resignation, he lay back down, pulled the blankets up over his shoulder and wrapped his arms around his wife.

It was going to be a very long night.

twelve

GILLIAN SNUGGLED MORE DEEPLY INTO THE WARMTH OF the blanket. "Berengaria?" she whispered. "Did you put another blanket over me?"

"Who is Berengaria?"

The deep voice startled her, then she remembered there had been none others about her but the three women.

"Why, you're the woman who found me and helped me. You're changing your voice like that in jest, aren't you?" She smiled, in appreciation of the humor. "My thanks for the covering. It feels as if it's been warmed near the fire."

"Ah," the voice stammered, then coughed. "Er, I'm pleased you're soothed," it said, sounding very raspy in its high tone.

"Why, I think you've caught a cold, my lady," Gillian said. "Perhaps you should have one of the others make you a potion. But not Magda. Is it true she burns everything?"

"Ah . . . um . . . aye, lass."

Gillian burrowed deeper into the warmth. "I feel so safe," she whispered. "You know, this is the safest I've felt since those first few nights in my lord Christopher's hall. Do you know, I'd never felt so safe before then? At Warewick, my father forbade me to bolt my bedchamber door against him. The times I tried, he broke it down, just as Christopher did. Only Christopher didn't beat me. My sire always did, and so soundly I couldn't move—oh," she exclaimed. "These blankets are suffocating me!"

The blankets loosened their hold and Gillian gasped in a breath. By the saints, they were strong!

She tried to lift her hands to push the quilt away, but she was being held too tightly. That made it all the more confusing. Was it Berengaria who spoke to her or did the blanket who had its arms wrapped around her have a voice? She knew if she could have opened her eyes, she would be able to tell the difference, but she was too tired to do so.

"You know," she said, with a deep sigh, "I truly didn't want to leave Blackmour. I know 'tis a most imposing and stern keep, but I darcsay I admired it from the first moment I saw it, when Colin let me stop and look. He complained loudly about allowing me the boon, but at least he didn't hit me. He frightened me badly, though."

"He'll be repaid," Berengaria's voice rumbled; then she coughed. "I mean, he'll be seen to," she continued, in her high, hoarse voice.

"I wouldn't, were I you," Gillian said. She stopped trying to force her eyes open. The warmth surrounding her was far too enjoyable to interrupt it with the sight of what was surely a crude hut. Berengaria likely couldn't manage anything else. "You see, I don't fear Colin. Jason told me Colin is afraid of heights, and I'm not. Should he shout at me, I'll simply flee to the battlements."

"Does it not occur to you," Berengaria said, sounding rather annoyed, "that your lord might be capable of seeing to him?"

Gillian hesitated, realizing the truth of the matter.

"He wouldn't bother. You see, he doesn't want me," she admitted. "I cannot fault him for it, for I am ugly and don't possess a smidgen of courage. I know he didn't wish to wed me and I cannot fathom why he did so, unless he was forced.''

''Now, Gillian—''

'' 'Tis true,'' Gillian insisted. ''He would not want me of his own will. Not that it matters if he ever did want me. He has sent me away.''

''But—''

''And even though he has sent me away, I won't go back to Warewick. My sire will kill me if I return.''

''You aren't going anywhere, girl.''

''I only wish that were true,'' Gillian said. ''You see, all I was trying to do was make Christopher need me. I heard the knights talking about how well Alice pleased them and I knew she could help me please Christopher so he would keep me.''

''Christopher is a fool.''

''Well—''

''He is a fool,'' Berengaria repeated. ''He should have listened.''

Gillian knew she should have defended her husband, but she couldn't help but agree with Berengaria. She could have explained it all well enough if Christopher had but given her the chance.

The tension began to slip from her, mostly because of the blanket who stroked her back soothingly. Perhaps Berengaria was a witch. Witches were surely the only ones who owned blankets with arms.

For the first time in days, she began to feel a true sense of peace. So this hadn't been the rescue she'd always wanted; it suited her well enough.

''Do you know,'' she ventured, ''I used to dream of being rescued?''

''Did you now?''

Berengaria's voice was sounding hoarser by the moment. Gillian promised herself she would rise and fetch the woman something to drink just as soon as she found the strength.

"Aye, I did," Gillian answered. "Especially when my father would shout at me. He did that often, you know. There were times I think it gave him greater pleasure to rage at me and watch me cower than it did to beat me. I always feared him more when he shouted than when he was striking me, for when he shouted, I would imagine how bad the pain would be."

She paused.

"Somehow the pain was always worse than I had imagined it."

"God damn his soul to Hell."

Gillian nodded, thinking those words a bit harsh for such a kindly old woman to say, but having to agree with her.

"Afterward, I would dream. You know, I think I have a fine imagination, if the tale were to be known."

"I daresay I'd have to agree with you."

"Shall I tell you of my rescuer?"

"Oh, please do."

Berengaria's tone was very dry. Perhaps she heard so many maids babble of their dreams that it was all she could do to stomach one more.

"He was tall and fair haired," Gillian said, "and so painfully gentle that even the thought of his kindness made me weep. He would appear at the hall just when my sire was raising his hand against me and force him to stop. Then my knight would gently invite me to be his bride. He would be quiet and patient, never making quick moves to startle me, never giving me any reason to fear him. He would have understood that I needed gentleness and understanding. He would have asked to do my bidding in all things, that he might never hurt me in any way."

"And you would have run roughshod over him inside a fortnight," Berengaria growled.

Berengaria's words tickled her so, Gillian laughed. "Somehow, I think that might be true."

"So, Blackmour is not at all to your liking, is that it?"

Gillian hesitated. Berengaria was starting to sound almost as curt and annoyed as Christopher.

"That cold in your voice is troubling you greatly, isn't it?" Gillian asked. "Should I fetch you something for it?"

"Nay," Berengaria snapped, "you can answer my question."

"I thought you liked Christopher," Gillian retorted, a bit stung.

"What I think isn't important."

"Then what could it possibly matter what *I* think?"

Berengaria swore. Or the blanket swore. Gillian wasn't sure who was who, but she suspected it was the blanket who had such a foul tongue.

"It matters, wench, because I say it matters. Now, tell me what you think of the dimwitted arse."

Now, that surely had to be the blanket talking. Berengaria held Christopher in high esteem. The blanket obviously had no such illusions about the Dragon of Blackmour.

"He is not dimwitted, though I will grant you, Blanket, he is dreadfully stubborn. He isn't at all what I had expected, nor what I had dreamed about."

The blanket's soothing hands stopped their motion.

"I can see how he wouldn't be."

"Oh, it isn't because of his blindness," Gillian said quickly. "Though I grieved for him because of it, I wasn't unhappy. At least he would never have to look at me, see my scars or my ugly face. Nay, 'tis that he is so harsh and ungentle. He despises me so. When I understood that he could send me away if the marriage weren't consummated, I knew he likely would."

"And where did you hear that?"

"From the kitchen wenches."

"Shouldn't listen to servants' gossip," the blanket said firmly.

"Aye, I know it, but it was truth this time. And you

understand why I couldn't bear the thought of going back to my father.''

"Aye, girl, I understand."

"He will kill me if I return."

"I know, Gillian," the blanket said, very softly.

"And so," Gillian continued, "I thought if I could give Christopher an heir, he wouldn't send me away. I hoped he would want to keep me on as a servant of sorts. I know 'twas wicked to want to obligate him, but I'm skilled at not drawing attention to myself. I didn't think he would begrudge me a little scrap of his floor to call my own in return for a child."

"Nay, Gillian, he couldn't have."

"I couldn't even muster up the courage to get past Alice's door, though. Christopher cast me from his hall before I could explain."

The blanket called her lord several very uncomplimentary names.

"I truly cannot blame him," she said. "I think he has been deeply hurt and I understand how it feels. Do you know I never trusted anyone besides William? Perhaps Christopher has been dealt with treacherously. It isn't easy to trust when you've been betrayed."

The blanket was silent for several moments, then it cleared its throat.

"But," it said very gruffly, as if it weren't comfortable expressing the thought, "perhaps you could trust Christopher."

Gillian thought about it for a moment or two, then shook her head.

"Nay, he would send me back to my father. 'Tis best I continue on to London. How far is London, anyway?"

The blanket sighed. "Much too far away for you, girl."

"Then what am I going to do?" she asked, but she didn't truly care about the answer. She was warm and, for the moment, she was safe. The rest of the world could go to the Devil.

"You will stay where you are," the blanket instructed, "and you and Christopher will have a talk in a few days and come to an understanding."

Gillian groaned. "I've no desire to talk. William promised me my knight would come for me one day and love me dearly. London is the only place my knight will find me. He certainly isn't going to brave Christopher's temper to fetch me."

"There will be no fetching of you, girl. You'll stay right where you are and you and your lord *will* come to an understanding. I've made my decision."

Gillian was too weary to argue, though she still didn't care for the blanket's words.

" 'Tis a pity Christopher couldn't come to love me," she said with a yawn.

The blanket spluttered.

Gillian smiled, finding the idea to her liking all of the sudden. "He is powerfully handsome, especially when he smiles. I don't much care for his bellowing, but I could avoid provoking him. Do you suppose he might kiss me someday?"

The blanket was speechless.

Gillian sighed. "I suppose not. You know, I met him several years ago, but I certainly don't remember him being blind. I suppose he knows then just how ugly I am. And, of course, I haven't his courage. He could never bear a wife who couldn't be as fierce as he, could he? Nay, Blackmour's lady should be as firm and immovable as the keep itself. I would likely shame him at every turn."

The longer she talked, and the more she thought about it, the more it hurt her.

"Ah, Blanket, I am in such a sorry state." She blinked back tears. "You know, I think Berengaria truly is a witch. I wish she could make me beautiful, for then Christopher would want me. Or perhaps she could give me courage. Which would be the more difficult of the feats, do you think?"

She yawned through her tears and pressed her face against the blanket's throat. Thinking about it anymore was just too tiring.

"Hold me while I sleep," she whispered. "Please."

The blanket did just as she asked.

thirteen

CHRISTOPHER DRAGGED HIS HANDS THROUGH HIS HAIR and stepped from the kitchens. The chill of the great hall hit him square in the face and reminded him of just how cold Gillian had been for two days while he'd been trying to find her. More and more he wondered how she had survived. Colin had said there had been no one in the hut, just signs of a recent fire. Gillian could have built that herself.

But then who was this mysterious Berengaria she talked to in her fevered dreams? Christopher shook his head, unable to answer his own question. Whoever the woman was, spirit or flesh, she'd kept Gillian alive long enough for him to find her and he was grateful.

He was also frightened. There was no use in trying to pretend otherwise. Gillian knew of his blindness; yet she wanted to stay. Or so she'd said. Had she truly been babbling aloud while dreaming, or had she been doing it apurpose, scheming to have him while his heart was softened?

He groaned silently. Saints, he was an untrusting whoreson! The girl had been out of her head with fever, calling for phantoms of her dreams and he was suspecting her of perfidy? The scars on her back alone should have convinced him that she had neither the stomach nor the heart for betrayal. How could she, when betrayal was what had cost her the most? Her father should have been the one soul she could have trusted and he had abused that trust.

An unaccustomed feeling of frustration washed over Christopher. He wanted Gillian to trust *him*, to look to him for comfort and aid.

Or did he? Did he want to open his heart to her, just to have her turn on him and rend him to pieces?

What he wanted was to sit down and rest until his poor head stopped turning in such circles. Saints, he'd never been so confused in his life.

A scream tore through the babble in the hall and Christopher jerked his head up. He ran to the stairwell, then sprinted up the stairs and down the passageway to his bed-chamber.

"Don't touch me!"

Gillian was screaming that at the top of her lungs. Christopher burst into the chamber and rushed over to the bed.

"My lord, 'tis the fever," Jason panted. "She was thrashing about so violently I had to stop her before she hurt herself. I vow I'm holding her down gently!"

Christopher pulled Jason away and found Gillian's shoulders. He pinned her to the bed, then put his knee over her legs.

"Gillian, stop it," he commanded. "You're dreaming. Nothing will harm you here."

"Stay away from me," she wept, flailing her arms and legs wildly. "Not again, Father. You're not going to hurt me again!"

"Gillian—"

Her knee caught him full in the groin and he gasped out an oath.

"Stop it!" he bellowed.

A blinding pain in the side of his head was followed immediately by the feel of cold liquid splashing over his chest and arms.

"My lord, she snatched the pitcher before I could stop her," Jason said quickly.

Christopher gritted his teeth, ignoring Gillian's continued screams. "Am I bleeding?"

"Nay, my lord, but you are very wet."

"Thank you, Jason," Christopher said tightly. "I daresay I couldn't have divined that on my own."

"Not again," Gillian sobbed. "You can't touch me again."

"Gillian, calm yourself," Christopher said, trying to sound soothing. He found her arms and pinned them to the bed. "Calm yourself!"

"I have a s-sword," she said, ceasing to thrash. Christopher felt the fight drain out of her. "I know h-how to use it," she hiccupped. "I have a b-bloody sword."

Her will dissolved into hoarse sobs. Christopher released her shoulders and she rolled away from him. He sat on the edge of the bed and felt for her, finding that she had thrown her arm over her head, as if to ward off a blow.

"My lord, forgive me," Jason said, his voice hoarse. "I never meant to distress her."

Christopher sighed. "It wasn't your fault, lad, as you well know. You told me yourself that it would take time to win her trust, and I can see now how true that is. We'll go slowly and prove to her that she has no reason to fear us."

"Then you're keeping her?"

"Of course I'm keeping her. She needs me," he added, surprised at how boastful his tone was. "She needs me desperately and I'm not about to send her away."

Aye, that was truth indeed. What he didn't add was how pleased he was over it. For the first time in three years, someone needed him. He'd spent so long relying on others, first on Colin and Jason to watch over him until his body was healed, then on them both to help him find his way about in his world of darkness. He relied on Jason to be his eyes, on Colin to be his ears and his strong arm, even on his garrison captain and personal guard to see to the rest of his rotating guardsmen and not reveal his secret. Never once had anyone needed him for other than their daily bread and a marginally comfortable place to sleep.

But now it was different. Gillian needed his name to hide under, and his strong body to hide behind. She needed him to protect her and he wouldn't fail her. He would be quiet and still and wait for her to come to him. And he would hope to heaven that she could endure his foul temper and occasional bouts of impatience, for he very much doubted he could amend either flaw.

"I'll see to her now, Jason," Christopher said, finding that merely saying the words made him want to stand up a bit straighter. "And I'll fetch her something from the kitchens a bit later."

"Shall I wait, my lord? To see if you need anything?"

"Nay, lad. Hie yourself off to the lists and tell Sir Colin I sent you there to humiliate him. I've no need of you now."

"Oh," Jason said. "Very well then, my lord. But I'll return soon, aye?"

"After supper, lad. I'm equal to caring for Gillian myself until that time."

"As you wish, my lord."

Christopher bolted the bedchamber door behind Jason, then returned to the bed. He stripped off his wet tunic, then stretched out over the blankets and put his arm around his wife. She was still feverish, but that was to be expected.

"Blanket?" Gillian mumbled sleepily.

"Nay, Gillian, 'tis Christopher, not your blanket. Blankets do not have arms."

"Mine does," she insisted.

He smiled. This was the Gillian William had told him about, the one who teased with enthusiasm and countered his verbal parries with sharp thrusts of her own. It was a pity she couldn't wake from her fever and retain her lack of defenses. Then again, perhaps that would be part of the challenge, to see if he could teach her to trust him, to let him see this side she had shown to no one but her brother.

"Come closer, Blanket," she commanded. " 'Tis bloody cold in here."

"I'll have to take off the rest of my clothes and come under the sheet with you if you want to be warmer."

"Don't be a dolt. Blankets do not have clothes."

"Of course not." He pulled away, stripped off his remaining garments, and slid under the coverings. She turned instantly and burrowed against him, squeezing as close to him as humanly possible.

She was very warm and Christopher immediately became that way too. He groaned. Three years of celibacy had been three years too long and his body was reminding him of that.

"You're not very comfortable," Gillian complained, seeking a place for her head on his shoulder. "Much too hard."

Perhaps it wasn't such a fine idea to teach her to trust him. He had the distinct feeling that the Gillian of Warewick who lay buried under all the layers of living would be a very outspoken Gillian indeed.

"But even though you are so uncomfortable, you suit me," she whispered. "Will Christopher let me keep you, do you think?"

"Aye," he whispered, pressing his lips against her hair. "I daresay he will at that."

He pushed away the terror that nagged at the edges of his soul. She was an innocent child who could do nothing to hurt him. Teaching her to trust him was a far cry from giving her his heart. In time, he might even bed her, but that would require nothing but his body. He could keep his emotions at bay, not let her close enough to hurt him. He would keep her safe and he would try to be kind. He had kindness for Jason and for Wolf; that much at least he could give her. She would make no demands on him. His defenses would remain intact.

Not even Gillian could breach those.

GILLIAN WOKE, DRENCHED IN SWEAT. SHE OPENED HER eyes to darkness. It was then that awareness of her surroundings came to her in a rush. She was in a bed. Her head was resting on a muscular shoulder, the palm of her hand was lying on a broad, smooth chest and her forehead was pressed against a whisker-roughened jaw. There was a heavy arm around her back and over her waist.

And she was naked.

Her breath began to come in gasps. Her worst fears were coming to pass. She had been taken prisoner and her captor was just waiting for her to wake up so he could torture her.

With a mighty jerk, she rolled away and continued to roll.

"By the saints—" a man exclaimed.

She shrieked and scrambled to her feet. She found herself suddenly caught up in bedcurtains and she went down to the floor with a great rending sound and a hearty thump.

"Don't move!"

If she could have disobeyed, she would have, but she was trapped in voluminous folds of cloth and couldn't tell which way to exit them so she could breathe. She heard the sound of feet coming closer to her and in panic she kicked out.

"Gillian, by the bloody saints, cease! 'Tis me, Christopher! Can you not recognize your own husband?"

Christopher? Gillian froze. Christopher had come for her, just as Berengaria had said he would. But what was she doing in his bed? And draped over him like a whore, no less!

Snatches of dreams returned to her, pouring her heart out to the woman with silver hair, praying Christopher wouldn't send her to her father, talking to a blanket with such incredible warmth.

She jumped as she felt hands groping over the bed-clothes.

"Damn me, but you've tangled yourself well," Christopher said. "Can you move at all?"

She tried, and failed. "I fear I am sitting on whatever end there is to the cloth."

"Give me your hands then, and I'll pull you to your feet. Then we'll unveil you."

"Oh, please, nay," Gillian said quickly. "I'm not wearing anything!"

"I hardly see how that would be a problem."

Of course not, as he couldn't see her at all.

"Oh, my lord," Gillian said quietly, "forgive me."

Christopher grunted. "I'll give it some thought, depending on how quickly you obey me. Now, give me your hands and let me help you up. I won't steal all your covering."

Gillian pushed her hands out and felt Christopher take them. The next thing she knew, she was on her feet, stumbling, then falling against him. He put his arms around her and steadied her. Then, keeping one arm around her, he pulled the bedclothes from off her head. He felt her hair, then smoothed his hand over it.

"Can you breathe now, my lady?"

Breathe? While standing in the embrace of a man who frightened her while she was awake and haunted her dreams while she slept? Nay, breathing was beyond her.

"Gillian?"

"Aye," she managed.

He put his hand against her brow. "Your fever has broken, it seems. You must be hungry. I'll wrap you up in my dressing gown and put you before the fire, then I'll fetch you something to eat. Have you a preference?"

She shook her head. "Nay," she said.

"Can you stand, or are your feet tangled in the bed-clothes still?"

"I can stand, my lord."

He turned and crossed the chamber. Gillian did nothing but stand stock-still, swathed in heavy cloth and gape at her husband. Never in her life had she seen a naked man. She wondered, absently, what she had expected, but it certainly hadn't been what she was seeing at present.

His broad back tapered down to a trim waist and lean hips. Tight buttocks melted into heavy thighs which lengthened down into muscular calves. His every move spoke of power and grace. His muscles rippled as he reached out to pluck a dressing gown from off the table; then he turned. She caught her breath. She knew she should have been looking at his broad shoulders, or the finely honed muscles in his legs, but all she could do was stare at his groin.

"Stop staring," Christopher growled.

Her gaze flew to his face. He was staring at her. She blushed furiously and had the unnerving impression that he could actually see her.

"I wasn't staring," she lied.

"Aye, you were." He folded the dressing gown over his arm and let it hang in front of him as he crossed the room to her. "I can feel the heat from your cheeks." He put his palm to her cheek and nodded, as if he'd just proved a great experiment to himself. "Aye, you're blushing."

"And you're . . . you're naked," she spluttered.

He grunted as he draped the gown around her shoulders. "Sight was certainly not wasted on you, my lady. Now, go sit you down by the fire and I will fetch you something to eat. And then you'll retire back to bed. You've fought this fever for the three days since I brought you home, and I daresay you fought it for a day or two before then."

She stared at him in fascination as he pulled on hose and boots and continued to stare as he built up the fire. He soon left the chamber, his chest bare. Once he had gone, she pushed off the bedcurtains and drew his dressing gown more closely around her, ridiculously pleased that he had given it to her.

Then she ruthlessly squelched her feelings. He likely would have done the same for any number of others. He hadn't meant to imply anything by the gesture. She took her place in his chair next to the fire and didn't move a muscle. She didn't even dare move the chair any. Nay, she'd learned her lesson. Christopher didn't like the unexpected.

She jumped when the door behind her opened. Then she rose from her chair and hastened to close the door for her husband. She stood with her hand on the wood and toyed with the idea of escaping out into the passageway. But was escape really what she wanted? She'd escaped before, nay, been sent away, and it hadn't served her.

She pushed the door shut. Christopher's hand on her shoulder startled her. He reached over her and bolted the door, then slid his fingers down her arm until he could clasp her hand.

"Come. Your supper is waiting."

"What time is it?"

"I daresay 'tis the middle of the night."

"I'm sorry," she said quietly. "That was a foolish thing to ask."

He squeezed her hand as he led her over to the hearth. "It was a logical question to ask of anyone but a blind man. But I'll not hold it against you." He felt for the arms of the chair, then positioned Gillian in front of it and pushed her gently down. Then he pulled over a small table and put her supper atop it.

"I wasn't sure what your preferences were, so I brought what I could find. Cook was conveniently senseless and would not rouse when I suggested he do so."

Gillian broke off a piece of bread and chewed on it, finding it hard to swallow indeed. She watched Christopher settle down on the stool opposite her, watched his expression turn serious and knew he was ready to tell her she was to be sent home. He flexed his fingers, as if he prepared to do battle. Then he leaned forward, looking in her direction.

"Oh, please," she blurted out. "Let us not speak. I beg you."

He looked momentarily confused, then shrugged and sat back. "As you wish, my lady."

She knew her reprieve was sure to be short-lived, but she enjoyed it just the same. She pulled her legs up into the chair with her and hugged her knees to her chest as she ate from Christopher's findings. She poured herself wine and savored the taste, knowing she would soon be drinking the piss-water her father preferred, if she were alive to have even that.

And she stared at her husband. She memorized the way his long, dark hair fell over his brow; the way he cocked his head to one side when he listened; the stern, unyielding strength of his face. She memorized how broad his chest was and how powerful his arms were. She watched his hands, remembering how he had brushed one of them over her hair, then touched her cheek with the other. She would never forget how beautifully he moved, all strength and grace. Everything about him was strong and dark and uncompromising. Just like his home. Neither Blackmour nor Blackmour's lord would ever yield to anyone less powerful or intimidating than they.

She realized suddenly how completely inadequate she was to be his wife. The thought echoed in her head, as if it had been something she'd dreamed. Aye, he deserved better than she. She sat back in her chair and sighed softly.

"Finished?"

She nodded. Then she remembered. "Aye."

He rose and walked over to the bed. Her heart sank as he picked up the bedclothes and began to reconstruct his bedding. It was obviously a task he did very rarely as he was hopelessly unskilled at it. Gillian couldn't bring herself to help him. The sooner he was finished, the sooner he would start talking and the sooner she would be on her way.

Far too quickly he flung the blankets over the lumpy sheet. She watched as he crossed the chamber and stopped directly before her. He held down his hand.

She rose without taking it. "I can find my own way, my lord. I thank you for the supper and for your hospitality. I would repay you if I could, but I daresay you wouldn't want to visit Warewick."

"What are you babbling about, woman?" He reached out until he'd bumped her nose with his fingers, then he put his hand against her brow. "Have you gone feverish on me again?"

"Nay, my lord," she began, feeling as miserable as she ever had before. Nay, this was worse. She'd been alone with Christopher of Blackmour in his bedchamber and seen him gentle and gallant. No amount of dreaming in the future could ever best this evening.

"You're overtired," he said, sounding displeased. "To bed now, Gillian, and no arguments."

"My lord, I know you will send me away," she blurted out, "so I beg you not to pretend otherwise. I would rather leave now, if it's all the same to you."

He looked heavenward, then slipped his arm around her shoulders. He led her to the far side of the bed, felt for the blankets and held them up.

"In, my lady. Before you chill more. I imagine your toes are blue by now."

"But . . ."

"In," he commanded.

"My lord . . ."

"Gillian, get you into bed, then we will talk."

Gillian's heart felt like lead in her chest. Why could he not just say it and have done? She wanted to protest again, but Christopher stood there so expectantly that she couldn't do anything but obey him. She crawled onto the bed, keeping the dressing gown around her. She listened to him bank the fire, move the table to where he had taken it from, and check the door. The soft sound of his clothes hitting the floor was followed by the creaking of the bed as he slipped under the blankets. He was silent. Finally the strain wore on her until she thought she would scream.

"My lord, I beg you—"

"I spoke rashly before," he said, his voice very gruff. "You remember when."

She didn't. He'd spoken rashly so many times, she had no idea which time he referred to.

"My lord . . ."

"By the saints, Gillian, must I grovel on my knees to have forgiveness?" He'd gone from gruff to angry more quickly than she could follow. "I never meant to say what I did about the affair with Alice. I regret I didn't go after you immediately and say so. I'm sure this will come as a surprise, but I'm not very patient and I have been known to be a bit pigheaded at times. I regret that my actions caused you grief. There. I've said it. Now can we sleep?"

Gillian was speechless. He was apologizing? And now he wanted to sleep? It wasn't what she wanted to hear, not at all. She wanted to know exactly when he planned to send her back. At first light? After she broke her fast? After supper?

"Damn me," he swore. He shifted on the bed and she felt him take her hand in both of his. "Are you vexing me apurpose, wife, or was my apology insufficient? I vowed to be patient with you, but I can see already that I'm not equal to the task. I demand to know if you've forgiven me or not. Yea or nay, lady."

And though his words were stern, he stroked her fingers with great care. Gillian hardly knew what to make of him. But it was his touch, in the end, that made up her mind for her.

She swallowed. "Yea," she managed. "I have forgiven you."

He grunted softly. "My ears think your response to be not overly enthusiastic, but perhaps I can hope for nothing more as yet. Now, may we sleep?"

"Aye."

"Your fingers are cold. Give me your other hand. And you may as well give me your feet too. I've survived several nights of your cold toes on mine; I daresay I'll survive a few more."

Gillian couldn't make her limbs move, but she didn't have to. Christopher moved her bodily. He covered her feet with his, then gathered her hands together and placed them against his bare chest.

"You need me to keep you warm," he said, his voice a low rumble somewhere immediately above her head.

She could only nod.

"Go to sleep, Gillian. Nothing will hurt you this night."

This night. His words echoed in her ear long after his breathing had become deep and regular and his grip on her hands had loosened.

But what of the nights to come?

fourteen

GILLIAN KNELT AT THE ALTAR AND PRAYED, AS SHE HAD been doing for much of the morning. She'd woken to find Christopher leaning over her, feeling her brow. He had announced that her fever was gone, but that she wasn't to leave the bed that day. He'd then departed, leaving her no less upset than she had been the night before. The only difference was her hands and feet were indeed very warm.

When she'd come to the chapel, she'd prayed for no one but herself, not sparing her father a thought, nor Christopher. She prayed that she would be able to remain at Blackmour, that she would be safe, that Christopher would never strike her. His hands were large and heavy and she knew he could have wrought damage she never could have recovered from.

"Gillian!"

The sudden sound of that deep voice made her jump in fear. She darted a glance over her shoulder and saw Christopher standing in the aisle of the empty chapel, a fierce frown on his face.

"Aye?" she said, her voice barely audible even to her ears. She rose on shaking legs. "My lord?"

"I thought I instructed you to remain abed," he said in a low, gravelly voice.

"Forgive me, my lord," she whispered.

"Come over here," he commanded, thrusting out his hand.

Gillian wanted to sink back down to her knees. Perhaps remaining at Blackmour would be worse than being sent home. She steeled herself for the worst as she crossed over to her husband and stood before him. *Oh, God, please don't let him hit me.*

"Please, my lord," she blurted out, "I beg your forgiveness."

"As well you should," he said roughly, reaching out and jerking her into his arms. His embrace robbed her of breath.

"Think you it was pleasant for me to return to my bedchamber expecting to find my wife lying obediently in bed where I left her, only to discover the chamber was empty? Saints, woman, I'd thought you'd left me!"

Gillian was too astonished to answer. Why should he care, when that was likely just what he wanted her to do? She stood in her husband's embrace, her face buried against his chest and remained silent.

"There are several other things you must needs pacify me for," he growled. He pushed her back, took off his cloak and draped it around her shoulders. "Perhaps you do not remember it, but I was awake several nights tending you and the worry has made me irritable indeed."

Gillian stole a look at him while he fumbled with the clasp at her throat. Why were his hands shaking so? Was he truly so angry?

The clasp caught and held. Christopher brushed his thumb along her jaw in a gentle caress. Gillian stood with his cloak draped about her and could do nothing but stare at his hand in amazement as he pulled it back.

"Gillian? You were about to appease me with a heartfelt apology?"

She stammered out the words, "I'm sorry, my lord."

"That is another thing," he said, frowning down at her. "Either you've forgotten my name, or it doesn't suit you. It might be wise to plead a poor memory, for the latter would not sit well with me at all. For all you know, it might be enough to force those horns out from atop my head."

Gillian looked up at him, bewildered. Was he teasing her? William had always teased her thusly, with mock gruffness, but she'd known he loved her. She knew nothing of the sort about Christopher.

"Has the cold numbed your mind and your tongue, lady, or merely your tongue?" Christopher lifted his hand and ran his fingers lightly over her face, touching her mouth in passing. "You're gaping, so I must assume the cold has chilled your mind past using." He slipped his arm around her shoulders. "Let me see you back to our bedchamber and build you a fire. You haven't eaten either, have you? Gillian, I vow I'll have to keep you close by means of a leash if you do not heed my words more closely."

She didn't answer him; her heart was beating in her throat and words were simply beyond her. Christopher of Blackmour, Spawn of the Devil, had just given her his cloak, presented her with a crusty bit of teasing, and now was mother-henning her with skill even Jason would have to admire.

In a gruff way, of course. He was a dragon, after all.

It had been so long since she'd felt anything akin to gentleness from anyone that it was all she could do to let him lead her across the courtyard, up the steps, through the great hall and on up to his bedchamber without breaking down and sobbing. She sat when he placed her in his chair, then watched him as he stoked the fire.

Gillian caught her breath as he turned to her, kneeling, and felt for her hands with small, hesitant motions. Then he took her hands in his and brought them to his lips, blowing on them to warm them.

Her eyes burned with tears. How could he be so kind when he knew he was going to send her away soon?

She pulled her hands away before they learned how it felt to be tended by his.

"Please don't," she begged.

"Gillian—"

"My lord, please," she said, avoiding his searching hands. "You only hurt me more!"

"I am trying to help you—"

She escaped the chair and fled for the door, praying she wouldn't weep. There was so little left to her; her dignity was perhaps something she could keep.

"Damn you, Gillian, wait!"

She ran to the only place she knew Christopher wouldn't follow her: the battlements. Her legs were unsteady beneath her as she flew up the steps, but she forced them to work anyway. Perhaps once she was outside, the chill would numb both her mind and her heart.

Within moments, she stood at the wall overlooking the sea. In spite of herself, she wept. The guards ignored her, the gulls below ignored her. Oh, Blessed Virgin, how much worse could her life become? She wished with all her heart that she'd never set foot outside Warewick's puny walls, never seen Blackmour, never been witness to Christopher's gentleness with Jason.

And that she had never had that gentleness turned on her.

Without warning, a hard body came to rest against her back. Arms flanked her, and hands slapped against the flat edge of the wall with so sharp a sound that she jumped.

"Why do you continue to run from me?" a deep voice demanded. "Gillian, I absolutely refuse to beg! I've spent the last three years of my life begging and I'll do it no longer."

Gillian took a deep breath and dragged her sleeve across her eyes to hide the evidence of her grief.

"You keep sending me away."

"Once!" he exclaimed. "I did it once and I was wrong!"

He took her by the shoulders and turned her to face him. His frown was formidable. Gillian backed up against the wall. Christopher followed her, allowing her no room for escape.

"But you intend to send me away still," she said miserably.

"Send you away still?" he repeated. "Why would I send you away?"

"If anyone should know your reasons, 'twould be you."

"Perhaps you should explain them to me," he said, sounding mightily irritated, "since you seem to know so much about them."

"You never wanted this marriage," she blurted out, forcing her chin to remain up and not burrow into her chest as it so wanted to do. "My father couldn't have coerced you, of that I'm certain. Why you offered for me I do not know, for I brought you nothing. Now, you realize your mistake. Is that not so, my lord?"

He closed his eyes as he lifted his face heavenward and released a deep sigh.

"Did William never tell you that you thought too much for your own good?"

"Aye," she said, forcing the word past the lump in her throat, "he did."

Christopher gathered her close and rested his chin on top of her head. "He was right." He held her for a moment, then released her and pulled the cloak carefully up to her ears. " 'Tis cold out, and I'll not have you chill. Let us go in."

"My lord, I am not above begging. Please send me away now. If I weren't such a coward, I could likely endure a few more days here, but I've no courage—"

"You are not going anywhere, Gillian, unless you continue to refuse to call me by my name," he interrupted. "Now, come inside."

He reached for her hand and pulled her along behind him. Gillian went with him, only because he wouldn't release her. He hadn't meant what he'd said and she was certain she'd learn the truth of it soon enough. She followed behind him as he walked along the battlements, his right hand lightly skimming the wall, his left holding onto hers firmly. He continued on before her down the steep steps from the battlements; then he caught her hand again and kept it in his as they walked down the passageway.

"Count the doorways for me, Gill," he said quietly.

Not even William had called her by that name. It sounded so gloriously familiar coming from Christopher's lips that she started to weep again as she touched each doorway. If only he would want to keep her in truth!

" 'Tis this one," she said miserably.

Christopher turned her toward him and put his hands on her shoulders.

"How is it I can grieve you by saying nothing at all? You're overwrought from the fever, aren't you? I never should have let you escape to the battlements. I'll be more diligent in the future."

He opened the door and pushed her gently inside the room in front of him. He gave her no choice in what she would do next, for he swept her up into his arms and carried her across the chamber to the bed.

"Rest," he commanded, laying her down and pulling a heavy quilt up over her. "You are still weak from your ordeal and you need to sleep. I trust I will return in a few hours and find you here, obeying me as a good wife should?"

"Aye," she whispered.

She held in her tears until Christopher had gone, then buried her face in his pillow. She wept until she couldn't breathe, and then she began to wonder if her tears would ever stop. She was weary of weeping, of never having the courage to face things that frightened her, of never feeling secure anywhere.

Christopher had never come right out and said he planned to keep her. And until he did, she knew she couldn't feel safe.

And, oh, how she wanted to feel safe.

SEVERAL HOURS LATER, CHRISTOPHER PUSHED INTO HIS private solar, waited until Colin had trudged past him, then shut the door. He turned and glared. Coddling Colin had not been in his plans for the day.

"We have privacy. What in hell's name do you want?"

Colin cleared his throat. "I want to know what you're doing."

"What do you mean, what am I doing?" Christopher replied, exasperated. "I'm bloody living. What else would I be doing?"

"Don't be dense, Chris. What are you going to do with Gillian? I walked past your chamber an hour ago and heard her sobbing. Did you bed her again?"

"Of course not! She is overtired. The fever was hard on her and I was foolish enough to allow her out of bed."

Colin began to pace. He sighed several times—sure signs his poor taxed brain was working harder than was good for it. Then his footsteps stopped.

"You could have it annulled, you know," he said.

"I don't want an annulment. Gillian has a wonderfully sharp tongue when she's out of her head with fever and I daresay she'll eventually learn to use it on me while she is herself."

Colin grunted. "You could teach her obedience, I suppose. Even the threat of a beating would be sufficient."

With a curse, Christopher flung himself in Colin's direction. Whether it was fate or skill he wasn't sure, but he managed to find Colin's throat conveniently under his fingers as they fell. He landed a very satisfying blow to Colin's face before Colin's returning fist caught him under the chin and sent him sprawling. Christopher groped for his brother-in-law's tunic, then jerked him close, hoping his expression was as formidable as it felt.

"Never, *never* say the like again, or I vow by the rood that I'll flog you myself," he said coldly. "Gillian is never to be threatened with that, not even in jest."

Colin pried Christopher's fingers from the front of his tunic, then pushed him away. "Saints, Chris, you know I wasn't in earnest. I'm powerful fond of the girl."

"Then do not even jest about such a thing. I've spent four nights in the same bed with her and heard her cry out as she dreamed of her father. You know the man and you can easily imagine how he terrified her. I'll not have her terrified again."

Colin sighed. "She'll not hear the like from me."

"Good." Christopher rose and walked over to the alcove. The curtain was drawn and he puzzled over it until he caught the faint whiff of roses. He immediately realized just who was hiding in his solar. He'd left his wife with specific instructions to stay in bed, but she was obviously incapable of following his simplest order.

"Chris, you'd think you were in love with Gillian the way you carry on."

Christopher whirled around, wondering how he could make Colin be silent without saying as much. His friend was powerfully clever on the battlefield but hopelessly inept when it came to understanding subtle gestures.

"My duty is to defend her," Christopher managed, putting his finger to his lips.

"Should I speak more softly?" Colin whispered. "Why? Has Gillian been screeching her demands at you?"

"Colin, damn you!"

"You know, she isn't as homely as the gossips say," Colin continued. "She may not be as beautiful as Lina was, but she's a good deal kinder."

"I've no mind to hear aught of Lina," Christopher said, groaning silently. All Gillian needed to hear was a long list of his first wife's attributes and find herself compared to them.

Colin laughed suddenly. "I remember when you came back from Warewick that summer. You said Gillian was all eyes and limbs."

"Your memory fails you. I said she was charming."

"Nay, my friend, you said she was coltish."

"Saints, Colin, she was a child of ten-and-five! What was I supposed to say?"

" 'Tis a pity she can't hear you defend her so sweetly. I daresay she'd be pleased."

Christopher groaned out loud.

"Do you ever plan to tell her about the vow you swore to William, to care for her after he died? Perhaps she'd find it chivalrous. I think she has taken a bit of a liking to you. She watches you all the time."

"Colin, you horse's arse, be you silent!"

And Colin, like the fool Christopher knew him to be, laughed again heartily.

"By the saints, Chris, I can't remember the last time you blushed. I think Gillian is good for you. You are going to keep her, aren't you?"

"I said I was," Christopher said through gritted teeth.

"When are you going to get her with child? I think it well past time you had a babe or two to torment you."

"Out," Christopher said, pointing to the door.

"But I'm not finished talking—"

"Aye, you are."

"Won't you walk me to the door, then?"

Christopher didn't have a choice. Colin took him by the arm and dragged him across the chamber.

"I knew she was in here," Colin whispered with a chuckle. "Want her to hear anything else before I go?"

"You blighted whoreson."

Colin guffawed and pulled the door shut behind him. Christopher turned away from the door and leaned back against it, wiping his hands on his thighs. Now what was he to do? Leave and pretend he hadn't known she was there? Or should he begin his lessons in trust now?

He walked over to the alcove, drew back the curtains and heard an almost silent intake of breath. *Almost* silent. He put one hand on the wall and leaned against it, effectively cutting off whatever escape she might have had planned. He shook his head and clucked his tongue.

"That wife of mine," he said with a sigh. "So obedient, remaining abed when I instruct her to do so, never doing aught but what I have given her leave to do. Aye, I am fortunate indeed. I could have had a wife who wept buckets of tears the moment I turned my back, then hied herself off to my private solar, hid herself in this very alcove and eavesdropped on a conversation that wasn't fit for her ears."

There was a soft gasp, and a rustle of skirts. Christopher caught Gillian about the waist and pulled her back into his arms.

"And just where are you going, lady?"

"I didn't know you'd come here, my lord."

Christopher frowned. "Who?"

"My lord . . . Christopher."

He kept his arm around her shoulders and pulled her over to the bench, leaving her no choice but to sit with him.

"I built you a fine fire. Why did you leave it?"

She said nothing, but he felt her shoulders slump.

"Gillian?" He slid his hand up her arm until he could put his thumb under her chin. He lifted her face, then trailed his fingers lightly over her cheek. His fingers came away damp. He brushed the moisture away. It was replaced instantly by more. He groaned inwardly and lifted his lady onto his lap. He took her hands and slid them up around his neck, then put his arms around her. It took nothing more than a gentle pat on the back to leave her sobbing in his arms.

"Gillian," he murmured, at a loss. Lina had never wept,

unless she'd been trying to coerce him into giving her some trinket she wanted. Her tears had been false, nothing but a tool to soften his heart. Gillian's tears came straight from her soul. He had the distinct feeling she was weeping for not only the past fortnight's events, but the whole of her life.

And so he let her weep. He held her shuddering body close and rocked her, not even thinking to complain about the dampness of his neck and tunic. Her tears broke his heart, for he could well imagine the hurt that forced them from her. God's truth, he wished he could shed like tears and rid himself of the pain still lodged deep in his heart.

Her tears finally turned to hiccups, then mere sniffles. Christopher continued to rock her, stroking her back soothingly.

"There, now," he whispered. "Nothing will ever hurt you again, you'll see. Now, tell me why you left that wonderful fire I burned my hands preparing for you. Did it not please you?"

"I couldn't enjoy it."

"And why ever not?"

She pushed away from him so quickly, she almost fell off his legs.

"You do not want this marriage! You made some sort of vow to my brother."

He clasped his hands firmly behind her back, keeping her on his lap.

"Did you want to wed me?" he asked bluntly. "When you heard who had offered for you, did you not throw yourself at your sire's feet and beg to be released?"

She paused. It was a very long pause.

"That was before."

"Before you noted that I had no horns," he asked dryly, "or before you saw for yourself that my eyes were not red?"

"I never truly believed that. About the horns, that is."

"I've no doubt you did." He reached up and smoothed

her heavy curls back from her face. "Gillian, had I not made my vow to William, I wouldn't have offered for you, but my reasons are not the ones you think."

She was silent for several moments.

"No doubt, my lord," she said, finally.

Christopher sighed. "It wasn't because of you, Gillian."

"As you say, my lord," Gillian said, very softly.

"I wouldn't have offered for anyone," he said unwillingly. By the saints, he had no desire to speak of this!

And so he didn't. Let her think it was because he loved his first wife. Let her think anything but the real reason, the gaping wound in his pride Lina's last words had left on him. Aye, Gillian would never know what his first wife had reduced him to.

"Should I go?"

Christopher realized how fierce his expression was. "Nay, girl," he said gruffly, drawing her to him. He forced himself to ignore the anger just thinking on Lina set to boiling inside him. "Just idle thoughts. Put your arms around me and remind me what my name is, and I'll be content."

Only one of her arms ventured to touch his waist, a far cry from the way she had slept slung over him during her fever, but it was a beginning. Christopher was very still, unwilling to frighten her.

"And my name?"

She paused. "Christopher," she said.

"Ah, that was the name my mother gave me. Should I do my best to embroider it on your sleeve, or will you remember it on your own?"

"I'll remember it, my lord."

"Who?"

"Christopher."

He smiled and leaned his head back against the wall. "Comfortable, my lady?"

"Aye, my lord."

"Who?"

She made a noise that sounded suspiciously like a small laugh. Christopher brushed his hand up her arm and over to her mouth on the pretense of arranging her hair, when in reality he wanted to see if she was smiling or not. She was. Satisfied, he snuggled her closer and closed his eyes.

"You are a rather exasperating man," she ventured.

"My fondest wish is to bring out the shrew in you," he said cheerfully.

"Are you going daft, my lord?"

"Who—"

"Christopher," she amended quickly.

"If I am, Gillian, I lay the blame at your feet alone."

But if going daft could possibly be a good thing, he couldn't have been happier about his poor brain turning to mush. Who would have guessed that marriage would have ever given him such quiet pleasure? Or that it would have given him back purpose? No longer would his days be filled with waiting for Jason to aid him or Colin to come amuse him with tales of the garrisons. Nay, someone needed *him*. For the first time in months, he had a reason to rise each day.

And that reason was currently making little snorting noises as she slept peacefully in his arms.

fifteen

"BY THE SAINTS," GILLIAN EXCLAIMED, JERKING HER thumb away from the needle. She put the offended appendage into her mouth to soothe it. Either she was growing more clumsy by the hour, or she had passed far too much of the past se'nnight sewing.

To be sure, it wasn't as if she wanted to be sewing. She wanted to be out in the garden, looking at herbs or snatching the odd moment to train. Unfortunately, Christopher was convinced she was still far from recovered from her fever and had decreed she do nothing more taxing than sew until he thought her fully restored. She had stolen up to the battlements a time or two to escape the confinement of Christopher's bedchamber, but only when she'd been certain he was occupied in the lists. She hadn't had the courage to do more than that.

Or the will, if the truth were to be known. The last se'nnight had been the most peaceful she could remember passing. No one disturbed her, no one demanded that she do aught. Jason came often to bring her meals and give her tidings of the goings-on in the keep. Christopher had come by as often as Jason merely to see how she fared and if she had been resting. At first, his unannounced visits had left her heart pounding in her throat so forcefully that she'd been incapable of speech. As time had passed, she'd found herself almost waiting for him to come. Indeed, it was a fragile peace between them, but one she was loath to have end.

"Gillian?"

Gillian looked up from her sewing, startled. Christopher stood at the threshold of the chamber. Gillian searched his features quickly, trying to determine his mood.

"Gillian, are you here?"

"Aye, my lord," she said, setting aside her mending.

He paused, then frowned. "You sound feverish."

She jumped up out of the chair. "Nay, my lord," she said, doing her best to sound as unfeverish as possible. "I feel perfectly well."

He grunted softly in answer. "I thought perhaps you might wish to go outside for a short time. I daresay you haven't seen much of the keep yet."

"Gladly," she said, hastening to fetch her cloak. She fetched it from off its peg, threw it around her shoulders and ran for the doorway.

And the next thing she knew, she had tripped over her hem and was falling against her husband. How it happened, she couldn't have said, but one moment she was falling and the next she was being held securely against Christopher's broad chest. He patted her back gently, then set her upright.

"I take it this means the idea suits you," he said, his expression lightening.

"Oh, aye," she said, as overcome by the idea of freedom as she was by the sight of his expression. It was but a small smile he wore, but it cheered her just the same.

"Then we're off," he said, trailing his hand down her arm until he'd captured her fingers with his. He gave her hand a gentle squeeze and pulled her along down the passageway with him.

Gillian followed, surprised. He was doing something to

please her. Surely this was an auspicious sign. And hadn't he told Colin he intended to keep her? She had very good ears and was certain that was what she'd overheard.

But for how long?

And as what?

Those two thoughts had fair consumed her over the past se'nnight. The conversation of the kitchen wenches she'd overheard had haunted her. Christopher still could put her away. She was fairly certain her marriage hadn't been consummated. Though she slept each night in the same bed with her husband, he made no move other than to warm her hands and her feet. And she had her doubts that would result in any heirs any time soon.

"Good morrow to ye, milord," a knight said to Christopher as they stepped out into the great hall.

Gillian looked up at the man in passing, then felt her face flame. She didn't know his name, but she'd seen him the day before as she'd made her way furtively up to the battlements. The knight had been pressing a serving wench up against the wall, in full view of anyone walking down the passageway. Gillian had ducked into an alcove, torn between revulsion and fascination. The wench had been moaning for all she was worth and this man had been matching her, moan for moan. Gillian had hidden in the shadows and watched as, a few moments later, the knight had come swaggering by. The wench had trailed after him, complimenting him on his skill and bidding him seek her out whenever he pleased. Gillian hadn't understood it. Surely the wench hadn't enjoyed it, had she?

Gillian suspected it was that moaning that resulted in children, but she wasn't at all certain she wanted to indulge in it with Christopher. It would probably be excruciatingly painful and Christopher would crush her without realizing it.

But if he didn't have a son, he could send her back to her father at any moment. That was the thought that terrified her. It was almost enough to make her want to suggest he be a bit more bold.

Almost.

Short of an heir, the simple words "aye, Gillian, I'm keeping you forever, for I simply cannot live without you" certain would have sufficed. But Christopher would never say the like; she was fast learning that Christopher never said anything he didn't mean. If he promised her he would scold her if she didn't nap as long as he thought meet, then scold he did. Though he had only done it once and apologized sincerely afterward.

"You'll stay close by," Christopher announced suddenly, as he opened the hall door. "Blackmour is large, much larger than Warewick, and I'll not have you wandering off and losing yourself."

"Of course, my lord." Then she jerked on his shoulder. "My lord, mind your step!"

He came close to slipping off the first step outside the great hall, but he checked himself immediately. He frowned at her.

"I knew that."

"Of course, my lord," she said meekly.

"Saints, child, you are becoming as irritating as Jason. Do not humor me."

"But, I wasn't humoring you . . ."

He folded his arms over his chest and frowned down at her. "Aye, you were. And in payment for your sport, I require two things from you."

Gillian stiffened in dread. "But I have nothing to give you," she whispered.

"Ah, but you do. The first thing I require is a saucier retort than merely 'I wasn't humoring you.' You can do better, can you not?"

Gillian sighed in relief that he demanded no more than that. Then she realized what he had asked. Being saucy with her brother had been one thing; allowing her tongue to run free at the Dragon of Blackmour's expense was another thing entirely.

"I wouldn't dare," she murmured.

"Dare, lady."

Gillian looked up at him. He seemed earnest enough, and was waiting patiently. That in itself was something noteworthy.

But he was also a hand taller than her brother and infinitely more fierce. She had trusted William with her soul; she couldn't say the same about Christopher. Nay, jesting with him wasn't something she could do.

"I have forgotten what we were talking about," she said, stalling.

He pursed his lips, as if he understood exactly what she was doing. "I haven't, but I will let it pass for now. The second thing I require is your attentions in the garden. The whole of my life I have wished to bring a saucy maid into the midst of my herbs. Put your arm around me. I wish for you to feel protected while we are out of doors."

He didn't wait for her to comply but drew her arm around his waist and kept it there by means of his hand. Then he put his other arm very carefully around her shoulders. Gillian felt a furious blush come to her cheeks, but she didn't attempt to pull away.

Christopher was silent as they walked, as if he were concentrating very hard, or listening. Perhaps both. Gillian suspected he was paying great attention to where they were going, for he made no misstep.

"Your know your land very well, don't you?" she asked softly.

"Aye," he said, drawing a deep breath and releasing it. "I have no choice in the matter."

Gillian had no idea how to respond. She wasn't sure Christopher would have appreciated sympathy and she certainly couldn't offer him counsel on how he should live.

"I'm sorry," she said, feeling that she needed to say something.

He stopped at the gate to the garden. "Are you? For yourself?"

"Me? Nay," she said, shaking her head. "I'm content."

"I surely don't know why."

The bitterness was apparent in his voice. Mayhap he thought of what he had lost. And the loss was great. He had lost warring, training, the simple joys of seeing his garden blooming. He had also likely given up any hope of a beautiful wife, though why any father would have turned down such a son-in-law was a mystery to her. Even blind, he was a lord to be reckoned with.

Christopher led her over to a mossy place that was sheltered by a small tree. He helped her sit, then stretched out at her side. Before Gillian knew what he intended, he had swung his feet away from her and dropped his head onto her lap.

"Hand," he commanded, holding up his hand for hers.

Gillian put her hand in his and continued to stare down at his beautiful face. Saints, having him so close was unnerving! His head was a heavy weight atop her legs and his shoulders against the side of her thigh were as malleable as a stone.

"Are you cold?"

"Nay," she managed.

"You're trembling. Surely you aren't afeared of me, are you?"

"Nay," she lied.

"If anyone should fear me, it should be that monstrous squire I have. You don't see him cowering before me, do you?"

"Nay," she said.

"And why do you think that is?"

Gillian paused and considered. "I think," she ventured, " 'tis because you love him."

"By the saints," Christopher spluttered, jerking upright, "whatever gave you such a foolish notion? He's my bloody squire! I'm sworn to care for him, train him, teach him to be a knight.''

Gillian wanted to point out to him that he treated Jason more like a beloved son, but she refrained. Christopher was scowling furiously and it didn't take much effort to understand that sentiment was something he didn't voice easily.

Which boded ill indeed for her peace of mind.

Christopher threw her a final frown, then laid his head back down on her thigh.

'' 'Tis also because I am the kindest of men,'' he said, curtly. ''I care well for what is mine.''

Gillian couldn't manage a response, so she merely sat with her back pressed up against the cold stone of Christopher's keep and left her hand in his. And she held her tongue.

Time passed in silence. The tension in Christopher's shoulders seeped into Gillian's leg and through the rest of her body. She was excruciatingly aware of her hand in her husband's and that he certainly wasn't caressing it gently as was his habit. She tried to ease her fingers away from his, but he tightened his grip immediately.

''You're my wife,'' he said gruffly. ''Think you I would treat you with any less care?''

She did indeed but didn't dare say as much.

''Gillian?''

''Nay, my lord,'' she whispered.

''Have you ever seen me raise a hand against Jason?''

''Nay.''

''Take a belt to him?''

''Nay, my lord.''

''Shout at him?''

Gillian felt the intense desire to squirm. Shout? Indeed, he did that regularly.

''Often, my lord,'' she ventured.

Christopher's short laugh surprised her. ''Aye, there is truth in that, I suppose. And I'll likely shout at you too.

The difference is, you may shout back. I wish you to think on that while I sleep. I'll expect a few shrewish shouts from you when I awake.''

With that, he closed his eyes and began to snore. Gillian shook her head. The man could blow from fair to foul more quickly than she could follow, but as long as the storm was over, she didn't mind.

She leaned her head back against the wall and looked out over Christopher's bailey. It was indeed enormous and so much finer than Warewick that she could hardly believe she was now mistress of it, at least in name.

The sun peeped out from behind a cloud and Gillian smiled in spite of herself. It felt as if she hadn't seen that blessed heavenly body in days. For some reason, the sight of it cheered her. It certainly cast a warmer glow on the surroundings, though Gillian had to admit a dozen such suns couldn't lighten the dark gray of the stone about her. Blackmour was a forbidding place, no matter the weather.

''How looks my keep in this fine sunshine?''

Gillian realized with a start that her husband was indeed very much awake and that his snoring had been a ruse. Saints above, had she been babbling her thoughts aloud?

''Ah . . . um . . . it looks only slightly less gloomy than it looks in the rain, my lord,'' she blurted out.

''No doubt, my lady,'' he said, with a short laugh. Then he merely turned his face toward her and smiled.

His smile caught her off guard. How much it softened the sternness of those rugged features. By the saints, it transformed his visage into something beautiful. For the first time, she looked at him and saw what William must have seen: a serious, yet amiable man whom her brother had trusted completely.

Gillian stared at his mouth, wondering if his lips felt as soft as they looked. She reached out her hand and gently touched his lower lip with her finger. Aye, it was soft indeed.

Then she realized what she had done and jerked her

hand away, her cheeks aflame. As if she should actually touch him like a lover!

Christopher caught her wrist, as easily and accurately as if he'd seen it.

"I command you not to stop."

"My lord . . ."

He sighed with exaggerated patience. "Fetch me needle and thread, woman. I can see I must needs sew my name into the flesh of your arm that you remember it more easily." He sat up. "Go on and fetch it. It will pain you greatly, but at least you will not forget who I am." He turned his head toward her. "Well? I don't hear you moving."

Gillian looked at him for several moments in silence, gathering her courage.

"I think you jest with me, my lord," she said, finally.

Christopher's expression softened. "Indeed I do, my lady."

And with that, he reclined once more and closed his eyes. Gillian didn't dare touch his mouth again, but she did leave her hand in his. In time, she felt him relax more fully. She doubted that he truly slept, for every noise made him stiffen slightly.

She leaned her head back against the stone wall and let the sensation of peace wash over her. At the very least, she felt safe. And she wanted to believe that Christopher cared for her, in a sisterly way of course. He wasn't the Devil's spawn the rest of England thought him to be. Nay, he was merely a man with a flaw that he wished no one to know about. Perhaps that was part of what kept him away from her.

She was ashamed enough of that thought that she began to blush. Christopher would never see himself as unworthy of her. The very idea was unthinkable. Nay, he was being polite. He would likely continue to be polite until she did something to show him perhaps a few less manners in the bedchamber would result in a few children.

She stared down at him for a goodly while. Then, when she was certain he was well and truly asleep, she leaned down and brushed a kiss against his forehead.

She blushed clear to the roots of her hair and prayed no one had seen her foolishness. As if Christopher of Blackmour would actually want her!

CHRISTOPHER WASHED SLOWLY, LOOKING FORWARD TO sitting before the fire and warming up before going to bed. The day had been eternally long and full of problems he hadn't cared to think about. The only light in the gloom had been his time with Gillian in the garden. He was more than pleased with how things had gone. She had called him by his name at least twice that he could remember and she had kissed his forehead. If that wasn't a sign of blossoming trust, he didn't know what was. A pity all he could think about was that he'd wished she had kissed him a bit closer to his chin.

On his mouth, for instance.

He plunged his hands into the freezing water and splashed his face. It was insane. The entire idea of wedding her had been absurd and the consequences only worsened with each passing day. He had nothing to offer her. Aye, he had his name and his protection, but that was nothing.

Considering he wanted to offer her himself.

All of himself.

He dunked his head in the basin this time and kept it there until the chill of the water and the need for air forced him to lift his face.

"My lord, what are you doing?" Gillian exclaimed.

Christopher felt a cloth put into his hands.

"You'll chill, my lord. Come over to the fire and regain your warmth."

He had warmth enough, and to spare. But she would never know that. She was just beginning to trust him. Bedding her would have to wait a few more months. Perhaps years. Perhaps never, if his common sense won the war against his loins. As if he could actually care for a child they might produce! He could hardly care for himself!

"My lord, help me with this wine, would you not? I fear I am hopelessly unskilled at mulling it."

Christopher ruffled his hair with a linen cloth, then crossed the room and knelt down next to his wife.

" 'Tis done easily enough," he said, setting out the cups and pouring the wine. He sprinkled in the spices, then he reached for the iron poker and plunged it into each cup. After he had put the fire iron away, he handed Gillian a goblet and smiled tightly. "See?"

"Thank you, my lord."

He drained his, then cast about for something else to do to take his mind off his wife.

"Oh, but I do have a terrible tangle in my hair," she muttered under her breath.

"Let me see to it," Christopher said, ignoring his instinct for self-preservation. He worked the tangle free of her silken curls, then indulged himself in a few moments of merely touching her hair. It smelled like roses. He sniffed his way up a lock until he suddenly found himself nose to nose with his bride.

"My lord?"

He ached to kiss her. Just a simple kiss. What could that possibly hurt?

"Christopher?"

She was trembling. He pulled away with a silent curse. Too soon. It was far too soon and he was frightening her.

"To bed, Gillian," he said hoarsely. "You've been awake long enough. I'll not have you tiring yourself overmuch."

"I'm perfectly sound, my lord."

The wench had the gall to sound annoyed. Christopher had half a mind to kiss her senseless and show her just how annoyed *he* had been since his damnable decision to give her time to trust him. Saints, he should have bedded her a se'nnight ago. He would have done it carefully and brought her great pleasure.

Nay. He rose and turned his back on the fire and Gillian. Carefully wasn't enough. Foolish or not, he wanted her to want him. And, more than that, he wanted her to realize the life she was consigning herself to. If she were still a virgin, he could release her and give her to someone else. Someone whole.

The thought made him grind his teeth.

The smell of roses wafted past him. He jumped when he felt cold, slender hands touch his arm.

"My lord, what have I done to anger you?"

The fear was back in her voice. Christopher groaned silently.

"Nothing, Gillian. It isn't you."

"Should I say something saucy to please you?"

"Aye," he said, feeling a weary smile come out.

She was silent. "I fear I cannot think of anything at the moment."

"Let us go to bed and you can think on it while we sleep. I'll expect something worthy of you first thing to-morrow."

"Very well, my lord."

"Gillian," he began, feeling powerfully uncomfortable. He wanted to ask her if she feared him, but he couldn't bear to hear the wrong answer. He fixed a gruff look on his face to cover his uncertainty. "If you steal my pillow as you did last eve, I'll be forced to take drastic mea-sures."

"I'll be more careful."

"Aye, you will. Indeed, I daresay we'll be forced to sleep a bit closer to each other tonight." The saints pre-serve him, he was setting himself up for a night of sheer misery! "Just so I can retrieve my bedding with greater ease, of course. No other reason."

"Of course not," she answered softly.

Christopher couldn't decide if she sounded sorry because he supposedly had no other reason to sleep close to her, or if she were sorry that she would be forced to endure his presence in such close proximity. And that doubt in his mind was enough to drive him to drink.

He was momentarily tempted, then remembered all the mornings he had suffered already thanks to too much drink over Gillian of Warewick, lately of Blackmour, and he knew he could not drink again to forget her.

He was, the saints pity him, firmly caught in a hell of entirely his own making.

sixteen

"NAY, JASON, LEAVE GILLIAN'S MEAL BE. I CAN SEE TO it myself."

Gillian watched her husband wave away his squire, then watched Jason's face fall. Jason's shoulders slumped and he moved away to take his place on a stool behind the lord's table. Gillian felt her heart go out to him. For a solid se'ennight Christopher had been telling the lad he needed nothing from him. Indeed, Gillian began to understand how it was Christopher kept his blindness from his household. He chose her meal carefully and skillfully, then over-saw her consumption of it with as much ease as if he'd actually seen her slipping things under the table to the dogs.

But when Christopher quit the hall with Colin and left Jason behind, Gillian stopped thinking about her husband and started thinking about his squire. The poor lad. It was obvious he felt his place had been done away with, and that was the last thing she wanted.

"Jason?"

"Aye, my lady?" he asked wearily, as wearily as only a lad of ten-and-six can.

"Perhaps you would care to walk with me? As part of your chivalry training?"

He smiled faintly. "It would be my pleasure."

"Up on the roof, where Sir Colin cannot torment us."

"Of course, my lady."

Within moments, they were walking along the battlements. Jason was unusually silent. Gillian knew the best way to cheer him would be to make him talk about something he loved. It was rather handy that the person he worshipped was the same one who figured prominently in her dreams also.

"Tell me of your time with Lord Blackmour," she said, attempting to sound only mildly interested.

"It has been a squire's life," he said, shrugging.

This wasn't going as she had expected it to and it was difficult to corner him when she was walking in front of him.

"I grow chilled," she announced, hoping she sounded the part of a grand lady. Jason was likely used to dealing with those sorts and it would put him at ease. "Let us retire to your lord's solar. I would have a bit of wine to soothe me."

"As you will, my lady."

A short while later, Gillian was warming her toes by a finely constructed fire. She reached for the bottle and poured more wine into Jason's cup. He downed it just as readily as he had the previous four cups.

"You knew him always?" she asked, refilling his cup yet again.

"Aye," Jason nodded, then drained the goblet. "He had squired at my father's keep and I had watched him from the time I became aware of the souls around me. He was a fierce and powerful lad whose bravery far surpassed those around him."

Wine had loosened Jason's tongue and Gillian couldn't have been more pleased about it. These were tales she was more than ready to hear.

"My father loved him dearly and treated him as he would have another son. He had no reservations about giving me to Lord Christopher at such a tender age. You might say," Jason said with a smile, "that I came along as part of my lord's outfitting. My father gave him a fine new stallion, armor and a page. My lord Christopher didn't even turn me over to the care of his mother, as is custom. He wanted to keep me near him, so as to watch over me." Jason's smile turned into a grin. "You might suppose I was a very spoiled little boy."

"Even if you were at first," Gillian said, returning his smile, "I daresay you've grown out of it. Now, tell me more. What things did you and Christopher do?"

"Marvelous things," Jason said, beaming. "Tourneys, battles, visits to court. He took me with him everywhere he went and cursed anyone who sought to deny me entrance. He was determined that I should learn as much of the world as I could while he was there to protect me from its evils. And he trained me, saints, how he trained me! My lord Christopher is one of the finest warriors I've ever seen, my father and my brothers included. He is rarely unseated in the joust and never bested with the sword.

"I wish you could have seen him when we traveled on the continent. He was a most impressive sight, dressed all in black and red. And how much gold he earned, vanquishing others at tourneys! I was the most fortunate of lads to have him as my master. There wasn't anything I wouldn't have done for him."

"He knows that, Jason," Gillian said softly.

Jason's smile faltered, as if he remembered why he had been so closemouthed.

"Aye, I know," he replied, just as softly.

"He needs you just as much as he always has. I could never take your place with him."

"I do not begrudge you his affection, my lady."

Gillian laughed softly. "There is nothing to begrudge, Jason. Christopher loves you well and that you know."

Jason sighed and rubbed his hand over his face. "My only wish is that I might have spared him this trial he faces now."

"Tell me of it," she said, trying not to sound as curious as she was.

"It was an ill-fated year that stole his sight from him. I should have pleaded with him not to wed her, but I too was blinded by her beauty."

Gillian stiffened. "A woman did this to him?"

"Nay, but his wedding her was the beginning of the troubles."

"Tell me of her."

"Her name was Magdalina of Berkhamshire."

Gillian gasped. "Was she of Colin's kin?"

"His sister. And she was as beautiful as Sir Colin is ugly. Pale haired and pale eyed, and with a face that could turn a man's reasoning to mush in no time. My lord fell under her spell the moment he saw her, and she under his. Or so we thought. My lord could see no one but her. It was only a few months after his wedding that he was out riding and was overtaken and wounded. Her Ladyship was distraught, so distraught she wouldn't speak to him, or go near him . . ."

Gillian had stopped listening. So Christopher's first wife had been beautiful. And he had been able to see no one but her. No wonder. The man deserved a beautiful woman.

Something Gillian knew she would never be.

Or would she? Was there some way she could make herself beautiful? Not that Christopher would be able to see it, but others might tell him and that would please him.

And then he would love her as much as he'd loved his first wife.

She rose and left the solar, leaving Jason still babbling behind her. She walked down the passageway, then stopped when she heard female voices coming from inside one of the chambers.

"I bought a potion and you know how it worked." A

laugh followed that. "I haven't had the peace to sleep in a se'nnight!"

"I paid for one too, though it tasted burned. But it worked well enough. Did you not mark how none of the men can stop looking at me?"

"And to think they live under the guise of midwives!"

"Aye," the first laughed again. "Who would have thought a love potion could work so well?"

"Oh, tell me where they are," a third voice pleaded. "I'll give you each a coin if you do."

There was a great deal of haggling, then forthcame the information Gillian wanted.

"Down in the poorest part of the village, the third hut past the beggar with the lame dog. Smoke ascends continuously from the hole in the roof. 'Tis easily found."

Gillian didn't have to hear more. She made her way quickly down the stairs.

The Fates were with her.

"OCH, BUT BUSINESS IS BRISK!" MAGDA EXCLAIMED.

"Magda, we won't be having any business if you insist on burning everything you put in that bloody pot! Lucifer's knees, you are a helpless nun!"

"Don't call me names, Nemain," Magda said stiffly. "I'll have you know, my potions have worked well enough so far. Without your help!"

Nemain grumbled under her breath as she put her finger into the pot and tasted. "Another pinch of comeliness. Nay, not that pot! That's wart dust, you pitiful novice! A pinch of that will turn your paying wenches into toads. Toads cannot earn money by scrubbing floors and you know what that means."

"Aye, it means no more coins. Nor anyone to aid," Magda added. She stirred the contents of the black kettle carefully. "Berengaria, you're staring out the window again. What do you see?"

Berengaria was watching the Dragon's wife slip out the

gate and make her way through the village outside the outer wall. She brushed aside an unsavory lout or two who eyed the young mistress of Blackmour with less than chaste thoughts. Then she turned Gillian's feet in the right direction and led her gently to the inconspicuous hut that sat among a score of other inconspicuous huts.

A knock sounded on the door. Berengaria smiled and went to answer.

"Gillian."

Gillian's green eyes widened. "Lady Berengaria? You weren't a dream?"

"Come in, child," Berengaria smiled, drawing Gillian inside. She led her to a stool, then shooed away Nemain and Magda, who stumbled over each other in their haste to offer Gillian something tasty to drink. "Do behave, you two," Berengaria scolded. "Magda, love, watch the pot. Your potion is burning again."

Gillian smiled. "I see I didn't dream her either."

"Nay, child, you did not. Now, tell me. How goes your life with the Dragon? I hear his temper is fiery."

"And his form is marvelously fine," Magda sighed dreamily.

"Magda, be you silent," Nemain grumbled.

Berengaria only smiled serenely. "Gillian?"

Gillian leaned forward, as if she feared the walls were listening.

"I need your aid, my lady."

"How so, child? You've the skill to win your lord."

"Nay," Gillian said, shaking her head miserably. "His first lady wife was beautiful and I know beauty is the only way to win him. Can you not make me a potion or give me a herb that will make me beautiful? Courage, too, if possible. That would serve me well." She looked at Berengaria pleadingly. "I have no gold now, but I will bring you whatever you ask for later, if I may."

Berengaria looked at Gillian thoughtfully. "Beauty and courage are all you require?"

"I would request a love potion too, but my lord wouldn't be affected by it. He's powerfully stubborn," Gillian admitted reluctantly. "But if I were beautiful and courageous, he might grow fond of me. And if he were fond of me, he might wish me to have his child. If I were the mother of his child, he might learn to love me." She paused. "Think you?"

Berengaria had many thoughts, one of which was how utterly suited for each other were Christopher and Gillian. Two souls so worried about their own flaws that they couldn't see the love waiting right there before them for the asking.

Blindness came in many guises.

"Of course, I'll aid you," Berengaria said gently. "Beauty and courage will be yours, my child. And my only request would be that you bring me word of your successes. That will be payment enough."

Berengaria rose and walked over to her private work-table. She pulled out her own stock of herbs and took a pinch or two of several things, mixed them together and folded them up into two leather pouches. She handed them both to Gillian, received a kiss of gratitude, then watched Gillian scamper off back up to the keep, her worries solved.

"What did you give her?" Nemain asked suspiciously. "You didn't take from the normal beauty and courage pots. I should know. I labeled them myself."

"I gave her something special," Berengaria said, smiling to herself.

"Hrumph," Nemain said, unconvinced.

"Don't question your superiors," Magda said to Nemain, parroting back Nemain's favorite axiom.

Berengaria sighed as the bickering began again. Of course she'd only used crushed rose petals, but Gillian would never be the wiser. The natural beauty she possessed and the stores of courage deep inside her would come out and blossom because of her belief.

And that was a magic more powerful than any wizard's thumb-bone could ever provide.

seventeen

COLIN OF BERKHAMSHIRE WASN'T A MAN TO BE TRIFLED with. He knew that, and he always made sure others knew that. It saved him a great deal of aggravation while trying to garner information. A mere frown was usually all it took to have his chosen interrogatees babbling their innermost secrets in an effort to escape certain punishment. Nay, he wasn't a man to be taken lightly.

Unfortunately, Gillian of Blackmour seemed not to realize that.

He followed her back up to the keep, scowling at peasant and knight alike and saving his unwitting mistress from several unsavory encounters. Gillian remained oblivious. If she'd but turned and seen his frown, she surely would have known she was ignoring the wrong man.

And she was betraying the wrong dragon.

Colin's ire rose with each step he followed her. Just what mischief had she been about in the village? She'd sought that witches' hut as easily as if she'd been going there all her life. Colin didn't believe in witches, nor in potions, but he'd heard the gossip. Whatever Gillian was contriving, it surely boded no good. And if the girl did anything to harm Christopher . . .

To say Colin felt kindly towards Christopher was simply an understatement. Christopher was not only his brother-in-law, he was his brother by affection. They had tourneyed together. They had gone off to war together. Christopher had saved his life and Colin had returned the favor. Only Colin hadn't been able to save Christopher's sight. That grieved him more than he cared to admit.

He didn't remain at Blackmour out of guilt. He had fiefs of his own, which he visited on occasion. Nay, he stayed with Christopher because Christopher was the only family remaining to him that he would break bread with. And because Christopher needed him. Colin took enormous pleasure in poking his nose in deserted corners and assuring himself that no one hatched any plots to harm the Dragon of Blackmour. He enjoyed being Christopher's messenger, in putting fear into the hearts of those who had any dealings with Blackmour.

Colin's eyes narrowed as he followed Gillian through the great hall. He never would have suspected this one of betrayal. She was a mouse. A marginally fetching mouse, but a mouse nonetheless. She might even have been pretty had she not spent so much of her time cowering. Not that he could begrudge her that. After seeing her torn gowns at Warewick, he'd marveled that she lived still.

Though if she harmed Christopher, she would think her past life at Warewick to be pleasant indeed compared to her future.

He followed her down the passageway to Christopher's chamber, then waited a few moments outside the door, wanting to make certain she had the evidence of her guilt in her hands before he caught her.

He eased the door open, then slipped inside the chamber. Gillian was standing at the table, dropping something into a cup.

"Do nothing else," Colin barked.

Gillian jumped and dust went flying into the air. Colin

strode over and saw the herbs scattered about her. He glared down at her.

"Poisoning my lord?" he demanded.

Gillian cried out as she dropped to her knees and tried carefully to retrieve the few herbs that had missed landing on the table and fallen to the floor instead.

"I said cease, you murderess!"

"They aren't for him," Gillian moaned. "They were for me!"

Colin was very rarely mistaken and he found the sensation to be quite unnerving.

"For you? Child, why would you want to take your own life?"

Gillian ignored him and continued to search for the bits of herb scattered about. Colin knelt and grasped her chin, lifting her face up.

"I asked why you would want to take your life."

"I don't," she whispered, her sweet green eyes full of tears. "These were herbs to make me beautiful and give me courage. So Christopher would love me."

Colin's eyes burned as badly as they ever had after being in a smoky hall. Merciful saints above, he thought he just might weep!

"I see," he said gruffly, trying to cover up his consternation. "Courage and beauty, eh?"

"And you've scattered most of it."

Never had an accusation wounded him more. He started searching with her, picking up every last bit of dust that remotely resembled anything edible. Then he found himself helping her capture the ones that had fallen to the table. Once that was done, he helped her put all the herbs back onto the scraps of leather.

"I actually couldn't imagine you trying to poison Christopher," he said, frowning deeply.

Gillian looked up at him, her cheeks wet with her tears. "I forgive you freely, though you have fair ruined my chances of winning Christopher now. Lady Berengaria gave me of her private cache of courage and beauty herbs. I daresay this was the last of the lot.''

Colin had his doubts about several things, mainly that this Berengaria creature was a lady and that herbs could actually make a person beautiful and courageous. But he chose not to say as much. Gillian was already terribly distraught, obviously because she thought the herbs would no longer serve her. For the first time in years, Colin found himself completely undone by a woman's sweetness. Aye, Christopher hadn't chosen poorly with this child.

And if she wanted to believe herbs would make her beautiful, he was perfectly willing to help her do so. But he would make damn sure she wasn't going to poison herself by mistake. Already Christopher was fond of the girl. Losing her would certainly trouble him.

''I don't suppose you'd care to share,'' Colin asked, trying to sound disinterested so she wouldn't suspect anything. ''Just of the beauty herbs, though. I've courage enough to spare.''

Gillian's shy smile was positively enchanting. Colin vowed then to tell Christopher just what a fetching wench he'd bought himself.

''Just a bit. I'll need most of them for myself.''

Colin nodded solemnly, as though he actually agreed such foolishness would work.

''I believe these are the ones. Here.''

Colin accepted a goblet of wine with a sprinkling of beauty on top. As he drank, he wondered in the back of his mind if it might truly make him handsome. Not that he cared, of course. Handsomeness never helped a man on the battlefield.

He waited. When he didn't begin to retch, he had the feeling Gillian wouldn't poison herself.

''How do I look?'' he asked.

''Well, there isn't much of a change.''

Colin watched the crestfallen look descend on her face and he cleared his throat hastily.

"You know, I've heard these things take at least a se'nnight to work. Perhaps longer in the case of a man. Try just a little each day, my lady, then be patient. I'm sure they will serve you quite well."

Gillian nodded and picked up her own cup of wine. She closed her eyes while she drank, as if she prayed sincerely for success.

"Gillian? Saints, Colin, I can smell you too," Christopher barked from the door. "What are you doing in here tormenting my lady?"

"Ah," Colin stalled, "we were discussing herbs."

"I'm sure you've discussed enough. Get you gone, Colin. I'll see to Gillian now."

Colin clapped Christopher on the back as he left the chamber. Then he headed down to the cellars, feeling the need of something very strong to drink.

CHRISTOPHER LAY IN HIS BED AND WAITED UNTIL GILLIAN fell asleep. He rose and dressed in hose and boots, then picked up his sword and left his chamber. He hadn't trained in a se'nnight and already he could feel a difference. Not only did parrying with invisible foes keep his muscles honed, it helped him keep his sense of balance.

The memories of just how long it took him to regain even that were ones Christopher didn't dwell on if he could help it. Ah, how much he had taken his eyes for granted! Even such a simple thing as swinging a sword had been a task to relearn. At first it had been all he could do to move his blade from side to side and still keep on his feet. He'd landed flat on his face the first time he'd attempted a forward thrust. That was, of course, ventured only after he'd learned to parry without losing his supper. Saints, even now, the very thought of the dizziness he'd suffered made him queasy.

He shook off the memories and strode forward. He could parry with ease now—and he'd earned every bloody stroke he could swing.

He hadn't walked five paces before he heard someone fall into step with him.

"Colin?"

"Damnation, Christopher, but you are too observant."

Christopher grunted as he strode forward. "I've nothing to say to you. I cannot wring a decent answer from my wife as to what you were doing in my chamber. Should you have even kissed her when I dare not, I will kill you."

"Me? Never. Not that she isn't a comely wench. Grows more beautiful with every passing hour, to my mind."

Christopher didn't answer. Gillian's beauty, or lack thereof, was the last thing on his mind. Bedding her was first and foremost in his thoughts. Continually. Day and night. Dreaming or awake. He could not force her delicate smell from his nostrils, nor could he erase the memories of waking each morning with her draped over him like a soggy blanket. But of course, she wouldn't want him. Why would she, when he had so little to offer her?

Christopher mounted the steps to the tower chamber, then waited until he heard Colin reach the landing behind him.

"Might we have a candle?" Colin asked.

"Aye, but fetch it yourself,"

Christopher stretched his muscles, then began working with his blade. Thrust and parry, parry and thrust. Strike the right, sever the sword arm, then seek the heart, always the heart. In his youth, Christopher had followed a more chivalrous method of swordplay, delaying the kill out of politeness. Now it was kill quickly, or suffer death himself. He knew if he ever faced a real opponent, he would be bloody lucky to come out with all his limbs intact, not to mention his very life. He had to strike for the heart and not miss his mark. It would be the only way he would survive.

Christopher stopped once he heard Colin making his way up the steps, then waited again while his brother-in-law settled himself with a grunt.

"Shall I tell you what I was doing in your chamber today?" Colin asked.

Christopher lunged with his thrust, then pulled back. "Suit yourself." He gathered himself for another thrust.

"Your wife went to see a witch named Berengaria this morn."

Christopher was caught in midlunge, and he almost went sprawling. "She *what?*"

"I followed her down to the village, then back again. I feared she had your death on her mind."

Christopher could only stand with his hands hanging down by his sides and gape. Berengaria? The same woman Gillian had called for in her fevered dreams?

"You jest," he managed.

"I do nothing of the sort. She was in their hut for a goodly while; then she returned home. And then I, fearing for your precious life, followed her into your chamber and accused her of being a murderess."

"And is she?"

Colin snorted. "You won't believe what I'm about to tell you."

"Tell me just the same."

"She has procured herbs to make her beautiful and give her courage. So she can win you—if you can fathom that."

Christopher felt for the wall behind him, then slid down to the floor. He stretched his legs out and merely sat, trying to take the tidings in.

"She wants to win me." He was stunned.

"Aye. And she thinks she cannot unless she is beautiful. Why that should matter to her, I don't know."

"She must have heard a tale about Lina."

"Not from me."

"Likely from my babbling squire," Christopher grumbled. "He was singing to himself in my solar when I found him this afternoon. Gillian had left him with four bottles of wine. I've no doubt he told her several things he shouldn't have. Now, tell me more of what my lady is about.''

''She's putting these witchly herbs into wine and drinking the bloody concoction. I don't think they will harm her,'' Colin added, ''for I tested them on myself.'' He paused. ''I daresay your lady wasn't too pleased not to see immediate results on my poor visage.''

''It would take more than herbs, my friend.''

''Well,'' Colin said stiffly, ''you might have come away with all the beauty, but you'll notice I have all the brawn and intelligence. Keep your pretty face.''

''And you keep your head atop your shoulders,'' Christopher suggested, ''and do it by leaving me in peace. I've much to think on.''

He heard Colin mutter under his breath, pick up the candle and leave the chamber. Christopher sat and thought. So Gillian wanted to win him. Why, by all the blessed saints above, would she want a blind husband? Because she could have no other? Or was it because she hadn't been given a choice?

Nay, if she didn't care for him, it would be a simple enough thing to endure his attentions and then take a lover. That was something that happened with regularity in the whole of England.

She wanted to win him. Why?

Not for his gold. She had that already. And surely not to use that gold against him. Through sad experience, he had learned that Gillian wasn't capable of betrayal. And it couldn't be because she wanted to hurt him. Hadn't she said while in her delirium that she loved him? It was entirely possible that such a thing were true, wasn't it?

To think she had sought out a simple village witch for herbs to make her beautiful so she could please him.

He rose and left the tower chamber, descending the steps without thinking and continuing on to his chamber. He entered it and bolted the door behind him. He walked si-

lently to the bed and undressed. Gillian didn't stir until he
slid under the blankets next to her.

"Christopher?"

"Aye," he said, reaching out and drawing her close.
"Come, let me keep you warm."

"Where have you been? I thought you'd fallen out of
bed."

Christopher smiled. Gillian was never too aware of what
she said when she was sleepy.

"Nay, girl, I was just out taking a walk."

"Hmmm," she murmured. "You'll stay now, won't
you?"

He bent his head and pressed his lips against her forehead. "Aye, I'll stay now."

"I feel so safe," she mumbled; then she fell asleep.

Well, there was simply no higher compliment than that.
Christopher wrapped his arms around her shift-covered
form and closed his eyes. Sweet, modest, gentle Gillian
felt safe with him. Who would have thought it? Only Gillian could have walked straight into the dragon's lair and
tamed the beast so thoroughly, something no other maid
in England had ever been able to do.

Not even Lina. Oh, she'd hurt him deeply enough with
her words after his wounding, but there were places in him
she'd never come close to touching.

Places Gillian had already claimed as her own.

Christopher felt the walls around his heart come tumbling completely down and he felt panic well up in his
breast. Oh, how easily she could destroy him if she turned
her back on him now!

Gillian stirred. Christopher remained perfectly still as
she smoothed her hand over his chest, petting him as she
was wont to pet Wolf when he was restless.

"Sshh," she whispered soothingly. "Christopher,
you're dreaming. 'Tis naught but a foul dream. Be at
peace."

For a moment Christopher couldn't quite tell who was

dreaming and who was awake. Then Gillian's motions slowed and finally ceased. Christopher let out his breath slowly and felt the tension drain from him. Gillian wouldn't leave him. She needed him.

And, God help him, he needed her. He needed her gentleness, her sweetness of spirit. Her heart was pure and innocent, such a contrast to his. Odd, but for the first time he realized that he needed to learn to trust just as badly as she did. He pressed a kiss against the top of her head.

"Don't leave me," he murmured, not at all surprised at the words coming out of his mouth.

And, as if she'd heard, Gillian tightened her arms around him.

Christopher wanted to weep.

eighteen

GILLIAN DRAINED THE GOBLET OF WINE, THEN SET IT carefully on the table in Christopher's bedchamber.

"I have courage," she repeated to herself. "Vast amounts of courage. Serving wenches do not frighten me. Why, if any of them so much as crosses me, I'll take my blade to them."

That said, Gillian put her shoulders back and left the chamber. The herbs were working. Indeed, she felt almost bold, if such a thing were possible after only a few days. She walked down the passageway with a confident air, feeling altogether pleased with herself and her life.

And altogether displeased with the condition of the rushes in the great hall. It was a marshy mess and she had every intention of seeing the floor covering changed that day and frequently thereafter. She marched straight into the kitchen and surveyed with a critical eye the servants lounging about. In the past she'd felt little more than a servant, so she could well sympathize with their plight; but each member of the household had tasks to see to, herself included. Christopher didn't shirk his duty to see his folk kept safe. She didn't shirk her duty to try to see Christopher appeased at all times. Christopher's servants were going to stop hiding from their chores. That was all that needed to be said.

She cleared her throat. All but Cook turned to look at her. Cook still intimidated her, but after a few more herbs, even he would find himself coming to heel when she called. She swept the remaining servants with a firm look.

"The rushes will be changed today."

Not a soul moved a muscle. One woman yawned, then gulped suddenly. Gillian caught sight of a movement next to her and looked to see Colin there at the doorway, a fierce frown of displeasure on his face. She tilted her chin up.

"I need no aid."

Colin grunted, then turned and walked from the kitchens. Gillian turned back to her staff.

"Fresh rushes await in the hall. Let us begin now."

A few more enthusiastic yawns greeted her. Gillian very carefully folded her arms over her chest. It was something Christopher did when he prepared to intimidate whomever had displeased him.

"Whoever would prefer to empty the cesspit is more than welcome to volunteer," Gillian added, keeping her voice level.

"I'll do neither," a dark-haired, heavyset woman drawled.

Gillian fixed the woman with her best frown. "My first worker. Anyone care to join her?"

"Who's going to make us?" another woman scoffed.

Gillian felt her palms grow damp. Saints, how was she to enforce her commands now? By fetching her blade and drawing it on the servants? Her knees began to tremble beneath her gown.

"Any number of her husband's guardsmen," Colin said curtly, suddenly appearing again at the doorway.

Gillian looked to her right and watched as six grim-faced warriors trooped past Colin and bowed to her. They waited, silent, for orders. Gillian put her shoulders back and gestured to the two women.

"Show these two the way to the cesspit. The others will be pleased to attend to the task I've set for them."

The two women were helped out of the kitchens and the rest of the servants jumped to do Gillian's bidding. She appointed a trustworthy-looking soul to be in charge of seeing the hall cleaned, followed them out into the great hall, then stood on the dais and watched to make sure the task was begun as she'd ordered it. Colin came to stand next to her, watching silently with her. Finally he cleared his throat.

"A fine showing," he said gruffly.

Gillian looked at him, feeling vastly relieved. "I'm grateful for the aid."

"Aid? You needed no aid from me. Besides, I had nothing to do with it. Christopher sent the lads, fearing your display of temper might reduce his hall to rubble."

"Nay," Gillian breathed. "Surely you jest."

Colin shook his head. "I don't. He was eavesdropping. A terrible habit of his, I might add. And he said to me, 'Colin, I vow that wife of mine has turned into a most ferocious wench. I'm beginning to fear her temper.'"

"He did not," Gillian said, feeling a blush steal up her cheeks.

"I never lie."

The front door opened and shut with a bang. Christopher himself plowed into a servant and almost went sprawling.

"By St. George's throat, what is going on here?" he bellowed.

Colin squirmed. "Well, I almost never lie," he muttered.

Gillian was torn between gratitude for Colin's thoughtfulness—crafty though it had been—and trepidation over Christopher's reaction. She waited for her husband to cross the hall, praying she could keep up her show of spine. Christopher stopped across the table from her and scowled.

"Tearing my hall to bits already?" he barked.

"I'm changing the rushes," Gillian offered. Christopher continued to scowl and her courage faltered. "If it would please you," she added.

"Who put the whip to the servants, Colin?" Christopher asked.

"Lady Gillian," Colin said, without a flinch. "She had even me trembling from head to toe. I'm surprised you didn't hear her shouting from where you were."

Christopher paused and stroked his chin thoughtfully. "So she yelled."

"Most ferociously," Colin confirmed.

"Then she has more courage than I. Come with me, Colin, and let us leave the fearsome dragonness to her work. I've no mind to feel the bite of her blade for interrupting her cleaning." Christopher inclined his head to her. "My lady."

"My lord," she murmured, her cheeks flaming.

Christopher leaned over the table, put his hand to her cheek and smiled. "I daresay she blushes very becomingly, don't you think?" he asked Colin.

"Very," Colin agreed. "A man with a tongue more skilled than mine would likely call it beautiful."

"Indeed. Then I will give her blushes a closer look later. Come away from my lady, Colin, lest you irritate her with your ugliness. A good morrow to you, wife."

Gillian watched, openmouthed, as her husband and his brother-in-law walked across the rushes and out the door. Then she had to sit down to regain her wits. Becoming? Beautiful? Nay, 'twas impossible. She'd have a sniff of Christopher's breath later on and see just what he'd been imbibing.

Though she had to admit Colin's looks had surely improved. He might never be handsome, but he was looking more tolerable by the day. Gillian took another look about the hall to assure herself that everything was proceeding according to plan, then she ascended the stairs with as much dignity as she could muster. Then she ran all the way to Christopher's chamber and shut herself inside where she could look at herself in peace.

She pulled out Christopher's polished mirror and walked over to the window slowly. She threw open the shutters and took a deep breath or two to give herself more courage. It worked well enough, for her hand hardly trembled as she held the mirror up and looked at herself.

Beautiful she would never be, but comely? It was hard to be impartial when so very much rode on how fair of face she was, but, well, that wasn't such a bad face, was it? She ran her fingers over her brows. They were curved, aye, almost pleasingly so. Her eyes were bright and greener than usual. Not a bad color, as far as eyes went. The freckles which had plagued her for so long had faded, likely from the lack of sun. Indeed, her skin seemed fair, and smooth as a babe's.

Feeling encouraged, she looked at her hair, her most glorious failing. To her surprise, it was no longer the texture of straw. It fell in soft curls around her face and over her shoulders. Gillian fingered a lock and marveled. Was it the food? Or perhaps the sea air? Nay, it had to have been the herbs. All the features she had looked at with such a critical eye over the years had softened somehow. Of course, she would never lose the crooked place in her nose, or the scars here and there, but they seemed less important now. She had a few redeeming features. That was more than enough for her.

She put away her mirror and smiled, feeling it come easily to her. It was happening. Soon she would be beautiful and Christopher would want her. He would get her with child, then at least care for her because she was the mother of his babe.

For the first time in her life, she looked forward to the future.

• • •

CHRISTOPHER DISMOUNTED AND HELD ONTO THE SADDLE until he found his bearings. What in the world had driven him to think breaking a new mount would be fine sport? The horse had bucked like a beast possessed and it was only by sheer luck and stubbornness that he had remained atop its back. Now he was so dizzy that he thought he just might lose his supper.

"My lord," Jason said quietly, "hand me the reins."

"The saints be praised," Christopher said weakly. "Help has arrived. Point me in the direction of something that doesn't move, lad."

Jason's hand on his back was unobtrusive but sure.

"Ten paces to the bench against the wall," Jason murmured under his breath.

Christopher counted, bumped the bench gently with his shins, turned and collapsed. He accepted hearty congratulations from his men, then readily recognized the disgusted snort of the soul who sat down next to him.

"You fool," the body said with another snort.

"Shut up, Colin."

"You're green as your bride's eyes, Chris. What in heaven's name moved you—"

"A contrary spirit named Gillian. I had to do something to distract myself."

"I would have rather chosen a wench than that devil horse you rode, but you broke him well. A gift for me, I presume? Or perhaps you should give him to Gillian. She'll likely tame him as well as she's tamed the servants. And you, of course."

"You'll not provoke me, try as you might," Christopher said. "I'm too befuddled to spar with you at present."

"Then prepare to fight with your lady, for here she comes and she's frowning already. Saints, Chris, those herbs *are* working for her. Why haven't I seen any change on my sweet visage?"

"Gillian had much to work with from the start. You, however, are completely past hope."

Colin elbowed him sharply in the ribs, then got to his feet. "Lady, your lord makes me ill just by looking at him. I leave you with the unenviable task of seeing to him. The saints be with you."

Christopher smelled Gillian's sweet scent as she sat next to him. Her cold fingers came to rest against his brow.

"Are you ill?" she asked.

"I broke a stallion this morn," Christopher said with a smile, feeling smug at the accomplishment. It was a feat worthy of any sighted man. "He left me without any sense of direction."

"Christopher!" Gillian made disapproving noises. "You come along now with me to the garden. You'll lie with your head in my lap and rest for a time. I'll not hear a word in protest."

Protest? Christopher had no intentions of doing the like. He allowed his wife to take his hand and pull him to his feet; then he followed meekly behind her as she marched purposefully in what he sincerely hoped was the right direction. He surprised himself by being so docile. Perhaps it had something to do with the fact that he'd never before seen Gillian be so bold and he wasn't about to discourage her.

He lay down obediently and let the touch of her hand on his hair relax him completely. And then he did something he hadn't done in three years.

He fell asleep out in his garden.

Christopher woke to the feel of lips pressing awkwardly against his. It took all his willpower not to stiffen in surprise—delighted surprise. Soft lips left his and he listened to his lady hum a lullaby. He might have thought she was singing it for him, but then a most astonishing notion occurred to him. A lullaby?

She wanted a child.

How convenient that he was right there to father one for her.

He almost smiled. Indeed, he would have but Gillian

kissed him again, a soft, hesitant kiss that he almost missed feeling. He waited until she'd straightened before he stirred purposefully.

"Did I sleep?" he asked with a yawn.

"Aye, my lord."

"And drooled all over your gown, likely."

Gillian's shy laugh was nothing short of enchanting. Christopher lifted his hand and trailed his knuckles gently along her cheek. Her skin was either warmed from the sun or from a blush. His vanity preferred to think it was the latter.

"So," he began conversationally, "did you leave the servants trembling again today?"

"Likely with naught but laughter," she said quietly.

"I'm sure that isn't so. You know, I've meant to tell you this for almost a fortnight, but it keeps slipping my mind. I'm quite pleased with the way you've taken things in hand. Brave and courageous of you, truly," he added. "Even Colin fears to cross you as of late."

"Think you?" Her voice was little more than a whisper.

"I do." He rolled up and rose to his feet, then turned and held down his hand for her. "I cannot remember a woman ever forcing me to retire to my garden. You have the questionable honor of being the first. And," he added, frowning darkly for her benefit, "you know I am not easily led."

"I've noticed that, my lord."

"Even your tongue has sharpened. William would have been pleased."

Her fingers twitched in his hand. "And you, my lord? Are you?"

Was he pleased? Was he overjoyed that she'd taken her courage in hand and kissed him? Was he thrilled that she trusted him enough to keep her hand in his? Had he not woken each morn for the past fortnight and given thanks for the tender-hearted lass sprawled over him with such innocent abandon?

"Aye," he said, smiling down at her. "I'm pleased enough with you. Of course," he added, putting his arm around her shoulders, "you could be bolder still. And much saucier. I've a thick enough hide to endure a sharper tongue from you."

"You wouldn't mind?"

He started back to the hall with her. "Mind? Nay, lady. I would enjoy it." And what he didn't say was that the bolder she became, the more fully he would know that she trusted him. And she couldn't trust him enough, to his mind.

Without saying a word, she stopped him. Christopher felt her hand on his chest and bent his head toward her, trying to listen to her movements. He was completely unprepared to feel her lips pressing timidly against his cheek.

"Thank you, my lord."

He heard the tears in her voice and had the feeling he'd just given her a gift of approval she'd likely had from no one but her brother. So he wrapped his arms around her before she could pull away and buried his face in her sweet, sun-warmed hair.

"Nay," he whispered. "Thank you."

"For what, my lord?"

Christopher hardly knew where to begin. He gave her a gentle squeeze.

"For enduring a foul-tempered old dragon who had enough sense to wed you and found himself a treasure in the bargain."

"Treasure? My lord, surely you jest. My dowry—"

Christopher chuckled and lifted his head. "I spoke of you, not your dowry."

She was silent for so long that he feared he'd said the wrong thing. He lifted his hand and searched her features gently. Her cheeks were wet.

"Me?" she whispered.

Saints, now *he* was going to weep. "Aye, you," he said roughly, pulling her back against him and tucking her head beneath his chin where she wouldn't see the moisture in his own eyes. "Daft child," he whispered, trying to sound gruff. "Come inside and let me smell your clean hall. Sentiment makes me uncomfortable."

HE KEPT HER WITHIN ARM'S REACH FOR THE REST OF THE evening, finding that having her close was pleasant indeed. He had the feeling he might actually dare to kiss her later and she wouldn't bolt the other way.

His reticence made him shake his head in disbelief. Never in his life had he doubted his skill betwixt the sheets, or wondered how his advances would be received. And now he was treading softly so as not to frighten a girl-child of a score and one who likely had no knowledge at all of the act of loving. It was astonishing.

Gillian begged to be excused immediately after the meal and Christopher let her go, surprised that she seemed to want to retire to their bedchamber. Did she intend to go mull some wine? Or something else entirely? The possibilities were intriguing—so intriguing that he found himself following almost on her heels.

Only it wasn't to find her waiting in his bed, it was to find her doubled up on the floor near the hearth.

"Gillian, by the saints, what ails you?" he exclaimed.

"Naught," she gasped. "I beg you to leave me be."

"I'll do no such thing. What did you eat today?"

"It isn't that," she moaned.

"Saints, girl, you are in pain!"

Her next moan sounded more like embarrassment than agony. "My lord, 'tis my time. Please, let us speak no more of it."

"Oh," Christopher said in a small voice. "Well, then, I see. Um, do you require . . . aid?"

She was slow in answering. "Could you put me to bed?"

Christopher lifted an eyebrow at that. This was a new request. Gillian was forever stalling, puttering about the chamber to prolong the time she was forced to crawl beneath the sheets with her naked husband. Perhaps this monthly curse was a boon in disguise.

"Of course," he said gently. He lifted her then found his bearings. He carried her confidently to the bed and held her easily with one arm while he flung down the covers with his other. He laid her down and took off her shoes. Ignoring her quick gasp, he managed to rid her of her dressing gown also. Leaving her shift, he pulled the blankets back up over her and carefully felt for her face. He put his hand against her brow and found it cool to the touch.

"Might I fetch you wine?" he asked.

"Nay, my lord. Thank you."

He found her hand and brought it to his lips. "Sleep well, my lady." He closed the bedcurtains and started for the door.

"Christopher?"

He paused. "Aye?"

There was silence for a moment. "You're not sleeping here?"

A more dimwitted soul might have thought she sounded disappointed. Christopher fingered the bolt on the door.

"Would you rather I didn't?"

"Oh, nay," she said quickly. "I mean . . . I . . ."

Christopher smiled. "I'll return, Gill. Your toes won't go unwarmed this night."

He wished he could see her face, to know if she were smiling or frowning.

"Well," she began, "don't be long, aye?"

Christopher cleared his throat to keep from choking. "I won't."

He slipped out the door and then leaned back against it. On one hand he was powerfully disappointed that her body chose now as the proper time to put her through the monthly torture. On the other hand, he wasn't unhappy at all. A se'nnight? Aye, much could happen in that time.

nineteen

GILLIAN ROLLED OVER AND LOOKED AT THE EMPTY PLACE next to her. It was the third night since Christopher had put her to bed so sweetly that she had woken to find him gone. Just where had he taken himself off to—his tower chamber? She remembered the night she'd gone there and seen Wolf standing guard before the door. What mischief was Christopher combining?

Gillian swung her legs to the floor and stood up, drawing a dressing gown around her. She had to make use of the garderobe, that was certain. The one she intended to use was conveniently close to the tower stairs. It wouldn't hurt to look, would it?

She saw to her needs, then paused at the bottom of the steps leading to the tower chamber. Wolf loped down the steps and nudged her hand. He at least seemed glad to see her. She petted his head, then climbed quietly up the steps. She paused on the landing to catch her breath. She pushed open the door the slightest bit and saw the shadows dancing against the wall.

The ring of steel against stone startled her and she jumped before she could stop herself. Christopher's hearty curses covered her gasp of surprise. She peeked inside

again and saw her husband reach down and pick up his
sword. He stood still for a moment, as if he regained his
balance, then took up a fighting stance.

Gillian could only gape at him, amazed, as he worked.
Why, she'd never seen a warrior his equal! There was certainly none in her father's guard with swordplay so fine.
Christopher parried against an unseen foe with strength
and agility. The candlelight caressed his bare, glistening
back, highlighting the crisp muscles in his arms and shoulders as he strove to fend off an invisible attack with his
great broadsword. He fought only in hose and boots, and
such poor covering hid nothing of his powerful legs. It
was no wonder Jason's father had sent his son to squire
with this man. Even if Jason did naught but watch Christopher, he would learn more than most lads would learn
with masters who could see them.

Christopher's attack became more vicious and Gillian
watched in fascination as he seemed to cut down a foe
shorter than he but perhaps as broad. And it occurred to
her, with a startling flash of recognition, that he was fighting her father. He plunged his sword into his enemy's
heart, then let his arm drop down by his side. Gillian
smiled, feeling as if the victory had been a bit hers too.

"I think he's dead," she said approvingly.

Christopher whirled around with a gasp. "Gillian!"

"Aye, my lord?"

"You frightened me witless, woman! Did no one ever
teach you never to sneak up on an armed man that way?"

"I kept behind the door."

Christopher grunted, unappeased. "Announce your presence next time."

Gillian smiled and walked past him to make herself
comfortable on the stone seat in the alcove. "Come,
Wolf," she called. "Keep my feet warm while we watch
our lord cut down my father once again."

Christopher pursed his lips. "How did you know?"

"I've done it often enough myself. I recognized the breadth of the target."

Christopher laughed and dragged his arm across his sweaty brow. "Indeed. Another night you'll bring your sword and I'll watch your technique. I mean," he stammered, "you'll tell me about it."

"There would be nothing to see," she said gently. "I'm a poor swordsman."

"I'll be the judge. Now, what is it you're doing out of bed? I left you moaning in pain."

"I'm sorry I disturbed you," she said, abashed. "You should have woken me."

Christopher shook his head. "I needed to train anyway." He resheathed his sword and picked up his tunic to mop his face and chest. "Back to bed with you, girl."

"Do you know," she said as he approached, "what it is people believe you do in your tower chamber late at night?"

"I shudder to think."

"Devilish deeds, my lord," she said solemnly.

Christopher squatted down before her and smiled dryly. "Deeds you never gave credence to, of course."

"Well . . ."

"Next you'll tell me that I change my shape too. What is it I become, a wolf? Ripping the throats from those foolish souls who dare set foot on my lands?"

"Christopher!" she said, with an uncomfortable laugh. "How did you know?"

He grinned. "Who do you think started such rumors?"

"You are a wicked man." She reached out and touched the top of his head. "Aye, I think I do feel a horn or two growing here. Perhaps there is some truth to the gruesome tales."

"The only gruesome tale that will soon be told is of the scolding you'll earn from me if you don't return posthaste to our bedchamber and go to sleep." He took her hand and pulled her to her feet.

"Won't you come?"

He hesitated, then smiled. "Very well, if you like."

Gillian kept her hand in his as she followed him down the stairs and back to his bedchamber. She lit a candle on her bedside table, then crawled under the sheets. She lay silently and listened to her husband wash, drink and then strip. He slid under the blankets next to her and reached out to touch her shoulder.

"How do you feel?" he asked quietly.

"Better, thank you."

He trailed his fingers down her arm gently. Gillian shivered in spite of herself.

"Hurt?"

"Nay," she whispered.

He slipped his hand up under her hair and began to massage the back of her neck gently. She groaned, then blushed hotly. Christopher chuckled.

"So you like that, do you?"

" 'Tis tolerable."

He grunted. "Saucy wench. Come closer so it isn't so much work, and I might please you tolerably for a moment or two more. If you vow to repay the favor," he added.

"Oh, but I wouldn't know how," she stammered as he pulled her closer.

"I'll teach you. Here, roll onto your belly so I might show you how to do this properly."

Gillian was quite certain she was going to die from the feeling of pleasure of Christopher's firm hand working over the muscles in her back gave her. He didn't say aught about her scars, but he touched her more gently when he encountered them. That shamed her greatly.

"Stop," Christopher whispered in her ear. "Don't pull away from me, Gill. You've no reason to hide them from me."

"They're powerfully ugly."

"I have my share of them, too. Give me your hand. Here, feel this long, ghastly mark over my ribs? Here on my shoulder? This one over my heart? Those are only the marks from my braver foes. On my back you'll feel the marks from the cowards, cowards like your father.'' He kept her hand in his and brought it to his mouth, kissing it firmly. ''Only a coward beats a woman or a child, Gill. You did nothing to earn these marks, but I'm proud of your bravery in enduring them.''

''I wasn't brave.''

''You survived. That took courage.''

''Nay . . .''

Christopher put his head next to hers on the pillow. He was so close, their noses touched.

''You were brave,'' he whispered. ''And you never need fear him again, Gill.'' He leaned forward and pressed his lips against hers. ''Never again. I'll keep you safe.''

Gillian wasn't sure if she were more surprised by his words or by his kiss. And she honestly couldn't decide which of the two had left her with the urge to weep, for both touched her heart.

Christopher began to trail his fingers through her hair gently.

''You were brave in the garden today,'' he said, as if he discussed nothing important. ''Bold, even.''

''And when was that?'' she asked.

''When you kissed me.''

She looked at him narrowly. ''You weren't asleep,'' she accused.

''I was until you kissed me. And damn me, but it was a fine way to wake up.''

Gillian couldn't help the bubble of soft, hysterical laughter that came out. She was lying in bed with the Dragon of Blackmour, discussing the fact that she'd kissed him as calmly as if she'd been discussing the merits of steel for blades with her brother!

''That amuses you?'' he growled.

''Nay,'' she said quickly, fighting her smile. ''Not that.''

"What then?" he demanded.

"This," she said, waving her hand to encompass where they were lying.

"Lying abed with me amuses you?"

"Discussing kissing with the Scourge of England while lying in his bed amuses me. There isn't a soul alive who would believe me if I confessed the like."

"The Scourge of England, eh? And what other complimentary names do you have for me?"

"Oh, there are so many, my lord. I don't know if I could stir myself to remember them all."

"You disrespectful chit, didn't you know I despoil five or six maidens about your size each morn before I break my fast? How dare you mock me so thoroughly. If I demand a list of titles, then you'll give it to me and quickly."

Gillian smiled at the gruff expression on the beautiful man lying next to her. Who would have thought she would be so close to a man and not fear him? She reached up and traced Christopher's cheek, the bridge of his nose, the long eyelashes that fanned over his cheeks. By the saints, he was handsome. She leaned over and kissed him gently on the cheek, as she had so often done to William. Only she entertained no brotherly feelings whatsoever for Christopher.

"Somehow, my lord," she said softly, "those names—despoiler, bane and scourge—just do not fit you. If England could see you as I see you now, they wouldn't believe the tales."

"And just what is it you see, Gillian of Blackmour?" he asked, opening his eyes.

"A fine man who has been very kind to me," she murmured, feeling color stain her cheeks. "And a very comely man, too," she added.

"And you are beautiful."

Her face fell. "Nay—"

He put his finger against her lips. "You are." He traced her features with his finger. "I feel no flaw here. Nor here,'' he added, lifting his hand and smoothing it over her hair. "You were fetching when last I saw you, Gillian."

"You said I was coltish."

He grinned. "I've a penchant for coltish women."

"I have grown uglier, if possible."

"Hush," he said sharply, but his features were gentle. "No one will speak of my wife thusly, my wife included. Colin tells me that if you were any more beautiful, it would be a poor thing for rumor would spread and I would be ever busy fighting off interested lads and then I would have no time to laze about in your bed discussing . . . what were we discussing, Gillian?"

She knew he was teasing about her fairness, but somehow it didn't hurt her so much. At least he was teasing her. That meant he must care for her, even if it were only a bit.

"Gillian?"

"Aye, my lord?"

"What were we discussing?"

"I vow I've forgotten."

"Ah, but I haven't. We were discussing your boldness in the garden this afternoon and how much I liked having you kiss me. If I pretended to sleep, would you kiss me again?"

"You're teasing me cruelly."

He rolled over onto his back, closed his eyes and began to snore.

"Christopher!"

"Sshh, I'm sleeping. Be bold, Lady Blackmour."

"Christopher," she groaned.

"I'm waiting," he whispered.

"Are you teasing me?" she asked, suddenly finding the game painful.

He opened his eyes. "Nay, Gillian, I'm not teasing you." And he wasn't, if his tone and expression told anything. "But I'll understand if you don't wish to kiss me.

In fact, I think I'll just go to sleep before the thought of that wounds my pride much further.'' He closed his eyes promptly.

Gillian looked down at him and weighed her alternatives. She could simply roll over and go to sleep. Or she could take Christopher at his word and kiss him. She knew he wasn't one to speak rashly, and he didn't seem to be teasing her at present.

She considered the matter until she felt the tension drain from him and his breathing become deep and regular. Once she was sure he was good and asleep, she carefully moved up a bit, then lowered her head and pressed her lips softly against his. She felt foolish doing it, but Christopher would never be the wiser.

She tried it again and tried to make her lips match his a bit better this time. There, that was a better effort. She kissed him a third time, feeling his lips press fully against hers. She lifted her head and smiled, pleased with her success.

"Again."

She gasped and jumped, startled. Christopher's arm was immediately around her waist, keeping her close.

"Where go you?" he asked.

"You are supposed to be asleep!"

"I am. I'm dreaming that my bold, saucy wife is kissing me. Now, come back," he coaxed. "Just kiss me one more time, Gill, then I'll let you go."

"Why?" she asked, pained.

"Because I like it. Don't you?"

She bowed her head. "Aye," she said softly.

"Then kiss your demanding dragon one more time so he'll have pleasant dreams."

She bent her head and obliged him. He was perfectly still until she raised her head. Then he smiled.

"You're very skilled."

She felt herself begin to blush. "I am not."

"Aye, you are. Perhaps you'll care to practice on me a bit more tomorrow."

Gillian allowed herself the luxury of believing he was only half-teasing. She turned on her side with her back to him and blew out her candle. She resettled her head on the pillow and smiled to herself.

"That depends," she said airily.

"On what?"

"On whether or not you scratch my back again as well as you did tonight."

Christopher gasped softly. "Why, you little mercenary! So now I must pay for my kisses by giving you pleasure?"

"It would seem so, my lord."

He grunted as he rolled toward her and draped his arm over her waist. "And they call *me* the Scourge of England. I'll be sure to warn the king next time we see him to keep his purse strings knotted well, lest you plunder the treasury."

Gillian smiled at his teasing, feeling wonderfully cherished. She grew accustomed to the heavy weight of Christopher's arm over her waist and the warmth of his chest against her back, burning her through her shift. It was the first night she had ever gone to sleep with his arm around her, and she found that she liked it very much indeed.

"Gill?"

"Aye," she murmured.

"This curse of yours," he said slowly. "When will it be finished?"

Gillian felt a rush of something go through her and she couldn't decide it if were excitement or terror.

"Two days hence, perhaps," she managed in a choked voice.

Christopher said nothing else, but felt for her hand and laced his fingers with hers. He must have felt her trembles, for he pulled her closer and whispered soothingly against her ear.

It seemed only moments later that his whispering became soft snoring. Gillian wished with all her might she could have rested so easily while contemplating the finishing of her courses. What was she to expect from her husband then? What would he expect of her? A pity a visit to Alice was forbidden her; at least Alice could have offered a bit of womanly counsel.

Gillian caught her breath as another idea came to her. Christopher shifted at her stiffening, grumbled under his breath, then drifted back off into sweet slumber. Gillian released her breath slowly, relief flooding through her. Aye, she had a place to go for aid, and go she would. First thing after daylight.

She snuggled back into her husband's arms and let his warmth soothe her into a peaceful rest.

twenty

COLIN OF BERKHAMSHIRE WASN'T AN UNTRUSTING MAN. Indeed, if he were forced to admit the truth of it, he was fair and just to a fault, always giving those he felt compelled to interrogate the largest portion of patience and long-suffering he possessed—and indeed he possessed those attributes in abundance. But when it came to practitioners of the shadier arts, surely he could be permitted a small modicum of distrust.

He'd been leaning against the wall, enjoying a brief moment of repose in the early morning sunshine, when he'd noticed a slight figure slip furtively out of the great hall. He'd known instantly who it was, and it had taken no great powers of perception to divine where she intended to go. She had that look about her. It had aroused his suspicions immediately.

And so he now found himself following after her down what seemed to be an unnaturally well-trod path through the lesser frequented part of the village. So, others had been seeking out herbs of various sorts. He stroked his face thoughtfully. Perhaps the herbs Gillian had shared with him had wrought a good work on his own features.

To be sure, he'd caught more than one wench staring at him with renewed interest of late.

But the saints only knew what sort of concoction these women would press upon Gillian this time. No matter the success he might have found himself; Gillian was another matter entirely. Christopher would be beside himself with grief if aught happened to his wife.

Colin lengthened his already long stride, sending peasants and animals alike scurrying for cover. A few more paces and he was directly behind his lord's lady wife.

"Lady Gillian?"

She jumped half a foot, then whirled around to face him. She clutched at her throat with her hand and made strangled sounds. Her face was quite red and Colin felt a thrill of fear race through him.

"Are you ill?" he demanded. He grasped her by the shoulders and began to shake her. "Have you already swallowed their foul brew? By the saints, I'll have them strung up by their warted noses!"

"S-stop," Gillian said, her teeth clacking together. "I've d-drunk n-nothing!"

Colin frowned down at her. She was still very red in the face, but indeed she appeared to be breathing as she should, which surely showed she hadn't been poisoned yet. Perhaps he had been mistaken and she was merely out for a bit of air. He was galled to admit it, but with Gillian of Blackmour, one just never knew.

He paused. Even if she had left the keep with a more innocent purpose, she had surely taken a wrong turn. There was no sense in allowing her to travel further on the ill-advised pathway she currently trod, for no matter where she thought she was going, he knew where it led. Colin folded his arms over his chest and assumed his most intimidating pose.

"I believe you are lost," he announced. He inclined his head back toward the keep. "The bailey is that way."

Gillian made a small motion with her hand, as if he had

been a pesky fly she was seeking to shoo away.

Colin lifted one eyebrow. "How was that, lady?"

"Go," she whispered, shooing him again. "Colin, please. I've things to attend to here."

"What could you possibly want with them this time?" he demanded. "Surely that last bundle of herbs served you—"

"Sshh!" Gillian whispered frantically, casting a wary glance about her. "We mustn't let on to their secret."

"Why not? It isn't as if anyone truly believes... ah..."

His speaking came to an abrupt halt at the look on Gillian's face.

Gillian looked away. "I believe," she said, very softly.

"Er... um..." he stammered, scrambling for his footing. By the saints, who would have thought Christopher's marriage would have wreaked such havoc on his own sorry life? Here he was on the verge of confessing a belief in sorceresses merely to avoid bruising this child's feelings. Indeed, he was going soft! "Ah..." he said, then cleared his throat, "er... well, then, so do I, lady."

"Do you really?" Gillian asked, looking back at him suddenly.

Colin took a deep breath. No sense in wounding the girl further.

"Aye," he said reluctantly. "I certainly can't deny that those herbs served you quite well." That was true, at least. "Indeed, Christopher can hardly speak of anything but you and he continually praises your courage and beauty."

She caught her breath. "Truly?"

"Aye," Colin said darkly. "He's completely ruined for decent labor of late."

"I can hardly believe he speaks of me," she whispered.

The beginnings of joy in her face caught him full in the chest. He blinked rapidly. Damned dusty pathways. A man never had to clear his eyes thusly on a sturdy cobblestone road.

"Believe it freely," he said gruffly. "I daresay those herbs have indeed aided you as you intended. Now, surely you need nothing more here, so let us return to the keep forthwith, lady."

She shook her head.

Colin shook his head also, unable to believe she wasn't snapping to do his bidding. Perhaps too many courage herbs in a woman wasn't a good thing.

"Let us return," he repeated. "Now."

"I've other business with them," she said, her face flushing again.

"What else could you desire herbs for?" Colin asked. "Wasn't the first batch sufficient?"

"I'm not here for herbs. I'm here for advice."

He frowned. "Advice on what?"

She ducked her head and muttered something under her breath.

"What?" he demanded. "What advice could you possibly need to seek here?"

She squirmed mightily and looked anywhere but at him.

"By the saints, my lady, speak!"

"Womanly matters," she blurted out suddenly. Then she clamped her lips shut and blushed furiously.

"Womanly—" Colin closed his mouth with a snap.

He found he couldn't say anything else. Who knew what *womanly matters* truly entailed? All he knew was that he wanted to know no more of them than he did at present.

He spluttered gruffly a time or two to cover up his discomfort, then gestured abruptly toward Gillian's goal.

"Go," he said, gesturing again. "I'll wait for you outside."

The color drained from her face. "You'll not listen, will you?"

Colin choked. "By the saints, of course not!"

She looked as relieved as he felt. Without another word, she spun on her heel and fled the last little distance to the hut. Colin followed more slowly. He watched a small, white-haired woman open the door, watched the woman's face light up when she saw Gillian, then continued to watch as the woman drew Gillian inside. The door closed softly.

Colin gave the hut an unsympathetic frown. The saints only knew what sorts of things Gillian might learn from a gaggle of witches. Surely nothing that would serve her. Well, there seemed to be only one alternative. He would have to put his own soul at risk and have a small listen. At least then he would know what foolishness to purge from her mind.

With grim determination, he took up a post outside the hut door. As inconspicuously as possible, he put his head close to the thatched wall. There was giggling aplenty, peppered with a frequent "Lucifer's toes, Magda, stir the bloody brew!" Colin frowned at that. He'd be wise to investigate thoroughly anything Gillian intended to take home with her.

He paused and gave that more thought. Perhaps Gillian would have a few more beauty herbs he could sample.

And so he would, he decided, at his earliest opportunity. No sense in Gillian putting her life in danger while he was about to save her from herself.

Time passed.

He could make out almost nothing of what was said. Indeed, the low murmur of voices was almost soothing enough to lull him into an uneasy rest, even standing as he was against the wall. He might have actually slept, had he not been so startled by the occasional witchly epitaph being flung about inside.

This was indeed a high price to pay for first taste of Gillian's findings.

Without warning, the door opened and Gillian appeared outside. Colin looked her over carefully, but could see no damage wrought. Her hands, however, were disturbingly empty.

"No herbs?" he asked.

Gillian was very red in the face and seemed incapable of speech. Colin turned a fierce frown on the open doorway, only to find himself confronting three white-haired, sweet-faced women of rather advanced age.

"Colin of Berkhamshire," one of the women said, the one who had welcomed Gillian initially. She smiled at him in a most maternal manner.

"You know, Berengaria," Gillian said, "he had a few of my beauty herbs."

Colin threw her a warning glance. As if he wanted these witches to know what he'd been about!

"I think they worked well enough on him," Gillian added.

"Then perhaps he'd care for something else tasty to drink!" a spoon-bearing sorceress said, pushing her flyaway hair out of her eyes with a plump hand. She waved her instrument of witchery at him. "I'll prepare something right away."

Colin would have backed away but the third old woman grasped him about the wrist with a grip that rivaled steel for strength.

"Best bring him inside," she said with a grumble. " 'Twill require something of mine for a marked improvement. Magda, move away from my pots! Lucifer's knees, 'tis a wonder I manage to concoct anything at all with you puttering about!"

The doorway opened up to receive him like the gates of Hell. Colin looked frantically about for Gillian, but all he saw was the flash of her cloak as she disappeared up the way. No help from that quarter.

"Come along now," the grumbly one said. "No need to dig in your heels, lad. Beauty doesn't come without work." She cast him a jaundiced glance. "I believe you'll require a *large* pinch of thumb-bone."

"The saints preserve me!" Colin blurted out.

"Nemain, don't frighten the lad," the first witch said. She removed Colin's wrist from Nemain's clutches. "I'm

Berengaria, my lord. Won't you come inside? I'll brew you a fine pot of soothing tea.''

"Tea," Colin repeated doubtfully. Well, tea didn't sound quite so nefarious.

"Perhaps with a few of my special herbs," Berengaria said, tugging him gently toward the hut.

Colin considered. 'Twas obvious Gillian hadn't come away with any. And he surely wasn't a man to overlook the possibility of success when he saw it.

"A small cup," he stated. "Liberally sprinkled."

"And you can have a taste of my special potion while you're waiting," the pudgy one said, almost leveling him with her spoon.

Colin rose from his recently assumed crouch, then paused on the threshold.

"Lucifer's knees, where is that bloody thumb bone!" greeted his ears.

Colin took a deep breath, cast one last prayer heavenward, and entered the hut.

The door shut firmly behind him.

GILLIAN WALKED BACK TO THE KEEP, BEWILDERED AND rather stunned. And she knew well enough where the latter feeling came from. Christopher spoke of her beauty and courage to others.

It was almost more than she could take in.

She likely would have had more success in doing so if she hadn't been so bemused by what she'd just learned in Berengaria's hut. She wasn't sure if she'd been comforted or led astray. Berengaria knew much of the birthing of babies but had been unwilling to divulge much of how they were conceived. Magda had been no help. The old woman, bless her pudgy self, had done nothing but giggle continually. Nemain, whom Gillian wasn't quite sure of still, had sat in the corner, aloof. Likely she had the most knowledge, for she alluded to many diverse experiences while in search of her potion makings. But she would divulge nothing, only nod in a very knowing manner.

Berengaria told her that a child was conceived when both parties generally wore very little clothing (and this was received by a long bout of gasping from Magda), and it was a fairly tolerable act. Gillian suspected there was kissing involved, and of course a good deal of moaning, but Berengaria hadn't said as much. Nemain had pursed her lips several times—that had been as good a confirmation as any.

In the end, Gillian had been admonished to be bold and trust in her newfound courage and beauty. Berengaria had told her to make her wishes known and Christopher would see to the rest. Magda's swoon and Nemain's knowing nod had convinced Gillian further of the truth of that.

So she would. A final packet of herbs were hidden in her cloak to aid her in shoring up her courage. Perhaps in a day or two, she would inform Christopher that she was ready to consummate their marriage.

And pray that he didn't either faint or flee the other way.

Nay, he wouldn't. She put her shoulders back and marched through the inner bailey. Hadn't Colin said that Christopher talked of her often? When he was with her, he surely seemed fond of her. Hadn't he demanded that she kiss him the night before?

Aye, that was reason enough to be a bit more bold. She would acquire a bit more courage; then she would see the deed accomplished.

twenty-one

CHRISTOPHER SHRUGGED HIS SHOULDERS UNCOMFORT-
ably, eager to have his mail off for the day. It had been a
rather successful day as days went of late. He'd jousted
for the first time in a fortnight and not been unseated once.
Of course, had anyone but his own guardsmen been there,
they would have thought it odd indeed the way Jason and
Colin yelled at him as he rode, but they were in truth
calling out to him agreed-upon signals to alert him to his
opponents' intentions. There were times it didn't work at
all and Christopher ended up on his back time and time
again. Today had been a success. He'd earned no bruises
and was feeling rather smug.

"Fetch my lady," he said, giving Jason a push.

Jason trotted off and Christopher continued on his way
to the high table. He sat down and endured Colin's hearty
thump on the back as his brother-in-law took the place next
to him.

"A fine showing," Colin grunted. "You almost im-
pressed me."

"Count yourself blessed that I'm blind. 'Tis the only
reason you ever find yourself remaining atop your mount."

"You smug bastard."

Christopher grinned. ''The truth pains you, my friend?''

''What pains me is the memory of you humiliating me at my own tourney, Blackmour. I've much to see you repaid for.''

''You challenged me. What was I to do? Let you best me, then face Lord Robin's wrath? He trained me to win, not to lose to palsied, bumbling oafs—''

Colin growled and Christopher soon found himself flat on his back with Colin's bulk crushing the breath from him.

''My lords!'' Jason exclaimed. ''I beg you to behave!''

''Why, you cheeky, misbegotten cur,'' Colin gasped, jumping up.

Christopher grabbed Colin by the foot and jerked backwards. Colin went down with a thump and a hearty curse. Christopher rolled over and looked up in the direction of Jason's panting.

''Where's Gillian?''

''She awaits you in your chamber, my lord.''

Christopher froze. She was waiting for him? He didn't have to count on his fingers to realize what day it was, but he certainly hadn't expected Gillian to remember. She obviously had. If her actions were any indication, she sounded for all the world like a woman who planned to welcome her husband to her bed that night.

''Why, Chris,'' Colin said, clucking Christopher under the chin, ''you're blushing, lad.''

Christopher threw a fist, not caring where it landed. It landed, quite nicely, in the middle of Colin's face.

Colin only grumbled. ''I'd see you repaid, but I wouldn't want to break anything important. Jason, fetch your lord something to strengthen him. He'll need it for his labors this eve.''

''Colin, be silent,'' Christopher snapped.

''And a wash for the lad. Wouldn't want little Gill to swoon because of his smell.''

''Colin, damn you, be you silent!''

Colin started to laugh.

"Ah, Chris, if you only knew." Then his laughter ceased abruptly. "Of course, it isn't as if *I* know," he said, sounding rather defensive. "I'm not in the habit of eavesdropping, especially when it comes to womanly—" he coughed. "Well, I'm off to see to . . . um . . . well, I'm off. Best of luck to you."

And with that, Colin's boots made a rapid flight to the door.

"I'll see to washing water for you, my lord," Jason said, sounding suspiciously sober.

Christopher sat up with a scowl. "Cease with your smirking, child!"

"Me?" Jason asked innocently. "Smirk? My lord, never. You never smirk and I've learned all my good habits from you."

Christopher made a grab for his squire but the lad was too nimble. Christopher cast himself down into his chair and put on his favorite scowl. No one troubled him, which gave him ample time to think. Was he reading more into Gillian's actions than he should? What else could she be doing? She wouldn't be toying with him.

He jumped at the hand suddenly on his shoulder.

"Your water is prepared, my lord."

Christopher jerked Jason over his knees and gave the lad a hearty whack on the backside. He pushed his squire to his feet, then rose and glared down at him.

"For teasing me."

"It was worth it," Jason said, the grin apparent in his voice.

"You wait, little lad. I'll be there at your wedding and you'll wish you hadn't used me so ill in your youth." He took Jason by the ear and pulled him toward the kitchens. "And as further payment, you'll spend your evening seeing to my mail."

"In your bedchamber, my lord?"

Christopher pulled harder and Jason yelped.

"In the hall," Jason gasped. "I vow it!"

Christopher grunted and allowed Jason to help him out of his mail. He had a wash, loaded Jason down with a wooden trencher of food and a bottle of wine, then headed up the stairs. He knew his face was flushed and had the feeling everyone in the keep knew that he intended to go upstairs and at least kiss his wife senseless. Bedding her might wait a night or two, but the entire keep likely knew that, too.

He stood outside his door and took a deep breath. Then he looked down at Jason.

"Not a word, imp."

"I wouldn't, my lord. Not in front of the lady Gillian."

Christopher felt a smile tug at his mouth. "Perhaps I'll keep you a few years longer instead of sending you home to your father in chains."

"My gratitude, my lord."

Christopher knocked softly, then poked his head inside the chamber.

"Gillian?"

"Aye, my lord."

"Would you rather I came back?" he asked gruffly.

He felt her tug on the door. "Come in, Christopher."

"Jason," Christopher rumbled, "set the meal down and go. We'll not need you tonight."

"Of course, my lord," Jason said respectfully. He set the tray down, then clapped Christopher on the shoulder on his way out.

Christopher leaned back against the door and slid the bolt home as unobtrusively as possible. He felt as nervous as a squire contemplating bedding his first wench. Nay, even more nervous. This was Gillian, not some serving wench. And he couldn't see a bloody thing. She could have been weeping silently and he wouldn't have been the wiser.

"Are you hungry?" he demanded suddenly.

"A bit," she answered.

"Come take the wine. We'll eat before the fire."

How he managed to get the food down from the table to the hearth he wasn't sure, but he did. He ate with the gusto of a man devouring his last meal.

"Are you eating at all?" he asked around a mouthful of bread.

"What I can steal of it."

Christopher felt himself color. "Forgive me. I've worked hard today."

"I know."

"How do you know?"

"I watched you."

Christopher sat up a bit straighter. "You did?"

"I did," she said. "You are exceedingly skilled, my lord."

"For a blind man."

"For a *mortal* man," she corrected.

Christopher puffed out his chest a bit. "Indeed."

"Christopher, you astonish me," she said softly. He felt her hand come to rest atop his. "Everything William ever told me about your skill is true. It is still true, despite your loss of sight. You are as fine a warrior, nay, even a finer warrior today than you were when you came to my father's hall six years ago. I know of no man who could stand against you."

Christopher couldn't remember the last time praise had given him such a swelled head. He made a few gruff noises, but in truth he thought his breast would explode from the pride he felt. A few simple words from Gillian had pleased him far more than any of Lina's insincere flattery. He raised his lady's hand to his lips and kissed her knuckles.

"Thank you, my lady. Your words have pleased me so well, I think I'll give you free rein over supper for a few moments. Eat your fill."

Christopher was perfectly relaxed until dinner was finished and he realized that the moment of truth was approaching. And he had no idea how to proceed. Had he been able to see, he could have seen Gillian's face and known her thoughts. Now he was fumbling in the dark.

And had the time for bedding her truly come? He'd had a few chaste kisses from her over the past few nights and those only after a great deal of coaxing. He wanted her to trust him fully and that would likely require more than just a single night of more intimate kisses and caresses.

He put the remainder of the food up on the table and took to pacing. And before he knew it, he'd run bodily into his bride. He caught her by her shoulders and kept her upright.

"What are you doing?"

"Pacing," she answered.

Christopher frowned and resumed his walking, trying not to run into Gillian as he passed her in midchamber. He heard her stop, then turned and faced her direction.

"Gillian—"

"Christopher—"

He paused. "Go ahead."

"Nay, you first."

"I insist."

"I wouldn't dare."

He folded his arms over his chest. "Speak, woman."

Gillian was silent for some time. Then she cleared her throat uncomfortably.

"About . . . about our marriage," she began.

Christopher's chest tightened painfully. *Oh, God, please nay* . . .

"I think . . . that is, don't you think . . . I mean to say, perhaps 'tis time we had it . . ."

Christopher waited. Then he waited some more. And then he felt as if his heart had been ripped from his chest and cast to the floor.

"What?" he asked hoarsely.

Gillian mumbled something.

"Speak up!"

"Consummated!" she exclaimed.

Christopher blew out his breath in relief. "I feared you would say annulled," he managed.

"Annulled," she gasped. "You mean . . . you want it—"

"—consummated," he finished.

Well, there. It was out now. Said. Spoken in words that couldn't be taken back.

Gillian hadn't said anything in return. Christopher cleared his throat.

"Gillian?"

"Aye, my lord?" She sounded as if something were choking her.

"Did you mean it?" he asked gruffly.

Her response, if she'd even made one, was lost in the thundering blood in his ears. He walked over to her, his hand outstretched. He found her and put his hands on her shoulders.

"Gillian? What say you?"

She was trembling so badly he thought she might knock both of them down.

"Aye," she whispered.

Christopher put his arms around her and gathered her close.

"My sweet girl," he whispered, pained. "Don't shake so. I won't hurt you."

"Y-you w-won't?" Her teeth were chattering.

"I won't," he said, hoping she wouldn't mind if he admitted the truth after the fact.

"But I've h-heard the s-servants," she said, shivering. "I think it p-pains them."

Christopher smiled against her hair. "Love, those are groans of pleasure."

"Oh, I truly don't th-think so."

"Trust me."

He continued to hold her close until her arms came hesitantly around his waist. Then he slowly rocked her from side to side, just a bit, and smoothed his hand over her long hair. It fell down her back in heavy curls and he smiled as he fingered a lock and felt it curl around his thumb.

"I love your hair," he murmured. " 'Tis very soft."

" 'Tis very disobedient. It won't ever stay under a veil."

"Then you'll never put it under a veil. Leave it free."

"If it would please you."

He paused. "Do you know what would please me?"

"What, my lord?"

"To see you," he whispered.

She swallowed, hard. "As you will, my lord."

He took her hand and led her over to the fire. He sat down in a chair and pulled her onto his lap.

"Comfortable?"

He knew she nodded because he had his hand under her hair at the back of her neck.

"Turn toward me a bit," he whispered. "I'll need both my hands."

She did, putting one of her hands on his chest. Christopher lifted his hands and gently trailed his fingers over her face. He felt the smoothness of her forehead and the soft silk of her eyebrows. He traced the thin bridge of her nose and smiled at the small crook there. Her eyelashes were like spiderwebs against his fingers, almost too fine to discern. He smoothed the tips of his fingers over her cheeks, her jaw, her chin. He memorized the shape of the end of her nose and the delicate curve of her lips. He slid his hands back, traced the outside of her ears, learned how it felt to bury his hands in her lush hair and feel it fall over his fingers.

"Gillian," he said, shaking his head in wonder, "how can you say you aren't beautiful?" He leaned forward and pressed his cheek against hers. "Your skin is flawless." He turned and pressed kisses over her closed eyelids, over her brow, down her nose. "Your features are perfect. Your nose is pert, just as it should be for you to look down it at me. Your cheeks feel rosy, your brow smooth. I know the color of your eyes, 'tis a deep green flecked with brown and gold. And your hair," he gathered a fistful of it to bury his face in, " 'tis wondrous fine. I vow I'll never tire of it."

Gillian hadn't moved. Christopher pulled back and carefully touched her face, trying to understand her expression. His fingers came away damp with her tears.

"Why do you weep?" he asked, pained. "Sweet Gill, what have I said to grieve you?"

"Nothing," she choked.

Christopher was unprepared to have her throw her arms around his neck, but he gathered his wits about him soon enough. He held her close and stroked her back, trying to soothe her.

"My love," he murmured, "don't weep, I beg you. It breaks my heart when you do."

"I feel as if I'm dreaming," she said miserably. "And I never want to wake up."

He smiled ruefully. "Don't I feel real enough to you?"

She was long in answering. "You'll change."

"What, and care for you more than I do now?"

Christopher froze, realizing what he'd just said. Gillian tried to pull away, but he kept his arms tight around her.

"See?" she whispered. "Already you have regrets."

He shook his head. "I regret nothing."

She pulled back slowly and he allowed it. He lifted his hand and examined her expression.

"Smile for me," he commanded.

It was a weak effort, for her lips trembled as they attempted it.

"Do you regret becoming my wife? Now that you know I have no horns?"

Her smile deepened, became a smile in truth. "I wouldn't regret it, even if you had horns."

"Then you're pleased."

"Aye."

"Because you've tamed the Dragon of Blackmour?"

She shook her head. "Because I love the Dragon of Blackmour."

"Of course you do," he said dryly. Secretly, though, her words caught him tight about the heart. Saints above, the woman could leave him unbalanced with naught but words!

"I do," she insisted.

"What you love, my sweet, is my terrible temper and my fetching blue eyes."

"Christopher, that isn't true!"

He blinked. "Then you don't love my eyes? Nor my temper? Nor all my other flaws?"

. She groaned and put her arms around him. "I love all your flaws."

"Nay, 'tis naught but my kisses that have won your heart."

He was pleased to hear her laugh for their words had become altogether more serious than he liked. It frightened him, the thought of loving the woman in his arms. Even now she could hurt him so greatly if she did but pull away from him.

Nay, she wouldn't. He would just keep her near him, by chaining her to him if he had to. Aye, here was where she would remain. And in time she would let him love her, and he would do his damndest to please her. He leaned forward to kiss her, then stopped when he felt her fingers touch his face. He held perfectly still as she traced his features gently, discovering his expression as fully as he had discovered hers the moment before.

"Are your eyes closed?" he asked.

"Aye."

He let her look her fill and smiled when she traced his lips with her fingers.

"You've changed," she whispered.

"How so?"

"You're so much gentler than you were before."

"I blame that on you."

" 'Tis a good change, Christopher," she said softly. "You frightened me dreadfully at first."

"And now, Gill?"

"I feel safe nowhere but in your arms."

Now, that was something he couldn't let go unrewarded. He dredged up every last shred of tenderness in his soul and poured it into his kiss. He encircled her with his embrace and let his mouth tell her what he knew he couldn't possibly put into words. He kissed her sweetly, praying she would know how deeply her words had touched him and, aye, even how happy she'd made him. It was unexpected, this joy she'd brought him, and all the more precious because of it.

"Trust me," he whispered against her mouth.

She nodded. He eased her off his lap, then pulled a fur off the chair and cast it to the floor. He drew her down with him, then laid her back on the fur and followed her, stretching out beside her.

He caressed her lips with his, doing nothing at first but tasting the fullness of her mouth. Then he carefully parted his lips and kissed her more fully. She didn't stiffen, nor did she pull away. Encouraged, he covered her mouth with his and gently touched the corner of her lips with his tongue. She jerked away, laughing.

"What do you?" she gasped. "It tickles me."

"Tickles? It *tickles?* Woman, that was to make you swoon, not laugh!"

"I see," she said. "Very well then, my lord, I will endeavor to swoon this time to please you."

"Saucy wench," he grumbled, then vowed to see that she swooned indeed. He ignored her mouth entirely and learned quickly that Gillian's neck was very ticklish and that kissing her ears made her squirm. He kissed her eyes closed, then scattered kisses over the nonticklish parts of her face. She sighed lightly when he kissed the line of her jaw and when he tilted her head forward again to kiss her mouth, he found her lips soft and parted. He fully intended to do anything but make her laugh again.

He let the feel of her hand on his shoulder guide him. The first time he captured her mouth with his and kissed her firmly, her hand pushed against his shoulder. He softened his kisses, teasing her until she arched unconsciously against him and her fingers dug into his shoulder, pulling him closer. He kissed her openmouthed until she started to make little noises that sounded suspiciously like moans. He stored up the memory to tease her with later when they weren't so occupied with more important matters. And when he thought she was completely absorbed, he kissed her deeply.

She choked so hard that he had to sit her up and pound on her back to stop her coughing.

"Merciful saints above!" she gasped. "Not so hard!"

Christopher rubbed her back until she regained her breath; he fought the urge to hang his head and laugh in despair. He rested his forehead on her shoulder and smiled to himself. Once Gillian was breathing normally, he lifted his head and kissed her cheek.

"Better now?"

"Aye," she managed.

"Ready to attempt it again?"

She shivered. "Aye."

Her voice was decidedly hoarse. Christopher laid her back down and leaned over her. He smiled as he trailed his fingers over her face again, just to make sure she wasn't weeping.

"I didn't frighten you, did I?"

"Christopher," she groaned, turning her face toward his arm, obviously trying to hide.

Christopher turned her face gently to him. Gillian was stiff in his arms and he knew she was waiting for him to invade her mouth again.

"Trust me," he said. "Rest easy, Gill. I won't hurt you."

"Will I know before you do that again?"

"You'll know," he promised.

He kept his word. He kissed her lightly, as before, then more firmly until she was kissing him back. And then very slowly and very deliberately, he kissed her fully. He felt the shock of pleasure all the way down to his toes. Gillian moaned, but she didn't stiffen. She did, however, start to tremble. Christopher fumbled for the blanket on the chair behind him, then tossed the blanket over her with one hand while he pulled her close with the other, trying to warm her.

"I'm not cold," she gasped.

"You're frightened."

"Not that either."

Christopher smiled. "I see."

"Nay, I don't think you do . . ."

He covered her mouth and cut off her words. She didn't think he understood, but indeed he did. He loved Gillian with his mouth, putting as much passion into his kiss as he could. He was more than surprised to receive like measure in return. Gillian kept nothing from him, giving him whatever he demanded from her, then making demands of her own. When he would have lifted his head to breathe, she tightened her hand in his hair and kept him where he was. He smiled against her mouth and she tugged sharply on a fistful of his long locks. Christopher felt like a youth, caught up in desire he half feared he couldn't control. But it was joyous. He laughed as he tore his mouth away to gasp for air, then laughed again at Gillian's complaints.

"You are insatiable. How am I ever to have strength to train when you drain it from me so thoroughly?"

"You've no one to blame but yourself," she said.

"You liked it, then."

A shiver went through her and she wrapped both her arms around his neck.

"Would I shame myself by admitting it?"

He shook his head. "Nay, Gill. I prize your honesty greatly."

"Then I liked it very much."

He pressed his face against her neck and relaxed. He tightened his arm around her waist and groaned softly when she began to scratch his back. As an afterthought, he sat up, ripped off his tunic, then lay back down and gathered his lady close. Her hands were hesitant on his bare skin at first, but his groans obviously encouraged her.

She was then quiet for so long, Christopher almost asked her if aught was amiss. Then she spoke.

"Will we have a child now?"

He smiled against her neck. "Soon enough, I'll warrant."

She nodded and continued to scratch. "I thought as much. Even though we were wearing most of our clothing."

Christopher froze. Then he lifted his head.

"What?"

"What?" she echoed.

Christopher swallowed very carefully. "Gillian—" He cleared his throat and tried again. "Gill, that was naught but kissing."

"My lord?"

Merciful saints above, the child was an innocent.

"Gillian, there is much more to it than just kissing."

"Aye, I know."

He suspected she didn't.

"What do you know?"

She made a small choking sound, but he waited patiently. 'Twas best he knew now the fullness of her ignorance.

"To start with," she said, sounding enormously embarrassed, "I believed we were to wear far less clothing."

"And?"

"And," she said slowly, "there was to be more moaning from both of us."

"Indeed."

"Aye. There was certainly kissing aplenty, but I daresay the lack of the other was a great oversight."

"I would have to agree." He fought diligently to suppress his smile. "Now, tell me where you learned all this."

"Berengaria."

Christopher groaned.

"Magda knew nothing. I think Nemain knew a good deal more than any of us, but she was rather closemouthed about the whole affair."

"I daresay she was."

"They told me to be bold and you would see to the rest. And you have—and nicely too."

Saints above, how had he managed to endure his life without this woman? He smiled as he leaned down and kissed her softly.

"Love," he whispered, "a child is conceived when a man's seed finds its way inside a woman's body."

"Oh."

"And that is accomplished in a certain way."

"Ah, I see."

She saw nothing of the kind; he knew that for a fact. And he wanted to make sure she understood, so he took her hand and drew it down his body. Her touch was featherlight, then her fingers found what he'd meant them to find. They stilled abruptly, clutching their discovery. Christopher winced. Perhaps a tactile demonstration hadn't been wise.

Gillian was silent for so long, he thought she might have fainted. Then she cleared her throat.

"Ah, I see," she said, in a choked voice.

He doubted she did, but she would soon enough. He smiled as he gathered her close. She came willingly, stiffening only slightly when her hips came into contact with his. He rubbed his hand lightly over her back to soothe her.

"Gillian?"

"Aye?" came the muffled reply.

"Did our kissing please you?"

"Aye."

"Then trust me about this. There is great pleasure in the act. I'll be gentle and slow. You believe me, aye?"

She nodded.

"Then in a few days I'll humor you and let you bed me. But only after you're blind with lust and you prod me to our bedchamber at the point of your sword."

Her laugh was muffled against his chest.

"Unchivalrous oaf."

He rolled onto his back, pulling her with him.

"Unchivalrous oaf? For that insult, I require several kisses to restore my good humor." He wrapped his arms around her waist. "Be about your work, wench, before I grow angry. You know what a fearsome temper this scourge has."

Gillian humored him, just as he'd hoped she would. He contented himself with her kisses and resigned himself to many hours in the lists over the next few days to rid himself of the desire that the shy touch of his wife's mouth on his sent coursing through his veins.

In spite of himself, Christopher found himself not giving the wait a single thought.

twenty-two

GILLIAN SAT IN THE ALCOVE OF THE TOWER ROOM AND watched her husband train. She toyed with a lock of her hair and stopped fighting the feelings just watching Christopher stirred in her. She couldn't look at his back without thinking of exactly how it felt to run her fingers over those heavy muscles. Looking at his arms brought to mind how it felt to be encircled by those thick limbs and pulled tightly against that hard chest. When he lunged, her eyes were drawn to his legs, unyieldingly solid legs that pressed up against hers when he kissed her.

Just the memory of it brought scalding heat to her cheeks and made her tug uncomfortably at her clothes. Though she'd been sorely tempted to hie herself down to Berengaria's hut one last time, she'd refrained. Instead, she'd drunk bottles of wine laced liberally with beauty and courage and prayed she would be equal to the task when the time came. The only relief she saw in sight was that when Christopher finally did take her she would have on less clothing, which would surely ease the heat that rose in her by simply looking at him.

She shifted on her seat, then noticed that Christopher

had stopped working. He was leaning against the wall opposite her, looking at her.

"What?" she asked defensively.

"Just listening to you watch me," he said, smiling.

"I wasn't watching you," she lied.

Christopher laughed and crossed the chamber to her. He captured her mouth before she could catch her breath, then eased her back on the bench. He leaned over her, bracing himself on his hands and one knee and kissed her until her breath came in gasps.

"Are you watching me now?" he asked, lifting his head.

"Aye," she breathed. "Both of you. Or perhaps there are three. I'm too overwhelmed to say."

Christopher shook his head and laughed again. "You've no one to blame but yourself for my insufferable ego, my Gill." He straightened and pulled her up to her feet. "Let me build up the fire for you, then I'll go wash."

And then I'll come to you. The words went unspoken, but Gillian didn't need to hear them. She'd had several days to become accustomed to the idea of consummating her marriage and she knew the time had come.

Christopher hadn't pressed her. Indeed, he seemed almost reluctant to touch her. He'd done nothing but kiss her for the past se'nnight and she found herself wanting more. Just exactly what that 'more' entailed, she didn't know. But Christopher knew and he would show her if she had to order him to—an idea she didn't find unappealing in the slightest.

After all, she had become a dragonness.

She sat by the fire in their bedchamber and waited for Christopher to return to their chamber. Jason brought supper, stammered out a greeting, then yelped when the flat of Christopher's hand caught his backside on his way out the door. Gillian watched her husband bolt the bedchamber door then come to cast himself down next to her. He smiled and reached out to take her hand.

"What does my lady desire of me?"

"Tonight, I should have my dragon sit close to the fire and partake of this fine meal his giddy squire has provided."

"And then shall you bed me?" he asked, with a teasing smile.

She wished he could see her expression, for then no words would have been necessary. She took his hand instead. She kissed his fingertips one by one then cradled his palm against her cheek.

"Nay," she said softly. "But you shall bed me."

Christopher almost fell over into their supper. Gillian laughed as she pushed him back up and put a goblet of wine into his hand. He downed it in a single gulp.

"Easy," she said with a smile. "Don't choke."

"Help me," he said hoarsely. "My hands are shaking too badly to cut my own meat."

Gillian moved the board so he could sit with his back to the fire; then she served him. And his hands did tremble. He finished his meal with great haste, then set the board aside. He found her hands and brought them to his mouth.

"Gillian," he said, "we can wait. I don't want you to fear me."

"If I feared you, I wouldn't have said what I did."

"Your hands are trembling."

"So are yours."

His smile was appealingly crooked. "Does this mean I'll need to call for Jason to help carry us both to bed?"

She shook her head. "We'll help each other."

He dragged his hand through his hair. "Saints, I'm unnerved."

"Then you want to wait—"

Immediately his arms were around her and he was lifting her onto his lap. "Let's not be so hasty."

Gillian smiled. "Perhaps you would like it if I ordered you about for a few moments more."

Christopher smiled. "Perhaps. What would milady have me do?"

"Take off your tunic, definitely." This was surely the first step.

Christopher obliged her immediately. Gillian moved off his lap and sat near him, facing his side. She dragged her fingers through his damp hair and watched him close his eyes and smile at the pleasure. And as she watched him, she marveled at how changed they both were. Of course, Christopher was as gruff and demanding as he had been from the first. Outside their bedchamber, that is.

When they were alone, his hard edges softened. He teased her, he laughed with her, he spent long hours brushing her hair or scratching her back. She was no longer afraid of the tall, intimidating man she'd faced so timidly in front of a priest. She only teased him about his terrible reputation, knowing full well that it hid a most tender-hearted and loving man.

She also marveled at the changes in herself. No longer was she afraid to speak her mind to Christopher, or to anyone else for that matter. Oh, Cook still intimidated her, but not nearly as much as he had at first. She teased Colin with as much enthusiasm as Christopher did. She mothered Jason terribly and she had even mustered up enough courage to greet Christopher's personal guardsmen when she saw them instead of scuttling by and praying they didn't speak to her.

And, hard as it was to admit, she had begun to feel beautiful. At least Christopher thought she was. Whatever his hands told him pleased him, for he touched her continuously whenever they were alone and never let her out of arm's reach when they were with others. He praised whatever feature he happened to have his hands on at the moment and he did it so sincerely that she had come to believe it.

More than that, she felt desirable. It hadn't even taken wine to pry from Jason the truth that Christopher hadn't

touched a woman since his wounding. Christopher had
pretended not to hear her when she'd brought up the question to him, which did nothing but convince her of the
truth of it. So their marriage had not been the choice of
either. He could have bedded her once that first night and
been done with it. That he had waited so patiently until
she was ready only convinced her that he wanted her and
her alone. That knowledge had done more to bolster her
courage than almost anything else.

"What are you thinking?"

She looked at him and smiled. "Oh, nothing much."

"You're thinking of me. I can tell."

"Actually, I was thinking that you might indeed care
for me a bit."

One side of his mouth quirked up in a smile. "Now,
what could I possibly have done to fill your head with such
a notion?"

Gillian reached up to touch his cheek. "You tell me I'm
beautiful," she said, feeling tears sting her eyes. "I don't
think you'd say it if you didn't feel something."

Christopher slipped his hand under her hair and kissed
the outer corners of her eyes.

"No tears, Gillian. I beg you."

She put her arms around his neck and held him tightly.
"You've just made me very happy. It was nothing any
other grumbly dragon couldn't have done with the right
amount of teasing."

The corners of his eyes crinkled when he smiled. "Ah,
but there was only one dragon for you, lady, and you have
him caught firmly about the neck. Perhaps you should find
a task for him besides catching a chill from your tears.
Rumor has it he's a powerfully fine kisser."

"I never trust rumor where my lord is concerned. I fear
I'll need to be convinced."

Christopher obliged her. And then his kisses turned into
something entirely different. Gillian felt certain she knew
where he was leading. When he cradled her in his arms

and rose, she knew he intended to take her to the bed.

When they reached the bed and he laid her down gently, she was prepared to have him remove his remaining clothes. She even managed to matter-of-factly help him remove her own gown and shift. Aye, she was fully prepared for what was to follow, for hadn't they kissed often enough in the past?

But when he lay down next to her and gathered her against his warm, unclad frame, she realized that nothing ever could have prepared her for the sensations that rushed through her.

By the saints, it wasn't at all what Berengaria had led her to expect!

IT WAS SURELY THE MIDDLE OF THE NIGHT BEFORE SHE could again breathe. She lay with her head on her husband's shoulder, trailing her finger idly over his bare chest. It had been a very long evening, full of things she'd never for the life of her expected.

And not that the last of it had been much to shout about, except for the discomfort. Gillian had held her tongue, partly because she didn't want to hurt Christopher's feelings and partly because of the very fact that she had been lying beneath the Dragon of Blackmour, a man feared over the length and breadth of England, and he had whispered her name harshly as he'd made her his. Complaining had been the last thing she'd been willing to do. Of all the names in England he could have ground out from between clenched teeth, it was hers, Gillian, that he chose.

He had trembled as he buried his face against her neck and tears had finally poured from her eyes. Christopher of Blackmour sought comfort in her arms. It was more than she could have ever hoped for.

A rough callused finger gently traced her cheek, then Christopher made a sound of distress.

"Saints," he groaned, "I've made you weep again."

"Nay," she said, shaking her head. " 'Twas not for the pain that I wept."

"Pain? You said there was no pain!"

"I weep for the love I bear you, my lord, naught else."

"Then you have given me more than the gift of your virtue this night, my lady, for never has another wept for the love of me, but you'll not evade the other so neatly. Did I not ask you if it pained you?"

"Aye, you did. And I answered as I saw fit."

He caught his breath, then chuckled. "Ah, sweet Gill, how cheeky you've become." He gave her a gentle squeeze. "I promise it will be better the next time."

Gillian snuggled closer. "As you say, my lord."

"You don't believe me?"

"It matters not."

"It matters not?" he echoed. "By the saints, Gill, how can you say that?"

"I love you, Christopher. If it pleases you, I am content."

"I want it to please *you!*" he exclaimed.

She blinked. "But it did."

"All but the last," he said grimly.

"Nay, even that wasn't completely unpleasant."

Christopher barked out a laugh. "Woman, you've no care at all for my ego, have you?"

"What would you have me say?" she asked, finding that blushes hadn't deserted her completely. "That I trembled so violently from pleasure that I thought I would fall from the bed?"

"Aye, that might do for a start!"

Gillian laughed helplessly. "Christopher, you are the most impossible man."

"Impossible, you say?" he demanded. He rolled onto his back, pulling her with him. She felt his features and realized he was wearing a formidable frown. "For that disrespect, you'll bed me the next time, then I'll tell *you* I found it merely endurable. We'll see how cheerful that makes you. Nay, don't move, you heartless shrew. The least you can do is soothe me by sprawling over me and keeping me warm.''

Gillian gave up trying to squirm away from him. After a few moments of embarrassment, she found that using her husband for a bed wasn't such a poor thing. She pulled up some of his pillow to make herself more comfortable, closed her eyes and tucked her head under his jaw. So he was worried that he hadn't pleased her. Surely that said something about what he felt for her. She smiled as she closed her eyes and tried to relax. Unfortunately, Christopher was strung too tautly under her for that.

''Christopher?''

''Aye,'' he said gruffly.

She propped her elbows up on his shoulders and rested her chin against his. ''You'll love me again after you've rested, won't you?''

''Why should I?'' he asked crossly.

Gillian suppressed her smile as she covered his mouth with hers. Imagine, Christopher of Blackmour wanting reassurance from her, Gillian of Warewick. It was a tale no one in England would believe.

She kissed her husband with all the passion she could find, trying to show him just how much she did love him. And how happy she was to be his. Perhaps he spoke truly, and it would become better with time. She wasn't quite ready to credit the kitchen wenches with moans of pleasure and not pain, but perhaps she would learn the whole of the matter eventually.

Suddenly, Christopher rolled her off him. Gillian caught her breath as he leaned over her. The kiss she had begun had quite abruptly become something he seemed intent on finishing. His hands moved over her, lighting little fires that blazed into big ones. And when he moved over her and took her, she felt no pain.

And, in the end, the pleasure was so intensely sweet, it was all she could do to clutch at his shoulders and be grateful he was holding her down for otherwise she surely would have trembled right off the bed.

The next thing she knew, she was lying on her back with Christopher kissing her softly. She reached up and touched his mouth with a trembling finger.

"You kept hold of me," she breathed.

"Of course," he said gently.

Then he took her mouth again and she knew that he was fighting his smile. She shivered as she felt the aftereffects of pleasure leave her. Christopher kissed her a final time; then he pulled away. He brought her with him, draping her over him as he might have a blanket, then began to hum cheerfully, tapping his fingers against her back in time to his song. Gillian managed a weak laugh as she snuggled close to him.

"You're pleased with yourself," she noted.

"Aye, pleased enough." He tapped some more. "You love me."

"Aye, my lord, I do."

His tapping turned to soft touches and his humming ceased altogether. After remaining silent for some time, he cleared his throat.

"Gill?"

"Aye, my lord?"

His hands twitched, as if he were uncomfortable. Then his hands stilled.

"I care too," he said gruffly. "Very much."

She had no idea why the words cost him so much, but they seemed to come dear. She closed her eyes and didn't stop the tears of joy that leaked out. He cared, very much. What more could she have asked for? She carefully pressed her lips against his neck and tightened her arms around him.

"Thank you," she whispered. "That means much to me."

He released the breath he'd been holding, then patted

her on the back, as if he were glad to have the sentiment over with.

"I pleased you."

It hadn't been a question.

"Very much, my lord."

He grunted. "I knew it, of course."

"Of course. You're powerfully skilled, my lord."

He grunted again and gave her a squeeze that fair robbed her of breath. "Go to sleep, Gillian. I need my sleep. For all the loving you're sure to demand when you wake," he added.

She smiled and fell asleep to the soft touch of her husband's hands against her back.

twenty-three

"My lord, I bring you greetings from Bernard of Warewick. He wishes me to inform you he will arrive within the fortnight to visit his beloved daughter."

Christopher reached for Jason's arm and pulled him down to whisper in his ear.

"Find Gillian and keep her busy. I'll not have her see that bastard."

Jason departed immediately. Christopher leaned back in his chair and drummed his fingers against the wood of the table.

"Tell Lord Warewick that his concern is most touching," Christopher paused and smiled a half smile that contained no warmth whatsoever, "but I've no time to see him at present and neither does his child."

"He bid me remind you he is your father-in-law."

Christopher let his features harden into the cold look that was famous from London to Hadrian's wall. Only a fool wouldn't have backed up a pace and cowered. He wished he could have seen the effect on Warewick's man.

" 'Tis only because you are his messenger that you will leave here alive. If Warewick comes again, rest assured he won't enjoy such luxury."

"He's heard rumors that you've tortured the girl!" the man blurted out.

Christopher laughed. The very thought was so ridiculous, he laughed again.

"Colin, are you listening to this drivel?"

"Listening and remembering," Colin growled from where he stood behind Christopher's chair. "And you know what a long memory I have."

"Aye, as long as my patience is short." Christopher stood. "Begone, you fool, and take this message back to your lord. He'll not see his daughter again and if he wonders why, tell him I am well acquainted with the treatment she received at his hall. As far as I'm concerned, he's no longer any kin of hers. And should he wish to see just how quickly and cleanly I can rid England of him, his vassals and everything he owns, I'll be happy to oblige him. Guards, see this misbegotten cur from my hall and allow no other bearing Warewick's colors inside the gates."

Christopher sat and assumed a very bored and arrogant pose until the hall door was closed.

"Arrogant whoreson," Colin muttered.

Christopher banged his fist on the table and swore. "How dare he! I'll *not* have him within my doors, terrorizing Gillian again. Nay, not even the sight of him will trouble her. Saints, Colin, I wish I could see. I'd slip into his house and murder him in his own bed, just to rid myself of the annoyance of having him alive."

The chair next to him creaked under Colin's weight. "What does he want, do you think?"

"Gold," Christopher said flatly. "What else would he want? He certainly isn't coming out of love for Gillian."

"I'd be more suspicious of him than that."

"What? Think you he'd steal her away from me?"

"Chris, he likely thinks you cannot bear the girl. How could he possibly know you're in love with her?"

Christopher scowled furiously but couldn't bring himself to deny the last. Colin never passed up an opportunity to tease him about it, but Christopher didn't mind. Let the whole of England know he was blind with love for her. It would please her. And whatever pleased her, pleased him.

He smiled to himself, wondering how it was he'd done without her for so long. A pity they couldn't have met in his youth. Aye, a pity he would have been too stupid to have looked at her in his youth. He could have wed her when she was twelve and carried her home, safe away from her sire. He would have bedded her the moment she was able and sired a score of lusty sons and sweet daughters on her. Aye, they had wasted these past ten years.

"Chris? *Chris?*"

Christopher blinked. "Aye?"

"Saints, lad, but you're dozing again! You've been in bed for over a se'nnight." Colin made a sound of mock surprise. "Nay, do not tell me you were doing aught besides sleeping!"

"Be silent, Colin," Christopher muttered, feeling himself color.

Colin's hearty laughter boomed out over the great hall. "By the saints, you are a besotted pup! I'll never see a decent day's labor out of you again, I'll warrant. Though little Gill might disagree with me on that score—"

A tremendous crash interrupted Colin's babbling. Christopher rose with a sigh and walked back to the doorway that led to the kitchens on the side of the hall.

"Merciful saints, 'tis Gillian," Colin whispered next to him. "Nay," he said, catching Christopher by the sleeve, "let her be. Jason has his hand on his sword. Saints, Chris, she looks powerfully angry."

"At who?"

"Cook."

Christopher paused and listened intently. There was a tremendous *thwack* and Colin chuckled.

"She just thumped Cook on the chest with his spoon. It would seem she grows weary of him never paying her heed."

Indeed that seemed to be so, for Christopher immediately heard his wife begin to speak.

"I am not a spirit," Gillian said curtly, "and you will cease treating me as if you saw me not. I am tired of listening to His Lordship crack his teeth on the rocks you cannot seem to sift from the bread and watching him choke on wine he must needs strain through his teeth to drink! Now, you will see that the fare is better, or you will be replaced!"

"By whose authority?" Cook grumbled.

"Mine. I am chatelaine here."

"Aye, and you're a hand shorter than me and thrice as skinny—"

The whisper of a sword coming from its sheath was accompanied by the gasps of the rest of the kitchen help. Christopher leaned close to Colin.

"Did Jason draw his blade?"

Colin choked. "Gillian drew Jason's blade. She holds it to Cook's throat—nay, Chris, leave her be. She handles it well enough." He laughed softly. "Ah, that you could see this! Your shy, demure wife is bristling like an angry boar and poor Cook is sweating himself dry."

Christopher leaned back slowly against the wall and smiled as Colin described with relish the goings-on.

"I think we might have something edible tonight," Colin whispered with a half laugh. "That is, if Cook doesn't cast himself into the pot merely to avoid another tongue-lashing from your lady."

"Now," Gillian said imperiously, "will I hear my lord curse about his bread again?"

"Nay, lady," a deep, trembling voice answered quickly.

"Or his wine?"

"Nay. It will be seen to immediately."

"Very well then. Here, Jason, take back your blade." She clapped her hands. "Back to work, all of you."

Colin sounded near tears from his suppressed laughter. "Chris, she is a wonder!"

"Aye, she is at that." He folded his arms over his chest and listened to his wife come toward him.

"What are you smirking about, Blackmour?" she demanded.

"Me?" He wiped the smile from his face. "Why, nothing, lady. I was just admiring your mode of handling the servants."

"Aye," Colin added. "Mayhap you would care to see to the garrison this afternoon."

"You are a pair of grinning fools and naught but," Gillian said, sounding displeased. "Jason!"

"Aye, my lady," Jason said breathlessly.

"See to your lord. Nay, on second thought, I will see to your lord. Take Colin away and see that none of the maids fight over him again. I vow he grows more handsome with each passing day."

Colin made a strangled sound and Christopher laughed. The one surefire way to unnerve the man was to compliment him and Gillian had learned that well. Then he winced at the sharp poke in his belly.

"Do I amuse you, my lord?"

"Nay," he said, trying to sober his expression. "Nay, lady. You frighten me. You intimidate me. I tremble in fear of your anger."

"You mock me and I'll not have it. Jason, did I not tell you to take Colin away? Make haste, boy. Christopher, come with me. I've a mind to speak with you alone."

Colin burst out laughing. "Poor Chris. There's never an end to your labors with this wench, is there?"

Christopher had the feeling Gillian's frown had been immediate and formidable, for Colin gulped.

"*Adieu*, my lord. Come, Jason, let us beat a hasty retreat before she skewers both of us on that blade of yours."

Christopher felt his hand taken and found himself being pulled from the kitchens. He laughed at Gillian's tugging.

"Gill, I've things to see to this afternoon, truly."

She stopped. "What sorts of things?"

"The men, the keep, my steward. Things that will keep food on your table and wood in your hearths."

Slender arms went around him and he felt her lips kiss his neck under his chin.

"How long will it take?"

"Three hours."

Her lips somehow found their way to his ear. He bent to make it easier for her, then wondered at his own stupidity. The reaction of his poor body to her gentle teasing was immediate.

"How long?" she breathed.

"Two hours."

"Too long."

He swallowed again. "An hour. No longer."

"Don't be late." She brushed her lips across his. "I'll have to come find you else, and you know how that will irritate me."

"God forbid," he said, with feeling. He listened to her go up the stairs, then leaned back against the table and tried to remember just what had been so bloody pressing a moment ago. His steward? Nay, the man could see to the hall well enough on his own for an afternoon. The men? Colin would manage them. The keep? It could fall down around his ears and it wouldn't have made a wit of difference to him. He turned and strode toward the steps. If Gillian wanted him in their bedchamber in the middle of the day, far be it from him to deny her.

He walked down the passageway to his chamber, then knocked and entered.

"Gillian?"

"Christopher!" There was the sound of scurrying and he wondered what she was about. "That wasn't an hour!"

"Wasn't it? It seemed more like three."

"Well, come back later. I'm occupied right now."

He frowned. "With what?"

He felt her hands on his arm. "Come back in an hour."

"What are you doing? Is there someone else here?"

"Of course not. Now, go."

She pushed him out the door and shut it behind him. Christopher walked over to the opposite wall, turned and leaned back against it. He ignored the servants who passed him. He even ignored Wolf, who was ejected from the bedchamber after only a few moments. He ignored everything but his frown, which became more dark with time. What was she doing? If she had taken a lover . . .

Gillian? A lover? Nay, the thought was ridiculous. He'd bedded her himself barely a se'nnight ago. She couldn't have tired of him so soon. Even if she had tired of his loving, she was still shy. It was only last night that she had relented and come to bed without hiding behind her dressing gown as if it were a shield.

He heard the door open, then heard Gillian gasp.

"Christopher, what are you doing?"

"Waiting," he growled.

"By the saints, you startled me."

He folded his arms over his chest and glared. "Is the hour passed yet, or must I wait longer?"

He heard soft footsteps, then felt her hands come to rest on his arms.

"You needn't wait longer, my lord," she said quietly. "Come into your chamber."

He let her lead him inside, then listened to her slide the bolt home on the door. Soon he found himself in his great chair with a cup of warm wine in his hand. Gillian brought him water to wash his hands and face, then left him alone while she puttered about the chamber. Christopher listened to her hum a charmingly off-key melody and felt his heart catch at the tremor in her voice. Was she nervous then? What did she have planned?

As if he couldn't answer that for himself. He had the feeling, smug and arrogant though it might have been, that his wife planned to seduce him.

Damn, but he was looking forward to it.

He heard her coming toward him, then felt polished wood be laid in his hands.

His lute.

He frowned. "What's this?"

"You need an afternoon of leisure, my lord. I thought this would please you."

"I see," he said, feeling unreasonably disappointed. "I thought you had something else in mind."

Her delighted laugh made him color. He scowled at her, but only received a fleeting kiss in return.

"You don't think I mean to hold you in your chamber all afternoon merely to sing for me, do you?"

"How should I know?" he grumbled.

She only laughed again. Christopher heard her settle into the chair opposite him. He could think of several things he would have rather been doing than tuning a bloody lute, but once his fingers touched the strings, he found he couldn't help himself.

And once the tuning of it suited his ears, there was no sense in not dredging up a ballad or two to sing.

And so he sang. And he listened to his wife laugh and weep and clap for him. By the time his fingers were too used to continue, he realized what a wonderful gift his lady had given him.

"I haven't played in years," he said, as she took the lute from his hands.

"I know, my lord," she said softly.

Christopher turned his face to the fire. "I suppose it was tolerable enough to listen to."

His hands were soon full of wife. She settled herself comfortably onto his lap and then put her arms around him.

"I could listen for days," she said, kissing him softly. " 'Twas a very great gift you gave me this afternoon."

If she only knew! He wanted to tell her how much it had pleased him, but he couldn't seem to find the words.

So he gathered her close and held her tightly, and said nothing.

"Your fingers must be sore," she remarked.

"A bit."

"I'll see that you don't abuse them further today," she said.

A jolt went through him as he realized what she was about. And he couldn't help but smile.

"The idea pleases you?" she asked.

"Well enough."

"Then put your arms around me, Chris," she murmured.

He did as she bid, undone more by her use of his shortened name than her request. When he would have kissed her, she pulled away and shook her head. He had no choice but to allow her full control. Her invasion of his mouth was shy at first, then more bold, likely because she felt him begin to tremble.

The longer she kissed him, the warmer he became until he knew he would die if he didn't take some of his clothes off. He was sweating when Gillian rose from his lap suddenly and pulled him to his feet. He opened his mouth to ask her what she was doing, then felt her hands fumbling with his belt. He suppressed a groan.

Her hands stilled.

"My lord?"

"Aye," he rasped.

"You're frowning."

"Nay, Gill, this is a look of desperation."

"Then I haven't displeased you." It was more of a statement. Christopher lifted his hand and touched her lips. He found the beginnings of a smile there.

"Nay, love. But you could likely tell that for yourself."

Her hand traveled down, then stopped. Her fingers investigated a bit more and Christopher shivered.

"I see," she said.

He could only smile miserably in response. Then his belt

fell to the floor and Gillian pulled his tunic over his head. He snatched it away and mopped his brow before he let her have it.

"Better?" she asked.

"A bit. I could be even cooler, though." He smiled hopefully.

She laughed. "Aye, no doubt. Sit, and I'll take off your boots."

"Nay," he said, stopping her. He pulled his boots off himself, then froze when his wife began to remove his hose. He tensed as she slid them down his legs, then put his hand on her shoulder for balance as he stepped from them. "Now you," he said reaching for her.

She pushed his hand away. "In my own good time, my lord. Now that you are cooler, sit you down again. Perhaps a bit of wine will refresh you."

What would have refreshed him was carrying his lady to the bed and losing himself in her. But, 'twas her day to have him at her mercy so it seemed. He sat down obediently and resigned himself to being slave to Gillian's whims.

It was a very cheerful resignation indeed.

He accepted his wine and his wife's slender form on his lap with a smile. The wine was cold this time and he appreciated the gesture. He drank, then offered her a sip. While she was drinking, he thought to sneak a touch or two and immediately found himself thwarted.

"Drink your wine, Christopher. Your hands are most disobedient and I'll not stand for it."

Christopher drank meekly, then handed her the cup when he was finished. He clasped the arms of the chair and smiled weakly.

"I'm at your mercy."

"Aye, you are. There was never any doubt about it."

He grinned at her arrogance, then caught his breath when her cool hands slid up his chest, past his neck and into his hair. Then he groaned when Gillian kissed him.

She kissed him until he was certain that, had he been able to see, he would have been seeing two or three of her. And sitting in a chair was certainly frustrating when what he wanted was to feel her pressed against the length of him.

As if she'd read his mind, she rose. He followed her up so closely, he bumped his nose against her shoulder. Her only response was a soft laugh. Christopher felt himself redden, but devil take her, what did she expect? He was eager, as eager as he'd ever been as a randy young squire, and his lady was completely to blame for it. He allowed her to lead him to the bed, then found himself sitting down. Gillian stood between his thighs and brushed her hand over his shoulder.

"I must remove my gown, I think," she said, as if she truly puzzled over her next move. "Sit here quietly, Christopher, while I see to it. It may take me a bit of time."

Not if he had anything to do with it. It took him only a few heartbeats to rid her of her clothes, haul her back with him on the bed and kiss her until neither of them could breathe.

"Christopher . . ."

He tugged on her long hair. "I am at your mercy. Isn't that what you wanted?"

"Aye, it was," she admitted.

"Then take me," he said, putting his hand behind her head and pulling her head down to his. "Take me and love me however you wish. Slow, fast, it matters not to me. I'm yours to do with what you will."

The idea obviously pleased her. Christopher tried not to groan as she discovered just exactly what pleased *him*.

"Chris?" she said, a few minutes later.

"Aye, my love," he rasped.

"You're at my mercy, you know."

"Don't I know it—" he gasped.

He suddenly and quite completely lost track of what he'd been meaning to say. All he could do was hang on and pray he wouldn't die before both of them found release. He clamped down on his own passions with an iron control until Gillian caught her breath. He instantly obeyed her hoarse plea for him to hold her.

And once she could breathe again, she propped her chin on her fists and yawned.

"I'm finished and ready for a nap. What of you, my lord?"

"Gillian!"

She laughed and leaned down to kiss him. "And here I thought perhaps you'd fallen asleep already. Forgive me."

"You are a heart . . . heartless—" he gasped and couldn't finish.

Having her love him wasn't what made him groan deep in his throat. It was what she was whispering in his ear.

Never had a woman told him what pleasure she gained from pleasing him. Servants had never been much for lavishing praise and noblewomen were too concerned with his purse, not his person, to tell him aught. Not even Lina had spared him much thought.

But Gillian, merciful saints, Gillian! The feel of him lying beneath her, naught but iron-thewed muscle pleased her. His harsh breath against her neck pleased her. His callused hands made her tremble. But that wasn't what pleased her the most. It was feeling the quickening of his body, when he lost control that pleased her the most. When he lost control . . .

When he came to himself, she was stroking his cheek with her fingers. Christopher blushed to think he'd been so undone. Hopefully he hadn't done anything to embarrass himself.

"You're blushing."

"You cannot see me," he bluffed.

"The bedcurtains are open. And now you're blushing harder." She laughed softly. " 'Tis very sweet, my lord."

Christopher forced her head down to his shoulder and wrapped his arm around her, keeping her immobile.

"I'll not be mocked this way," he said, mortified.

He felt her smile against his neck and released her reluctantly when she pushed up. Her lips were soft against his.

"Tell me I pleased you," she whispered.

"If words are required after that," he said dryly, "then I'll give them to you. You pleased me well enough."

"Well enough?"

"All right, you bloody well killed me. Does that satisfy you?"

She only laughed and pressed a soft kiss against his cheek. "Christopher," she chided.

He smoothed her hair back from her face. "Gill . . ." he paused helplessly. "I've never felt the like before. And 'twas not only my body you pleased." He traced her lips with his fingers. " 'Twas my soul."

"I love you. Do you know that now?"

"Had I any doubts from before, I would have them no longer." He snuggled her close and closed his eyes. "Gillian?"

"Aye, my lord."

"Thank you."

"My pleasure."

"Nay, 'twas mine." He gave her a gentle squeeze. "I've a beautiful, passionate, courageous wife who loves me and I couldn't be happier." He pressed his lips against her hair. "Gillian of Blackmour, I—I love you." He felt a suspicious moisture gather in his eyes. "Aye," he repeated softly, to himself. "I love you deeply." He ran his hands over her back. "Are you uncomfortable? Do you wish to move?"

"Nay, my lord."

He could have sworn he felt hot tears against his neck. They matched his own.

"Will you stay with me?" he murmured.

"Forever, my lord."

He pulled a blanket up to cover them both, then laid his head back and closed his eyes. Gillian wrapped her arms around his neck and buried her face against his throat. Christopher had the feeling she had no intentions of letting him go any time soon.

Nothing could have made him happier.

twenty-four

GILLIAN SPRINKLED THE VERY LAST OF THE BEAUTY AND courage into her goblet of wine. She swirled the rich liquid about for a moment and said her accustomed words of blessing over it.

"I am beautiful," she murmured. "I am courageous. My husband loves me." Her heart caught in her throat at that. She knew Christopher loved her. He told her he did. And now she had the beauty and courage to hold him.

Or so she prayed.

It was only in the back of her mind that she worried. She was her father's daughter. Would his blood rise to the fore? Destroy the faint hints of comeliness she'd managed to acquire? Turn her into a cowering, pitiful waif of a girl again?

She lifted the goblet and drank. She drank fully, ignoring her need for air, ignoring everything except draining the cup of beauty and bravery. Then she set the goblet down and held it with both hands.

"I'm beautiful," she whispered. "And I *will* hold him. I will not lose him to Magdalina's ghost or my sire."

That said, she felt a smile creep over her features. After all, she had bested Cook. Not even Christopher dared cross the man. Aye, she had bested both the Dragon and his cook and that was a feat worthy of any minstrel's song.

She walked over to the alcove and threw open the shutters. Glass didn't enclose the windows here for it would have been futile. The first good storm would have destroyed the panes instantly. Gillian fingered the warped, sea-worn wood of the shutters and smiled. Only rock survived long here at Blackmour. Wood was far too puny and cowardly a substance to endure the elements. Gillian wanted to believe she was made of the sterner substance. Christopher certainly was.

She stared down the cliff that made up Blackmour's foundations and watched the sea beat against the shore. The sight never ceased to fascinate her. She loved the white spray, the churning waves, the tang of the salt air and the mist against her face. And out of the corner of her eye, she saw just a hint of rocky shoreline. For a moment, she wondered what it would be like to walk along that shore. Was the ocean cold or warm? What did the water taste like? Christopher told her it was salty and not fit to drink, but she couldn't imagine that. Water was water.

"Gillian? Where are you?"

She turned and smiled. "Here, my lord. By the window."

She watched Christopher walk toward her and marveled anew that this man was hers. How powerful he was, tall and strong. Aye, and lordly too. His arrogance showed in every line of his body, in his walk, in the way he held his head high. She very much suspected there was none to equal him.

He walked into her arms and gathered her to him.

"What are you doing holed up in our bedchamber?" he asked, his deep voice rumbling in his chest.

"Watching the sea," she said, with a contented sigh.

"Don't lean out the window. You're liable to fall and then where would I be?"

"I'm not sure. Where would you be, my lord?"

"Bereft," he whispered, tightening his arms around her. He rested his cheek against her hair and fell silent.

"Christopher?"

"Aye, love."

"Is the sea warm or cold?"

He stiffened, then pulled back. "You've never felt it?" There was disbelief in his voice. "Merciful saints, Gill, but you've led a sheltered life." He smiled down at her and tucked an unruly curl behind her ear. "Would you care to feel it for yourself?"

She took Christopher's hands and put them to her face so he could tell for himself just how much the idea pleased her. He laughed softly then slipped his finger under her chin and gently closed her mouth.

"Answer enough, sweet one. Find a warm gown and I'll help you change. Even though 'tis summer, the shore will be chilly. And wear your sturdy boots that you don't hurt your feet on the rocks. I daresay you'll want to crawl down from my mount and play, won't you?"

"Oh, aye," she threw over her shoulder as she ran for her trunk.

She pulled forth a heavy woolen gown and impatiently tried to pull the one she was wearing over her head. Strong hands aided her in her task, then stilled when they brushed over her bare shoulders. Gillian pushed Christopher's lingering hands away and shoved her gown at him.

"Help me."

"Ah, but I planned to."

"Have you but one thing on your mind?" she asked, exasperated, trying to avoid his hands.

Christopher only laughed. "And this from the woman who would not let me from my bed this morn until well after sunrise?"

"I couldn't stop myself," she said, blushing hotly.

"Stop yourself from ravishing me?" Christopher grinned. "Perhaps it would be wise to forgo the journey to the shore and retire to bed. You look exhausted."

"I look nothing of the sort," she said, snatching her gown away. She donned it herself, finding that all she could do was laugh at Christopher's attempts to thwart her.

"A nap when we return," he insisted.

"If it pleases you."

He started to respond, but she quickly put her hand over his mouth.

"Cease," she said with a half laugh. "I know what you were about to say, you lecherous old dragon."

He caught her hand and pressed a soft kiss in the middle of her palm.

"Vow you'll remember every word and promise to act on them all or I won't take you."

"I promise."

Christopher kept her hand in his as he led her toward the door. "I'll collect later. The sea air always does improve my appetite. For many things," he added solemnly.

"Christopher!"

He only grinned.

A short time later Gillian found herself sitting behind her husband, astride his huge black warhorse, surrounded by half the castle guard. Christopher grumbled his displeasure at what he deemed a very serious invasion of his privacy, but he sent none of the men back. Gillian started to say something to soothe him, then heard him mutter under his breath.

"It isn't as if I could bloody well protect her myself."

She pretended not to hear. It had been at least a month since Christopher had last said anything like that. She wondered what had changed; then it occurred to her that it had been a month since they'd first lain together. She couldn't quite bring herself to believe that it was the physical expression of her love for him that had wrought the change. More than likely, she thought dryly, it was that he never allowed her from his bedchamber and therefore never worried about her.

Christopher's horse needed little guidance to descend

the path to the shore but even the knowledge of his sure-footedness didn't ease Gillian's unease. She wrapped her arms around Christopher's waist and clung to him, praying they would reach the shore safely. She buried her face against his back and closed her eyes.

"We won't fall," Christopher growled softly.

"It isn't you I doubt," Gillian mumbled against his cloak. " 'Tis this treacherous path!"

"If you think this to be treacherous then the very sight of the climb to the Lord's Hall will reduce you to tears."

"The Lord's Hall?"

"My father's refuge from my mother."

She would have asked more, but Christopher's stallion stumbled. Christopher immediately jerked on the reins.

"Steady," he commanded.

The beast obeyed and resumed his calm pace. Several moments later Christopher sighed in relief and the tension eased from him. Gillian lifted her head and caught her breath. They were on the shore, so close to the water that she jumped the first time a wave crashed against the rocks. She watched in fascination as the water slithered back into the deep.

Christopher dismounted and held up his arms for her. Gillian put her hands on his shoulders and smiled reflexively at the care he used while setting her on her feet. She put her arms around him and hugged him.

"Thank you."

"For what?"

"For the gift of this."

A slight smile softened his features. " 'Tis repayment for the gift of my lute a few days back. Now, hold my hand while you explore. You know the sea monsters will snatch you away if you venture out too far, don't you?"

"Nay," she breathed, moving closer to him.

He hugged her tightly. "Aye. A tasty morsel such as you would make a fine meal for one of the beasties who lies in wait near Blackmour."

She pulled her head back and looked up at him. "Are you teasing me?"

"Might be."

Gillian smiled as she reached up and put her arm around his neck. She pulled him down, unresisting, and kissed him softly on the cheek.

"You're very sweet."

"Pray keep that a secret between us." He brushed his lips across hers. "Go play, Gill. I think I'd be wise to wait for you here."

"Nay, come along."

He shook his head.

She slipped her arm around his waist and drew his arm over her shoulder.

"Trust me."

"Gillian—"

"Trust me," she repeated. She took the hand that rested over her shoulder and laced her fingers with his. "You've given me so much, Chris. I am so seldom able to repay you."

He smiled ruefully. "You do not fight fairly, lady. First you compliment me, then you call me by the name you rarely use outside the bedcurtains. How can I say you nay?"

"Good," she said, giving his hand a squeeze. "Might we walk a bit along the shore? Well out of the reach of the monsters?"

"Aye, we might. But have a care that you don't walk me into a half-rotted tree."

"I'll take wonderful care of you, my lord."

"You already have," he said softly.

His words echoed in her mind as they walked along the shore. Every time she bent to examine a particularly interesting bit of rock or shell, she heard his words.

"Do you want to feel the water?" he asked.

She looked up and found that he was smiling gently.

"Dare I?"

"I'll draw my sword to hold the beasts at bay."

"You know I believed all of William's tales in my youth."

"Love, you believed William's tales until the time we were wed. Sweet Gill, you've a trusting soul."

"What you mean is I'm naive."

He shook his head. "Trusting. Innocent. And delightful to tease. But I'll still hold your hand. The water might suck you away if you're not careful."

"And that would grieve you?"

His expression sobered. "Aye. It would grieve me deeply."

"Then hold my hand, my lord," she said softly. "For I'd not lose you so soon."

"Choose a smooth place and let us venture out. Not too far," he added. "Catch up your skirts, too. There's no sense in soaking them."

Gillian held onto Christopher with one hand and her skirts with the other. She crept down a few steps and frowned as the water receded in front of her. She followed it, but it fled yet more. Then, before she could back up, the waves came in. She shrieked and jumped backward so quickly that Christopher stumbled.

But he only laughed. "Approach again, Gill, but not so close. Let the sea come to you."

Gillian grabbed her sodden skirts with one hand and reached down with the other, trying to touch the water. Immediately she felt Christopher take hold of a fistful of the back of her gown.

"Thank you, my lord."

"Think nothing of it, my lady."

"A little further out, Christopher. The sea is afeared of your mighty frown."

She reached out and let her fingers slide through the chill water. It soaked her feet and shins as well, but she didn't mark it. She was far too busy feeling the sand slipping from under her feet and trying to keep her balance.

Christopher held his place as steadily as if he'd been standing on firm ground.

"You, my lord, are as immovable as your keep."

"Aye, I'm too heavy to be troubled by this puny tide. 'Tis a good thing you have me, else you'd be washed out to sea by now. Now that you've felt the sea, might we go home? Your gown is soaked clear to your waist and I'm sure your hands and feet are like ice."

"Might we come another day? To swim?"

Christopher paused. "Swim?"

"Aye. I think it would be fine sport."

He smiled as he shook his head. "What a brave one you've become, my lady. You're willing to face the sea monsters?"

Gillian moved easily into his embrace. "Aye, if you're there to protect me."

"Like as not, you'd be protecting me—"

"Stop it," she said, surprised at the sharpness of her tone. She bit her lip and waited for Christopher to respond. She didn't dare look at his expression.

At least he was still holding her. Soon his hand was skimming over her hair. Gillian closed her eyes and let out her breath slowly. Whatever he was feeling, it wasn't anger. She tightened her arms around him.

"I'd have no other," she whispered.

"Not even a man with two good eyes?" he asked quietly, but there was no despair in his voice. Indeed, there was only a kind of sadness she'd never heard in his tone before.

She shook her head against his chest. "Nay, my lord. You see more clearly than anyone I've ever known."

"I wish I could agree with you."

Gillian looked up at him. "Please, Christopher, speak no more of it, I beg you. I love you as you are. Indeed, I'm grateful you cannot see, for you would never have chosen me else and I cannot bear to think of how unhappy I would have been."

He only smiled gravely and pulled away. "Let us go home, Gillian. We've both need of a hot fire and warm wine."

Gillian nodded and slipped her arm through his as they walked back along the shore. She looked up at the cliffs, then stopped when she saw the stone house perched atop one of the steepest. It was large, as far as houses went, and seemed sturdy enough. But the path leading up to it was indeed very steep and looked dangerous. Jagged rocks lined the winding route. It was easy enough to see how one misstep could mean disaster.

"What are you staring at?" Christopher asked.

"I'm not sure. There is a house of sorts there above the cliff."

" 'Tis the Lord's Hall. My father's folly, if you will."

Gillian remained silently, waiting. Christopher had never said much about his family and she had begun to wonder about them. When he remained silent, she nudged him.

He sighed and dragged his hand through his hair. "The entire tale, eh? I take it you've nothing better to do with your day."

"The entire tale, if you please."

Christopher released her hand, then bent and felt for a handful of rocks. He turned unerringly toward the sea and began to cast them out, one by one.

"My father was the second son. His older brother, Gervase, died while out hunting boar. The title fell to my sire, which in truth was a pity for he was completely inadequate to the task of maintaining my grandfather's enormous wealth and properties." He flung another stone into the sea. "The Lord's Hall is just another in a long list of his extravagances. He married my mother when he was a score and she but ten-and-two. After a few years, he got her with child and realized his mistake." A grim smile twisted his mouth. "My mother found childbearing not at all to her liking and complained of the grief I caused her from morn

till eve. It was then that my father began to build himself
his own private escape.''

"The Lord's Hall," Gillian murmured.

"Aye. In truth, I cannot blame him for my mother was
impossible to endure. I escaped to Artane as soon as I
could and was more than happy to be free of her harping.
My father escaped to his folly.''

"Your mother never came to fetch him?"

"Up that path? Gillian, you can see for yourself that the
way is perilous. The means of ascent up the back is just
as dangerous for the cliff is separate from the mainland,
just as is Blackmour. My mother never fetched my sire,
but she did brave the climb once, while he was away
squandering more gold. She stole his sanctuary right from
under his nose, thinking he would come for her.''

"I take it he didn't.''

Christopher snorted. "Of course not. He claimed the
climb was too steep and left her there to rot. She never
saw the inside of Blackmour's walls again, for she was
just as stubborn as my sire. I cannot blame him. I wouldn't
have gone after her either.'' He looked out over the sea
and his blue eyes were dark and cold. ''A man would be
daft to attempt it. Now, does that satisfy your curiosity?''

"More than amply, my lord.'' In truth, she was very
sorry she'd asked, for the telling of the tale had certainly
fouled Christopher's mood.

She guided him subtly as they walked back up the shore.
Her heart was heavy and she forced herself to ignore the
stone dwelling that perched on the edge of the cliff like a
vulture overlooking its domain. It said so very much about
what had gone on during Christopher's youth. A pity he'd
never known love from his parents.

The irony of the thought wasn't lost on her. Her mother
had died soon after her birth and it certainly wasn't as
though Bernard had been lavish with his affections. But at
least she'd had William. Christopher likely hadn't had anyone.

Christopher mounted, then held down his hand and pulled her up in front of him. Gillian twisted so she sat over his powerful thighs and she pressed her cheek quickly against his.

"I love you, my lord," she whispered.

"What inspired that, lady?"

"Nothing," she lied. "It seems that all it takes is the sight of you to bring the words to my lips."

Christopher smiled briefly, then turned his mount and headed back up the path. Gillian relaxed in his arms and rested her head against his shoulder, closing her eyes. The gentle motion of the horse and Christopher's warmth came close to putting her to sleep.

"Riders approaching!"

The cry startled her. Christopher cursed and spurred his stallion on. Gillian remained as still as she could, trying not to distract him.

"Ranulf, who is it?" Christopher demanded.

"Too far to tell," Captain Ranulf said from beside them.

Gillian didn't open her eyes until Christopher had stopped inside the inner gates and swung them both down from the saddle. He started barking out orders and she wondered if her father had suddenly decided to lay siege to Blackmour just to annoy his son-in-law. Then Jason came running toward them. He plowed into Christopher and Christopher almost lost his balance. He made a grab for his squire and shook him.

"Mindless babe!" he bellowed. "What are you about?"

"My lord, 'tis my sire," Jason said breathlessly. He was grinning from ear to ear. "And both my brothers. Aren't you pleased?"

Gillian didn't pay any attention to Christopher's expression. She was far too busy trying to control her own unease. Christopher she could manage. Even Colin didn't intimidate her and surely Cook was under her sway. But Jason's family? Strange men? Nay, that was something she couldn't face.

She started toward the keep and suddenly found herself nose to chest with Colin. The saints only knew where he'd come from, and Gillian cursed his appearance. He folded his arms over his beefy self and looked down at her with a frown.

"Where are you scampering off to, my lady?"

"I forgot something in my chamber."

"No doubt you would like to believe you forgot your courage but I know for a fact that you have it right there with you."

"Colin, please," Gillian begged, sidling past him.

He took two large steps and blocked her path again. "Cease," he whispered sharply. "You've nothing to fear from Robin of Artane or his lads. Women, the lot of them. His boys are whelps and Robin himself will likely weep if you look at him crossly. Now, what you should be worrying about is meat and drink for your lord's table. And if you cannot stomach that simple task, have a care for his heart's comfort. If you think he relishes these tidings, think again."

Gillian ventured a look at her husband. He'd stopped bellowing his orders. He stood in the midst of the activity, still as stone.

Looking stricken.

Colin gave her a gentle push, but she hardly needed that. She had no idea why Christopher wasn't anticipating with joy a visit from his former master, but she could easily speculate on the possible reasons. From all she'd heard, Robin had loved him like his own son. Christopher's reaction likely had a great deal to do with his loss of sight.

By the time Gillian reached her husband's side, she was in a fine temper. Damn Robin of Artane if he thought to make Christopher feel inadequate. Gillian took her husband's hand and tugged. She tugged more forcefully when he didn't move.

"Christopher, we'll go in now," she said firmly. "It isn't fitting that the Dragon of Blackmour greet his guests in the courtyard like an insignificant lord. Come inside and sit in your great chair. Artane may seek you out there.''

She busied herself seeing to her husband's comfort, praying that Lord Robin was truly as womanly as Colin had made him out to be. It would be easier to kill him then if he upset Christopher.

Then again, she might just do it if he were as fierce as her husband.

twenty-five

CHRISTOPHER PACED FROM THE DAIS TO THE HEARTH. HE likely would have paced straight into the fire if he hadn't run into his wife. He mumbled an apology, then turned and walked back to his high table. He ran into that too, and the pain in his thighs was enough to make him cease his movement.

He leaned his hands on the table and bowed his head. Saints, he wasn't prepared for this. Robin never arrived unannounced. Christopher always had several days to accustom himself to the idea of having his former master about, to steel himself against Robin's kindness and understanding, to shield his mind from the memories that the very sound of Robin's voice brought back to him. But this meeting had come upon him too quickly. His heart was open, assailable, unprotected. If only he'd had more time!

The doorway to the great hall opened. Robin must have entered, for Christopher heard Gillian squeak. And, in spite of himself, Christopher felt his heart lighten. Obviously the lord of Artane had lost none of his intimidating presence. Christopher could sympathize with Gillian and her reaction, for he remembered well his own first sight of Robin of Artane.

He'd been but a lad of seven—and a terrified lad of seven, if the truth were to be known. His father had seen fit to escort him to Artane, but Christopher had paid the price in the tales his father had told him along the way. By the time they'd reached the keep, Christopher had been convinced Robin would beat him to within an inch of his life if he made even the slightest misstep.

Robin had been standing in front of the hearth when Christopher had entered the hall. Christopher had hidden behind his father, too terrified to speak. And then his sire had begun to list Christopher's faults and he'd almost lost what little food he'd managed to ingest that morn. He'd been certain Robin would take him outside and thrash him for his past bad behavior. The blood had been thundering in his ears so loudly that he hadn't heard his father call him to step forward—but he certainly had felt his sire's sharp cuff to his ear.

And so he'd come to stand in front of Lord Robin, shaking so hard he could barely remain upright. When Robin had commanded him to look up, Christopher had—but very slowly. He'd started at his new master's feet, then given more than a passing glance to those large hands and upward to those broad shoulders. He'd forced himself to meet Robin's eyes steadily and tried his best not to break down and weep in fear. Saints, but the man had seemed huge! Christopher had come to realize later that Robin had been but a man of five-and-twenty at the time, but to young eyes he had seemed very old and very intimidating. Indeed, Robin had seemed so lordly and fierce, Christopher had been hard-pressed not to turn tail and flee as quickly as his shaking legs would carry him.

Then Robin had reached out suddenly, taken Christopher's trembling hand in his own and drawn him to his side.

"I'll take him," had been Robin's only comment.

His father had grunted and advised the young lord of Artane to be liberal and harsh with his beatings. Christopher had felt his stomach begin to violently protest that thought when a most astonishing thing had occurred. Lord Robin had squeezed his hand. Christopher had looked up, unsure, only to receive a wink in return.

And thusly his life as page had begun. There had been no beatings, no undeserved bellows, no listing of his faults. There had only been joy in serving a man who treated him fairly and with great affection. Because of that small first gesture, Lord Robin had earned Christopher's unswerving loyalty. There wasn't anything Christopher wouldn't have done for his lord.

The sound of firm footfalls coming his way brought him back to the task at hand. Christopher heard Gillian's sharp intake of breath and surmised that Robin was frowning. He frowned back, out of politeness.

"What, no greeting?" Robin barked. "No kiss of peace? No 'my dearest Artane, how happy I am to see you?' I've trudged over your God-forsaken bits of soil for two days looking forward to a warm welcome, fine food and drinkable wine. And here you cannot even come outside your hall and acknowledge me?"

Christopher clasped his hands behind his back and smiled gravely.

"Well, my lord, I would have had a score of naked dancing girls awaiting your pleasure if you'd but given me more warning."

He heard Robin's soft laugh suddenly break through the air like sunshine through a cloud. "My Anne would have me skewered for the like and you know it well."

"Then I bid you welcome anyway, such as it may be."

Christopher found himself in a bone-crushing embrace and he pounded Robin on the back as best he could. Then his former master took his face in his hands, kissed both cheeks, then ruffled his hair as if he'd had been a lad several years younger than Jason. Christopher cursed him thoroughly. Robin only laughed.

"Whelp, you act as if I embarrassed you in front of

some wench! Where is this woman who makes you keep up such appearances of manliness?"

Christopher knew Gillian was standing near the fire, so he turned to her, held out his hand and smiled encouragingly. He heard her unwilling feet come slowly toward him. Her cold fingers soon came to rest in his palm.

"My wife," Christopher said, giving her fingers a gentle squeeze. "Gillian of Warewick."

"Warewick," Robin repeated sharply. "I am hard pressed to understand why you would have aught to do with him, Christopher. Or with anything of his."

"I have nothing to do with him," Christopher said grimly. "But I've taken Gillian gladly."

Robin swore. "I should have killed the man myself years ago. After I saw what he'd done to William—"

"My lord!" Christopher interrupted hastily. "This isn't the place for recounting past events." By the saints, that was all Gillian needed to hear, a retelling of what her brother had suffered.

"William?" Gillian echoed. "Christopher, what is this of Will—"

"Later, Gillian," Christopher said, tightening his grip on her hand. " 'Tis naught. Nothing to fret over."

"Jason wrote that you'd wed," Robin rumbled, "but he said your wife was so ferocious, she even had Berkhamshire tamed. Somehow I expected a woman as large as you are and with a visage as ugly as Colin's. Surely this isn't the dragoness my son sang the praises of."

Christopher eased Gillian in front of him and wrapped his arms over her chest to keep her there. She tried to elbow him in the ribs, but he merely tightened his embrace.

"Here she is," he said, suppressing his smile. "Talons and all."

"Hrumph," Robin said, sounding unconvinced.

Gillian trembled and Christopher rubbed her arms. "Courage, Gill," he said softly. "And you, my lord," he said to Robin, "leave her be."

"I'm merely having a look at her," Robin said. Then he clucked his tongue. "Nay, this child is far too beautiful for all that fierceness. Where have you hidden your true lady, Christopher? The one who Jason claims has even tamed you?"

"Why, the miserable little wretch!"

"Ah, so the tales are true."

"They are not," Christopher snapped. "I'm not tamed. I am lord of this keep still and Gillian jumps to obey my every whim. Isn't that so, wife?"

"Aye, milord," she said, " 'tis true."

Robin grunted. "Someone is lying here but damn me if I can't divine who it is. Christopher, release your bride. I'll question her over by the fire, where I can use the irons if she proves reluctant to divulge the entire tale."

"Very well," Christopher said, fighting his smile.

"But Christopher!" Gillian gasped.

"Go with him, wife. I'll come rescue you if I hear flesh singeing."

"Oh, Christopher, please," Gillian begged, backing up against him.

Christopher bent his head to whisper in her ear. "He teases you, Gill. Besides, 'tis evident you've tamed me, so you should have no trouble doing the like to Artane. Surely you're fierce enough to face a paltry lord from the north."

His wife paused. Christopher could sense her gathering her courage about her. Then he felt her shoulders go back and her trembles cease. Almost.

"Humor the dotard, Gill, while I'm about my business. I have a squire to find and thrash."

"As you wish," Gillian whispered.

"Come, Lady Blackmour," Robin said, in his not-quite-fiercest of tones, "let us leave your lord to his play. I've a few questions to put to you."

Her gulp was painfully audible. Christopher gave her shoulders a final squeeze before he released her. Robin would do her no harm. Snarl and snap though he might, underneath he was quite tenderhearted.

Christopher recognized the same failing in himself. Gillian certainly never hesitated to make use of it as often as she could. Perhaps she had tamed him after all.

But, there was no sense in the rest of the realm knowing as much.

"Jason!" he called. "Bring yourself over here, boy! I've a mind to speak to you about your correspondence!"

GILLIAN STRUGGLED TO STAND TALL AS ROBIN LED HER over to the fire. The return of his intimidating frown did nothing to bolster her courage. She watched Christopher walk off and knew her last hope of escape had just fled. She continued to walk only because she was being pulled—and by Artane, of all people!

The tales she'd heard about him hadn't exaggerated. The man was huge. He was likely only a finger or two taller than Christopher but somehow that small bit was enough to make him seem enormous. His clothing wasn't covered with buttons and jewels and all manner of baubles as her father's was when he was trying to style himself a fine lord. Robin's simple garments spoke volumes about a man who needed no adornment to appear powerful and important.

She'd watched him stride across the hall with a grim expression. Christopher's had been equally as grim. Watching the two men standing naught but a foot apart, she'd readily recognized the similarities. Both were proud. Both were excessively arrogant. Both were powerful warriors to the depths of their bones and were used to having their own way. Indeed she fancied that Christopher would seem very much like Robin when he had acquired that glint of silver at the temples. He already had the arrogance. Now all he needed was age.

But presently her husband had escaped to wrestle with Jason, leaving her to face this man who wore such a fierce frown.

He gestured for her to sit. "So," he began, taking a seat across from her and looking at her with steely gray eyes, "you wed him."

She nodded, casting a nervous look over her shoulder to see what had become of Christopher. Jason had been found and was currently being shaken.

"Why?"

She looked back at Robin. "I beg your pardon?"

"I asked why, woman. Why did you wed him?"

Gillian clutched her hands in her lap. "I was given no choice in the matter, my lord. He offered for me and my father accepted."

"And when you learned of the offer, did you rejoice because you knew you would soon be wealthy?"

Right on the heels of the realization that she truly should be offended at Robin's question came another more startling revelation: Robin was just as concerned about Christopher's happiness as she was. She felt some of the tension ease from her and she even managed a small smile.

"In truth, I pleaded for my father not to send me here."

"For what reason?" Robin's expression hadn't softened any.

"I thought Christopher had horns."

A corner of the man's mouth twitched. "I see. And what did you do when you learned he didn't?"

"I fell in love with him."

"Before or after you knew his secret?"

Gillian lifted her finger to her eye with a questioning look. Robin nodded carefully.

"After."

For some reason, the answer seemed to please him. He relaxed back against the chair and a smile came to his lips. And then Gillian understood why Robin of Artane's smile alone was enough to set any queen's lady to swooning. His smile was pure mischief and she knew where Jason had come by his charm.

A tremendous crash made her jump and she jerked

around in her chair in time to see Christopher take down two men his size onto a bench that collapsed under their collective weight. Jason stood nearby, laughing heartily. Gillian would have risen, but Robin put his hand on her arm.

"Leave them."

"But they might hurt him! Who are those knaves?"

Robin's eyes twinkled merrily. "Those knaves, lady, are my two eldest boys."

Gillian was torn between embarrassment at having possibly offended the intimidating earl of Artane and worry that said earl's rambunctious children would injure her husband. And then Christopher caught a fistful of Jason's clothing and jerked him down into the fray. At least her husband wasn't being thrashed. Only slightly relieved, she turned back to her husband's guest and fought to ignore her blush.

"Forgive me, my lord. I meant nothing by it."

Robin waved aside her words. "As I have done nothing for months but listen to those two whine for me to pay a visit to Christopher, I can't help but agree with your assessment of their characters. Now, let us talk of something less tedious. You're seeing Christopher fed well?"

"Aye, my lord."

"And you bathe him now and then?"

Gillian couldn't stop her intense blush. She pulled at the neck of her gown, trying to ease her discomfort. Bathe Christopher? Though she had never been overfond of the practice, Christopher seemed to find it quite to his liking. But if Robin only had an inkling of the times Christopher had lured her into his bath and bathing had been the very last thing on his mind!

Robin chuckled. "Ah, say no more. I can plainly see that the lad's ears cannot help but be clean. Now, tell me of yourself. Blackmour agrees with you?"

"Very much, my lord. He is a wonderful man."

"Nay, child, I spoke of the keep. How do you like this dismal place?"

Gillian smiled reflexively. "'Tis the most wondrous place in England, I'm sure. Much finer than my father's hall."

"Saw you no other?"

She shook her head.

Robin smiled gently. "I'll have Christopher bring you to Artane for the Christmas feasts and you'll have aught else to compare this gloomy hole to."

"I like this gloomy hole," she insisted.

Robin laughed. "Ah, child, you are a fitting mate for him. Jason didn't exaggerate your fierceness. But you must come this winter just the same so you might see the place your lord passed his youth and the damage he wrought on my hall."

"I would like that very much," she admitted, "but I fear Christopher will not accept."

Robin was silent. He waited patiently, one eyebrow lifted in question.

"He won't leave Blackmour, you see," she said softly. "I fear he is very proud, my lord. Here he requires no aid, for he knows every stone and twig, but outside the gates . . ."

Robin nodded. "Say no more, Lady Gillian, for I understand well Christopher's pride. And," he added with a dry smile, "I can blame no one but myself for it, for I fear I encouraged it in the lad for many years. I daresay it has served him in the past and likely serves him well enough at present."

"Aye."

"But it doesn't do much to allow you to see much of England and you should. My family was fair bursting with curiosity about the child who had finally tamed the Dragon and I'll admit I was sent here for the express purpose of discovering the details." He laughed softly. "I could not refuse my lady her request, for she does love a good romance. Aye, you must come, simply so my womenfolk will leave me in peace. Leave Christopher to me.''

Gillian nodded, but she had the feeling Robin would be wasting his breath. Christopher wasn't a man to change his mind.

''Papa! Papa, did you see my lord? He bested Phillip and Kendrick both without breaking a sweat!''

Gillian watched Robin laugh as Jason bounded over, fair frothing at the mouth with boasts of Christopher's prowess. Robin caught Jason around the neck and pulled him down for a hearty kiss.

''Aye, I saw enough, young one. Fetch chairs for your lord's guests, Jason, and see to their comfort. Show me that Christopher has taught you something besides the finest swordplay south of Artane.''

''But 'tis just Kendrick and Phillip, Papa. Surely they can use the floor.''

''Jason!'' Christopher exclaimed, coming up behind him and trying to look stern. ''You will see to their comfort immediately. Remember, they are our guests—as unsavory a thought as that is.''

The two young men standing next to Christopher gave him slurs in return, but they were grinning as they did so. They were also sweating and looking rather rumpled. Gillian felt pride rise up in her breast. Artane's sons were as tall as Christopher, yet he had bested them both. She sat up a bit straighter in her chair.

Then she realized they were looking at her and her courage deserted her with a rush. They were likely pitying Christopher that he was saddled with a homely wife. Had she ever considered herself beautiful? Nay, she'd been a fool.

She rose, looking down and trying to hide behind her hair. ''I'll see to a meal,'' she mumbled.

Christopher caught her before she could move away. ''Nay, Jason will see to the like. You will see to me. These two curs think me a gelded stallion and I'll not have it.

I'm as untamed as the day you wed me, Gill, and you'll stay here and attest to the fact.''

"Christopher, please," she whispered.

"Gillian, what is it?"

If she could have died, she would have. It would have been preferable to the scene her husband was causing.

"I beseech you to let me go," she whispered frantically. "Please!"

"Why?" he whispered back.

Gillian felt all eyes in the room riveted on her. She leaned up and put her lips against Christopher's ear.

"I do not wish to shame you," she whispered hoarsely, tears burning her eyes.

"What is this?"

"I am not beautiful . . ."

Christopher wrapped his arm around her and drew her close, then cupped his hand against her ear. "Foolishness, Gill. You're very beautiful. And you've courage to equal mine. If I can face these souls, so can you."

He kissed her quickly, then turned her around and pulled her back against his chest, folding his arms over her shoulders.

"Lads, meet my lady, Gillian. Gill, one of these is Phillip, Robin's eldest and heir."

A dark-haired, gray-eyed younger image of Robin inclined his head.

"Lady Gillian."

The other young man grinned. "Just remember him as the fastidious one. The only reason Christopher bested us is because Phillip didn't want to muss his clothes."

Phillip threw an elbow to shut his sibling up and Christopher laughed at the second young man's strangled grunt.

"The objectionable one is Kendrick." He paused and Gillian watched him listen carefully for a moment or two. "I don't hear your shadow babbling flatteries to my serving wenches, Kendrick. Did he finally meet his end on some lord's gibbet?" he asked hopefully.

Kendrick only laughed. "Not as of yet, my lord. Royce is merely off roaming the countryside. He's too restless to make Blackmour his home for a few fortnights."

"A few fortnights?" Christopher choked. "Surely you have business elsewhere, lad, that will require your attention soon? Perhaps you and young Royce could hie yourselves off to the continent and make mischief there."

"But why ever would we want to do that?" Kendrick asked.

He wore the same look of innocence Gillian had seen on Jason's face a score of times. Now she knew where Christopher's squire had come by it.

"Your larder is well stocked enough for my tastes, I'm sure," Kendrick continued. "And the scenery here is the loveliest I've seen in months."

Gillian looked at her husband in time to see the fierce frown he threw Kendrick's way.

"Aye, 'tis most fair," Christopher said curtly, "and you'd do well not to admire it overmuch."

Gillian looked from her husband to Kendrick and back, but couldn't divine for the life of her why her husband was scowling and Kendrick was grinning. Perhaps Kendrick had made himself too much at home in Christopher's garden at some point in the past. She could well understand why her husband might be annoyed at possible future plundering of his herbs.

"As you can imagine, Gillian my love," Christopher said, with another dark look cast in Kendrick's direction, "Kendrick is the one who's given Robin all his gray hairs. Isn't that so, my lord?"

"Between you, Christopher, these two and Jason," Robin replied with a smile, "aye, I'd say I've earned all the white in my crown. At least you've found a lass to control you. Now if I could rid myself of Phillip and Kendrick in like manner, I might have some peace in my household."

"You'll never have it with Phillip's betrothed underfoot," Kendrick grinned. "Christopher, you should see the wench. I vow she's never had a wash, nor combed her hair. The only reason Phillip wants her is that she will bring him a rich holding."

"She's a fine woman," Phillip growled.

Kendrick threw back his head and laughed heartily. "Aye, if you could find her under all that filth! Saints, Phillip, her hall is such a sty, I daresay you'd misplace her and never run across her again. Not that you'd be there long enough to try. How long was it you managed to stay the last time? Two days before she had her guards toss you into the moat?"

Phillip shoved Kendrick, who backed up into Jason and almost upset the tray of cups he was carrying. Jason cursed his older brothers fluently, then presented himself to Christopher.

"Wine, my lord."

"And chairs?"

"Seen to, my lord."

Robin laughed. "I can't believe it, Christopher. My youngest lad has acquired manners."

"Aye, in spite of himself," Christopher said, taking his seat.

Gillian allowed Christopher to draw her down onto his lap and was grateful for his closeness. Conversing with men was not something that came easily to her, especially when the men were so intimidating.

Phillip was the spitting image of his father, both in word and movement. Kendrick was no less handsome than his brother, nor was he any less lordly. Jason had told her numerous stories about Kendrick's escapades, which always seemed to include some sort of conquest, be it in the bedchamber or on the battlefield. Looking at Kendrick's half grin as he listened to Phillip discuss his betrothed's holdings, she could readily believe either. But charming or not, she couldn't meet his eyes, nor Phillip's. They were uncharted territory and she had no idea how to, nay, not even the desire to speak to them and learn for herself if they would treat her poorly. Dangerous men were not something her wavering courage permitted her.

Then she realized the irony of it all. Dangerous men? Why, she was sitting in the lap of the most dangerous man in England. Oh, she'd heard stories about Robin of Artane. William had told her tales, and she'd heard her father and his men discuss Artane's prowess in battle. Their admiration had been grudgingly given, but given freely enough. Robin of Artane was a fierce warrior and a powerful lord. But he was, after all was said and done, merely a man.

Not like the Dragon of Blackmour.

Not a soul in England spoke of Christopher of Blackmour without crossing themselves. His reputation, his deeds, aye, even his very temper was reported to be black as night and fierce as Hellfire. His past triumphs might have equaled Robin's or they might have been lesser—it mattered not. He was Christopher of Blackmour, warlock extraordinaire, and there wasn't a soul who dared face him.

And there she sat, smack in the Dragon's lap, nestled as close to him as if he'd been a harmless pup.

The very thought made her breathe out a laugh.

"What are you smirking about, woman?" Christopher growled softly into her hair.

"Nothing at all, my lord," she whispered.

"I don't believe you."

She leaned up and pressed her cheek against his. "I was just thinking that I love you and I am glad to be yours. Not every woman in England can boast of spending an eve ensconced in Blackmour's arms."

"Nary a one save you," he said, a smile touching his lips.

"Enough," Kendrick drawled. "Woo your lady after we've supped, my lord. Seeing you holding such a comely maid makes me powerfully jealous of your good fortune and I'll likely need a great amount of food to soothe my injured feelings."

Phillip snorted. "You could likely find yourself a maid if you weren't such a bumbling idiot."

"Better an idiot than an affected bugger who can't leave his tent without a dozen glances in the mirror to see that his clothes are on straight."

Phillip lifted one eyebrow and looked at Christopher. "My lord, you don't mind a bit of blood on your floor, do you?"

"Never mind the mess," Kendrick retorted. "Phillip bleeds tidily."

Jason jumped out of the way as Phillip lunged and shoved Kendrick out of his chair. Christopher sighed.

"Robin, perhaps we should retire to the table now and let the children play. You'll find the fare to be edible enough. Gillian has taken charge of Cook and, believe me, he doesn't dare anger her."

Gillian fought her smile as Christopher purposefully stepped on Phillip on his way to the table.

"Oh, sorry, lad," Christopher said, straight-faced. "Didn't see you."

"You're next, Blackmour," Phillip vowed, panting. "Kendrick, you dolt, let me up! Father, disinherit this fool!"

Robin only laughed and leaned over Gillian's head to whisper conspiratorially to Christopher.

"Children," he stated. "May you have a dozen lads to torment you."

Gillian groaned before she could stop herself.

"Perhaps only half a dozen," Christopher said, with a wince.

Though as Gillian sat next to Christopher later and listened to the good-natured bickering that went on between Jason and his brothers, she found the idea of so many sons for her husband to be not a bad thing at all.

twenty-six

CHRISTOPHER PULLED THE TUNIC DOWN OVER HIS HEAD, then indulged in a hearty stretch. He'd spent far too much time at the table last eve, talking to Robin about the state of affairs in England and doing his best to ignore Kendrick and Phillip's squabbling. The lads were both older than a score each, but somehow they managed to irritate each other as thoroughly and competently as only two young children could. Christopher couldn't truly blame them overmuch, as their father and uncles had set the example for them, fighting one minute and laughing together the next. Christopher shook his head. Life at Artane was never commonplace.

"Are you off then, my lord?"

Christopher turned in the direction of his lady's voice and smiled at her. "Aye, Gill. I daresay Cook has prepared something quite edible this morn. Shall we go down?"

"Ah . . . I think I'll be along later."

Christopher paused, surprised by the hesitancy in her voice. He walked over to her, then reached out to touch her.

"Are you unwell?"

"Nay, my lord. 'Tis merely that I have a pair of things that need my immediate attention."

He frowned. "And those things would be?"

"Ah, several things. Most pressing and noteworthy."

To be sure, he couldn't bring anything pressing to mind. They had enjoyed a lengthy interlude of marital bliss earlier that morn. Then he'd spent a goodly amount of time telling her how pleased he'd been by her courage in facing Robin by herself. Short of remaining bolted in their chamber with him, Christopher couldn't think of anything else that would require more of her attentions than breaking her fast would.

And then he understood. Obviously the thought of seeing their guests unnerved her still.

"Ah, Gillian, my love," he said softly, pulling her into his arms, " 'tis only Robin and his lads."

"Aye, my lord, I know."

She patted his back, as if she wanted to be soon finished with the conversation and have him be on his way.

"Robin wasn't unkind to you last eve, was he?"

"Nay, my lord." She patted him some more.

"You've nothing to fear from them, my love."

"Aye, I know it," she said, her voice quavering just the slightest bit. "Best be off to the table, husband, before Artane thinks you've slighted him."

Christopher leaned his cheek against her hair and smiled to himself. "Let him think what he likes. I daresay I'd rather spend my time with you. Perhaps I'll send Jason to fetch us something to eat and we'll both remain here."

"Oh, Christopher, nay," she said, sounding shocked. "You couldn't disappoint him thusly."

"He's not the king, Gillian. He's just a man."

"Of course, my lord." More patting ensued. "Run along now. I'll follow in time."

He pressed his lips against her hair. "Then you'll leave me to go down and face them alone?" he murmured.

She turned him toward the doorway. "Aye," she said, without hesitation. "Off with you."

"As you wish then, my love. But you'll be down soon, aye?"

"Aye, my lord. Soon enough."

"After you've given your important items their due attentions?"

"Er . . . aye, Christopher. Make haste, that I might begin my labors."

Christopher was tempted to force her to come with him, then thought better of it. He quit the chamber before his lady wife ejected him bodily. He smiled to himself, but the smile felt pained. He would fetch her later in the day, after she'd had a chance to work herself up to meet the challenge. After all, if she could face Cook and come away victorious, she could surely best Robin. She had no inkling of what a soft heart Robin possessed.

Perhaps he would do well to tell her of it. Indeed, perhaps he would spend much of the afternoon seeing to it. It would give him a perfect reason to excuse himself from his guests and pass the remainder of the day with his wife alone in their bedchamber. Robin had already deprived him of one afternoon tryst. Christopher had no intentions of missing out on another.

He made his way down the passageway, then stopped at the top of the stairs. What he wanted was to thump down them with his normal haste, but he thought better of it. The last thing he wanted was to take a tumble and wind up sprawled at Robin's feet. So, he very carefully descended, but with his head held high and his shoulders back.

He heard the scrape of wood against stone the moment his foot touched the great hall floor.

"My lord," Jason said, coming immediately to him, "my father and brothers are awaiting your pleasure."

"And have been for some time," Robin called, "but we've made do. You've become a late riser, my lad."

Christopher heard Colin choke, and he wished he'd been just that much closer to his brother-in-law so as to continue to silence him once he recovered his breath.

"I had things to see to," Christopher said, coming to take his seat next to Robin. "Most pressing items that needed my complete attention." He shoved a cup at Colin. "Drink, man. And once you can breathe again, keep drinking. I daresay I've no stomach for what I'm sure you intend to say."

"My lord," Jason said, from behind him, "where is the lady Gillian? Shall we wait for her?"

"She'll be along after a bit. Best prod Cook to put forth his creations now."

"Is Gillian unwell?" Robin asked.

Christopher shook his head. "Nay, not unwell." He smiled faintly. "Shy, perhaps."

"Ah," Robin said, "I see."

Christopher leaned back against the chair and looked in Robin's direction. "Do you, my lord?" he asked softly.

Robin was silent for a moment. "Perhaps I don't, Christopher. Last night your lady seemed to have little stomach for guests, but I assumed 'twas because she hadn't had much experience with the like. Warewick kept her quite sheltered, didn't he?"

"Aye," Christopher said grimly, "as sheltered as you would a prisoner."

"Surely he was simply protecting her."

Christopher shook his head. "You saw William's scars. Gillian suffered in his stead after he left to page."

"Merciful saints above," Robin whispered.

"Say nothing, Robin. It would only distress her."

"Damn him," Robin muttered. "I can hardly think of him without reaching for my blade."

"Neither can I," Christopher said. "If I could slay the man and be done with him, I would."

"Has he troubled you since you took Gillian to wife?"

"Only once," Christopher said. "He sent a messenger

to see how she fared and to announce his impending arrival. I daresay the words I sent back disabused him of that notion soon enough.''

''If I'd known yestereve, I wouldn't have growled at her so,'' Robin said, sounding rather apologetic.

Christopher smiled. ''She survived well enough. It will take a day or two, but she'll accustom herself to you and the lads. She seems to have misplaced her courage at the moment, but she'll find it again.''

Colin elbowed him in the ribs. He was obviously eavesdropping again. ''Tell Artane how she drew Jason's blade,'' he said, chewing vigorously, ''and threatened to stick Cook with it. A damned fine showing, if you ask me. The fare has certainly been better since.''

''Indeed,'' Robin said. ''Do not let us distract you from the full enjoyment of it, my lord Berkhamshire. I daresay you're showing me more of your pleasure than I care to see.''

Christopher smiled into his cup at Colin's muttering. Robin never passed up an opportunity to irritate Colin. There was surely more to the story, but Christopher had never asked for the entire tale. One of Colin's uncles had had Robin's death on his mind for a time, but things seemed to have turned out well enough. Perhaps Robin merely strove to repay the entire Berkhamshire clan for having troubled him at all.

''Will she descend later?'' Robin asked. ''I give you my word not to grieve her further.''

''I've no doubt she will,'' Christopher said.

''The lads will leave her be also,'' Robin added. ''Won't you, sons?''

Kendrick and Phillip chorused their assent, though Kendrick's agreement seemed a little less enthusiastically given than his brother's. Christopher threw Kendrick a warning look just on principle. The saints only knew what the whelp would interpret his father's meaning to be.

''Your sire meant to say,'' Christopher said, suddenly

deciding he should clarify his position on the matter, "that you likely should give her a wide berth, lads."

"But—" Kendrick began.

"A *wide* berth," Christopher repeated. "You, my little lord Kendrick, should no doubt be *especially* careful that you don't grieve her. I shudder to think what might become of you else."

"Hmmm," was Kendrick's only reply.

Christopher growled, then felt Robin's hand come to rest on his shoulder.

"I'll see to it," Robin said.

"If you value the child's life, I daresay you should."

Robin only laughed. "I'm sure he'll take your warning to heart, Christopher. Now, let us speak of something less perilous. Tell me how you've fared of late. How went the planting this year?"

These were tidings Christopher could relate easily enough. He talked and answered questions until his meal was finished. It gave him pleasure to tell Robin of the prosperity of his holdings, likely because Robin had been the one to teach him how to see to them. Christopher had been an apt pupil and his lands showed as much.

By the time Colin had slurped and gulped his way through his meal, Christopher had exhausted all the details he could give of the present workings of the keep. Robin seemed eager to see things for himself, so Christopher rose to oblige him. He had the feeling Gillian wouldn't come down until the lads had quit the hall anyway, so there was little sense in remaining at the table.

Colin held him back as the Artane lads made their way to the doorway.

"I'll wait to look after her, if you like," Colin offered gruffly, "so you can see to His Lordship. 'Tisn't meet I should show him about the place in your stead."

"Aye," Christopher agreed reluctantly. "Perhaps you could suggest she come find me when she descends."

"Aye."

"And keep those lads well away from her."

"With pleasure."

Christopher nodded, then walked away. He would have sooner spent his time with his wife than showing his former master things he could no longer see, but politeness demanded otherwise. Odd, how things had changed. A year ago, he wouldn't have believed he could feel thusly. Gillian had indeed wrought a mighty change in him.

"Christopher, are you with us?" Robin called from the doorway.

Perhaps Robin's advancing years would insist he take a small rest soon. Christopher nodded to himself over that thought. Robin would have a rest and Christopher could sequester himself in his garden with his lady and enjoy her sweet ministrations.

"Christopher?"

"Coming," Christopher said, starting toward the hall door. "Let us make haste, my lord. I vow you're beginning to sound rather weary."

GILLIAN CREPT DOWN THE STAIRS WITH GREAT STEALTH. She hadn't heard any voices from the top of the stairwell, but that meant nothing. Like as not, Lord Robin and his lads were having their fill of the morning's repast and could not speak for their eating of it.

She peeked out into the great hall. To her immense relief, 'twas empty. Perhaps all the men had gone out to the lists for the morning. If she were clever enough, she could slip down the way and out the front gates without being marked. A pity she hadn't chosen something more manly than skirts to wear. She could have tucked her hair into her tunic and passed herself off as a lad if she'd been thinking.

Ah, well, there was no time for regrets now. She had to act, and soon. She hadn't thought another trip to the village would be necessary, but she hadn't planned on Jason's kin, either.

She opened the great hall door and looked out. No sign of her husband or his guests. That boded well. She left the great hall and ran down the steps. Perhaps it would be easier than she'd anticipated.

Gaining the inner curtain gate was easily accomplished. She then slipped through the tunnel and out into the sunshine on the other side. Then she paused. She could see Christopher and Robin walking down the way to the outer wall. There was no sign of Phillip or Kendrick. Gillian chewed on her lip. That made things more difficult. It wasn't as if she could flee past her husband and his guest without saying a word. 'Twas clear she would have to wait until they'd turned aside to the lists before she could continue on her way.

It didn't take as long as she'd feared. She watched Christopher lead Robin off to the right toward the training field. Praying Robin wouldn't turn and see her hastening toward the outer gates, she put her foot to the path and started on her way.

"Ahem," a voice said sternly, from behind her. "And where would you be off to, my lady?"

Gillian sighed. She should have known Colin would be lurking about. She turned to face him. "I'm out to take some healthful air."

He grunted, wearing an expression that said he doubted as much. "You've plenty of it about you."

Gillian set her jaw. "I fear, my lord, that there simply isn't enough here."

"And I say there is," he said, folding his arms over his chest. "Indeed, I would suggest that you've had more than enough healthful air for the moment. You've no need to traipse down to the village for more."

Gillian sighed. Colin had a look about him that warned her he would be rather difficult about the whole affair. 'Twas obvious he wouldn't simply allow her to go alone . . . but—

"Perhaps you'd care to come with me," she said suddenly. Surely he couldn't refuse such an offer. "I'm certain Berengaria would be happy to see you."

Colin scowled. "Like as not, they'd press some undrinkable potion upon me and spell me into downing it."

"And would that be such an ill thing?"

"Depends upon who is stirring the pot."

Gillian could not help but smile. "I suppose there is truth in that. Poor Magda."

"At least she hasn't come to the keep, demanding to assist Cook in the kitchens," he said darkly.

"Cook would never survive it," she agreed. "I think it would be more amusing, though, to see him go at it with Nemain."

"By the saints!" Colin exclaimed, shuddering. "I wouldn't touch another morsel at the table if I knew she was anywhere near a cooking fire. Now," he said, frowning down at her, "why don't you run off and see to Christopher? I daresay he missed you at the table this morn."

But Christopher was walking with Robin. She shook her head.

"He's far too occupied at present," she said, feeling her breath begin to come in gasps, "with his important guests."

"Bah," Colin said, waving a dismissive hand, " 'tis only Artane."

Gillian shook her head vigorously. "I couldn't."

"You managed the feat last eve."

"Barely."

Colin opened his mouth to say something, then shut it. Then he merely stared at her for several moments in silence. Gillian watched him study her and wondered if he was coming to agree with her assessment of her own failing courage.

"Is it Robin," Colin asked, "or his lads?"

Gillian looked at Robin, who walked alone with her husband. She stared at the man and turned over in her mind her memories of last eve. Robin certainly hadn't used her ill. Indeed, once he'd discovered that she loved Christopher in truth, he'd become quite cheerful. And, if she were careful, she could sidle up to her husband, take his hand and perhaps avoid attracting all that much of Robin's notice. Aye, that she could do. She stood up a bit straighter.

"I can manage Artane," she announced, dredging up more courage.

Colin grunted. "Then manage him. I'll go down to fetch something to aid you with the lads. *If* you scamper off right now and see to your lord."

Gillian looked at him in surprise. "Truly?"

"Aye," he muttered.

"You don't mind?"

"Nay," he said, even more gruffly.

"Ah," she said, suddenly understanding. "I see."

"You see nothing," Colin grumbled at her.

"Of course," Gillian said, inclining her head. "And I know it isn't as if you truly *wish* to ingest any more beauty herbs."

Colin only scowled. "Off with you, child. I won't go until I see you making good on your part of the bargain."

Gillian started across the field toward Christopher, smiling. 'Twas obvious Colin had volunteered so as to have a taste of whatever was on the fire at the moment. For a man who claimed not to believe in witches, he certainly was eager to visit a trio of them.

She felt a laugh bubble up inside her. Someday she would have to sit down with Berengaria and discuss men and their tender hearts—and their vanity. To think the fierce Colin of Berkhamshire was ready to venture down to a witch's hut merely to drink all manner of things to improve his aspect. What a tale!

"Pray, lady, tell us what brings forth such a joyous sound from you," a voice said from behind her, "that we might inspire it in you again."

Gillian whirled around, her hand to her throat. Kendrick and Phillip stood not three paces from her. Gillian felt her

breath come in gasps and she thought she just might faint.
Why, she hadn't even heard them come up behind her. Yet
there they stood, looking at her full in the face, waiting
for her to respond.

What she wanted to do was turn tail and flee the other
way. Her feet, though, seemed to be rooted to the spot.

"My lady," Phillip said, a frown creasing his fair brow,
"are you unwell?"

Kendrick elbowed him in the ribs. "We've given her a
fright, dolt." He dropped to his knees in the dirt, jerking
his brother down with him. "Lady Gillian, we mean you
no harm," he said, looking up at her intently. "We merely
heard the sound of your lovely laughter and could not bear
the thought of hearing no more of it. Will you not forgive
our rudeness in coming upon you unannounced and yet
again grace us with such a heavenly sound?" He clasped
his hands together in a gesture of pleading.

And then he smiled at her.

Gillian took a pace backward in spite of herself. Where
these Artane lads had come by such smiles was a mystery.
'Twas no wonder Jason had a handful of castle maids
mooning over him at any given moment. He would no
doubt find himself just as handsome as his brother when
he reached a score of years. Kendrick had a smile that
could certainly turn a woman's reasoning to mush.

Gillian paused and considered that. To be sure, Kendrick's smile should have turned her own thinking into
something akin to gruel; yet she found herself in complete
control of her faculties. She leaned her head to one side
and studied the young lord from Artane. He was indeed
very fair of face. His eyes were a most interesting shade
of green. Ah, and then there was the little mark in his
cheek that appeared when he smiled. She folded her arms
over her chest and continued to look down at him. A most
beautiful young man, yet she found herself unaffected.

She turned her attentions to his brother. He looked much
like his sire, save his expression was far more sober. His

hair was a shade darker than his brother's, and his eyes were a steely gray. Gillian suspected he would look very much like his sire when he attained Robin's years. Already she could see how his broad shoulders were preparing themselves to take on the future burden of his father's title. Despite his preening, Phillip was a man to be reckoned with and would be a most imposing lord in his turn.

Gillian stood, silently contemplating the two powerful young men who knelt in the dirt at her feet. By all accounts, she should have been made giddy by the very fact that they paid her any heed at all. Even had that failed, their combined beauty should have rendered her speechless and caused an abrupt loss of her wits.

But, somehow, she remained quite unmoved.

She realized, with a start, that she simply preferred the snarling and snapping of the Dragon of Blackmour.

Just as suddenly, another revelation occurred to her. She had not only faced Christopher of Blackmour and lived to tell the tale; she had won his love. What could she possibly have to fear from these lads whose smiles were pleasing enough, but left her knees steady beneath her?

She clasped her hands behind her back and inclined her head at them.

"My lords, I fear I cannot indulge you in more laughter at present, though I regret the grief this will no doubt cause you. I must seek out my lord, for I daresay he wonders where I have gotten myself to." She smiled at them. "One doesn't deny him his whims."

"Indeed," Kendrick said, leaping to his feet. "Then allow me to escort you to him immediately, my lady."

"Nay, I will," Phillip said, rising and dusting off his knees. "If you will permit me, Lady Gillian—"

"You are betrothed, fool," Kendrick said, shoving Phillip out of the way and extending his arm toward Gillian.

"And she's wed!" Phillip exclaimed, jerking Kendrick's arm away.

Kendrick only ignored his brother and extended his bent

arm again. He smiled down at her. Gillian smiled in return. Indeed, she was so surprised at the ease with which she did so that she smiled again.

"My lady," Kendrick said, quietly, "the gift of your smile is one I will treasure always."

Gillian put her hand on his arm and felt quite at ease. "Why, my lord," she said, touched by his gallantry, "you are indeed a very sweet boy."

"Boy?" Kendrick repeated. He suddenly went very red in the face.

Phillip shouted with laughter from behind them. Gillian looked behind her to see Artane's heir doubled over, guffawing. She looked back at Kendrick, almost curious enough to ask what had tickled his brother so. But before she could speak, Kendrick made her a low bow.

"My lady, I have a small matter to see to. If you might take a few steps away, then wait for me? I will be at liberty to escort you very soon."

Gillian nodded and walked several paces away. Phillip's laughter ceased abruptly. She turned to determine what had become of him, but all she could see was a very great cloud of dust. Ah, a display of brotherly affection. But such a violent one! 'Twas little wonder Robin had acquired so many white hairs. His lads certainly gave vent to their emotions with little provocation.

She wondered if it would be rude to leave them to their play. There was certainly no sign they intended to cease with it any time soon.

She shrugged and began to walk. And then she froze in midstep. She put her foot down and simply stood, taking in the realization.

She had faced Kendrick and Phillip.

With her own unaugmented store of courage.

She paused and considered her actions from all angles. Aye, she had confronted them unflinchingly. She had spoken with strange lords and lived to tell of it. Why, she hadn't cowered once!

She strode forward, inordinately pleased with herself. Indeed, now she regretted having sent Colin on his errand, for she fancied she needed no more herbs for courage.

She espied her husband standing some distance away from her, talking to Lord Robin. Gillian put her shoulders back. She would perhaps even go so far as to apologize to Lord Robin for not having been at the table that morn. She had best do it while her courage flowed through her veins like strong wine.

She smiled as she walked across the field. She had encountered Artane's lads and bested them! What a tale to tell Berengaria the next time she saw her.

"I'll see to her," a voice growled from behind her.

"Nay, I will!"

"Phillip, lad, you've a tear in your tunic—oof!"

Gillian looked over her shoulder in time to see Phillip plant his fist quite firmly in Kendrick's middle. Robin's second son bent over with a gasp. Gillian paused and waited for Phillip to limp over to her. She refrained from remarking about the bloody knee that showed through his torn hose. After all, the lad did pride himself on his tidiness.

Phillip stopped at her side and bowed. Then he held out his sleeve.

"Ah, forgive me," he said, pulling his arm back. He dusted off the cloth, then extended his arm again. "If you will permit me, my lady, to see you safely to your lord?"

Gillian looked him over. There was dust in his dark hair, too, but she decided against telling him as much. And there was surely no sense in commenting on his rapidly swelling eye.

"How gallant you are, my lord," she said, bestowing her second-best smile on him. She would reserve her finest for her husband. He wouldn't be able to see it, but perhaps Robin would be good enough to describe it for him. Gillian put her hand on Phillip's arm.

He led her off and she went, surprised at how simple a thing it was. She hadn't taken ten paces when she heard the sound of someone approaching from her other side. She looked over to find Kendrick limping alongside her. He seemed quite incapable of straightening up all the way, but he held out his dusty sleeve just the same.

"Take it, I beg you," he wheezed.

"Well, I do have two hands," she said, slowly. She placed her right hand on his torn sleeve, avoiding the bleeding scrape on his skin. His hair was even dustier, if possible, than Phillip's. He had obviously come out worse for the wear from their little friendly tussle.

As Gillian made her way in a stately manner across the lists, she marveled at what a fine morn it had been. Though the day had started off less than splendidly, it had certainly shaped up nicely.

She looked up and found that Colin was trotting across the field toward Christopher. He must have traveled quite swiftly to have reached the village and come back in such a short time. Perhaps he hadn't stayed for anything to drink.

She watched as he and Robin talked to Christopher, and wished she could have heard what they were telling him. Christopher's expression, even at that distance, gave nothing away.

But by the time she reached her husband, she could tell he was fighting his smile. Colin had his elbow resting on Christopher's shoulder and his hand over his own mouth. Perhaps she was mistaken and Magda had indeed pressed something rather charred upon him during his visit. Then she looked at the lord of Artane and found him to be smiling fondly at her. She hastily tested her courage and found it steady beneath her; she looked at Robin and returned his smile.

"My lord Christopher," Kendrick croaked, "your lady is safely delivered to you."

Christopher's mouth twitched. "I understand you had a rather rough time of it, lad."

Kendrick could only groan. Gillian watched as Colin's eyes began to water. She frowned at him.

"Drank you something amiss?" she demanded.

He only held out a pouch of leather and dropped it into her hand.

"There you are, my lady," Colin said, coming out from behind his hand and shaking his head slowly, "though I daresay you won't have need of them. Best give them to Artane's lads." And then he started to laugh. He turned and walked away, still giving vent to his mirth.

Gillian watched as he finally reached the bailey wall. She frowned. He had doubled over and fallen to the ground.

"Christopher, I fear Colin has ingested something foul," she noted. "He seems quite overcome."

Her husband reached out and drew her into his arms. He was chuckling.

"Ah, Gill," he said, with another laugh, "you are a treasure." He lifted her face up and kissed her softly. "You have made wrecks of us all." He smiled down at her. "Your pressing matters are attended to, my love?"

"Most satisfactorily, my lord."

"Then will you not remain by my side today?"

Gillian only held him more tightly. "I would be nowhere else, my lord."

"That's one hand taken care of," Kendrick said faintly, "but there's yet another to be seen to. If I might offer my own humble self—"

"Nay, I will," Phillip interrupted. "My sleeve is far cleaner."

"It won't be for long," Kendrick growled.

Robin began to laugh. Gillian looked up at him from the shelter of her husband's arms.

"My lord," she said, "I fear these lads of yours are given overmuch to displays of affection."

Robin only shook his head, grinning. "You have made fools of my sons, lady. And now that you have made your conquests for the morn, perhaps you would see to your lord whilst we take a turn about the lists? He is most impossible without your gentling influence."

"I am never impossible," Christopher corrected. "Move out of my way, Kendrick. Here, Gillian, don't step on them while they're rolling about in the dirt. Nay, Robin, I am fierce and untamed, but never impossible."

"Impossible and stubborn," Robin insisted, nudging Phillip out of his path rather ungently with his foot. "Do you not remember the time you refused to come in from the lists in that driving storm—"

Gillian listened to the conversation going on over her head and soon found herself walking between the two men, her hands on their arms. She couldn't help but smile. Here she was, strolling between the Dragon of Blackmour and Robin of Artane, two of the fiercest men in England, and she felt nothing but pleasure in the sunshine and their company.

And she'd managed the feat by herself.

It had been a most noteworthy morn.

twenty-seven

CHRISTOPHER LEANED BACK AGAINST THE BAILEY WALL and scowled. Saints, what a fortnight! Much as he loved Robin, he was to the point of admitting he was heartily sick of all his guests. Especially Robin's sons. He'd passed the greater part of the past two weeks listening to Kendrick and Phillip fight over who would either sit next to Gillian, or sing to her, or escort her here or there. The only benefit to all the skirmishing was that the lads kept each other so busy fighting that they hadn't had much time to stir up mischief.

A pity the lads couldn't have finished each other off at some point in the past se'nnight. It would have surely saved him his current aggravation.

"Your horse, my lord," a page said, interrupting his thoughts. "Do you not wish to mount now? Lord Kendrick seems to grow restive as he waits."

"No doubt," Christopher said, swinging up into the saddle.

As much as Christopher would have liked to lay the blame for what he faced presently on Kendrick, he knew it rested squarely with Colin. He should have made certain Colin's plate was fuller that morn. If the man had been working his way through larger portions, he likely would have had less time for making polite conversation. And it was just such polite babble that had led to Robin's discovery that Christopher had been jousting.

And once Colin had spewed that detail forth, he seemingly hadn't been able to restrain himself from suggesting that perhaps Robin might wish to see the feat himself.

Christopher reached down and rubbed his stallion's neck to soothe him. At least Jason was keeping Gillian occupied. No sense in being humiliated before his former master *and* his wife all in one morning.

If he'd had a choice, he would have been strolling along the seashore with his lady. Had he been feeling particularly generous, he might have invited Robin to come along. The lads too, as long as they maintained a decent following distance of several hundred paces.

"Christopher?" Colin called.

Christopher muttered a curse under his breath. He'd done such a fine job of staying out of the lists over the past pair of weeks. He'd distracted Robin with the details of running the hall, with the improvements made in the village, and with an afternoon or two walking along the strand with Gillian. In truth, he couldn't deny that he enjoyed sitting in front of the fire in the great hall, doing nothing more than conversing with his former lord over inconsequential matters. It was during those times he almost forgot about his lack of sight and the things he'd lost. Pleasant speech with Robin, and Gillian's hand in his—what more could he want?

"Saints, man, wake up!" Colin said irritably.

In answer, Christopher lifted his lance.

Colin called the start. Christopher was less than enthusiastic over the fact that he was facing Kendrick, but the whelp had been determined. Phillip he could have managed, but Kendrick was definitely more his father's son in matters of warring. Even had he still possessed his sight, he might have been led to break a sweat unhorsing Artane's son. Blinded, 'twas another matter entirely.

"I'll fetch some wine!" Colin bellowed.

Wine in a cup in the right hand—Christopher hardly had to think about the signals anymore. He moved his lance immediately to the right and down.

Christopher heard the impact before he felt it, and he definitely heard Kendrick's hearty curses. He fancied he'd heard Robin's gasp as well.

"Again," Colin called from the wall.

"Damn," Christopher muttered. He rode to the end of the lists and let the black turn them about on his own.

"My lord, another lance," one of his men said from his right.

Christopher tossed aside the broken lance he held and grasped the new one. He balanced it in his hand and waited, feeling even less pleased about his immediate future than he had before the last pass.

Colin called the start again. Christopher set his heels to his mount and the stallion leaped forward. He lowered his lance as if he could actually see where he intended it should go. Colin said nothing, so Christopher knew he was close to the mark.

"Shield up!" Colin blurted out.

Christopher lifted his shield higher but kept his lance trained where it had been. The impact almost knocked him from his horse.

"By the saints!" Robin exclaimed.

Christopher wheeled his mount around and waited for word.

"He's down!" Colin called, sounding inordinately pleased.

Christopher turned his mount toward Colin's voice and trusted the black to stop before he plowed into anyone, for he had no more stomach for concentrating.

"Well done, Christopher!" Robin said.

Christopher felt Robin take the reins. He dismounted while his ego was still intact. He found himself grasped by the shoulders and shaken vigorously. It had to be Robin doing the like. Only Robin would wrench him about as if he were again a lad of twelve summers.

"Did you watch, Berkhamshire?" Robin demanded. "I trained this lad, you know. A bloody fine job I did, if you're curious."

"I wasn't," Colin grumbled.

Robin only laughed and gave Christopher another shake. "Saints, Christopher, but you've lost none of your skill. I couldn't have chosen better for my son."

Christopher sighed. "A pity all he can do is watch me fight the air."

"'Tis enough," Robin said. "I'm more than content with what he can learn with his eyes alone."

Christopher couldn't help but feel relief at the praise, for there were times he truly wondered if Jason wouldn't have been better off with someone else.

"Aye," Robin said, "you've made a fine showing this morn. And, Chris," he added, his voice suddenly quiet, "I wouldn't have known the difference, if I'd been a stranger to you and your trial."

Christopher felt a rush of pride sweep through him. There was no pity in Robin's voice; there was only wonder and satisfaction. Perhaps it hadn't been a wasted morn after all.

"Thank you, my lord," he said, just as softly. "I have trained hard to accomplish the feat."

"I've no doubt you have, lad."

"There are times I don't succeed," Christopher admitted.

He heard Robin's soft chuckle. "Well, lad, if the truth were to be told, there are times I don't succeed either. But I tend not to speak overmuch of them."

"I shouldn't think you would."

Robin only laughed. "Ah, Chris, I do miss you. Come, leave your mail behind and let us seek out your lady and pass the rest of our day pleasantly. We've had enough of warfare this morn. Here, careful that you don't step on Kendrick."

"Thank you, Father," Kendrick gasped. "What I need is a hand up, if you don't mind."

"Ask your brother. Christopher and I are off to find his lady."

"Wait for me!" Kendrick called after them.

"Can't," Robin called back cheerfully.

Christopher smiled in spite of himself. "You have a cruel streak, my lord."

"Thank you," Robin said, sounding as if he were smiling. "I do what I can to torment my children. They've already wrought their work on me. Now, where do you suppose your lady is keeping herself?"

"The saints only know," Christopher said, "but we'll find her soon enough."

Though he doubted it could be soon enough. An ache welled up in his heart, a desire to see her that was suddenly so strong that it stole his breath. Saints, but he hadn't passed enough of his time with Gillian. He'd hardly been able to, what with Kendrick and Phillip slobbering over her like hungry hounds. He frowned. Perhaps it was time Robin returned to Artane, before something happened to his heir and second son.

GILLIAN CAST A CAUTIOUS GLANCE ABOUT HER, THEN looked back at Jason. "You're certain?" she asked. "No one will see?"

Jason shook his head. "Nay, lady."

"But what if your sire comes from the lists?"

"My lady, he will not. Have you ever seen him in the garden?"

Gillian fingered the hilt of the wooden sword. "Nay," she agreed slowly. Perhaps she would indeed have privacy for training.

Jason had caught her pretending to slay her father in the tower chamber a pair of months earlier and had immediately volunteered to train with her. After the first day, when she hadn't been able to lift her arms to feed herself because of the soreness, she'd almost quit. After all, training with a substantial opponent was far different than sparring against air—no matter how vividly she imagined that air to be her formidable sire.

In the end, she'd reasoned that training with Jason was almost like training with Christopher himself and that had finished thoughts of ceasing. If nothing else, she might be able to guard Christopher's back if the need arose.

"Now, you must come at me truly," he announced. "I vow, my lady, that you've been overly kind these last few days." He lifted his sword and beckoned with the other hand. "Pretend you are irritated with me."

Gillian smiled. "Oh, but I never am, Jason. You're a very sweet boy."

Jason scowled. "I'm no boy, lady. In a few years I'll have my spurs and be a man indeed. Now, come. My lord has no trouble feigning irritation with me."

Gillian blinked. "I daresay he feigns nothing."

Jason only laughed. "No doubt, my lady." He reached out and slapped her blade lightly. "Now, what did we practice yesterday?"

"Controlled fury."

"Aye," Jason stated in a fine imitation of Christopher, "and you are far from having mastered it. You don't know that such a skill will save your life someday. I know it has saved my lord's. My sire's too," he added. "Let us begin."

Gillian gripped the sword in both hands and fended off Jason's very tame attack. He held the wooden sword with one hand, as if it weighed nothing. Then again, compared to a true blade, it likely seemed naught. Though Jason's sword wasn't so heavy she couldn't lift it with relative ease, it was a far sight more substantial than a wooden blade. Christopher's sword was even heavier than Jason's. Though Gillian could lift it, it was far from being balanced for her hand. Christopher wielded it with ease. It must have taken him years to build the muscles necessary to use such a weapon—

"Ouch!" she exclaimed. The mark the flat of Jason's blade had left on her arm stung.

"That was for dreaming. Do so in a real battle and you'll feel no pain at all because your head will be resting on the ground beside your crumpled form. Now, again."

Feeling irritation was no trouble for her now. She found herself for the first time actually taking the offensive. Jason's look of bored patience didn't leave his face. That only irritated her the more. She swung wildly, wanting nothing more than to rid him of his look.

The next thing she knew, her sword was on the ground, Jason had spun her around by the shoulders and the flat of his blade was pressed against her throat.

"You're dead," he said grimly. "Lady Gillian, you let your passion get the best of you. If you must feel, let it be fury and let it be controlled!" He backed away and gestured to her fallen sword. "Fetch it and let us begin again."

"I don't have to do this," she muttered.

"Quitting would be . . . cowardly," Jason finished slowly.

Gillian flipped her blade up with her foot, her eyes not leaving Jason's. She glared at him.

"Wisely done, lady." He made her a small bow. "Think of me as someone you would like dead and let me see if all these hours have been wasted or not. Does anyone come to mind—"

Gillian didn't let him finish. Somehow, at her fingertips, lay all the anger she'd ever felt for her sire. First the fury made her shake; then it passed, leaving her feeling as hard and sharp as Christopher's deadly blade. Everything she'd ever learned from William and all that she'd learned from Jason in the past two odd months came to her clearly. She went at her husband's squire calmly, as if she'd done the like every day for the past score of years. The sword became light in her hands and she wielded it with skill she didn't know she had.

She pretended Jason was her father. She laughed grimly the first time Jason didn't jump quickly enough and the blunted edge of her blade caught him under the ribs. She followed that up with an attack that left him stumbling backward. Pressing her advantage, she continued to push him back until he was stopped by a wall. She sucked in air, savoring a heady feeling of victory. She put the dull point of the wooden blade to his throat.

"You're dead, little lad," she said, with a grin.

Jason's eyes were wider than she'd ever seen them, he was sweating and he was speechless—a condition she'd never expected to find him in.

Then she realized Jason wasn't backed up against a wall; he was backed up against his father. She looked up and met Robin of Artane's gray eyes. He looked as surprised as his son.

So did Colin, Kendrick and Phillip, who were standing in a perfectly formed line next to Robin.

It was Gillian's turn to be speechless. Color flooded to her face and she would have given anything to have been able to hide amongst the herbs and disappear from those warriors' scrutiny.

"Merciful saints above, Chris," Colin whispered in awe, "she just bested your squire."

Gillian's eyes flew to Christopher's face. He stood next to Colin, his expression inscrutable. She dropped her sword and hurried to him.

"My lord," she began softly, "I'm sorry—"

Christopher grabbed her by the waist and lifted her up high into the air, laughing as he did it.

"Aye, you should be! Saints, Gill, the boy will likely never recover from such a thrashing." He set her back down, kissed her hard on the mouth and laughed again. "Did you see that, lads?"

"Amazing," Phillip said.

"Beyond belief," Kendrick said. "I want to train with her next. Phillip, wait your turn like a good lad. Here, Jason, help me off with this mail, then give me your sword. Let us see if our sweet Gillian can best us all this afternoon."

Gillian put her arms around Christopher and held on. She pressed her face hard against his chest and would have crawled inside his clothes if she'd been able, for she had no desire to face any more of the Artane brothers over blades. Christopher, though, was actually trying to pry her away.

"Go on, Gill," Christopher whispered. "I for one would like to see Kendrick humiliated."

"But I didn't humiliate anyone," she protested.

"Nay," Jason said, recovering his powers of speech, "but you bested me fairly. Here, we'll bind Kendrick's right hand to his waist and make him fight with the left. Aye, I'll wager a piece of gold on you, Lady Gillian." He laughed. "I daresay you could take him should he fight with the right!"

Kendrick shoved his brother. "Christopher won't mind if I thrash you for your cheek, brother. I'm sure you have fond memories of how well I can do just that, so watch your tongue."

Christopher unclasped Gillian's hands from behind his back. "Go on, Gill. Just don't hurt him too badly."

It was the beginning of a very long afternoon. Gillian bested Kendrick, though she was the first to admit that he spent more time flattering her than he did attending to his swordplay. Phillip was also easily dispatched. He cried peace after she tripped him into a puddle of mud.

After a bit of refreshment, Robin himself took up the blade against her. Gillian begged off after only a few moments. She pressed Colin into the service of humoring Lord Artane and sought the shelter of her husband's arms as he lay in the shade of the hall. He pulled her down onto the mossy place next to him and kissed her soundly.

"Such a fierce dragoness," he said. "How is it I hold her?"

" 'Tis either your fiery temper," she said, "or your fetching blue eyes, my lord. I vow I never can decide which I love more."

He smiled in return. "I can see why not, as both are so appealing."

Gillian smiled as she laid her dirty palm against his cheek. "I haven't seen nearly enough of you of late as I like, my lord."

"My thoughts exactly."

"Think you we might slip away for a time? Perhaps for an hour or two at the shore?"

"Slip away?" Kendrick echoed from where he sat behind her. "Without us? Surely not, lady."

Gillian watched Christopher's expression darken considerably.

"As you have been bested twice this morn, whelp," Christopher said with a growl, "perhaps you would care to retreat to your chamber and take your rest."

"Rest?" Kendrick said, bounding to his feet. "Don't need one. I feel as rested as if I'd passed the night on the king's finest goosefeather mattress. Come, my lady Gillian, and let us wend our way to the shore."

"No doubt *my* lady Gillian is faint with pleasure over the idea," Christopher said, wrapping his arms tightly around her. "I daresay, however, that she needs a cloak for the journey. Why don't you press on ahead, my lad, and see to a comfortable spot? We'll join you straightway."

Gillian watched as Kendrick herded his father and brothers out of the garden, onto their mounts and through the inner gate.

"Sir Ranulf!" Christopher called.

Gillian watched as her husband's captain made his way across the inner bailey to the low garden wall.

"My lord?"

"Lock the gates for the afternoon, won't you?"

"But, Artane and his lads—"

"—will be quite occupied at the shore for a few hours. When Robin begins to threaten my ability to continue the Blackmour line, then you may let them in. Until then, I've a mind for some peace with my lady."

"As you wish, my lord."

Ranulf disappeared down the way. Gillian watched her husband lie back and hold up his arms for her. She stretched out beside him and rested her head on his shoulder.

"Ah," Christopher said, with a long, heartfelt sigh, "this is what I've been lacking the past pair of weeks."

Gillian smiled. "And what is that?"

"A saucy maid in the midst of my herbs." He pressed his lips against her hair. "What say you we throw Robin's baggage over the walls and keep the gates locked for another few months?"

"Oh, Christopher," she said with a laugh, leaning up on her elbow and looking down at him. "Surely you don't mean it."

He put his hand around the back of her neck and pulled her down to kiss her firmly on the mouth. "Ah, but I do, my love. Much as I'm fond of him, I've seen too much of Robin and not nearly enough of you."

"You see me every night."

Christopher shook his head. "It isn't enough. We haven't napped in the afternoon in over a fortnight. I haven't had the peace or quiet to sing for you in at least that long. Saints, Gillian, I haven't even talked to you enough to know which servants you've been tormenting of late!"

"I haven't tormented anyone," she said, with a shake of her head.

"Other than Kendrick."

"I've hardly tormented him."

"But you have," Christopher grumbled. "The lad groans continually about your wedded state. As if you'd have him if you were free!"

"He's full of flatteries, my lord," she said, smiling at his gruff expression, "but I daresay he doesn't mean them."

Christopher frowned. "Of course he does. And well he should. The lad has a keen eye for beauty and 'tis obvious he cannot say enough about yours."

Gillian felt herself begin to blush. "Oh, my lord—"

"Perhaps 'tis merely that I begrudge him the looking at it," Christopher said with another frown. "Aye, it irritates me mightily that he can see what I cannot, though I will admit I have enjoyed his descriptions of it."

"He *is* given to excessive speaking," Gillian admitted.

Christopher grunted. "Aye, that is truth indeed. And I daresay I could stomach it if his tormenting of me ended there," he continued, obviously warming to the topic. "As if it weren't enough to listen to him babble on for hours, what does he do next but send for minstrels! Saints, but I can hardly bear the thought of another ballad!"

"Silence can be pleasing," Gillian offered.

"You can hardly blame me for tiring of it after two weeks of nothing but."

"Nay, I cannot."

"And the way they linger at the table," Christopher groused. "You would think those two determined to eat through my larder! I'm almost to the point of suggesting they return home and decimate their father's stores." He scowled up at her. "What think you?" he demanded.

"Well, my lord—"

"And while we're discussing it," Christopher finished, "let me say that Kendrick is the very last person I want to speak of. Now that we've managed to rid ourselves of him for a time," he added.

"Oh, Christopher," Gillian said, with a laugh. "You are the most impossible man."

"I'm a bloody poor host and I couldn't care less."

"I think you're a wonderful host," she said, leaning down to kiss him softly. "You've made them feel most welcome."

"Then I've obviously been remiss," he grumbled. "The lads at least should have felt some urge to head home by now."

Gillian laughed. "Oh, Christopher, how I do love you. How did I pass the whole of my life without your grumbles?"

"You were likely quite bored," he stated. "What I wonder is how you survived without my kisses. Indeed, I daresay you have suffered overmuch from the lack of them as of late. Come you here and make up for it."

Gillian couldn't stop her smile. Flattery from those Artane lads had given her a fleeting pleasure, to be sure, for it was indeed a novel thing to have handsome lords singing praises to her beauty. But how could that flattery possibly compare to Christopher's grumbling? Or his demands for her attentions? Or his scowls when he felt as if he hadn't seen her as much as he would have liked to during any given day? Aye, this was a love to be treasured.

Gillian smiled down at him. "Will you have kisses first, or should I tell you of the day, my lord?"

He pulled her head down and kissed her soundly. "A little of both, I think."

"And where shall I begin?"

"You shall begin by telling me first how weary I look and how you're certain a nap would be just the thing for me."

"I daresay you don't look overly weary as of yet."

"Then talk me to death," he commanded. "I'm sure I'll be quite tired by the time you finish."

Gillian smiled as she traced his lips with her finger. "Do you really wish me to?"

He smiled suddenly, a rueful smile that charmed her. "Perhaps my nap will wait for a few moments. Tell me of the day, my love," he said, reaching up to touch her hair. "And then tell me what you're wearing, and how your hair looks in the sunlight. Then tell me what blooms in my garden. Tell me of it all, Gillian. I hunger for nothing so much as the sound of your voice and the touch of your hand."

The earnestness in his voice made her want to weep. She leaned over and kissed him until she felt the tears recede from her eyes.

Then she did just as he asked.

twenty-eight

ROBIN OF ARTANE WALKED DOWN THE PASSAGEWAY, HIS curiosity getting the better of him. He'd seen the light flickering in the tower chamber and had heard the tales of Blackmour weaving his dark arts there. Robin had always dismissed the rumors as sheer foolishness, but he wasn't above a bit of snooping to see just what mischief young Christopher was combining at night.

Robin froze when his foot touched the bottom step. The growl that greeted his ears wasn't a welcoming one. Robin remained still as the black shape loped down the steps, then let out his breath slowly when the wolf sniffed his hand. Robin carefully scratched the beast behind the ears.

"Good boy. You protect your master well. Go see to your mistress now. I'll watch over Christopher." He pointed back down the passageway. "Go to Gillian."

The wolf whined and bumped Robin's hand. Robin sighed and relented.

"Very well, then. Come along. And let us see what your master does to ruin his sleep."

Robin climbed the stairs silently and paused at the threshold of the tower chamber. The door was ajar. Robin pushed it gently open and slipped inside the chamber.

Christopher was training. Robin leaned back against the wall and watched his former squire work. He smiled sadly. Ah, Christopher had been without peer. There had been times that, had Robin been entirely truthful with himself, he would have had to admit that he'd met his match in the young lord of Blackmour. That was no small admission.

Even now, Christopher had lost very little of his skill. His balance was less than perfect, but his art was still there. Robin couldn't begin to count the nights he had gone out to the lists with a torch and dragged Christopher inside, trying to impress upon the lad that training into the middle of the night wouldn't serve him. Christopher, in that sober, serious way he'd had, had pointed out to Robin that he'd been famous for the same thing in his youth. Robin smiled at the memory. Aye, he'd loved Christopher like a son, gladly taking him from a father who couldn't manage the responsibility of himself, much less a son who deserved careful and thoughtful training in both swordplay and governing a stronghold the size of Blackmour. Robin had taken on both tasks willingly, teaching Christopher all he could about living through wars and peacetime alike. Christopher had never had to hear anything twice. Once heard, the instruction had stayed with him always.

A pity Christopher hadn't been willing to be cautious where Magdalina had been concerned. Robin had no use for anyone from Berkhamshire, save Colin, and had pleaded with Christopher to drag the betrothal out. And then he'd seen how blinded with love Christopher had seemed, how often he had laughed, how happy he had appeared. Robin had kept his mouth shut and wished the lad all the happiness possible.

He had never believed the tale that Christopher's wounding had been an accident. It reeked of something foul. It had happened on one of Warewick's holdings, which was even more disturbing. Now Warewick had a tie to Blackmour. Robin couldn't bring himself to believe Gillian would have any notion of it. Saints above, how she loved Christopher!

But the entire affair had to be more than it seemed. A pity no one would ever likely know the truth. Magdalina could have been behind it, but there was no way of telling now. Christopher had his share of enemies, but Robin could think of none with the spine to come against him, especially when Blackmour's strongest ally was Artane. There wasn't anything Robin wouldn't have done for the child who had fostered at his home for so many years and the rest of England knew it.

He looked up when he saw Christopher stop parrying. Christopher dragged his sweaty arm across his equally sweaty forehead, then turned and looked straight at Robin. Robin blinked in surprise.

"Can you see me?"

"Of course not," Christopher grumbled. "But you have this bloody annoying habit of muttering under your breath when you think too hard. I vow I could hardly work for the distraction. My lord," he added.

Robin smiled to himself as he crossed the room and sat down in the alcove. "Forgive me. Continue with your play. I had merely come to see what devilish deeds my former squire combined in his tower room. The isle is aflame with speculation."

"And I suppose you heard these rumors from my wife," Christopher said dryly. "I vow she looked for horns for the first fortnight of our marriage."

"She's a beautiful girl, Christopher. You chose well."

Christopher sighed and came to sit down on the bench across from him. "I had no choice in the matter."

"You could have turned your back on her."

"I made a promise to William."

"It was a promise well kept."

Christopher fingered the hilt of his sword, his head bowed. Then he lifted his head slightly. "Is she fair to look upon? Not that it matters to me, of course."

Robin smiled. At the moment, Christopher seemed that same shy lad who had first gaped at a girl when he was ten. Ah, what a memory.

"She's enchanting," Robin said, smiling. "She's comely, but not so beautiful that the queen's ladies will poison her when you take her to court. Her gentleness of spirit shines in her eyes and that is a beauty that will not dim."

Christopher nodded, then leaned his head back against the wall. "Aye, she's a treasure. I couldn't be more pleased with her. What I am not pleased with, however, is those lads of yours slobbering over her." He frowned deeply. "That Kendrick is a womanizer of the first water—"

Robin laughed. "Harmless flirting, lad. You know Kendrick wouldn't dare the like."

"I know several other lords who would say he would."

Robin shook his head, amused. He hadn't expected jealousy from Christopher. The lad was truly in love.

"I'm in earnest, my lord," Christopher growled.

"I know," Robin said, suppressing his grin. "I daresay your frowns have told quite a bit of the tale, but if you like I'll warn him off further."

"You do that," Christopher said curtly.

Robin gave in and laughed. "Ah, Chris, it does my heart good to see you so besotted." He paused, then threw caution aside. "Bring her to Artane," he urged. "Anne wishes to meet her. And it will be good for Gillian. She needs the company of other women from time to time. Not that Colin isn't womanly enough," Robin added with a chuckle.

Christopher's smile was strained. "Colin will have to suffice her."

"You know Anne won't grieve her," Robin said, trying a different tack. "Neither will the children. I don't know the extent of what she suffered at Warewick's hands, but if it was anything like William—"

"It isn't that."

Christopher rose abruptly and walked to the middle of the floor. He took up a fighting stance, then lunged, thrusting viciously. He would have skewered five men with that strike. Robin dragged a hand through his hair and rose. He came up behind Christopher and put his hand on the younger man's shoulder.

"Christopher . . ."

He lowered his sword and turned around. "I appreciate the invitation, but I must respectfully decline."

Robin suppressed a sigh. Ah, such pride! He sighed again, then stepped back a pace.

"Then indulge me. I've lacked sorely for swordsmen of your mettle. Not even my brothers have your skill."

Christopher blinked. "You jest."

"Nay, I do not. They are all bumbling pages and give me no sport at all."

"Not that," Christopher said impatiently. "I cannot parry with you!"

Robin looked down at the wicked edge of Christopher's sword and realized the possibilities of injury. "We'll use blunted training swords, then. I'll go fetch a pair."

"Nay!"

"Then I'll fetch wooden swords—"

"*Nay!*" Christopher's exclamation was full of anguish. "Damn you, Robin, I cannot!"

"But of course you can," Robin said, surprised at the outburst. "Saints, think on how well you joust! We'll work out a like system for swordplay." He nodded to himself. "Aye, I'll send the lads home and stay on for an extra pair of fortnights. Then when you come to Artane—"

"Damn you, cease!" Christopher thundered. He cast aside his sword and grasped the front of Robin's tunic in two clenched fists. His breaths were harsh in the stillness of the chamber. "I cannot parry with you," he ground out. "I cannot see you to fight!"

"We'll hone new skills—"

"*Stop!*" Christopher cried out, as if he'd been struck.

"Merciful saints above, Robin, don't you think I wish I could? Don't you think I come up here each night and train, wishing I could actually see something besides blackness? Don't you think I weep tears of rage and frustration, knowing what I was yet faced with what I've become?"

Tears streamed down from his sightless eyes. Robin's heart wrenched inside him at the sight.

"Don't you think I want to come to Artane?" Christopher asked hoarsely. "I lie awake at nights dreaming of my days there. I imagine how it would be to take Gillian there, to show her the places I roamed as a youth, to present her to the man I loved more than I ever loved my own sire.

"Don't you think I want to see you, Robin? To be the man you made me into and see in your eyes that you are pleased with me? Doesn't it occur to you that I would wish to look at the Lady Anne and remember how I loved her sweetly in my youth and prayed for a gentle woman just like her to love me?"

A sob escaped him. "Don't you think I wish to look on my lady? Can you not imagine how badly I want to watch her birth my children, then look down at the babes and see myself in their features? Don't you think every day of my life is torture, knowing the things I want and knowing they're forever out of my reach?"

Robin felt his own tears slide down his cheeks and he did nothing to check them.

"Ah, Chris," he whispered roughly, reaching out to draw the sobbing younger man into his arms.

"Nay," Christopher said, pushing him away. "Leave me. For pity's sake, Robin, if you have any mercy, just leave me be!"

"I would do aught to ease—"

"There's nothing you can do! Just go." Christopher turned his back. "Please."

The last was nothing more than a whisper. Robin wanted

to stay, but he knew Christopher wouldn't appreciate it. Though he believed that Christopher possessed a great deal more than just his pride, it was obvious the lad didn't believe it himself.

So Robin left.

He walked down the stairs and down the passageway. He almost stumbled into Gillian before he realized what he was doing. He caught her by the arms and steadied her.

"Forgive me, lady," he said. "I didn't see you."

"Christopher?"

"In his tower chamber. As is his wont, I gather."

She smiled gravely. "Practicing his dark arts, no doubt."

Robin couldn't return her smile, even though he appreciated her wry sense of humor.

He stopped her as she moved past him with a soft goodnight. "Gillian, if I could presume . . ."

"Aye?"

"Leave him be. For the moment."

She went still. "My lord?"

"I spoke to him of coming to Artane."

Gillian winced. "And I take it that grieved him?"

He nodded, though that was likely unnecessary. He was certain Gillian could read the entire tale in his expression.

" 'Tis his damnable pride," Robin said, with a sigh.

"I fear, my lord," she said, "that there are times he doubts his own worth."

"Fate has not been kind, my lady."

"Hasn't it?" she mused. "In his mind, nay, it has not. But in truth, I cannot grieve overmuch for his loss of sight."

Robin gasped. "You jest."

She shook her head. "He never would have wed me else. 'Tis most selfish, I know, but I love him desperately. He never would have wed one as ugly as I."

Robin smiled, pained. "You both undervalue yourselves, Gillian, for you are a comely maid and Christopher is no less a man for being blind. Perhaps in time, you will both learn to see yourselves as you truly are.''

"Thank you, my lord.''

Robin took her hand and tucked it into the crook of his arm. "I've no doubt he will come to you soon enough and he will be prickly. Have a care with his tender heart, won't you?''

She nodded solemnly. "I will.''

Gillian looked up at him as they stopped before her bed-chamber door. Then she leaned up and kissed his cheek softly.

"Thank you for loving him, my lord. He values that greatly, though he may not show it overmuch.'' She smiled gravely. "I've learned that about you men. Scaly for the most part, but possessing very soft underbellies. My fierce husband is scalier than most, but I prefer him that way.''

With that, she slipped inside the chamber and closed the door. Robin stared at the wood for a moment or two, trying to digest the whole of the evening. Then the tension eased out of him and he had the feeling Gillian would be able to handle whatever sort of fit Christopher decided to throw. After all, Blackmour's temper was legendary.

And Robin sincerely hoped Christopher didn't ruin everything by letting it get the best of him.

twenty-nine

GILLIAN STOOD ON THE FRONT STEPS OF THE HALL AND watched as Robin and his sons made ready to depart. Christopher's mood was foul. Gillian watched her husband stand near her with his arms folded over his chest. His very expression was enough to discourage any and all attempts at conversation. Gillian suspected she knew the reason why he had no desire for speech. Even though Robin had remained silent about Artane since the night he had spoken to her, the invitation still seemed to hang between him and Christopher like heavy smoke.

"What, no smile from my lady for me to carry away on my journey?"

Gillian looked into Kendrick's dusty green eyes and grimaced.

"I've seen better, but that will do for now," he said. He took her hand and bent over it. He looked up from under his eyebrows and winked. "I'd kiss it, but I like my head atop my neck and your lord is in no mood to be trifled with, I fear."

"Leave off, dolt," Phillip said, pushing Kendrick aside. He took Gillian's hand, swept her a gallant bow and kissed her very carefully and chastely on the fingers. "It has been a great pleasure, lady. Give me leave to bring my bride here, won't you? I'd have her see your fine example of gentility."

"And cleanliness," Kendrick added, with a grin. "But I daresay you'll have to give that wench of yours a bath before you dare bring her here—"

Gillian's view of the ensuing fight was blocked by Robin's large frame as he drew her gently into his arms and gave her a fatherly hug.

"You take good care of my boy," he said quietly. "And bring him to Artane as soon as you can manage it."

Gillian nodded, finding it difficult all of a sudden to speak past the lump in her throat.

"I'll do my best, my lord," she whispered.

Robin smiled down at her, then released her and turned to embrace Christopher. Gillian watched her husband's stern visage and knew that he was steeling himself against any more of Robin's invitations. Robin was obviously too wise to say more than he would see Christopher again soon, leaving Christopher to take it however he would.

Gillian stood on the steps until the portcullis had come down behind Robin and his sons, then turned to look at her husband. She laid her hand on his arm.

"Shall we go to the shore today, my lord?" she asked softly. "I vow the sun will shine sweetly, just for you."

Christopher shook his head and pulled away, unsmiling. "I need to train."

And with that, he turned and walked back toward the hall.

Gillian stared after him, unsure what she should do. Christopher had been taken by foul moods before, but she had always been able to tease him from them. Judging by the set of his shoulders, this was more than a simple bout of surliness. She had the feeling even a few bold and saucy remarks wouldn't cure what ailed him.

"I'd leave him be," a voice said from her side.

Gillian looked up at Colin. "Think you?"

He nodded. "For the day, perhaps."

Gillian chewed on that for a moment or two, then met Colin's eyes again. "It isn't anything I've done . . ."

He shook his head. "You know it isn't."

She nodded, but she felt doubt nag at her. Colin walked away, but she didn't call him back. She was far too busy examining her actions over the past few days. Nay, surely she had done nothing to offend. Christopher had worn a grim expression since the night Robin had talked to him in the tower chamber.

Gillian sighed. Perhaps it was merely what she had thought from the start: Christopher was grieved over Robin's invitation. And perhaps Colin's counsel was the best. She would leave her husband be for the day and pray his foul mood would disappear with the setting of the sun.

SHE WOKE THE NEXT MORNING, ALONE. SHE REACHED over and touched Christopher's side of the bed. It was cold. She was fairly certain he'd been there, though, at some time during the night. The warmth of her hands and feet testified to that. Perhaps he had risen early to see to his men.

She broke her fast with what was left on the table, for she had overslept and missed the fullness of the meal. It took hardly anything to satisfy her, for her stomach seemed to share her anxiety over Christopher's mood.

The inner bailey was empty, except for the lone figure standing there, facing the gates. Gillian ran down the steps and hastened to her husband's side.

"My lord?"

He only shook his head, slowly. His expression was very grim.

"My lord, what troubles you?"

He only shook his head again, then turned and walked back toward the hall. Gillian watched him go, hating the feeling of helplessness that washed over her. Perhaps Christopher only needed to be comforted. She could offer to merely hold him, or fetch his lute for him, or—

"It will pass."

She looked up to find Colin suddenly standing next to her, much as he had the day before. He looked at the empty doorway Christopher had just passed through, then met her gaze.

"I think I would leave him be," he suggested

"Again?"

He nodded. "Aye."

"Is there nothing I can do?" she asked.

Colin shook his head. "Nay, my lady. You cannot aid him."

Gillian suspected he spoke the truth. Christopher had his own demons to wrestle with. She could not do battle in his stead.

" 'Tis far worse than usual," Jason said grimly, coming to a stop on her other side.

"Aye," Colin agreed. "Much worse."

"Usually he suffers for a day, then 'tis finished," Jason explained. "I haven't seen him in this state since they carried him back from Braed—"

"Jason!" Colin exclaimed.

Gillian looked from Colin's blazing eyes to Jason's suddenly blanched face. Jason looked at her miserably.

"My lady," he began, "forgive me . . ."

"For what?"

Colin reached around behind her and cuffed Jason smartly on the back of the head.

" 'Twas nothing, my lady," he said curtly. "The lad was babbling things he didn't intend."

Jason gulped and nodded.

Gillian turned to face her husband's squire. "Were you going to tell me of Christopher's wounding?"

Jason clamped his lips shut and remained silent.

"But, you won't grieve me," she said, surprised at his reticence. "Is it that you think Christopher should be the one to tell me?"

Colin cleared his throat pointedly and Jason remained firmly silent.

Gillian sighed. "Come, Jason, and let us leave Sir Colin to his grumbles. Christopher's dark mood has become ours, so you may as well tell me more of the details. He certainly hasn't spoken much of it—"

"And neither will we," Colin said, taking her by the arm. "Let us go sit on yon bench and enjoy the sunshine. While it lasts," he added, casting Jason a black look.

Gillian opened her mouth to protest, then thought better of it after noting the unyielding set to Colin's jaw. She could see there would be little point in arguing.

So she let Colin lead her to Christopher's favorite seat outside and she sat, because he gave her no choice. He stood at the end of the bench and folded his arms over his chest. He stared grimly over the bailey, wearing his unwillingness to talk like a cloak. Gillian looked down at Jason who had sat in the dirt next to her feet. His head was bowed and his shoulders slumped.

She put her hand on his dark hair. What a gentle heart Artane's youngest child had, to grieve so much for his master. Jason looked up at her, his blue eyes full of tears. His voice cracked when he spoke.

"I never meant to say anything about—"

"Jason, by the saints, enough!" Colin thundered. He looked more enraged than Gillian had ever seen him before.

"Colin," she said, surprised and very uneasy at his furious expression, "he has said nothing."

"He's said more than he should," Colin growled.

"I truly would like to know more of what happened," she ventured. "Christopher has told me so little. Jason has already told me a bit when I first arrived—"

"You told her?" Colin exclaimed. "You mindless babe!" He hauled Jason to his feet and began to shake him. "She was never to know it happened at Braedhalle!"

Gillian blinked.

"Braedhalle?" she asked.

Colin froze. He looked at Gillian, his mouth working silently for a moment or two.

"Ah . . . I mean," he began, "er . . ."

"Braedhalle?" she repeated, in a very small voice.

Misery was etched into every plane and angle of Colin's face. He and Jason both stared at her, silently, with pity and anguish mingled in their glances.

By the saints, it had been Braedhalle. The echoes of the word tumbled out into the bailey and then back at her, pelting her with the truth over and over again.

Braedhalle.

She couldn't breathe. By all the blessed saints above, Christopher had been wounded at Braedhalle. On her land.

She felt the air around her begin to spin. *On her dower land.* Oh merciful St. Michael, he had been blinded on *her* land. How could he even bear the sight of her?

The irony of that struck her like a slap and she started to laugh. He didn't have to bear the sight of her because he couldn't see her—because he had been ruined on *her* land.

"Now, Gillian," Colin began.

How could Christopher touch her without bringing it to mind? How could he hear her name spoken and not think of her dowry and what that bloody dowry had cost him?

She evaded Colin and fled into the hall. She ran up the steps, down the passageway and up the steps to the tower chamber. Oh, by the saints, why hadn't someone told her sooner?

She put her hand on the door and listened intently. No sound came from within. She eased open the door and looked inside.

Christopher sat against one wall, his sword on the floor next to him, Wolf lying at his feet. Gillian pushed the door fully open. What could she say to him? *Forgive me? I knew nothing of it? I love you and I would give my own eyes if it meant you could see again?*

"My lord?" she managed, tears streaming down her face.

Christopher didn't lift his head. "Leave me, Gill."

"Oh, Christopher."

He didn't move.

"Please," he whispered.

It was the please that undid her.

He was no doubt thinking of his blindness—and where he'd lost his sight.

Her dower estate.

She turned and fled down the steps. She ran to the chamber she shared with her love, then realized she couldn't go there.

It had happened on her land.

She ran through the great hall, down the steps past Colin and Jason and toward the inner bailey gate. The portcullis was down. She backed up and looked at Captain Ranulf, who stood on the parapet.

"Open it," she ordered.

"Now, milady, it isn't wise—"

"Do it!" she shouted. "As Lady of Blackmour, I command you to open this bloody gate!"

He hesitated.

"Open it!" she screamed. "Open it, you fool, and let me go!"

The man looked genuinely startled and at another time she might have laughed at his expression. Perhaps she had turned into a dragoness after all.

The gate slid upward. One moment Gillian was staring wildly at the metal-clad wooden spikes, then the next she was sobbing and could no longer see them as they rose up into the gatehouse. Why had no one told her?

The moment the portcullis was raised far enough for her to duck under, she threw herself forward and started to run. Where all the people had come from, she surely didn't know, but moving forward was almost impossible. She pushed and shoved and fought to get away from the inner bailey, trying to get out of the gatehouse tunnel. She heard Colin and Jason calling her name, but she ignored them.

Far too soon, she felt Colin take her arm and try to halt her progress, but she put her head down and struggled forward more determinedly.

"Gillian, cease," Colin begged.

Somehow he managed to put himself before her. She pushed against him, but he was as immovable as the flagstones beneath her feet.

"Let me pass," she said, through gritted teeth.

"You'll not run from this," Colin said.

She looked up at him, barely able to make out his form through her tears.

"You expect me to stay?" she asked hoarsely.

"It isn't your fault," Colin said, stubbornly.

"It was on *my* land!"

"As if you had anything to do with it! Saints, child, do you not think Christopher knows that?"

"He doesn't want me here."

"Of course he does."

"Nay," she said, shaking her head violently, "he just asked me to leave. I can't stay, Colin. I can't put him through more misery by remaining."

"It isn't you, my lady," Colin said. He put his arms around her and patted her on the back in a gruff sort of way. " 'Tisn't you, Gillian."

Gillian struggled a moment longer, then surrendered. She collapsed against Colin and wept. She cried for what Christopher had lost; then she wept more for the pain she had caused him by just being near him. No matter that she had known nothing of the affair. It was on her land. Surely he couldn't help but think of that each time he heard her name.

"My lady? My lady Gillian?"

Gillian heard Jason, but couldn't respond.

"My lady, 'tis my doing. You never should have known. I vow my lord isn't troubled by it."

That was enough to make her look up. "How can you say that?" she cried. "By the saints, Jason, he cannot help but be troubled!"

Jason shook his head. " 'Tis the thought of going to Artane which has distressed him so. My lord Christopher is always thusly after my sire comes." He reached out hesitantly and patted her shoulder. "He loves my sire, 'tis true, and no doubt wishes he could travel to Artane to see him. I think, though, now he's thinking how much he wishes he could take you to Artane." He smiled hesitantly. "Don't you see?"

Gillian dragged her sleeve across her eyes. She couldn't make herself speak.

"My lady, if he didn't love you so well, he wouldn't grieve for what he thinks he cannot give you. Surely you must believe that."

"I wish I could," she said, blinking hard. If only she could stop weeping long enough to see.

Jason pulled her away from Colin, then took her hand and drew it through the crook of his arm. "Leave him be for the afternoon."

"Nay," Gillian began.

"Just for a few hours," Jason insisted. "I vow he will return to his normal self by then. You'll see, my lady. I daresay he would be powerfully irritated if he found you'd done aught but enjoyed the peace of the garden for the afternoon."

Gillian paused. "I think I should just go," she said, but her heart wasn't in it. As distraught as she was by what she'd learned, the thought of being without Christopher was far harder to bear.

"I think you should stay," Jason said. He nodded back over his shoulder. "See the merchants who come up the way? You'll get lost amongst them and then where will we be?"

"Much better off," she muttered.

He smiled gravely. "Ah, but you know that isn't true,

my lady. Come, let us go back to the hall. We'll find a few trinkets for you, or if you can't do for yourself, then do for me. A few items of interest to warm the hearts of the maids I will woo in the coming months would be most gratefully received, I assure you." He slipped his arm around her shoulders and turned her around to face the hall. "Come with me, lady."

Gillian didn't pull away. Perhaps she and Christopher truly could come to an understanding in the end.

She let herself be led away from the gate, only slightly soothed by Jason's words and Colin's grumbling. It would take more than those things to ease the ache in her heart and the shame that coursed through her. Nay, it would take far more than that.

She was almost to the hall when she turned and looked at Jason.

"Merchants, did you say?"

"Aye, come to tempt you sorely, no doubt," he said, with a smile.

"But it isn't market day, Jason."

She felt Colin stiffen at her side. She spun around. The bailey was full of men who had come in with their carts.

Carts that flung off their coverings of cloth and food-stuffs to reveal armed men.

Gillian heard Colin draw his blade and push her back toward the hall door with one motion. She searched the bailey frantically for some sign of who the men might belong to.

Then her eyes fell upon the leader of the ragtag group of men who had come into the inner bailey.

It was her father.

And he was looking at her with murder in his eye.

"Go inside," Colin growled, pushing her again.

Gillian wanted to move, to speak, to cry out a warning, but the sight of her sire standing so boldly in Blackmour's inner bailey left her rooted to the spot.

"Jason, take her inside, then fetch your lord."

"Nay," Gillian croaked.

"Take her inside and fetch Christopher!" Colin snapped. "Do as I say, boy, or you'll feel the bite of my blade!"

Gillian felt Jason clutch her by the arm and drag her toward the door. Once she found that her limbs would move, she was surprised at just how quickly they accomplished the task of carrying her into the great hall and up the stairs.

"Lock yourself in your chamber, my lady," Jason said, his tone strained. "I'll come for you when it's over. I'm off to fetch Lord Christopher."

"Nay!" Gillian cried out, but it was too late. Jason had disappeared further into the darkness of the passageway.

Gillian burst into her chamber and ran for the trunk. She would get to her father first, before Christopher had a chance. Without giving it more thought, she threw up the lid and dug through the clothing for her blade.

Then the thought that she really should change into something more serviceable than a gown crossed her mind and she hastily took her own advice. She made quick work of braiding her hair. It behaved perfectly, something she might have taken pleasure in at another time.

Now all she could think about was the man she would have to kill.

She ran from her chamber, tripping over her own feet in her haste and fear. She would have to face her sire, but the thought of it terrified her so that it was as if she had frigid seawater in her veins.

But, she realized with a start as she fled down the steps, it was no worse than the fear she'd felt before her father beat her.

She took one last, great gulp of air and leaped down the final steps. She would run through the great hall and out into the bailey. Then she would engage her father before he had time to gather his wits about him. He'd found her naught but a cowering child before; he would find her a far different woman now.

She threw herself into the great hall, then skidded to a halt.

She'd expected to find the hall empty.

It wasn't. Her father stood in the middle of the floor with his men behind him.

Christopher stood facing him.

Gillian felt as if she'd been turned to stone. Her husband faced her father, without his eyes to guide him. Gillian would have cried out a warning, but she found her voice wouldn't work.

She had come too late.

thirty

CHRISTOPHER STOOD WITH HIS ARMS FOLDED OVER HIS chest, forcing himself to remain calm. By the saints, this was not how he'd planned to pass this morning!

Yesterday as he'd bid his former master farewell, he'd decided he would spend the day locked in his tower chamber. His mood had been black and it had seemed the safest course of action. No sense in making those around him as miserable as he was himself. He'd been determined to stay there through the night and possibly well into the next day, just to give himself time to work out his rage and frustration with his blade. Robin's leave-taking always affected him thusly; only this time the pain was greater. He'd wanted to travel to Artane in the past, merely to see Lady Anne and the other sweet souls there. Now, the ache was worsened by wanting to travel back to Artane and take Gillian with him. He longed to show her where he'd passed his youth. It would have also pleased her to see where William had left his marks on Artane's hall. Aye, the time could have been passed most pleasantly.

He'd kept his silent vigil well into the night. Somewhere around the second watch, he'd relented. Gillian hadn't been awake as he slipped into bed next to her, so she hadn't marked his frown. Even in sleep, she had turned to him and reached for him. He'd held her close and tried not to weep. Ah, all the things he longed to give her, but couldn't!

He'd returned to the tower well before dawn, prepared to pass another day training. His peace had been interrupted suddenly by Jason's bursting into the chamber, babbling something about Warewick and peasants and carts of armored men. Christopher had been certain the lad had taken a sharp blow to the head that had addled his wits. Now, he realized his squire had spoken naught but the truth. By sweet St. Michael's throat, this was a disaster! If he survived, he would send a missive to Robin and curse him thoroughly for having left a day too early. Aid from Artane was something Christopher never took lightly.

Now what was he to do? Feign indifference and pray Warewick was too stupid to see it for the fear it was? What he wanted to be doing was drawing his blade and plunging it through Warewick's chest. Unfortunately, he couldn't see to do that. A pity. Gillian deserved to have her father repaid for his treatment of her.

"I don't recall inviting you, Warewick," Christopher said curtly, praying he was looking in the right direction.

The hiss of a blade coming from its sheath brought gasps of disapproval from Christopher's household. He knew it was from his men and not Warewick's because Colin had barked out a particularly hair-raising oath of displeasure.

"I'd suggest you leave," Christopher said, keeping his voice even, "while you can still walk out of my gates."

Warewick laughed and Christopher realized he had misjudged his father-in-law's position. He turned toward Warewick's voice immediately.

"Leave?" Warewick scoffed. "When I collect what is due me, what should have been mine. Aye, I'll have it—"

"When I'm dead," Colin boomed. "And I've no intentions of meeting my end so soon—"

"Nay," Christopher said, putting out his hand sharply. "He's mine."

"Am I?" Warewick asked. "Then draw your blade, Blackmour, and let's see if you fight as poorly as you eat. I remember you to be quite bumbling the last time we met. Perhaps your eyes were blurred from too much wine. Or the sight of your new lady's ugliness. Or perhaps you can't see me at all."

"He'll never need to see you," Gillian shouted from a distance, "because I'll send you straight to hell!"

"Gillian," Christopher exclaimed, "by the saints—"

He heard the ring of metal against metal, then the sound of a resounding slap and Gillian's cry of pain.

And then there was complete chaos. Christopher turned this way and that, trying to hear what was going on about him. Gillian made no more noise and that worried him more than anything. If aught had happened to her!

He heard men cry out as steel pierced flesh. He smelled blood. Then he felt the sting of a blade. It was instinctive to draw his own blade and swing. He felt it bite deep and prayed he hadn't killed his wife by mistake. Warmth trickled over his fingers. Whether it was his blood or someone else's he couldn't tell. He was far too furious to care. By the saints, he was a useless piece of refuse!

"Back to back, my lord," Jason panted, bumping up against him. "Kill whoever comes within reach!"

"Where is Gillian?"

"Captain Ranulf guards her. Warewick struck her, but she'll recover, I'll warrant."

Christopher bellowed out his war cry, more out of frustration than warning.

He kept his back against Jason's and swung his sword viciously in an arc before him. Either his foes found him poor sport or they thought better of stepping into the path of his blade, for none came against him. Christopher continued to swing, praying his own men were careful enough not to get themselves backed into his steel.

And then it was over. Christopher came to himself to find Jason telling him as much and asking him to cease swinging. Christopher dropped the point of his sword to the floor and gasped for breath.

"All dead but Warewick and three of his men," Colin said. "Shall I finish them?" he asked, sounding positively delighted by the prospect.

"Nay," Christopher growled, smarting from the rescue, "I will."

"But, Chris—"

"I said I will!" Christopher snapped. "Where is the bloody whoreson?"

Warewick's laugh told the tale immediately.

"I knew it," he exclaimed. "You blind fool! Ah, this is a tale worth telling—Gillian of Warewick's fitting mate: a blind man! God, how perfect! If I'd known this would have been the result of that pitifully executed ambush, I would have counted it a success."

Christopher froze. "What?"

"You'll have the whole tale, will you?" Warewick taunted. "Where should I start? Perhaps we should pull up chairs and settle in. 'Tis a story long in the making. I wouldn't want you to tire during the telling of it."

"Speak, while you're still able," Christopher managed, reeling. An *ambush?*

He heard what could have been Warewick shifting positions and he raised his sword instinctively.

Warewick made a sound of annoyance. "Do you think I would slay you before you learn the truth? Put away your blade. I'll not finish you so soon."

Christopher put out a hand to stop Colin before he felt his brother-in-law move. Colin's oath was particularly foul, but he kept his place. He was obviously none too pleased about it.

"Now," Warewick said, "where shall I start? Shall I

begin with the wealth I drained from your sire whenever I was able? I was certain a few more years of poor crops—aided to failure by my men—would have finished him.''

"But it didn't," Christopher pointed out, with a grim smile.

"Aye, you saw to that yourself, didn't you, whelp? You and your glories on the continent.'' Warewick spat. ''I watched you come home with enough gold to purchase the king's favor for a dozen keeps. It was then I realized how you had aided me. I would see you slain, then have Blackmour and your gold both.''

"Neither of which you have,'' Christopher said pointedly.

"Yet,'' Warewick said. ''Yet. But I will. Now to the part I think you will find of the most interest. What shall I describe first? The night Magdalina of Berkhamshire first crawled into my bed, or the night we planned your murder?''

"You lie,'' Christopher said flatly.

"Do I? I think you knew Lina better than that. I promised her Warewick and Blackmour both if she'd wed with you, something she truly found abhorrent. Of course the wench never had a head for strategy. You were to come to Braedhalle with just her. It would have been so much easier to finish you properly if you hadn't brought so many men along to protect your wife.''

Christopher was too surprised to do aught but continue to listen.

"After she bungled the plan so thoroughly, I didn't have much choice but to finish her. A pity. If you had died, as you were supposed to, I would have wed her and had Blackmour and Warewick joined sooner than now. Of course, I would have been lord of both. I will yet be lord, once you're dead and I have Gillian home again. Who knows what sort of accident she'll meet with on the stairs?''

Shock numbed Christopher completely and left him with

naught but coldness inside. He was ruined because of
Warewick's greed. One man had taken away from him his
sight, the one thing he wanted more than anything, simply
because of his lust for gold.

"You bloody whoreson," Christopher choked out.

"Indeed," Warewick said cheerfully. "But a bloody
rich one. Or I will be."

Christopher wanted to sit down in the rushes and weep.
He'd never suspected Magdalina to be that calculating. To
learn she had ruined him in such a coldhearted fashion
rocked him to the very core.

And then to learn Warewick had been behind it all!
Christopher tore through the memories he had of Gillian's
sire, through recollections of time spent with William at
his home. Not once could he remember Warewick being
aught but arrogant and blustering, his usual demeanor. But
to realize Warewick had been planning his death for years!

"One last thing," Warewick added. "Braedhalle is my
poorest bit of soil, to be sure, but that wasn't why I selected it as Gillian's dowry. Perhaps you can think on it
and divine the real reason."

Gillian's sob broke through the silence. "You bastard!"
she cried.

"Silence," Warewick bellowed, "lest you have your
words back tenfold! I have a long memory. Now, Blackmour, tell me. Wasn't it clever of me to give to you the
very place where you'd lost what you hold most dear?"

Christopher couldn't speak. His rage choked him and it
was all he could do to breathe. Saints, he wanted nothing
more than to kill Warewick with his bare hands!

Which, of course, he couldn't. There he stood, encircled
about by his men and a handful of enemies alike and he
was powerless. It had been drilled into him from his earliest years: your duty is to protect others. At Artane, he
had honed that skill into something akin to artistry. Now,
he stood helpless, unable even to tell if the blood covering
him was his or someone else's. Before him stood a man

responsible for his own grief and years of grief suffered by William and Gillian alike.

And he was unable to do a damned thing to him.

"Come, Gillian," Warewick commanded. "Come home and let me reward you for how poorly your husband has treated me over the past few months."

Gillian caught her breath.

Christopher felt anger surge through him. That was the last thing he would let happen! He would die protecting her if he had to.

He raised his blade.

"You may have ruined my sight," he said, "but you'll not ruin anything else that's mine."

"And how will you keep me from it, blind man? By fighting me?"

"He won't have to," Colin growled. "It'll be my pleasure to do it in his stead."

"Nay," Christopher said, "I'll do it myself. Come at me, Warewick, if you've the spine for it."

Christopher prodded the air with his sword, but touched nothing.

"On your left!" Colin exclaimed.

Christopher whirled to his left and lashed out. The meeting of blade against blade sent tremors through him. But the tremors were pleasant ones.

"Perhaps it won't be as easy as you think," Christopher said curtly. "Care for another go, Warewick?"

"From below," Colin said suddenly. "Saints, Chris, watch out—"

Christopher felt the blade bite deep into his thigh. He gritted his teeth and swung, but he made contact with nothing. Colin called out directions, but Christopher was hard pressed to make sense of them. Warewick's few men had begun to shout and Christopher could barely hear Colin over the din.

Christopher lunged suddenly, praying he would survive it. He felt his sword meet bone and halt. Warewick swore viciously. Christopher pulled back, prepared to deliver more such blows.

But that was when the battle became something he couldn't fight himself. Gillian's sire only taunted him, nicking him time and time again.

And then the unthinkable happened.

His sword went flying.

Christopher stood there, empty-handed, and thought he would be ill. By the saints, how would he ever—

"Stay," Warewick bellowed. "Berkhamshire, put away your blade."

Colin put his hand on Christopher's shoulder.

"Chris, let me," Colin begged.

Christopher heard the ring of metal against the stone of the floor. It was followed by a lighter sound, as if a small blade had been cast aside also.

"I am unarmed," Warewick said placidly. "Let us see what you can do with merely your fists, boy."

Christopher felt some of his pride come back to him. Perhaps now this would be on more equal terms. At least he would be able to keep Warewick close. Hadn't he wrestled with Jason and Colin often enough—and bested both of them?

He felt his head snap back before he realized he'd been hit. Before he could regain his balance, another fist plowed into his belly, doubling him over. Hardly had he straightened before another blow caught him full in the face.

Warewick was a large man. He shouldn't have been so agile.

But he was.

Christopher struck out, but his fists met nothing. He moved forward and extended his hands.

Nothing.

And then Warewick began to laugh.

It was the laughter that undid Christopher. Never before had he lost control of himself in battle, even when he'd been young and green. But he lost control now. He came at the sound of the laughter and swung wildly.

The blood thundered in his ears. The confusion in the hall only added to his dizziness and unease. Christopher lost his sense of direction, lost the sound of Colin's voice, and lost his reason.

Another blow caught him and sent him reeling. He stumbled backward and lost his balance. Colin caught him, then shoved him back to his feet.

"Enough of this," Colin pleaded.

Christopher jerked away from his brother-in-law and dragged his hand across his mouth.

"I haven't finished with him," he said. "Come at me, Warewick, if you've—"

He didn't feel the impact of Warewick's fist. All he felt was the floor as it came up to meet first his back, then the back of his head. The pain was blinding.

"Enough!" Colin thundered.

Christopher shook his head, trying to clear it. But he couldn't. His body burned from cuts of the sword and the remains of blows. He sat up with an effort, then felt Colin's hands under his arms. He didn't curse Colin for aiding him back to his feet. To be sure, he couldn't have gotten there on his own.

"Go, Warewick," he rasped, leaning on his Colin. "You'll live to see another dawn."

"Because you cannot kill me? How kind!"

"Does the reason matter? Go before Colin is unable to restrain himself further and finishes you himself."

"Pitiful whelp," Warewick spat. "You're not even man enough to protect that bitch I sired."

"Let me take him," Colin begged. "Christopher—"

Christopher shook his head. "If I cannot do the deed, it will not be done. See him and his men out the gates, but leave him alive."

"Your generosity moves me to tears. You'll leave me alive to finish you another day—"

Christopher found himself suddenly standing on his

own. Then he heard the distinct sound of fist meeting flesh. Warewick's chatter ceased abruptly.

"I may not be allowed to kill him, but I don't have to listen to him," Colin growled. "Come, lads. Let us heave this refuse over the wall before his stench makes us swoon."

Christopher felt shame flood through him. Saints above, he couldn't even defend himself!

And to think Gillian had witnessed it all.

"My lord?"

Christopher stumbled back from her. His wife was the last person he wanted to have see him in this state. She'd already seen too much as it was.

"Christopher, let me see to you—"

He shook his head sharply. "Nay," he said. "Where are the stairs?"

"But—"

"The stairs!" he shouted.

He felt her hand on his arm and she turned him gently. When she stopped, he jerked his arm away and limped toward the stairwell.

"Christopher, please—"

Christopher ignored her. He'd been humiliated by her sire, unable to protect her himself, unable to do aught but stand there and be beaten almost senseless. Warewick was right, he wasn't worthy of her.

Hadn't Lina said the same thing about him? *You're not man enough to do aught but sit on the front steps in rags and beg for what you need. I'll have a man who's whole, or none at all.* At least Lina had gotten what she deserved.

But Gillian deserved better. She deserved a man who could keep her sire from her, protect her with not only his name but his arm. She deserved better than he could give her.

He walked alone to his tower chamber, shut the door behind him and sat on the floor, leaning back against the wall. The battle fever was leaving him, allowing him to feel his wounds in full measure. Not even that pain could equal the agony in his soul.

He had failed her.

He had only one choice, a choice he should have been courageous enough to make when he'd first begun to love her.

He'd send her away to someone who was whole.

thirty-one

GILLIAN STOOD IN THE GREAT HALL, UNABLE TO MOVE.
She cradled her right arm against her chest. It was numb
from the shoulder down. She hadn't counted on the
strength of her father's arm. It had taken only one clashing
of swords with him to send pain shooting up through her
limb. Her sword had dropped from her lifeless fingers.

Her face, however, was not numb. Her cheek ached
from where her sire had struck her. That wasn't the only
thing that pained her. Her pride stung mightily, for she
realized how unprepared she had been to meet her father
and best him.

If only the agony stopped there.

She looked at the stairs her husband had just climbed.
Christopher certainly wanted no further part of her. Saints
above, it wasn't enough that her father had stolen Christopher's sight three years before. Now, because of her, a
new humiliation had been added—being thrashed like a
lad before most of his household.

Gillian picked up her sword and turned toward the
hearth, as if not looking at the hall with its layer of blood
and bodies would ease her discomfort. She had brought

Christopher nothing but pain and ruin. Would to God that her father had finished her long ago!

A movement caught her eye. She looked to her left to see Jason going up the stairs to the upper floor. Against her will, and her better judgment, her feet turned in that direction and carried her with them up the stairs after her husband's squire. She knew Christopher would want nothing to do with her, but mayhap she could take one more look at him, fill her eyes with the sight of the man she loved more than life itself. And then she would do what she knew she had to.

She would leave.

To murder her father.

She stayed well behind Jason. It was an easy thing to remain unmarked. She'd done it so often at Warewick that the skill was perfected. She followed Jason down the passageway, waited in the shadows of an alcove while he went into Christopher's bedchamber and came back out again with a basin of water and cloths. It was no mean feat to follow him up the steps to the tower chamber, but she managed that, too.

She stood outside the threshold in the shadows, drinking in the sight of her husband, her heart breaking more fully with each moment that passed.

He sat with his back against the wall, his hands resting limply in his lap. Jason stood nearby, the basin still in his hands.

"My lord, should I not tend your wounds?"

Christopher lifted his head slowly, as if it were a very great effort.

"It matters not, Jason."

Gillian bit her lip to keep from weeping out loud. Never before had she seen her husband look so completely defeated, as if he no longer had any will to go on.

And the blame rested squarely with her.

"Should I call for the lady Gillian?" Jason asked.

Christopher shook his head. Gillian could have sworn

she saw dampness on his cheeks. Perhaps it was from the exertion of the thrashing he had just taken. Or perhaps he wept because of the pain she had caused him.

"Nay," Christopher said, his voice nothing more than a whisper. "That is the last thing I would have you do."

Gillian turned away. She crept down the steps, leaving her heart in pieces behind her. She had heard it from his own mouth. There was no doubt about it now. Christopher wanted nothing further to do with her. In truth, she couldn't blame him. She could hardly bear to live with the grief she'd caused him. How could she expect him to feel any differently?

She walked to Christopher's bedchamber and bolted the door behind her. She laid her sword on the bed and walked to her trunk. It wasn't as if she owned a great deal, but she did have a small bag of gold hidden beneath her most patched pair of hose. Christopher had given her coins now and then to spend at market, instructing her to purchase nothing with them but things for herself. She'd hoarded the gold, certain that someday she would have enough to buy him something fine and beautiful.

She pulled the bag out and fingered it thoughtfully. This would pay for aid in slaying her father. She couldn't think of a better use for the gold.

She retrieved the finely tooled scabbard Christopher had given her, then sheathed her sword in it. Her sword, gold and her cloak were burdens enough to carry with her. Perhaps a small stop at the kitchen would be wise. She would merely put her hand to her sword hilt and Cook would give her exactly what she wanted—and remain silent about the giving of it.

Slowly, she closed the lid to her trunk; then she ran her fingers over the smooth wood. 'Twas certain she would never see it, or this chamber again. Kill her father she would, or die in the attempt. If she survived, she would seek out another place to live. Whatever the outcome of her meeting with her sire, she knew she would never return to Blackmour. How could she, when she would only grieve Christopher by her very presence? Aye, leaving him be was the only thing besides her father's well-deserved demise she could give him.

She left the chamber before thoughts of her husband overcame her. Tears were something she could ill afford now. She would weep later, after the deed was done. Perhaps then she would think on what she had lost this day.

A short while later, she left the kitchens, her sword and her gold in one hand and a small bag of foodstuffs in the other. Cook had looked mightily puzzled when she'd bidden him a final farewell, but she hadn't given him any explanation. To be sure, he hadn't demanded one. If she could have managed a smile, she would have. The Dragon's cook had been tamed indeed.

She crept through the great hall, ignoring the blood still on the rushes and the stench of death. Aye, this was her fault. She had no one else to blame for her father's arrival today and the subsequent war that had ensued.

And Christopher's humiliation.

Her throat tightened again at the memory of her father toying with him, taunting him with mocking laughter and little pricks of his sword. If Captain Ranulf hadn't had her in such a death grip, she would have finished her father herself.

This time she would, once she'd had a chance to think of the most painful way to do it to him. She would need some sort of aid, too. Brave though she might be, she was no fool. Even with the number of her father's guardsmen Colin and his lads had sent to meet their Maker, there would still be knights aplenty at Warewick. Perhaps a few mercenaries could be purchased with her coin. Aye, that was wise. She would find men to get her inside the gates, then she would finish the deed herself.

She slipped out of the hall and down the steps. Once her feet hit the dirt, she walked forward with an arrogant swagger, as if she were nothing more than an errant knight, off to do deeds worthy of song.

The portcullis was open but guards were clustered about it thickly. Gillian kept her head down and continued through. If she could but reach the outer bailey, she would be halfway to freedom. She strode forward as best she could, elbowing men out of her way in what she hoped was a manly fashion.

She had almost reached the far end of the tunnel when she felt her feet leave the ground. She flailed about, but there was no escaping whomever had taken her by the back of her cloak and held her suspended a goodly ways up off the ground.

"And just where do you think you're off to?"

"Oh, Colin," Gillian groaned, "put me down."

"I don't think so—"

She elbowed him in the belly, but instead of leaping aside as the others she had dealt blows to had done, Colin only grunted and held her higher.

"I'd head right back inside the gates, were I you."

"You aren't me, so don't tell me what to do."

Colin set her down and turned her around, his heavy hands firmly grasping her cloak.

"Dragoness, I have no fear of your talons, so don't be talking as if I did. You've more courage than to run away, haven't you?"

She met his gaze squarely. "I'm not running away; I'm going to kill my father."

Colin blinked. "I see."

"Aye," she said, nodding, "I think you do. I'm off to buy myself a few mercenaries, then I'll go to Warewick and slay the bastard in his bed. Or in some other painful fashion." She looked up at him and frowned. "I haven't decided how, as yet."

Colin sighed.

"Think you I cannot?"

His expression was suddenly quite grave. "Warewick is

a warrior with many years behind him, Gillian.''

She stuck out her chin. "Then my youth will serve me well.''

"I meant that he has been warring for most of his life,'' Colin said slowly. "To be sure, you have the courage to take him—"

"And so I will.''

"—but even I would be hard-pressed to best him with the sword,'' Colin finished.

Gillian opened her mouth to speak, then realized there was nothing she could say to that. Colin was a fierce warrior. If he thought it would be difficult to fight her father, what did that say of her skills?

She felt some of her bluster leave.

"Indeed,'' Colin continued, " 'twould take most all my strength to see the deed done.''

The rest of her courage deserted her with a rush.

She bowed her head, defeated.

"I wanted to avenge Christopher,'' she said quietly.

"Aye,'' Colin said gruffly.

"You know why.''

"Aye, I know why.''

She looked up at him. "Did you throw my sire over the wall as you said you would?''

He shook his head. "Mussed his clothes quite a bit and let my fists tell of my displeasure, but I only threw him out of the gates. I didn't want him dead before I could find him later and kill him.''

Gillian felt her spine stiffen of its own accord.

"*I'm* going to do it.''

Colin only grunted. "We'll see. Now, come along back to the hall with me. Time will tell who will have the privilege of finishing the wretch.''

"I'm not going back,'' she said, pulling away. "Perhaps I don't have the skill to kill my sire myself, but I'll find someone who does.'' She paused and a name came immediately to mind. Why she hadn't thought of him before, she surely didn't know. "I'm going to Artane," she announced. "I'll pay Lord Robin to do the deed in my stead."

Colin's mouth fell open. "Artane?"

"Aye," she said, feeling heartened at the very thought. And then another thought occurred to her. "I'll pay Lord Robin to train *me!* Then I'll have the skill to see the deed done myself." She smiled up at him. "What think you?"

Colin's eyes were open very wide and his mouth seemed to be working quite hard, though no words were forthcoming.

"Aye," she agreed, " 'tis a most sensible plan."

"By the saints!" Colin spluttered finally.

Gillian pulled her cloak out of his fists, then leaned up and kissed him softly on the cheek. "Many thanks, Colin, for your kindnesses. I will never forget you. I will send word when my sire is dead." She turned around and faced the end of the tunnel. "Now, Artane is north. I think that is on my right hand when I leave the outer barbican."

Colin made a strangled sound from behind her, but Gillian didn't turn around to look. No doubt he was trying to wish her well but simply couldn't find the words.

Gillian was halfway down the path to the outer gates when Colin suddenly appeared at her side. Gillian looked up at him with a faint smile.

"You needn't see me to the gates," she said. "Those I can find by myself."

"You are *not* traipsing off to Artane," Colin managed, still very red in the face.

She reached out and patted his arm. "Don't fret, Colin. I'll find it."

"You can't tell bloody north from south!" Colin exclaimed. He strode ahead, then turned and planted himself before her. "You aren't going alone."

Gillian felt her heart warm at the thought of Colin's loyalty to her. But it wouldn't do to take him from Christopher.

"You must stay," she said, with a smile. "Though I do appreciate the offer of aid—"

"You are *not* going alone," Colin repeated stubbornly. "And you aren't going all the way to Artane. 'Tis a hard ride and you have no horse." He looked at her rather triumphantly.

"Then I'll walk."

"Then think on this, my lady. Your sire is not far outside the gates." He smiled and his smile was anything but warm. "With the send-off I gave him, I doubt he'll be moving much in the next few days. Nevertheless, we will not wish to be wandering the same roads as he will be."

"I could take him," Gillian said, but even as she said it, she wondered if it might be more difficult than she thought.

"After you train with Artane for a few weeks, aye, you likely could. But now, I think not." He folded his arms over his chest and looked down at her. He was silent for a moment or two, then his look brightened. "Perhaps a few more herbs would serve you. Let us hie ourselves down to those witches and see what they can offer."

Gillian opened her mouth to say him nay, then thought better of it. Her courage was returning, 'twas true, but a few more herbs couldn't hurt. She nodded slowly.

"Aye, that might be wise."

"Then let us be off," Colin said, taking her by the arm and tugging her down the path.

As she trotted alongside him, Gillian wondered at his change of heart but refrained from commenting on it. At least he was for her. She wasn't about to discount his aid. Perhaps when the deed was done, he would return and tell Christopher that she had been the one to avenge him. Though it would never atone for the hurt that had been done him, at least he would know she'd done her best.

She clutched her sword, her gold and her small bag of food and wondered if there were perhaps a herb that would improve her swordplay.

• • •

BERENGARIA STOOD AT THE THRESHOLD OF HER MODEST hut, breathing deeply. She'd been standing there most of the morning, trying to catch her breath—and it wasn't Magda's most recent recipe to drive her outside. She'd been privy to the sight of what had transpired in Blackmour's great hall. Why her Sight had failed to alert her to Warewick's arrival, she couldn't say. Christopher had indeed paid a heavy price for her lack of foreseeing.

She looked to her right only to see Gillian running to keep up with Colin of Berkhamshire's long strides, strides that were currently eating up great stretches of ground as Colin came toward her. Gillian's mood was difficult to determine; she was obviously merely trying to catch her breath.

Colin, on the other hand, seemed to be about some specific business. Berengaria found herself only mildly surprised at Colin's reappearance. He'd come to fetch a few herbs for Gillian a fortnight past but had fled almost immediately. Perhaps the sight of Nemain grinding up bone into a cup had been what had done it.

Colin came to an abrupt halt before her. Gillian was panting too much for speech, so Berengaria looked up at her keeper.

"She's off to kill her sire and needs herbs," Colin announced.

Berengaria felt her eyebrows go up in spite of her desire to look calm. Colin, who moved to stand directly behind Gillian, wore a distinctly pointed look, as if he strove to tell her aught merely with his eyes.

Berengaria didn't need to hear what he meant to tell her, for she knew what Gillian was about. She'd seen the outcome of the small war in the keep and knew what Christopher had suffered. Even without her art, she would have known where Gillian's thoughts would have led her. And now to think the child had gathered the remains of her faltering courage and put her foot on a path that would lead to Warewick . . . Berengaria looked at Gillian and smiled gently.

"I daresay you've the courage for it," she said.

Gillian nodded.

"But now you seek aught to improve your swordplay?"

Gillian's mouth fell open. "Aye," she breathed. "How did you know?"

Berengaria only smiled.

"She's off to Artane," Colin added. "To have Lord Robin train her." He shook his head violently and wriggled his eyebrows a time or two.

"Ah," Berengaria said, nodding. "A wise choice, Gillian, for I hear his swordplay is as flawless as his features. And he did train your lord."

"Aye," Gillian said, "my thoughts as well."

"Artane is a *long* journey," Colin said.

"Indeed," Berengaria agreed. "And I fear my cache of skill herbs is quite depleted. It would take me a few days to gather more. You would likely wish to remain here until that time."

Colin nodded vigorously.

Gillian hesitated. Berengaria watched her struggle with herself, as if she weighed the delay against the benefit of the herbs.

"A se'nnight," Berengaria offered. "No longer."

An expression of pain crossed Gillian's features. "But where will I go until then?"

"You'll return to the keep," Colin stated.

Gillian shook her head. "Nay, I could not do that. It would only grieve Christopher."

Berengaria looked at her gently. "I have to agree with Lord Berkhamshire," she said. "It would surely be safer if you waited at the keep. Then you could send for Lord Artane. Travel in these times is quite dangerous."

Colin positively beamed his approval.

Gillian shook her head. "I cannot stay at Blackmour, my lady."

"Oh, Gillian," Berengaria said softly. She reached and put her hand on Gillian's arm. Gillian's sword was clutched in her hand, and Berengaria's heart wrenched at the sight. How courageous this child had become, to take steel in her hand and face her greatest fear, all out of a desire to ease her husband's pain.

"Artane is much too far away, my child," she said. "I think you would do better to remain close to your lord."

Gillian's eyes began to fill with tears. "But 'twill only grieve him. I must go—"

"—to Blackmour's Folly," Colin announced suddenly. "Your sire will never manage the climb. Artane likely couldn't either, but we'll solve that later. 'Tis certainly close enough for the delivery of important herbs."

Berengaria watched as Gillian considered this new plan. She gave the girl's arm a gentle squeeze.

"This is a wise choice, my dear," she said, with an encouraging smile. "You'll be quite safe there. I'll send what you need with one of Lord Berkhamshire's men."

"In truth?" Gillian asked.

Berengaria nodded. "Of course. I daresay 'twill be a most comfortable place to wait for Lord Robin to come to you."

Gillian was still for a moment or two, then nodded. "Perhaps 'tis for the best."

"Well done," Colin said, grasping Gillian by her sword arm. He bowed to Berengaria. "Our gratitude, lady." He started back up the path, Gillian in tow. "I'll fetch the men; then we'll make our way to the cliff. 'Tis a most treacherous climb, so we must needs . . ."

His voice trailed off. Soon Berengaria could see them no more. She nodded thoughtfully. At least Gillian would be well protected, what with the fierce lord of Berkhamshire watching over her. And in truth Blackmour's Folly was as unassailable a refuge as Gillian could have wished for.

And it was close enough that Christopher could send for her.

Assuming he came to his senses in time.

The door behind her was yanked open and Nemain came stumbling out into the sunshine, coughing. A black cloud followed her.

Nemain gasped, clutching the doorframe. When she could breathe again, she fixed Berengaria with a steely look.

"I told you she couldn't cook!"

Nemain stumbled off, cursing under her breath. Berengaria cast a glance heavenward, took a deep breath and turned toward the doorway. At least this problem was simply solved.

'Twas far easier than tampering with matters of life and death.

thirty-two

CHRISTOPHER SAT IN HIS GREAT CHAIR BEFORE THE hearth in his bedchamber with a cup of wine in his hands and stared pensively into the flames. Staring was, of course, a misnomer for what he was doing. He was looking blindly into the flames, as blindly as he did aught else in his life. Indeed, the whole of his life was nothing but darkness, though now it was a more complete darkness than usual. It had been so for a fortnight.

Since the day Gillian had left him.

He had planned to send her away. He had wanted her to go to someone who could care for her properly. He had sat on the floor in his tower chamber, too numb to even flinch at the stitches he had eventually allowed Jason to take in his flesh, and turned over in his mind a list of allies to whom he could send her. He knew he had sunk to new lows when he had seriously considered giving her to Kendrick of Artane, the womanizing whelp. Not that Kendrick wouldn't have cared for her well. It was just the thought of anyone else, especially someone as flagrantly charming as Kendrick, touching Gillian's soft skin that had made him grind his teeth in fury.

Christopher had passed a day or two in misery, not mov-

ing except to take care of the most pressing of needs. He'd
had the presence of mind to wonder why Gillian hadn't
come seeking him, but he'd assumed she'd had the good
sense to simply leave him be.

He had assumed incorrectly.

Jason had read him the letter Gillian had sent along soon
after her flight, a letter full of apologies for having been
the cause of his grief. She blamed herself for all the ills
that had befallen him, from his inability to protect her from
her sire, right down to his blindness itself.

Christopher cursed softly. He couldn't even muster up
the energy to fling his goblet against the wall as he might
have another time. Even cursing was almost too much of
an effort. What good would it do him anyway? It wouldn't
heal his eyes and his eyes alone were what could have
made the difference. That truth resonated in his soul, shaking his very bones with the force of its vibrations.

If he'd been able to see, he would have cut Bernard of
Warewick to ribbons. Slowly. Methodically. Likely with a
bit of artistry, to pay the whoreson back for every moment
of pain he'd caused Gillian over the years.

If he'd been able to see, he wouldn't have let feelings
of worthlessness distress him when Jason's kin had departed. He would have ridden back to Artane with Robin
to show Gillian the only true home he'd ever known. He
wouldn't have fled to his tower like a bastard son, shamed
by what he could never be.

Aye, and if he'd been able to see, he would have likely
come to his senses about Lina on his own and cast her far
from him. He never would have been hurt, he never would
have felt scorned. He never would have known how it felt
to have a beautiful woman look at him and find him so
terribly lacking. His pride would be intact, not hanging
about him in shreds. Aye, he would have remained the
proud, peerless warrior, sallying forth to tourneys across
the whole of France and England merely for the sport of
it. He would have multiplied his wealth again many times

merely from the knights he would have held for ransom. He would have held a few barons and earls for ransom while he was at it.

If he could have seen them to best them.

And if he'd had his sight, he also would have been too stupid to realize what a beautiful soul Gillian of Warewick hid under her unruly curls and not-quite perfect face.

But he studiously ignored that thought.

The door opened softly behind him to his right and Wolf whined a low greeting. Christopher lifted his head.

"Colin?" he asked hopefully.

"Nay, my lord. 'Tis Jason."

Christopher smiled grimly. "I should have known. A horrendous stench did not attend your entrance."

He fell silent and listened to Jason seeing to his usual tasks of cleaning mail and putting away clothes. It must be morning again. Christopher hadn't left his chamber in so long that he'd completely lost track of time.

"Fair weather or foul, lad?"

"A bit of a chill, my lord. It would seem the summer begins to wane already."

So soon? Christopher shook his head in disbelief. Surely he couldn't have passed an entire summer with Gillian already. Of course, much of that time he'd spent lazing in bed with her. It was understandable that the days had gone by without him having noticed them.

He ruthlessly pushed aside the memories that threatened to overwhelm him. Gillian's name hadn't been spoken since she left and he fully intended that it remain that way.

Now, Colin's name was a different story. Christopher knew full well that Colin had gone with Gillian to keep her safe. It was somehow fitting. Gillian had tamed all of them and Colin was no exception. Christopher found it amusing how his fiercest of friends hovered over the lady of Blackmour like a nursemaid. Or he might have been amused, had he not been so hurt that Gillian had obviously found Colin's companionship preferable to his. Aye, she had found him lacking indeed, despite her pretty apologies to the contrary.

"Any message from Colin?" Christopher asked, then marveled that the words had come from his mouth. It had been the very last question he'd intended to ask.

"Aye," Jason said, sounding understandably hesitant.

Christopher froze. That wasn't the answer he'd been expecting. He set his cup down carefully next to his chair.

"In truth?"

"Aye, my lord, two missives. Shall I read them to you?"

Christopher very carefully leaned back in his chair and folded his hands in his lap. "Well, it isn't as if I can bloody read them myself." He gestured to the stool across from him. "Out with it, lad."

Christopher heard Jason drag up the stool and sit, then listened while Jason unrolled the parchment.

"I daresay Lord Colin didn't write this," Jason said. " 'Tis in a very fair hand. Why, I've no doubt the lady—"

"Content yourself with reading the words, Jason," Christopher interrupted.

"Of course, my lord," Jason said softly. "It reads: 'Christopher, you blighted whoreson,' " Jason coughed, then continued, " 'send me stores! I'm freezing my arse off up here while you're roasting your toes next to a cheery blaze. Wood, food and several bottles of wine would be well received. More to follow later.' " Jason cleared his throat. "To be sure, Lord Berkhamshire must have dictated that word by word. Surely the lady—"

"Indeed," Christopher said shortly. He drummed his fingers on the wood of the chair. That Colin had sent word must mean Gillian hadn't traveled far. But where were they?

Christopher chewed on his next words a good long time before he spat them out with as much haste as possible.

"And where do you suppose the whoreson is keeping himself?"

Jason cleared his throat. "The Lord's Hall. Or, more precisely, in a tent next to the Lord's Hall. It would seem that the hall itself is being occupied . . . by . . . er—"

"I see," Christopher said hastily, sparing Jason another tongue-lashing like the one he'd given his squire the first time the boy had said Gillian's name in his presence. "Well, that is news indeed."

"Would you care to hear the other missive now, my lord?"

Christopher waved him on. " 'Tis unlikely it is any more offensive than the last."

Jason unrolled the second letter. " 'Chris, I'm writing this myself as I can't let on what I'm telling you. Damned stubborn woman you've wed, and no mistake. She's fixed on the idea of killing her father to avenge you and won't be trained in swordplay by anyone save Artane himself. I'm supposed to have sent for him, but haven't yet. Thought you'd want to know what she's about first. The wench has spine, I'll give her that. I'll keep her here until I've heard from you, what you want done and all that. Berkhamshire.' " Jason rerolled the missive. "Shall I fetch aught to reply with, my lord?"

Christopher shook his head. "Not as yet, lad." He rubbed his hands together, then flexed his fingers. "Best hand me the first one, Jason. No sense in having it be lost."

"And the second?"

Christopher gave his squire what he hoped was a silence inducing frown. Jason gulped and immediately pressed a scrap of rolled parchment into Christopher's hands.

"There it is, my lord. The first one."

Christopher waved toward the door. "I need nothing now. Hie yourself down to the kitchens and find something to eat. You sound hungry."

"Thank you, my lord."

Christopher waited until Jason had gone before he leaned his head back against the chair. He ran his fingers over the parchment he held. It was something she'd touched, held, perhaps even wept over. Christopher dragged his sleeve across his eyes quickly. Saints above, 'twas simply a letter.

But it made him realize yet again just how much he missed her.

But Blackmour's Folly! He rose suddenly and began to pace. Why, by all the saints, had she fled there? The one place she'd chosen was the least likely place he'd ever be able to manage. Even sighted, he would have been a fool to tread that path. It was the only reason his father had built the bloody place as a haven from his shrewish wife! It was safe from any siege, friendly or not. How Gillian had managed it was a mystery.

Christopher's only faint satisfaction was the thought of Colin huddled on that pitiful bit of soil in a tent, shivering from the damp and from the continuous winds that buffeted the place. Death by ague would be a fitting end for the traitor.

His pacing took him to his window and he threw open the shutters. The chill wind off the water hit him full in the face. And if he felt it, Gillian felt it too. She would be cold. The girl's feet and hands were particularly susceptible to the chill. He remembered how it felt to have her appendages seeking his warmth during the night. And once he had woken to warm her hands, well, there hadn't been any reason not to warm the rest of her, had there? Christopher closed his eyes and let the memories wash over him.

Gillian under him with her body open to him, welcoming him with soft sighs and words of love. Gillian pushing him back onto the bed and loving him boldly, the heat from her cheeks telling him that she was blushing furiously. Sweet, gentle Gillian who had turned out to be a terrible tease, a sharp-tongued jester, a passionate lover.

She had blossomed before his very sightless eyes. He had given her safety and she had given him her soul.

And then she had taken it away from him because she thought she was the cause of all his troubles.

Christopher pushed away from the window, blaming the chill of the wind for the tears coursing down his cheeks. If only he could see! Then Gillian would have no reason not to love him. She would never have any reason to leave him. And even if she might be so foolish as to think she had caused his woes, he could bloody well climb that treacherous path to the Lord's Hall, jerk her to him and never let her from his arms again.

Christopher dragged his sleeve across his face again, then carefully set her missive down on his table. Then he left his bedchamber. His feet seemed to know exactly where they wanted to go, a place his mind wasn't ready to acknowledge.

He didn't believe in magic.

Bloody hell, he didn't believe in witches either!

BERENGARIA WATCHED IN SURPRISE AS THE DRAGON LEFT his lair and walked purposefully across his inner bailey. In her mind's eye, she saw him come through both gates, cross the heavy stone bridge, and stride through the village. She was so surprised that she hardly managed to scatter the obstacles from before him and lead his feet in the right direction.

Moments later a sharp rap sounded on the door. Magda answered it before Berengaria could stop her. And then Magda swooned, right into Nemain's arms. A smile touched Berengaria's lips at the sight of Nemain struggling to hold onto Magda and gape at the Dragon at the same time. It was a sight she was certain she would carry to her grave.

"I seek Berengaria," the deep voice said curtly.

"Aye, m-my lord," Nemain said, overcome.

Magda's swoon ended conveniently and she regained

her footing. "Of *course*, my lord!" she exclaimed, taking Christopher's arm and pulling him inside. She waved her spoon about excitedly. "We're so *honored* to have you visit us! Let me prepare something warm for you to drink."

"Nay, I'll do it," Nemain broke in, pushing Magda aside. "You'll burn it, little abbess."

Magda turned and thwacked Nemain smartly on the hand with her spoon. "You stop calling me that!"

"I'll stop it when you learn to prepare a decent love potion!"

"Enough," Berengaria said, pushing Nemain and Magda both toward the door. "If you've a mind to give His Lordship something, give him peace and quiet. Go forage for herbs and do not come back until I call you."

Protests were vociferous, but Berengaria prevailed. She shut the door on her two companions, then saw Christopher settled on the only chair in their hut. She drew up a stool and sat down before him. And for the first time in her life, she had a good look at Gillian's fierce and intimidating husband.

He looked neither at the moment. His handsome face was drawn and haggard, as if he'd suffered much over the past fortnight. His hair hung into his blue eyes. His hands were clasped loosely between his knees and his shoulders were bowed. Berengaria's heart broke at the sight. How she grieved for what this sweet lad had suffered in his lifetime.

She brushed away a tear or two and laid her age-spotted hand on his knee.

"My lord?"

He cleared his throat and lifted his head. "You are Berengaria? Gillian's Berengaria?"

"Aye, my lord. That I am."

Agony twisted his features. "Then I've come to ask a boon." He shifted restively on his chair, as if he would have much preferred to be up and pacing.

"My lord," she began, but he held up his hand.

"I beg you, allow me to finish." He took a deep breath. "I've seen much in this world that I cannot explain. I always considered myself to be fairly learned. I could read and I knew my numbers well enough when I could see them. And I'll tell you now that I've never had any use for witches." He paused. "But that was before . . ."

"Before you lost your sight?" she finished softly.

"Aye." He took her withered hand in both of his and clutched it. "I beg you," he said hoarsely. "I'll do anything, give anything. Just make me see again. It's all I ask. I'll give up all I have. All," he repeated. Tears slipped down his cheeks. "None of it matters to me."

Berengaria put her free hand over his. "For what reason, my lord?"

He swallowed hard. "For Gillian." He bowed his head. "So she'll have a husband who's whole."

Berengaria's heart broke at the sight of such a proud man so bowed with grief. And she would have given anything, aye, everything she'd ever possessed or hoped to possess if she could have done what he'd asked of her.

But she couldn't.

"My lord," she began softly, "if I could . . ."

He lifted his head and looked in her direction. "Then you . . . cannot?"

"Nay, my lord," she said, as softly as before. "God knows I wish I could. It is far beyond my art."

"But the herbs you gave Gillian—"

"Crushed rose petals."

Christopher's sigh came straight from his soul. "Of course. In truth, I think I knew it all along."

He started to rise, but she stopped him by holding onto his hands.

"There is something," she offered.

He sat back down. "There is?"

Oh, the hope in his voice! Berengaria smiled through her tears.

"Aye, there is. 'Tis the magic of belief."

A small smile touched his lips. "Lady, you speak to me as if I were a small lad, still swayed by tales told at bed-time."

She smiled in return. "Can you doubt the truth of it? You and I both know I gave Gillian nothing but simple herbs, but did she?"

"Nay. She believed it fully."

"And because of her belief, she gained courage and beauty, did she not?"

"She was never ugly, lady."

"In her mind she was."

Christopher laughed, but it was without mirth. "And so you tell me if I believe it strongly enough, I'll regain my sight?"

"I think, my lord, you know exactly what I mean."

He sighed and looked heavenward. "If I believe she loves me then she truly will."

"She loves you already. 'Twas your disbelief in that love that made you doubt her. And it was your disbelief in your own worth that finally drove her away. The thought you avoid most diligently is the heart of the matter, my lord. Had you had your sight, you never would have learned to love Gillian. You would have been wed still to Magdalina of Berkhamshire. The outer beauty of her face would have soon faded and left you with a woman whose inner ugliness would have driven you from your own home. Your life would have been a series of meaningless tourneys and travels on the continent merely to escape her. Your dissatisfaction would have grown until it hardened your heart into stone."

Christopher swallowed, seemingly speechless.

"The Good Father above does not gift us useless blessings," Berengaria continued. "The loss of your sight forced you to see with the eyes of your soul. It was with them that you saw Gillian and loved her. Think on the joy she has brought you! She will give you beautiful, strong children. Your life will be filled with true, stalwart friends who will be more than willing to be your eyes for you in return for the gift of yourself you've given them, a gift that cannot be measured by coin.

"When Jason leaves you to seek his own way, his uncles will send sons to be trained by you; then Jason will send his own sons. You will teach the lads more than swordplay, you will teach them to be men, to be grateful for what they have and take nothing for granted. And all along this course set out before you, you'll have a sweet, gentle girl by your side, a woman-child who loves you more than she loves herself, who sees your blindness as a blessing, not a flaw. And she will only call you a fool if you do not go to her!"

Christopher held up his hands in surrender and a small, nervous laugh escaped him. "I vow you've convinced me. Pray, lady, do not draw your blade!"

Berengaria loosened her hold on Christopher's hands when she realized she was nigh to drawing blood. She patted his hands in apology and smiled.

"I do tend to the passionate at times, lad."

Christopher leaned back against his chair and folded his arms over his chest, cocking his head to one side as if he listened intently.

"Are you a witch? In truth?"

"In truth?" she said with a smile. "In truth, I have a few gifts, a handful of which aid me when I need them to."

"And those would be?"

"The Sight," Berengaria said softly, not wanting to grieve him.

"That must serve you well," he replied, just as softly.

Berengaria smiled. "We live in perilous times, my lord. Marauding knights take what they want for their own, when they want it and the cost to others be damned. For myself, I can only say I've never been caught with my kettle still on."

Christopher laughed softly. "Indeed, lady. Then I'm pleased your Sight has served you so well. Now, what other gifts does a full-fledged witch possess in these perilous times? I've often wondered. Perhaps I could borrow a few to add to my own reputation."

Berengaria wished Christopher could see her smile. What a gentle creature this dragon was under all his fire and smoke. Gillian could not have been blessed with a finer man.

"I fear my gifts may not serve your reputation, my lord. I have a knowledge of herb lore. Also of midwifery. Though she knows it not, I brought your lady into the world."

"And a fine job you did indeed, mistress."

"I tend to believe such," Berengaria said modestly.

Christopher sighed and dragged his hands through his hair. Then he gave her a weary smile. "What does your Sight tell you at present? Other than the fact that your two companions are fair to falling through the wall in their effort to hear what we are saying?"

Two gasps and a shuddering of the unstable wall lent credibility to Christopher's words. Berengaria laughed.

"You are more observant than I, my lord. What my Sight tells me is that you'll have need of a midwife soon enough and I would hope you would remember where you could find one."

Christopher smiled. "You are a witch in truth then, lady, for I had considered procuring a nurse or two for my future children."

"Three!" a voice called from without. "A nurse or *three!*"

"Three, then," Christopher agreed. Then he stopped short. "How soon will I need you?"

"Within the half year, I should expect."

Christopher paled. "You jest."

Berengaria patted his knee and rose. "Hurry off to the keep, my lord. We'll be there when you need us."

Christopher rose, looking dazed. He left their modest hut, looking none too steady on his feet.

Berengaria watched him go, scattering obstacles out of his way and leading his feet in the right direction. She smiled to herself. Perhaps not giving him a full list of her talents had been a good thing.

She struggled to keep her feet as Magda and Nemain rushed past her into the hut. She stared into nothing and watched Christopher enter his hall. Already his step was more confident and his shoulders squared. She closed her eyes and tried to ignore the noise Magda and Nemain were making.

"I say we fashion him a potion in gratitude!" Magda exclaimed joyfully. "I'll put something on right away."

"Lucifer's nose, Magda, we must pack!" Nemain exclaimed. "I can't gather my things if you're puttering about amongst my pots. Now, leave off, novice, and let me be about my work. Lord Blackmour will be having guests for the birth, perhaps again from the north. I may be replenishing my thumb-bone sooner than I'd hoped!"

Berengaria stepped outside for peace. She cast her gaze to the future, praying she might see something to aid Christopher.

She saw nothing. She struggled to brush aside the darkness that hovered over coming events like a heavy fog.

It was useless. Either her gift had departed, or the future was too uncertain to be seen. For the first time, she understood a bit of Christopher's frustration.

And she prayed the darkness was just her own failing.

thirty-three

GILLIAN SAT ON A BOULDER AND STARED DOWN THE PATH that led up the steep side of the cliff from the shore. Every time she looked at it, she marveled anew that she had managed the climb. But managed it she had, partly thanks to Colin's having pulled her halfway up the incline behind him. Once at the top, the last thing she'd wanted to do was try to get back down. At least the steepness of the way reassured her that her father wouldn't come seeking her. It was a comfort knowing she had safety enough to prepare to meet him.

Her ascent had been accomplished nigh onto three weeks ago. Now she sat, stranded on a bit of land that was separated from the rest of England just as Blackmour was. Safe though she might have been, she'd never felt more alone in her life.

She looked out pensively over the ocean. She forced herself to look straight forward and not to her right. To her right, Blackmour hovered out over the sea like a huge beast of prey. Gillian half wondered if any of the fishes in the ocean dared approach. She certainly wouldn't have, in their place. Blackmour was every bit as harsh and intimidating a keep as it had seemed the first time she'd seen it.

Only she knew the warmth that waited within.

Had waited within, rather. The warmth would be gone now, but at least he would be at peace. And in a few months, she would deliver his babe and that would perhaps please him. At first, she'd thought to merely send the child to the keep and remain at the Lord's Hall. Now she knew she couldn't let her child go. It was the only part of Christopher that remained to her.

Though keeping the child might still be in question. She'd missed her monthly courses but twice. She might have suspected nothing except that she was so violently ill at the mere smell of food.

She shifted at the thought. She might have shifted more easily, but Colin had piled every fur and blanket available around her, as if he expected her to die from a chill at any moment. She wore them all to humor him. It was easier than fighting him.

"Gillian," Colin boomed from behind her. "It grows chilly."

"True enough, my lord," she called back over her shoulder.

His grunt of displeasure almost made her smile. It was no wonder Christopher kept Colin about the hall. Baiting him was good sport.

"I said *it grows cold*," Colin said from directly behind her. " 'Tis well past time you were inside."

"Go away, Colin. There is nothing to do inside."

"There is nothing to do *outside*."

"I can stare at the water out here."

"You can stare at the fire in *there*."

"Colin, you're a pest."

Without warning, he plucked her up, furs, blankets and all, and carried her inside the large, stone hall. Gillian sighed and surrendered. If she did what Colin asked, he would cease bothering her.

He deposited her in a chair by the hearth and sat down across a chessboard from her. Gillian rolled her eyes.

"I don't want—"

"Chris enjoys a fine game of chess. 'Tis past time you learned to play."

"I don't like chess."

"I don't give a pig's arse what you like."

Gillian looked at him so long, silently, that he started to squirm. Then she spoke.

"I'll hardly have the chance to play with him, Colin."

"You don't know that," Colin said gruffly.

"I do know that. He would never come for me, and I surely don't expect him to."

"He'll be here," Colin said stubbornly, "when the time has come for it."

Gillian looked away. "Not that it matters. Robin will arrive soon; then I'll begin my training. 'Tis hard to believe it has taken him this long, but I'll be patient a bit longer. After all, he is an important lord with many things to see to."

Colin coughed. "Indeed."

Something in his voice caught her attention. She fixed him with her most piercing stare. "You sent the message to Artane."

He squirmed. "Aye, I sent a message or two."

She threw off the furs and blankets. "There was the one I wrote for you to Christopher," she said, counting on her fingers, "then two or three more by your own hand." She felt unease begin to build in her. "Surely one of those was to Lord Robin."

Colin frowned fiercely and remained silent.

"Colin!" she exclaimed. "You vowed you sent it!"

"What I vowed," he muttered, "was to save my own sweet neck and even you will have to admit that it'd be the first thing I'd find severed if Christopher thought I'd actually done such a thing."

"But I have to be trained!"

"What you have to do is wait for Christopher to see to Warewick," Colin threw back. " 'Tis his right to repay your sire for what he's done and I'll not rob him of the sport."

Gillian jumped to her feet. "But my father will kill him!"

"Sit, child. Your sire will do nothing of the sort."

"You've no idea what the man will do." She folded her arms over her chest. "Very well, then, my lord Berkhamshire, I'll go myself."

"You will go nowhere."

"Aye, I *will*. 'Tis obvious I cannot trust you to do as you've promised."

She pushed her chair back from the chessboard and cast Colin a displeased glare. Saints, but the past three weeks had been wasted! She could have been to Artane and well on her way to being trained by now.

She pulled her cloak off the back of her chair and drew it around her shoulders. The climb to the shore was still possible that day. Indeed, she could be to the shore and halfway to Blackmour by noon.

"You cannot go," Colin said.

Gillian ignored him. She would have to have a horse, obviously. Christopher had several in his stables. She would choose what looked to be the fastest mount, then be on her way to Artane before sunset. At least she had a few training herbs left her. She'd saved them against the time Robin would come. She would need double the amount now, for she had half the time in which to perfect her skill.

"But where did I leave them?" she muttered to herself.

Colin cleared his throat. "You cannot go."

Gillian fixed him with a steely look. "And why not?"

He looked at her for several moments in silence, his face turning redder by the heartbeat.

"Because 'twill hurt the babe," he said finally, in a strangled voice.

Gillian froze. "The babe?"

"Aye, the babe."

She clutched the back of the chair. "How did you know?"

"You puke up everything I cook for you," Colin said, sounding rather irritated over the fact. "I daresay you aren't doing it out of worry over me freezing my sorry arse off outside."

Gillian felt the floor become unsteady beneath her. She leaned heavily against the chair. Saints above, she hadn't considered harm to the babe. Even if she trained until her skill was matchless, she might still lose. How could she put her child in that kind of danger?

She sank down into her chair.

"I fear you're right," she whispered.

"I daresay I am."

Gillian felt tears begin and she looked up at the ceiling in an effort to stop them from slipping down her cheeks.

"I wanted to see Christopher avenged," she said, blinking hard. "I have failed him even in that simple thing."

"You've failed him in no way, lady. You'll bear him a strong son."

She shook her head. "Somehow it doesn't seem enough."

" 'Tis a far better work than killing."

"But my sire—"

"If you wish to spite your father, think on what bearing Christopher a son will mean. The child will inherit all of Warewick and Blackmour both."

"I hadn't thought of that," she admitted.

"I'm certain your sire has."

Gillian nodded. He no doubt had. For all she knew, her sire suspected she was with child.

"I wonder," she mused, "if Berengaria has an herb for the bearing of a healthy babe."

"I've no doubt she has anything a maid might imagine she needs," Colin said.

Gillian looked at him and found herself smiling. "Think you?"

"Aye," he said. "Saints above, but I've never seen so many pots in one hut before in my life!"

Gillian leaned back against her chair and smiled. "And you would know, my lord, as you've spent ample time peering at them."

"Sshh," Colin whispered, casting her an irritated glance. "It isn't as if I wish everyone to know!"

Gillian shook her head, amused. The saints only knew what Colin had ingested on his various and sundry trips to Berengaria's hut over the past three weeks. Whatever brew he'd drunk didn't seem to have harmed him. Perhaps he'd partaken of a few herbs of wisdom along the way. Though she hardly agreed with his methods of keeping her at Blackmour's Folly, she couldn't disagree with the results.

"I suppose you're right about this," she admitted.

"Aye," he agreed. "I am."

"I don't care overmuch for your deception."

"Were you ready to listen to reason a fortnight ago?" he asked.

She paused, then shook her head. "I daresay I wasn't."

"Then perhaps my deception served its purpose."

Gillian sighed and looked into the hearth. The fire was warm, but it failed to soothe her. Giving up her vengeance was not an easy thing. She'd lain awake nights plotting it, praying the doing of the deed might ease Christopher's pain. And now to turn away from it?

She sighed. It was the better choice. She could use her strength to fashion a healthy babe. It was something that required nothing but her own humble skills. It certainly was a better work than killing. Her sire would likely meet his end on the end of someone's sword eventually. It didn't have to be hers.

"The saints only know what my father will do once he's back to himself," she said quietly.

"Well," Colin said, "I've a good idea of what *you'll* do and that will be to stay here until Chris comes to fetch you. And while you're here, you'll learn to play chess."

"But I don't want—"

"You're as stubborn and irritating as your lord, Gillian. You deserve each other. You'll drive each other daft in short order and I mean to be there to watch. Now, we'll discuss again the pieces and their purposes. You'll never best Chris unless you listen to me."

"Colin . . ."

"For every time you win, I'll let you sit outside."

She folded her arms over her chest. "I'll go outside when I please anyway."

Colin lifted one eyebrow and smiled a very dangerous smile. "Is that so? Perhaps you forget who sits across from you."

Half a year ago, Gillian would have been sweating with terror. Now she only laughed. And she was so surprised by her courage that she laughed again.

"Aye, I know well enough. The fiercesome Colin of Berkhamshire whose underbelly is softer than my dragon's. I do not fear you."

"Warren!" Colin barked at one of his men, who jumped to his feet immediately and rushed to Colin's side.

"Aye, my lord!"

"What did I do to the last lad who said he didn't fear me?"

The blood drained from the man's face. "My lord, I beseech you not to make me say. I'm still having foul dreams on account of it."

Colin waved the man away and he went to join his fellows on the other side of the small hall gladly. Colin looked back to Gillian and raised one eyebrow arrogantly.

"Well?"

"Would it soothe you more if my teeth chattered, or shall I burst into tears?"

Colin looked at her from under his eyebrows. "Saints, Gillian, I do believe those herbs worked in truth. Even Chris trembles just a bit when I turn fierce. And here you sit with me without so much as batting an eyelash."

Gillian's smile faded. "He doesn't fear you either. He loves you dearly."

Colin scowled and coughed gruffly a time or two. "He loves you more. Now, to the game before all this talk irritates me. My men will weep if I truly become angry."

Gillian nodded and let Colin distract her. It was certainly easier than letting her thoughts wander, especially since they always chose to wander back to Christopher. She pulled one of the knights off the board and fingered it, trying to pay attention to Colin's explanation of its purpose. Gillian knew very well what a knight's purpose was for she had one at home that she was very much in love with; only he certainly wasn't made of carved wood.

What was Christopher doing? Could it be possible he was thinking of her, or had he forgotten her the moment she'd left?

"Gillian, pay attention."

Gillian gave Colin a weary smile and struggled to do as he asked.

CHRISTOPHER FINGERED THE DULL EDGE OF THE WOODEN sword. He smiled in spite of himself. It had been years since he'd held the like. He'd had his own when he was a child, of course, but his sire had never stirred himself to demonstrate the use of it. Nay, those weren't the memories that made Christopher smile. It was thinking of the first time he'd put one in Jason of Artane's pudgy three-year-old's hands. Jason had waved the sword about, in ecstasies of delight, only to turn and wallop Robin squarely in the—well, in a most tender spot. Robin had doubled over with a gasp and Jason had fled around to the back of Christopher's legs. Christopher had found himself being used as a shield by both Jason and his instrument of torture. At ten-and-nine, Christopher had well understood Robin's discomfort, but he'd indulged in hearty laughter once Robin had limped off to recover. Saints, what a memory!

"My lord?"

Christopher inclined his head toward the door. "Come in, Jason."

"You seem in a fine mood, my lord," Jason said, sounding as if he were smiling because of that discovery.

"Idle thoughts," Christopher said, with a smile. "Tell me, lad, did you fetch Ranulf?"

"Aye, my lord. He comes presently."

"Well done. We'll see if this works any better tonight than it did yestereve."

" 'Tis a fine idea, my lord. I don't know why we haven't done it sooner."

" 'Twas your father's idea, Jason. When he was here he suggested it, but I said him nay."

"Why, my lord?"

Christopher shrugged and smiled faintly. "Too much pride, I suppose. I remember how it felt to cross swords with him and I couldn't bear to have it be less than it was."

"I understand, my lord."

"You know," Christopher continued, "when I could see, I never saw your father smile when he faced me over blades."

"Neither did I," Jason agreed. "He was working far too hard to keep you at bay, my lord. Ever he says that you are the only sport left for him."

"Were," Christopher corrected.

"Aye, my lord," Jason said softly. "But I daresay you will be again."

Christopher doubted it very much, but he shook aside the thought before it troubled him. He turned at the footfall behind him. "Ranulf?"

"Aye," his captain said, closing the chamber door behind him. "I've brought the other sword. May I catch my breath from climbing the stairs, or will you begin straightaway?"

"Saints, old man," Christopher said, "you tire so soon?"

"I'm resting against what you'll put me through, my lord," Ranulf said, sounding exhausted by the thought.

And for some reason, Christopher found himself cheered by it. He balanced the wooden sword in his hand and felt something akin to pleasure flow through him. He was training—and against something that breathed. A month ago, he wouldn't have dreamed he'd be doing the like.

It had been Colin's revealing of Gillian's plans that had brought him to this pass. The thought of his wife trudging up to Artane to beg training from Robin so she might slay her sire had been simply more than Christopher could take. Here was a girl who had screamed aloud at night while dreaming of her father, yet she'd found the courage to wish to face him and best him. Christopher had been humbled by the strength of her resolve.

And by the love that prompted that resolve.

So he'd made a resolution himself. He'd decided to take Robin's suggestion and work on his swordplay.

At first, Jason had aided him, calling out the signals Christopher was accustomed to use while jousting. After almost a fortnight of that, Christopher had realized how poorly such a thing would serve him. He hadn't been able to hear Colin's directions the last time he'd faced Warewick; he likely wouldn't be able to concentrate on signals the next time either.

So he'd learned to rely on his ears. He used Ranulf's voice and the whisper of his clothing to understand where his captain was and where he was moving to. And he'd discovered firsthand that the only way to keep his captain at bay was to be continually on the offensive. The moment he pulled back, he was lost. At least when he was on the attack, Ranulf didn't have the time to mark anything but the arc of Christopher's blade. The moment he ceased to press forward, Ranulf seemingly had the presence of mind to search out and make use of Christopher's weaknesses.

To say that he hadn't earned his share of splinters would have been a lie. But he'd given his share too. And for the first time in three years, Christopher felt confident in his skill. He'd spent so many hours parrying against unseen foes. To parry against a live one again was a heady pleasure.

"Let us begin," Christopher said, raising his blade. "Agreed?"

"Agreed," Ranulf said, from behind him.

Christopher whirled around and wood met wood. And then he had no more time for thinking. He poured all his energies into listening and attacking.

Time and time again, he struck out at his captain. He earned only a few scratches, and gave more than his share. He fought until his arms ached and his head pounded from the effort of listening.

"My lord, I beg you! Peace!" Ranulf exclaimed.

Christopher dragged his arm across his sweaty brow.

"Ranulf, you woman, why do you cry peace?" he demanded.

"Torment your squire, my young, lusty lord. Just until I catch my breath."

Christopher ground his teeth in frustration. "If I use my squire as sport, I'm liable to put this bloody wooden sword through his eye. If Jason dies, Robin will slow-roast me on a spit over a weak fire. On the other hand, if you die, your father will likely send me several bottles of his finest in thanks."

"My father is already dead," Christopher's captain panted.

"Then what have you to worry about?" Christopher said, fighting a smile. "Another hour, old man, then a rest. I feel as fresh as if I'd just stepped from my tent on a cool morning."

"You certainly don't smell that way, my lord."

Christopher barked out a laugh, declining to censure his captain. The man ten years Christopher's senior was normally very taciturn, executing his duties with a grim thoroughness. But to banter again while parrying was a long-missed pleasure. To do anything besides concentrate on keeping himself from swaying with dizziness was a pleasure. Perhaps he was now repaid for all those hours spent training. At the time he'd done it simply to cling to the thought that he was still a warrior. Now he could taste the fruits of his labors and they were sweet ones indeed.

He would find Bernard of Warewick and see him repaid for Gillian's scars and his own humiliation. Then he would have Gillian fetched home. And then he would demand that she never again do something as foolish as leave—

"Saints!" he exploded as Ranulf's polished wooden blade found its mark on his ribs.

"I thought you were attending me!" Ranulf exclaimed. "Damnation, Christopher, cease with your daydreaming!"

"I daresay he was mooning over the lady Gillian," Jason said wisely.

"Of course I wasn't," Christopher said crossly, rubbing his side.

"You were wearing that look, my lord," Jason noted.

Christopher snatched Ranulf's sword and flung it where he knew his squire was sitting in the alcove of the tower room.

"On your feet, child. You'll pay for your sport."

Jason didn't give him the benefit of an answer and Christopher cursed him thoroughly for it. And damn Artane's brat if he wasn't as silent as a ghost! Christopher prodded the air with his sword, seeking some kind of resistance. He came up with nothing.

The sting of a wooden sword across his arm had him whirling toward his squire. He found Jason's blade and countered with a thrust of his own. Jason gasped and Christopher followed the sound with a merciless attack. But Jason hadn't learned his craft from the Dragon for naught. Christopher was pleasantly surprised at his squire's returning parries.

And he was even more surprised at his ability to counter them.

Everything he'd ever learned, all the countless hours spent in the lists repeating the same stroke hundreds of times to perfect it, came back to him fully. Jason's blade found its mark a time or two, but Christopher's reflexes saved him from being more than touched. Then with a duck and a lunge, Christopher came up under Jason's blade, caught his squire by the wrist and pushed him back against the wall, immobilizing him. He laid his wooden blade across the lad's throat and grinned down at him.

"You're dead, little lad."

"And gladly so," Jason panted.

Christopher cast his sword aside and pulled Jason into a rough hug. "You've become a fine warrior, Jason. I'm powerfully pleased with you."

Jason returned the embrace fiercely, then stepped back quickly. "Thank you, my lord."

Christopher slung his arm around Jason's shoulders and listened for Ranulf. "What think you, old man, of this lad of mine?"

"You've trained him well, my lord," Ranulf said, clapping Christopher heartily on the shoulder. "His father couldn't have chosen a better man to do the deed. *Now* may we seek out some ale?"

"Aye," Christopher grinned. "Ale for us and a handsome wench for the young one here. He's earned a bit of play."

CHRISTOPHER'S GOOD HUMOR LASTED UNTIL HE FINALLY reached his bedchamber much later that evening. He cast himself down on a fur before the fire and listened to the wood crackle and pop in the hearth. Had Gillian been beside him, he would have pulled her underneath him and loved her until they both wept from exhaustion. Then he would have carried her to his bed, curled up with her and slept, content to hold her slender body next to his.

He groaned at the thought. Gillian was likely freezing to death. He'd seen more supplies sent out to her, but he wouldn't rest easy until she was back home where she belonged.

And he would have her fetched. Soon. Once he had remastered his art and once her father was no more. He would send some foolhardy lad up that perilous path to bring her home.

Then he would never let her from his arms again.

thirty-four

GILLIAN WOKE WITH A GASP. THE DARKNESS IN THE HALL was stifling. She could find no air to breathe. She fumbled for kindling to throw on the coals left in the hearth. Only when she had a hardy blaze going did she manage to relax enough to catch her breath.

Something was terribly wrong. She could feel it. It had everything to do with darkness. Oh, how she wished she'd never left Blackmour! At least she could have slept outside Christopher's door and been his eyes for him. But now she was too far away to help; she knew deep inside help was what he needed, and soon.

She got to her knees and began to pray.

CHRISTOPHER WOKE ABRUPTLY, HIS HEAD STILL FULL OF his dreams. They had been evil ones indeed. He rubbed his hands over his face and took a deep breath. He let it out slowly, forcing away the lingering unease that filled him.

He stretched out his hand and rested it on the place where Gillian had lain for so many weeks. Saints, but he never should have let her stay away this long! He'd been bloody stubborn and far too proud. He could have just as easily allowed Colin to finish Warewick. In spite of the hours he'd spent parrying with Ranulf, it wasn't as if he himself could walk into Warewick's bedchamber and do the deed himself!

It did no good to think on it, given the hour and his mood. He swung his legs out of bed and sat up, forcing himself not to heed the chill of the wood beneath his feet. It had been months since he'd had such foul dreams. He'd dreamed poorly since then, but nothing as black as what he'd just experienced. He paused, realizing when they'd lessened.

When Gillian had begun to sleep in his bed.

He rose abruptly. No matter the weather, he would have Gillian fetched home today. Berengaria had spoken truly. 'Twas but his pride that had kept him idle for so long. He didn't wish to be remembered as a fool in matters concerning his lady.

He dressed quietly and then felt for his sword. The house was quiet, a sure sign there wouldn't be any soul overanxious to do his bidding. Perhaps a few hours spent training would pass the time and clear his poor brain. He walked to the door and slid back the bolt.

"Come, Wolf," he said as he stepped out into the passageway. He pulled the door closed behind him and leaned back against it for a moment to gain his bearings.

Indeed, no sounds save Wolf's claws against the wooden floor broke the stillness of the night. Christopher was certain he hadn't slept long. Even on those rare nights when he managed to sleep more than a few hours, he slept poorly. Saints, he had grown far too accustomed to Gillian in his bed. How many times had he woken at night only to have her soothe him back to sleep?

A low noise startled him from his reverie. He stood still and strained to hear anything else. Mayhap it was merely a serving wench making her way back from some nightly tryst.

Wolf whined softly and bumped Christopher's hand with his nose.

"Then you heard it, too?" Christopher murmured.

Perhaps it was only Cook fumbling about in the larder. The man certainly never seemed to lack for girth about his middle. Christopher frowned. Perhaps he would do well to stroll about the keep in the middle of the night more often. Who knew what sorts of things truly went on?

A soft footfall came his way, startling him.

"Reveal yourself," he commanded.

" 'Tis me, my lord."

"Ah, Jason," Christopher said, relaxing.

"Aye, my lord. I heard you stir. Is there aught I can do for you?"

"Perhaps you can. Heard you any strange noise?" he asked.

"Aye, but I thought it was you," Jason said.

"Indeed," Christopher mused. "For all I know, it could have been."

"Foul dreams, my lord?"

"Aye, lad. 'Tis one of the blessings of a long and mis-spent youth, no doubt."

"As you say, my lord. But it wasn't a cry I heard. 'Twas more of a thumping noise. Shall I have a look in your chamber and see if aught has been displaced?"

Christopher nodded.

He heard Jason move, then stop abruptly at the low sound. Indeed, 'twas more of an echo of a sound than the noise in truth. Christopher felt the hair rise on the back of his neck.

"That wasn't in your chamber," Jason breathed.

"Aye," Christopher agreed, "it surely wasn't."

"Shall I fetch my sword, my lord?"

"Aye, and a pair of crossbows." The bow wasn't Christopher's weapon of choice, but as of late he'd begun to regard it with more favor. Chances were should he discharge a bolt in the direction of an enemy's voice, he would likely strike his target. Not to mention the pleasant distance a bow allowed one to keep between oneself and an opponent's sword.

A chill ran through him. It was the same cold feeling of dread he'd experienced before every battle he'd ever been in. That he should feel such unease in his own passageway was troubling indeed. Warewick couldn't have breached the gates. No one ever had. Blackmour was unassailable. Artane may have intimidated by sheer size; Blackmour did it by mere positioning. Only a fool would have braved the shoals around the island, and only an even greater fool would have attempted to scale the walls. Christopher could remember only one such attempt. By the time the man had reached the top of the walls, he'd been so exhausted by the climb it had taken but a gentle push by a guard to send him tumbling down to his death.

Surely Warewick was not that foolhardy.

"Bows and quarrels," Jason said, breathlessly. "Where now, my lord?"

"To the great hall," Christopher said, turning toward the stairs. "And quietly, Jason. Perhaps 'tis nothing more than someone who has ingested more ale than was meet."

"Hmmm," Jason said, but he didn't sound convinced.

Indeed, Christopher thought with the faintest of smiles, Jason sounded almost eager. He sighed. Ah, the poor lad. He'd missed out on much during the past three years.

Christopher counted the steps as he descended them silently. He paused at the entrance to the great hall and listened carefully.

Nothing but the snoring of men and hounds.

"Jason, do you see anything?" he whispered.

He felt Jason peer around him. "Nay, my lord. No one stirs."

"To the kitchens, then. Perhaps Cook is at his bread making earlier than usual."

Christopher eased his way out into the hall, hoping he wouldn't step on anyone by mistake. Blessedly, he encountered nothing but a stray bone lurking in the rushes. Gillian would have been in a fine temper if she'd found the like.

He paused at the entrance to the kitchens. There was no sound save Cook's hearty snoring.

"Saints," Jason muttered from beside him, " 'tis a wonder any of us sleeps."

"True enough," Christopher agreed. "Perhaps we'll have Gillian take him to task over it when she returns."

Jason was silent for a moment. "Then she's coming home?"

"Aye," Christopher said softly, "as soon as we finish our business here. 'Tis past time. Now, see you anything amiss?"

Christopher heard Jason shift at his side, then take a step or two out into the kitchen. Then he stepped back.

"Nay, my lord. Everyone sleeps."

Christopher frowned. 'Twas certain he had heard something, but where had it come from?

Wolf leaned against his leg and Christopher reached down to scratch the beast between the ears.

"What do you see, my friend?" he whispered. "To be sure, your eyes are better than mine tonight."

Wolf nudged his hand with his cold nose but offered no further opinion on the matter.

Christopher leaned against the wall and contemplated. Though he could hear nothing amiss, he was yet uneasy. Hadn't just such a premonition of something amiss been what made him trail Colin in the battle of Conyers? Had he not done so, Colin would have died. Berkhamshire's skill was enviable, but there came a point when even the most skilled can be outnumbered.

Christopher rubbed his stubbled jaw thoughtfully. Warewick had been cunning enough, gaining the inner bailey under the guise of a merchant. The man bore watching. The saints only knew what he knew of Blackmour's defenses. If the man and Lina had truly been lovers, and that was something Christopher did not want to dwell on, there was no telling what the man had discovered. Lina had shown no interest in the inner workings of Blackmour, but perhaps that too had been a ruse. Saints, but sight hadn't served him. He hadn't seen what was going on under his nose.

"My lord," Jason whispered, "perhaps we should venture to the cellars."

Christopher felt his heart leap uncomfortably at Jason's words. The cellars could conceal any number of intruders. But how, by the saints, would they have gained such a place? Ranulf had doubled his watchfulness since Colin's departure. Christopher had no doubts his captain hadn't been lax in his duties. And there was surely no other way in save the front gates.

Except for the seaside tunnel.

Christopher felt his flesh break out in a chilling sweat.

"*Merde*," he breathed, shocked at his own stupidity.

"My lord?"

Christopher shook his head. "Come with me, Jason. Here, give me one of those bows. Keep a sharp eye on the shadows, lad. I fear we may be facing Warewick sooner than we'd hoped."

"As you will, my lord. Here, follow me," Jason said, stepping in front of him. "There are bodies curled up everywhere here."

"Alive?" Christopher asked sharply.

Jason sucked in his breath. "Aye, my lord. Why wouldn't they be?"

"Get me to the cellars, lad. I'll tell you there."

"I'm with you, my lord," Jason said "Follow me."

Christopher put his hand on Jason's shoulder and held the crossbow lightly with the other. Why he hadn't thought of the passageway inside the outer walls sooner, he surely didn't know. It made horrifying sense. Before he'd wed, few people had known of the passageway. Colin and Ranulf were the only ones who came to mind.

Yet he remembered all too well the night Lina had come to him, terrified that they would be assailed from without— or within. He'd been tremendously proud of his defenses and had boasted that Blackmour couldn't be taken by force. He'd even gone so far as to tell her of the rocks that blocked the seaward tunnel that led to the passageway through the walls. He'd assured her that no one would breach the outer rock covering, much less find the way inside and into the larder. The only thing she had to fear might be a few rats. After all, no one knew of the existence of the passageway.

Christopher had the sinking feeling Lina's interest had been more than concern for her own safety. He let out his breath slowly, trying to calm his racing heart. If Lina knew, then Warewick knew as well. Christopher had no doubts the man wouldn't have hesitated to make use of what he'd learned.

He surely wouldn't have dared mount a siege. He would have had to keep one eye on the keep and one eye behind them looking for Artane and Wyckham and half a dozen other allies of Blackmour's. Aye, stealth would have been his choice. Christopher gritted his teeth as he made his way down to the kitchens. Saints, he had been blind!

They reached the bottom of the cellar steps and Jason stopped.

" 'Tis black as pitch, my lord," he said, hesitantly. "I can see nothing."

Christopher strained to hear aught amiss. The only thing he could make out was the faint echoes of Cook's snores.

"We need to search the east wall," he said, at length.

Jason was silent for a long moment. "East, my lord?"

Christopher smiled to himself. "The stairs are on the north side of the cellar, lad. We are facing south. East is to our left, aye?"

Jason put his hand on Christopher's arm. "My lord, I . . . I think I am beginning to understand. How it must be."

Christopher turned Jason east. "I hope you never learn

the whole of it, Jason. Now, as quietly as we can, let us search for the loose stone. It was well hid the last time I was down here."

"Loose stone?" Jason echoed, in a whisper. "In the wall? But—"

"What did you think filled the walls? Rubble? In some places, aye, but not this wall. And the outer side of this wall is twice the thickness, to make up for the passageway. I at least credit my father with some sense about that. If he'd carved out the passageway and left the outer wall but a pair of arm lengths thick, the kitchens would have slid into the sea long ago."

"As you say, my lord," Jason said, with a gulp. "Your sire's good sense on this matter be praised."

"Aye," Christopher agreed. He walked carefully, feeling ahead of him with both his hands and feet. Once he reached the wall, he slid his hands over the surfaces of the stones and, more importantly, in between. The mortar was solid in all the places he touched. He swore silently. He hadn't been in the passageway for years, but surely he hadn't forgotten the place of entry that easily.

"Wait, my lord, I think 'tis here."

Christopher felt the mortar around the stone Jason had found. It was indeed loosely packed. He dug at it with a crossbow quarrel and heard Jason doing the same.

"Perhaps it will come free now, my lord."

Christopher helped Jason pull on the stone and it dislodged with a suddenness that made them both jump back in surprise. It landed on the floor with a muffled thump.

"Bloody hell," Christopher muttered. "Nay, Wolf," he said, quickly, feeling his hound brush his leg. "I'll go first."

"My lord," Jason whispered, "wait. It seems less dark in there. Think you some of the outer wall has given way?"

Christopher leaned forward into the passageway. It was miserably damp, but no chillier than the cellar. If rock had fallen away, surely he would have felt some sort of stirring of the air.

Jason caught his breath. "My lord, the light flickers. I daresay 'tis from a torch."

Christopher pulled Jason back and climbed into the passageway. "Stay behind me," he said grimly. "I have the feeling we won't be alone for long."

"Nay," Jason breathed. "You cannot think Warewick—"

"I would credit him with almost anything. Come along behind me and keep as quiet as you can. Wolf, no noise, boy."

The passageway was large, as it should have been, given that the walls of the keep were some twelve feet across. Christopher judged the passageway to be two full paces wide. Enough to maneuver in, should he meet someone he needed to slay.

He hadn't walked for long when Jason caught him by the shoulder.

"It grows even lighter ahead, my lord."

Christopher pursed his lips. Saints, Warewick was cunning! Christopher blessed his intuition yet another time. Perhaps a bit of Berengaria's Sight was finding home in him. He would have to tell her the tale the next time he saw her.

"Bloody Hell!" Jason's exclamation was immediately followed by shouts up ahead.

Christopher lifted his crossbow and fired it. He heard a scream, heard Jason's bolt fly past his ear, and heard another scream. Christopher heard footsteps running toward him and cursed fluently. Saints, he hadn't counted on how difficult it would be!

Wolf snarled and Christopher could only assume his hound had attacked, because a man yelled in pain. Wolf cried out. Christopher pulled Jason behind him and strode forward. He thrust out with his sword.

The same man gasped in pain, then was silent. Christopher pulled his sword out of the man's body, feeling it had been altogether too simple.

"Wolf?" Christopher asked Jason.

"He seems to have lost part of his tail, my lord. He'll live."

"And Warewick's men?"

"Just Gillian's sire, my lord," Jason said quietly. "He stands some twenty paces in front of you."

"Aye, whelp," Warewick snarled. "That's how far away I am. Will you count for your lord while I come to him to slay him? And while you're counting, I'll be complimenting your master on his cleverness. How did you know, Blackmour, that I would come? Perhaps you aren't as blind as I thought you."

"Are you come to slay me in my bed, like the coward you are?" Christopher demanded.

"Coward?" Warewick choked. "It requires skill and cunning to slip in and out of a keep unnoticed. And more courage than you have, child," he added derisively.

Christopher ignored the slur. "What weapons does he have?" he asked Jason quietly.

"Sword and knife, that I can see."

Christopher started forward, then stopped abruptly as his foot came into contact with the corpse directly before him. Saints, the body was close! Which meant the man's sword had been just that close.

A shiver went through him that had nothing to do with the dank chill. He could have lost his head and never been the wiser.

Panic flooded him. By all the saints, what was he thinking! To parry against an enemy who wanted him dead? It was one thing to spar with his captain, or Jason. They wanted him to succeed. But Warewick? Unbidden, and certainly unwelcome, came the memories of just how easily Warewick had humiliated him before. Half the blows he'd anticipated. It had been the others which had left him bruised and battered, the ones that seemed to come from out of nowhere.

And now to cross swords with the man?

Christopher took a deep breath.

What other choice did he have?

To be sure, he could turn and run—and then live with his cowardice for the rest of his days. What would Gillian think when she learned? If she were even left alive to learn of it! Warewick would seek out his daughter and then her life would be over. Or worse, he would repay her daily for Christopher's cheek.

Christopher hesitated. If he fought, could he win? What might he lose in the fray? A limb? His very life?

"Come, Blackmour," Warewick said, his voice echoing off the stone, "come at me, if you dare. Let me finish you as I should have weeks ago. You've stood in my way for too long. Now, come at me and let us be done with this foolishness."

A fight it would be.

For he had no other choice.

He put his foot on the corpse's back and slid forward until he felt solid stone on the far side of the body.

"Ah," Warewick said, with a laugh, "you make it easy for me. Aye, come closer, son."

Wolf growled and Christopher put his hand out.

"Enough," he said, quietly. "I can do this myself."

Jason's hand on his shoulder stopped him.

"I can shoot the torch from his hand, my lord," Jason murmured.

Christopher smiled grimly. This was aid he could accept.

"Aye, Jason, you do that."

The arrow flew past Christopher's ear.

"You little bugger!" Warewick exclaimed.

"Got his hand too," Jason said. "Right through the wrist."

Christopher promised himself a good laugh over the smugness in his squire's voice. But that would come later. Now would come a fight on his own terms.

He stepped forward, feeling his way further past the lifeless body of Warewick's man. He heard Warewick cursing in the darkness. He took another step forward.

"How does it feel, Warewick?" Christopher asked. "Frightening? And know this: You've seen your last bit of light. The next glow you see will be the fires of Hell."

"I'll kill you anyway," Warewick spat. "See if I don't. I've waited too long, paid too much to see you dead. All my life I've wanted your land and I'll be damned if I'm going to lose it now, when I'm so close to having it. Draw *your* last breaths, Blackmour, for I've no intention of dying this day."

Christopher listened to Gillian's father continue to boast of what he would do once Blackmour was his. Christopher said nothing; he was far too busy listening and marveling at what a fool Gillian's sire was. Had he no idea his voice was all Christopher needed to find him?

And once found, he would be dead.

Christopher stopped and waited for Warewick to come to him. And when he was close enough, Christopher swung in an arc guaranteed to disarm.

At least it had worked well enough with Ranulf.

Christopher felt sword meet sword, then heard the ring of Warewick's blade as it left the man's hand and slammed against the stone wall.

"You bloody whoreson," Warewick exclaimed.

Christopher listened to the man fumbling in the dark for his steel.

"Think you that will stop me? Aye, I'll find my blade soon enough and then—"

Christopher swung with all his might.

Warewick screamed. Christopher heard the man stumble backwards. He didn't wait to see what Gillian's sire would do next. He continued to press forward, swinging and thrusting without pause.

"My eyes!" Warewick screamed. "You cut my eyes!"

It was so perfect that Christopher almost paused to savor it. To blind the man was perfect recompense for the destruction Warewick had wrought on him. He was momentarily tempted to allow Warewick to live, to enjoy in full measure the repayment of his own vile deed. There was a part of him that wanted with all his soul to see Warewick pay for every lash mark on William's back, every scar Gillian bore, and his own blindness.

But if he left Warewick alive, who knew what mischief the man would combine? His fury would be endless and Gillian would spend the rest of her life wondering when her father would appear.

So he thrust deep. Blade hit bone and Christopher pushed harder, burying his sword to the hilt.

"Damn you to Hell," Warewick gurgled.

"Not if you'll be there," Christopher returned.

He shoved Warewick away from him, not wanting any chance encounters with the man's dagger. He heard his father-in-law fall to the floor with a heavy thump.

And then there was silence.

Christopher stood there for several moments, listening for the slightest movement.

"My lord?"

"Fetch a torch, Jason."

He heard Jason scramble back out into the cellar, and still he didn't move. He listened with all his might for the sound of a footfall he might have missed or the sound of Warewick suddenly sucking in air for one last struggle.

But all was silent.

It seemed an eternity he stood there, waiting for a single sound, bracing himself for the possibility of an attack he couldn't see.

Christopher heard footfalls behind him. He eased away

from Warewick and lifted his blade against this possible new menace.

"'Tis me, my lord," Jason said. "Here, let me see what damage you've wrought."

Christopher lowered his blade, then heard Jason gulp. Jason's hand was suddenly on his arm tugging.

"Let us be away," he said, his tone strained. "He's very dead, my lord. I'm merely grateful I wasn't forced to look after breaking my fast."

"You've been too long out of battle, my lad," Christopher said, following Jason. "Lost your strong stomach, have you?"

Jason's only response was to walk faster.

Christopher followed his squire to the cellar entrance, then felt for the opening. Once he'd found it, he stayed on his feet long enough to find a handy wall to lean against, then he sat down with a thump.

It was only then that he allowed himself to shake. The terror that washed over him was like nothing he'd ever felt in battle. By all the saints above, how had he possessed the cheek to fight to the death? Warewick could have slit his throat by sheer luck!

Suddenly, on the heels of that thought, came another.

He had fought to the death.

And he was still alive.

It was almost enough to make him laugh. Saints above, he had done it! He had stared blindly at death, and come out victorious.

"My lord? Are you unwell? You look worse than I feel."

Christopher shook his head, feeling vastly relieved. "Unwell? Lad, I've never been less unwell in my life."

"As you say," Jason replied, doubtfully.

Christopher reached for his sword and then rose to his feet. He couldn't explain to Jason the feelings that coursed through him. Saints, for the first time in three years, he felt completely himself! The loss of sight hadn't made him less a man. No matter how often Gillian had told him so, he'd had to prove it to himself.

And now that he'd proved it, he could go on. Gillian would come home and know that she need never fear her sire again. William's soul could be at peace, knowing he'd been avenged. Christopher would live out his days knowing he could protect his lady if need be.

But God help him if he had to face another night such as this.

"Come, Jason," Christopher said, resheathing his sword. "Let's see to Wolf's tail and then find Ranulf. I've no mind to have those bodies rotting inside my walls."

"And then, my lord?"

Christopher put his shoulders back. "And then," he said purposefully, "I've another thing to see to."

And see to it he would. He'd just faced Warewick and lived to tell of it. His day was off to a bloody fine start. And it would finish out that way, if he had anything to say about it.

thirty-five

GILLIAN STARED INTO THE FLAMES OF THE FIRE IN THE hearth. She'd been at the Lord's Hall for over a month and nary a word from Blackmour or its lord. Her only accomplishment over the past five weeks had been besting Colin in chess.

It was a hollow victory.

But what had she expected? For Christopher to come running to fetch her? He likely wouldn't have if it had been a straight path from his door to hers. The path below was anything but straight.

One of Colin's men had fallen just the week before and broken his leg. The more Gillian thought about it, the less she wanted to see Christopher coming up that path. He would kill himself and then where would she be? Mistress of Blackmour, without her lord by her side? The thought wasn't worth contemplating.

She sighed deeply. As if any thought about a life together with Christopher was worth contemplating. She certainly hadn't had any messages from him. Obviously he'd agreed with her reasons for leaving. Her father had humiliated him one too many times. The first had come at her wedding by means of her pitiful dowry. As if dowering her with Braedhalle hadn't been painful enough! Saints, but it must have galled him to accept that.

Her sire had continued his assault by making Christopher look like a bumbling page in his own hall before his own people, then laughing while he told of Magdalina's perfidy. It was no wonder Christopher wanted nothing to do with her.

In truth, she couldn't blame him. Each time he realized she was near him, he likely thought of those hateful memories. Nay, 'twas best she left him be. The Lord's Hall could be made comfortable in time. Already she'd fashioned a clumsy bit of needlepoint for a pillow. Tapestries would follow, over the years. Her son wouldn't grow up in Blackmour's splendor, but at least he'd be warm and well-loved. Gillian had nothing else of value to offer.

The front door banged shut and someone stomped his feet.

"Out, lads," Colin said. "Clear out and pack your gear. We're leaving immediately."

Gillian watched, openmouthed, as her guardsmen filed out of the hall obediently. She was left looking at Colin who stood at the door. His very expression warned her not to question him.

But she did so anyway. "You're leaving me?" she asked in disbelief.

Colin cleared his throat. "I daresay you've no more need of me."

"But, Colin, that isn't true!"

"Aye, it is," he said curtly. He made her a low bow. "Good morrow to you, lady."

"Colin!"

He turned to leave and she jumped up.

"You can't go. I forbid it!"

Colin looked back over her shoulder. "You what?"

"I forbid it, damn you."

He turned to face her. "Both you and your lord have the most annoying habit of forgetting that I am not your vassal. The second son I may be, but I've lands of my own. I owe you no allegiance.''

Gillian blinked, feeling as if she'd been slapped. ''I see,'' she said, her courage faltering.

''So you do.''

She looked up at him. ''Then you'll not stay out of friendship?''

Colin made several gruff noises, cursed a time or two, then rolled his eyes heavenward and strode across the floor to her. He put his arms around her in a hug that almost crushed her ribs. He released her only to kiss her roughly on both cheeks and ruffle her hair.

''You've no need of me. You'll manage perfectly well with what you have here.''

And with that, he turned and stomped from the house, banging the door shut behind him.

Gillian looked at the closed door and felt the silence descend. It grew so quiet that the sound of the fire crackling was startling. She turned and walked back to the hearth. She sat, then realized sitting was a poor idea.

So she paced. She paced the length of the large chamber, then its breadth, then the length again, all in an effort to stave off the panic she felt descending. She wouldn't survive. She would starve. Or freeze to death. Damn Colin! He knew it as well as he knew anything.

Anger replaced her fear and she strode over to the door and threw it open. She stalked out onto the bit of ground that served as a courtyard and looked down the rocky path, ready to bellow her displeasure to her reluctant keeper.

Only it wasn't her reluctant keeper she saw descending the path.

It was someone entirely different.

Climbing up.

Merciful saints above, it was Christopher. Gillian fought to catch her breath. She cried out a warning as she saw him fall. As if he'd seen her, he raised his head and struggled to his feet.

Gillian sank to her knees.

She prayed, eyes open and watching her love. Christopher had come for her. She knew in that moment just how deeply she mattered to him, how deeply he truly loved her. Why had she ever allowed Colin to talk her into coming up to this accursed place?

She watched her husband struggling up the treacherous path. Her heart was too full of the sight for anything but painful joy to find home in her breast. She vowed with all her soul to never again leave him. Lina had left him, for different reasons of course, but she had gone. Gillian knew she could never do the like again. Not a day would go by that Christopher didn't hear numerous times just how much she loved him and how happy he'd made her. He'd given her so much more than just a safe haven, a powerful name and a skilled arm to hide behind.

He'd given her his love.

She jumped to her feet and ran inside the house. He would be cold when he arrived, and likely thirsty. She tossed more wood onto the fire, ignored the splinters in her hands, and put a bottle of wine on the hearth to warm. She piled up furs for his use, brushed her hair and made sure that all her clothes were on straight. Then she fled back outside and hugged herself against the wind as she watched her lover toil up the last hundred paces of steep incline.

The closer he came, the more clearly she saw what the climb had cost him. His face was scratched. His tunic was torn and a bruised and bloody knee poked through his hose. The late afternoon mist had plastered his hair to his head and soaked his clothes. But he didn't falter. He merely continued on his way, a determined look on his face, a confidence about him she hadn't seen before.

The wind began to howl but Gillian didn't move from her place. Christopher struggled against not only the terrain but the wind too, yet he didn't pause. Gillian called to him, but the wind blew her voice back behind her. So she merely waited, fighting the tears that threatened to blind her.

Ten paces and he would be before her.

Five paces.

Then one.

She threw herself against him and he staggered, but regained his balance soon enough. Gillian pressed her face against his chest and wept, great wrenching sobs of relief.

"Oh, Gill," he said hoarsely. "Hush, now." He held her close. "Let's go inside, love. You'll have to help me find the door. The climb was all I could manage."

She nodded and put her arm around his waist. She led him to the door, then helped him shut it against the wind. Christopher pushed his hair back from his face and sighed deeply.

"Just a bit of sport," he said, smiling crookedly. "I think I'll go break a few stallions, then perhaps build myself a new keep or two before sunset."

Gillian wrapped her arms around him and clung to him. "Christopher, I'm so sorry!"

"Don't," he said quickly. He buried his face in her hair. "Don't, Gill. You were worth it. I vow it. I would have crawled here on my knees if I'd had to." He tightened his arms around her. "I came to fetch you home."

She lifted her face. "I would have come home weeks ago, but I feared you didn't want me."

"How could you think such a thing? Saints, Gillian, I love you!"

She paused. How was she to tell him all she had feared over the past few weeks? She stood in his embrace, searching for the right words.

"I followed Jason up to your tower chamber," she said, at length. "He asked you if he should fetch me and you said it was the last thing you wanted him to do."

He shook his head and pulled her closer. Gillian stood with his hand skimming over her hair and closed her eyes.

"I didn't want you to see me thusly," he said softly. "Can you not understand why?"

"But it was my fault," she whispered.

"Nay," he said forcefully, "it wasn't. It had nothing to do with you. It was all your sire's doing. Saints, I won't even call him that again. It was Warewick's plotting and scheming that wrought what damage was done." He held her more tightly. "Don't you realize yet that you are the only joy in my life? And if you think on it rightly, Warewick did nothing but make it so we found each other."

"But—"

"You had nothing to do with any of the other," Christopher insisted. "I wouldn't trade my life now for what I had before for any amount of gold. And if losing my sight means that I've found you, 'tis a trade I will gladly make."

"Christopher!" she said, aghast. She pulled back to look at him. "Surely you can't—"

"Aye, but I do mean it," he said. "And if it takes me the rest of my life to see you believe as well, then it will be time well spent."

Gillian stared up at him. He looked sincere enough. And to be sure, he held her tightly enough.

She had the courage to believe him. Didn't she?

"Truly?" she asked, giving him one final chance to say her nay.

"Truly," he whispered. He bent his head and kissed her gently. Then he smiled down at her. "And now that we've settled that, perhaps you would care to lead me to the fire and sit with me while I regain my warmth? Perhaps I can do the same for you. I've no doubt your toes haven't been any color but blue since you crawled up to this place."

"They have been rather chilled," she admitted.

"Then come with me," he said, taking her hand, "and let me see what I can do for them."

"Nay," she said, pulling him toward the fire, "I will see to you first. Sit here and let me clean you up. You look to have had a rough time of it."

Christopher sat where she placed him, but he followed her movements with his head. She bathed his bloody knees, then cleaned the rest of his scratches. Then she stopped as he reached out to her. His strong hands traveled lightly over her arms and down, finding her waist, then coming to rest over her belly.

He paused and an expression of wonderment settled on his features. Gillian looked at him, surprised.

"You know," she breathed.

A smile spread over his face, as beautiful as morning sunlight from the east. "I had it on excellent advice from a witch named Berengaria," he said. Then he put his arms around her and drew her close, resting his cheek on her belly. "I love you," he said quietly. "I love you deeply, Gillian, and I vow I'll never drive you away again."

"But you didn't—"

"Aye, I did." He lifted his head and looked up. "I've so much to be grateful for, Gill: you, this babe, lads about me who don't see my blindness. There is much good I can do even without my eyes to guide me. If you'll help me now and then."

"Not that you'll need it," she said gently.

His smile was rueful. "I'm not too proud to disagree. I'll need it often, and I won't begrudge myself the asking for it. If you won't mind giving it."

"You know I won't."

His smile faded, to be replaced by an expression of soberness. "You've no idea what losing you did to me, Gillian, even for that short time. I couldn't bear it again."

She put her trembling hand against his cheek. "You'll never have to, my lord."

He pulled her down onto his lap, then kissed her firmly on the mouth. "Aye, I won't, for I'll never let you from my arms. And I vow, Gillian of Blackmour, if you ever lead me on such a merry chase again, I'll chain you to me!"

Gillian laughed in spite of herself. "I'll remember that,

my lord." She smiled. "Shall we go home?"

"Tomorrow."

"Tomorrow?"

"Aye. You'll be far too busy this afternoon."

"Will I?"

"Aye," Christopher said firmly. "I don't suppose you've been sleeping in something besides this chair, have you?"

"I might have a fur or two thrown close to the fire."

Christopher had her off his lap and onto her feet so fast, her head swam. She clutched his arms until she'd regained her balance.

"Are you unwell?" he asked.

"Nay," she said, laughing as she took a deep breath. "I must have stood up too fast."

"All the more reason to lie back down soon. Go bolt the door, would you?"

Gillian smiled to herself as she did what her husband had asked. Then she turned and ducked to miss Christopher's hastily discarded tunic.

"You'll chill, my lord," she called to him, feeling wonderfully cherished.

"All the more reason for you to be bloody quicker about coming back over here to warm me," he said pointedly.

Gillian walked across the floor and into her husband's arms.

"You're wearing too many clothes," he stated.

"Think you, my lord?"

And that was the last thing she managed to say for a very long time.

GILLIAN LAY WITH HER HEAD ON HER HUSBAND'S SHOUL-der, her palm resting on his muscular chest. She took note of the new scars and, in spite of herself, felt grief over the sight of them.

Christopher caught her hand and brought it to his mouth.

"Cease," he commanded.

Gillian sighed. "As you wish, Christopher."

He rubbed his hand over her arm for several moments in silence, then stopped his motion. Gillian lifted her head and looked down at him.

"My lord?"

His expression was very grave. She sat up and looked down at him, feeling faintly alarmed.

"Christopher, what is it?"

He sat up slowly, then pulled the blanket up to tuck it around her shoulders.

"I have aught to tell you," he said quietly.

His tone made her uneasy. "And that would be?" she asked.

" 'Tis something I've done," he admitted.

She felt herself beginning to frown. She couldn't seem to help herself. "What?" she demanded. "Surely you and those Artane lads haven't been off—"

"Saints, nay," Christopher exclaimed, sounding horrified. "I killed your sire, Gillian. What did you think I'd been about?"

"Oh," she said, relieved. "I feared you'd been out—" She shut her mouth with a snap and looked at her husband. "You did what?"

He sighed. "He's dead. By my hand."

"By your hand?" she repeated. She put her hand on his shoulder and forced him around, looking him over carefully for other wounds she might have missed. Then she ran her hands over his chest and down his belly.

"Stop," Christopher said, with a half laugh. "Saints, woman, I'm telling you I finished off your sire and all you can do is gape at my scars."

"Oh," Gillian said, sitting back and putting her hands in her lap. "Well, what else am I to do?"

He took her hand in his. "I daresay I shouldn't suggest you grieve for the man."

"Nay, you shouldn't."

He rubbed his thumb over the back of her hand. Gillian

waited for him to speak, but he remained silent. After all, what was he to say? He'd only done what she herself had intended to do. He surely shouldn't apologize.

Gillian looked at him, sitting before her with his head bowed and she felt a shiver go through her. How, by all the blessed saints above, had it all come about? When? And how had Christopher managed it?

"He didn't mark you," she said, finally.

"Of course not," Christopher said, giving her a haughty look. "After all, I am the Dragon of Blackmour—"

"Scourge of England and all that," Gillian finished for him. "Aye, I know many names for you, my lord, but they don't give me the answer to this riddle."

"Hrumph," Christopher said, looking faintly displeased. "Then you think my reputation wasn't enough to do the old bugger in?"

Gillian pursed her lips, wishing her husband could see her expression. As an afterthought, she brought his hand to her face and let him feel it for himself.

Christopher frowned. "Very well, then, here is the tale. I woke from a foul dream without anyone to soothe me—"

"The saints be praised for that."

Christopher frowned at her, then continued, "I thought I had heard a noise, so Jason, Wolf and I descended to the cellars. We found Warewick creeping inside a passageway in the sea wall and it was there I finished him."

"You could have been killed!" she exclaimed.

"I'd been training with Ranulf and Jason," Christopher said defensively. "I was ready for the deed."

"He could have felled you with an arrow, you fool!"

"Saints, Gill, 'twas in the dark."

"And that makes a difference?" she demanded.

"It certainly made one to him," Christopher retorted. She paused. "Ah," she said, slowly, "now I see."

"And he didn't," Christopher said, "which is likely why I managed the feat."

"Oh, Christopher," she said, feeling a tremor start in

her knees and work its way up, " 'twas a very great chance you took."

He gathered her up and pulled her onto his lap. "Colin wrote and told me you intended to do the deed yourself. When I heard of your courage, how could I have done anything less?"

Gillian could only hold onto him and tremble.

"I had to do it, Gill," he said quietly. "For my own sake, if you would rather think on it thusly. I had to prove to myself that I am still the man I was."

She thought about all the things she could have said to him, beginning with *Couldn't you have proved it to yourself another way* and finishing with *What were you thinking, you fool?* But she said none of them. He might have claimed the deed had been done for his own sake, but he had surely been thinking about her, too. And William.

She pulled back and touched his face with her fingers. "You risked much, my love."

"How could I have done else?"

She shook her head. "You couldn't have. I'm simply grateful."

He smiled faintly. "And I'm grateful you had the good sense to stay here instead of traipsing off to Warewick."

"Artane. I was going to Artane."

"Even worse."

"I could have found my way," she said.

He looked at her in disbelief. "Think you?"

She smiled and put her arms around his neck. "Perhaps not. I suppose, then, my lord, you will have to take me to Artane yourself. The saints only know where I might wind up if I tried to find it on my own."

"The saints preserve me from another pair of nights spent scouring the forest for you."

She smoothed his hair back from his face. "Will you, Chris?"

"Will I what?"

"Take me to Artane?"

He pursed his lips. "You, lady, do not fight fair."

"You've bested Warewick," she pointed out.

"Aye."

"You've climbed to Blackmour's Folly."

"That, too."

"You were wise enough to wed me."

"Surely my most noteworthy feat."

She paused before she dealt the killing blow. "Robin and his lady wife will want to see your son."

"As I said, lady, you do not fight fair."

Gillian smiled as her husband laid her back on the fur. She knew he thought to distract her with his sweet kisses and gentle touches, but she wouldn't distract that easily. It wasn't meet that the Dragon of Blackmour leave anything unconquered.

She would see to that.

For she was his wife, after all, and a dragoness herself.

It was well past nightfall when Christopher finally succumbed to slumber. Gillian rose quietly, checked the bolt on the door one last time, then built up the fire. Then she sat down in the chair she'd occupied for so many days and stared down at the man lying before her.

The firelight flickered over his beloved features, softening them. It glowed against his shoulders, shoulders that bore the burden of keeping her safe. It caressed his large hands, hands which could either wield a sword again in her defense or touch her so gently as to bring tears to her eyes.

She sat watching him for a goodly while, thinking on the events that had brought them to this place and time.

She closed her eyes and gave thanks for the bitter and the sweet, for both had, in the end, brought her joy.

Then she rose and slipped under the blanket next to her husband. His arm came around her and drew her close.

She smiled, content.

epilogue

GILLIAN WATCHED ARTANE RISE UP BEFORE HER IN THE distance and felt the same awe she'd felt the first time she'd seen Blackmour. Artane was, well, immense. It was a major holding, being close to the border and all, and it showed that it had been built with that fact in mind.

"Can you see it yet?"

Gillian shut her mouth and turned to her husband. "Aye," she managed.

He laughed. "Ah, sweet Gill, I wish I could see your face. Do you look as surprised as you sound?"

"You never said it was this big."

"You never asked."

"You, my lord husband, have this irritating habit of leaving out the most important of details. Such as how very large this keep is and how completely adorable your son would be. You vowed he would be ugly till he turned a score."

"I didn't want you to be disappointed," Christopher said modestly.

"Shall I hold him now?"

"Later, Gill. He'll require a firm hand until we reach the gates."

Young Robin of Blackmour looked anything but restless at the moment. He sat in his father's lap, his two-year-old's curiosity blunted by the nap he'd just had. Black hair stood up all over his head and he looked out sleepily on the world through his father's deep blue eyes. Gillian's heart tightened within her at the sight of her husband holding their babe so securely with his large hand. Aye, Christopher was proud enough of the lad, and well he should have been.

"I love you," she said quietly.

Christopher cocked his head her way. "Is that in repayment for finally bringing you to Artane, or did I do something else to please you?"

She laughed softly. "The first, assuredly, since I have been threatening to lead you on a merry chase here for a pair of years now. And for the other, nay, I was simply glad that 'tis you who holds my son. He and I are both very fortunate to have you."

Christopher reined in his mount, felt for her, then kissed her full on the mouth.

"Nay, 'tis I who am fortunate," he said softly. "You've given me joy after joy, my Gill. There's hardly room enough in my heart to receive—"

"By the saints, not again!" Colin exclaimed, nudging his horse forward between them. He gave Gillian a disgruntled look. "That is the fifth time today, Gillian, that you have caused the entire company to halt from your mooning. Or is it you who is at fault?" he asked, turning to Christopher. "Chris, you lovesick whelp, I'm in sore need of ale and a taste of Lady Anne's fare and you're doing naught but making me wait the longer for both. Now, must I ride between the two of you, or can you forgo these sickeningly sweet sentiments until we are safely behind the walls?"

"You could leave us in peace," Gillian suggested pointedly.

"Alone?" Colin gasped, horrified. "The last time I left

you alone 'twas in Blackmour's Folly and I didn't see either of you for a solid fortnight. The saints only know how many children might result from another such oversight on my part. Move out, lads! I've a mind for some ale!"

Christopher turned to Gillian as Colin rode on. "I rather enjoyed that fortnight, my love. Perhaps when we return, we'll have ourselves another such pair of weeks."

"As you wish, my lord," Gillian said cheerfully.

They rode on until they'd reached the outer gates. Gillian looked at her husband.

"You will show me where you roamed as a youth?"

"I promised I would. I doubt much has changed."

Gillian reined in her mount as Christopher did. He sat still, listening for several minutes.

"Chris?"

He smiled reflexively. "Just thinking. Nothing to fret over."

"Robin will be happy to see you."

"And I him."

She waited, but still he didn't move.

"Shall we go in?" she asked.

He reached for her hand and clasped it tightly. "Aye, we will." He looked at her. "Can you bear to be at my side night and day for the next month or two? I'll need more than your eyes for this, Gill."

Her only answer was a gentle laugh and another kiss.

"OH, BUT THEY DO LOOK HAPPY," MAGDA SIGHED. "Don't they, Berengaria?"

Berengaria smiled. "They do indeed."

"And to think 'twas us who brought them together!" Magda said, tears standing in her eyes.

"Hrumph," Nemain said from where she rode behind the other two in the Dragon's company. "All *you* succeeded in doing was using up the last of my thumb-bone! It was Berengaria's herbs that accomplished the deed, though I'm still not sure about her methods. Those certainly weren't the approved beauty and courage herbs.''

"I'm quite sure my potion would have helped," Magda insisted, "had I just had time to perfect it—"

"They wouldn't have been able to drink your brew for the taste of it!"

Berengaria only smiled as she rode along on Blackmour's gentlest mare. The Dragon and his lady were most generous with both their affection and their means. They also thought nothing of harboring women who were rumored to be witches. Then again, Christopher had no room to criticize, what with his own black reputation flung from one end of the isle to the other.

She watched him dismount with his son tucked in the crook of one arm, then reach up and pluck his lady from the saddle as if she'd been a child herself. Berengaria smiled through her tears. Ah, here were two who had overcome themselves to reach out and heal the other. What joy was theirs because of it!

"Do you require aid, mistress?" a gruff voice asked.

Berengaria accepted a bit of aid from Colin of Berkhamshire and beamed her approval on him.

"Very gallant, lad. You're coming right along."

Colin grunted. "As if I needed chivalry. What I need is a few more of those beauty herbs to improve my visage. I don't suppose you brought any along, just for emergency's sake, did you?"

"Oh, I'll mix you something up right away," Magda said, falling from her mount and making a grab for her saddlebag along the way. "Just let me get set up inside, my lord, and I'll have something tasty prepared in no time."

"Ah, perhaps too much beauty is a bad thing," Colin stalled. He hastily bowed to the three of them and then bolted for the great hall.

Berengaria watched Christopher and Gillian be welcomed by Robin and his lady Anne, then saw them go into the hall. She almost followed, when she was interrupted by a tall lad coming to a halt before her. This had to be the young lord of Artane, Phillip. He was fashioned perfectly in his father's image.

"My lady."

"Good morrow to you, my lord," she replied.

"My lord Christopher says you are healers?"

Berengaria didn't ask why he wanted to know. The young man was covered with bruises and scratches. She lifted her eyebrows in question.

"My betrothed," he said, smiling sheepishly. "A duller man might suspect she wanted nothing to do with wedded bliss."

Berengaria laughed. "Of course. It must be her Scottish temperament."

Phillip blinked. "How did you know?"

"Scotland?" Nemain echoed, her ears perking up. "I've a mind to go to Scotland. Seen any wizards in those parts, my lord? I'm in sore need of a thumb-bone."

"Wizards?" he echoed. "Thumb-bone?" He shuddered. "None that I've run across."

"We'll have to remedy that, won't we?" Nemain said, hopping spryly down from her horse. She grasped him by an unbruised bit of skin and pulled him toward the hall. "My specialty is brides who haven't the mind to be brides. I'll be happy to give you my aid."

Magda pushed her white hair out of her face with her pudgy, gentle hand and toddled off after Nemain, who was already knee-deep in her list of needful ingredients. Phillip was still shuddering.

Berengaria counted on her fingers, then smiled in relief. She could aid the young lord of Artane yet still be at Blackmour in time to birth Christopher's yet-to-be-conceived daughter.

Och, but business was brisk!

• • •

"I TELL YOU, HE LOVES HER! HAVEN'T YOU SEEN THE way he is ever holding her hand?"

"Sister, he's blind," a deep voice whispered soberly. "I daresay she's helping him."

"Kendrick, you're lying! I'm telling Papa and he'll take a strap to you."

The young man laughed. "Empty threats, Mary. And I don't lie."

"He doesn't need aid. Why, the other day, I saw him stop her before she stepped into a puddle! He's simply the most perfect man ever created and you're bloody jealous."

"Aye, I'm jealous enough of his happiness," Kendrick agreed. "And if you wish to moon over him so powerfully, put away your mending. You're drooling on Phillip's favorite tunic. 'Tis no wonder he always wants to ply the needle himself."

There was the sound of a maid bursting into tears, a hasty apology from her brother, followed by the sound of light feet fleeing from the chamber. Booted feet followed, carrying with them more apologies.

Christopher let out the breath he'd been holding.

"Never again," he vowed. "Never again will I let you talk me into hiding behind curtains, Gill. Saints, what possessed you to think this bloody alcove would be a fine place for an afternoon tryst? We have a perfectly good bed in Robin's finest chamber to use. Here I find myself holed up in this cramped space, struggling to not breathe too loudly—"

"That should be the least of your worries," Gillian said. "Did I or did I not hear you say you were thinking of giving young Robin to Kendrick to squire? By the saints, Christopher, the lad will never survive it!"

"My lord Artane would never let anything happen to his godson," Christopher said, praying that was true. Had he truly said anything to Kendrick? Saints, that was all young Robin needed! Son of a warlock and squire to an arrogant, womanizing—

"Christopher, you're going to break me if you do not loosen your grip."

Christopher forced himself to relax. "Forgive me, my love. Let us speak of something besides squires and nefarious reputations. Now, you had a purpose for spiriting me off to this place?"

"You need a daughter, my lord. Berengaria told me to begin my labors right away."

"Saints," Christopher laughed, "you four women give me no rest at all, what with your orders!"

"You seem to be holding up very well. Now, come here, husband, and let me soothe you."

Christopher allowed his wife free rein for a few moments before he escaped her sweet kisses and merely held her close.

"Gill?"

"Aye, my lord."

"I don't hold your hand merely to have you aid me."

"I know, Christopher."

"I like to hold your hand."

"I know, Christopher."

"But I am glad 'tis your hand that guides me."

"Nay, Chris, 'tis yours that guides me."

He smiled against her hair. "Of course it is. I did save you from the puddle yestermorn. I would have walked you into it, though, if you hadn't squeezed my hand."

" 'Twas merely a show of affection, my lord."

"Promise me such shows of affection far into the future, my lady, and I'll be content."

"Always, my lord."

Christopher closed his eyes and silently gave thanks for the blessings that were his. He had a fine, strong son who delighted him and Gillian both with his antics and childish babble. He had friends that did indeed see past his blindness to the warrior he had been and still was.

And he also had eyes that saw not the world around him, but past it to what he never could have seen otherwise. For it was with those eyes that he had seen his lady.

And she was the greatest blessing of all.

He held her close and didn't stop the tears that leaked out to dampen her beautiful, unruly curls. Ah, how sweet were the gifts he had been given!

It was all he ever could have wanted, and surely more than he deserved.

He could ask for no more.